BY ROBERT HOLDSTOCK FROM TOM DOHERTY ASSOCIATES

The Merlin Codex

Celtika

The Iron Grail

The Broken Kings (forthcoming)

The Mythago novels

Mythago Wood

Lavondyss (forthcoming)

The Hollowing (forthcoming)

THE IRON GRAIL

Book Two of the Merlin Codex

ROBERT HOLDSTOCK

TOR®
fantasy

A TOM DOHERTY ASSOCIATES BOOK
NEW YORK

This is a work of fiction. All the characters and events portrayed in this book are either products of the author's imagination or are used fictitiously.

THE IRON GRAIL: BOOK TWO OF THE MERLIN CODEX

First published in Great Britain in 2002 by Earthlight, an imprint of Simon & Schuster UK Ltd., a Viacom Company.

A Tor Book
Published by Tom Doherty Associates, LLC
175 Fifth Avenue
New York, NY 10010

www.tor.com

Tor® is a registered trademark of Tom Doherty Associates, LLC.

ISBN 0-765-34987-6
EAN 975-0765-34987-3

First Tor edition: February 2004
First mass market edition: January 2005

Printed in the United States of America

0 9 8 7 6 5 4 3 2 1

Dedication

For the Sisters Three: Sarah, Nancy and Rachel

. . . your country under bondage
    cattle straying on the ways
for five tear sodden days
    hardship and a long sigh
one against an army
    your own blood a red plague
splashed on many a smashed shield
    on weapons and women red eyed
the field of slaughter growing red . . .

from *The Bull Raid on Cuailnge*,
from the Irish Celtic legend

Is this the Warped One?
We'll have corpses'
shrieks in our enclosures,
tales to tell.

ibid.

Contents

THE ISLAND OF ALBA, TERRITORY OF THE CORNOVIDI, 272 BCE

CHAPTER ONE

—

Three of Awful Boding

The great fortress of Taurovinda, its causewayed heights rising steeply from the Plain of MaegCatha, bloody playground of the Battle Crow, stood abandoned, burned and silent. The brooding forest encircling the plain had encroached deeply into the empty land around the hill. Twisted blackthorn, briar rose and scrub oak whispered at the base of the ramparts, edging closer, clawing at the towering earthen walls. The high watchtowers, blackened by fire, seemed to drift against the clouds. Nothing had passed the outer gate, however, save for the birds, the Dead, and those who lived outside of Time.

The oldest of the Five Fortresses of Alba, stronghold of the warlord Urtha, mournful Taurovinda still defied the land that sought to bring about its corruption. It stood strong against the storm of nature. And for days, now, it had been calling to me: an urgent whisper, a sound-scent summoning me, drawing me from the seclusion of my hidden valley, away to the west.

I crossed the plain from the evergroves, Taurovinda's gloomy sanctuaries, spread along a curve in the mysterious river Nanto-suelta, whose fords at this point the fortress guarded. I was aware, as I followed the traces of the path between groves and gate, that I was watched from the shadows of grey rocks and stooping oaks, which had grown as fast as weeds since the desertion of the hill. It was early spring, but the plain and the groves might have been in early summer.

Enormous, steep embankments enclosed the hill, capped with high palisade walls of dark oak rising rank upon rank, enclosing a maze of roads. Five gates opened along these winding approaches between the earthen banks, the first carved with twin bull skulls, the second with the interlocking antlers of stags, the third with the leering faces of wolves, the fourth with human skulls grinning from hollows carved from elmwood columns, the fifth hung with the long-bones of two horses, tied in bundles, wrapped in horse-hide and topped with the red-painted skulls of Urtha's favourite war-steeds. This was the Riannon Gate. The horses had pulled the king's chariot in raids and carried his three children in fun. He had mourned their slaughter as he would mourn the death of a brother.

It was a long climb, a gloomy climb, an ascent made in shadow and silence. From the Riannon Gate I surveyed the sprawl of houses and lodgings, animal sheds and barracks. The king's hall lay ahead of me, long, steep-roofed, its great oak doors closed. It had been much repaired after the sacking of the fort and as I walked around the boundaries of the enclosure I saw the colour and sheen of shields lining its northern wall, the arms of ancestors and champions. But who had undertaken this renewal?

I walked as far as the western gate, which looked out over willow marshes and a distant, untidy forest. Beyond that were rocky gorges, reaching to the edge of the Realm of the Shadows of Heroes itself: Ghostland, playing ground of the honoured dead and the as yet unborn.

In the centre of Taurovinda was a dense orchard of apple trees and berry bushes, hazel spinneys and shimmering birch. This was the druids' place, the place of deep shafts, deep tombs, stone shrines and bone shrines and the effigies of those who were invoked during the cycle of the year.

Apart from the wind in the foliage, this too lay in silence.

When the first sounds came, they were a surprise. I had expected to hear the same whispering summons that had called me to the fortress, but now I picked up a plaintive mewling, the sound of pain, three voices murmuring with pain, I thought. I noticed, also, the creaking of rafters, steady and slow. The crying seemed to come from the king's hostel, and I walked past the wall of broken shields to the wide, double door of carved and red-painted oak.

Now the doors were open; I could see they were broken, the intricately carved faces of horses and hounds battered, their colour fading. I entered the gloomy interior of the hall, but enough light streamed from narrow smoke holes in the roof to illuminate the grim and gory sight of three naked women hanging by the neck from the central rafter. Their hands were tied, their bodies flayed from throat to thigh, but they showed the sharp glitter of life and expectation in their eyes as they watched me, giving the lie to their apparent condition.

Though I gagged for a moment, I had seen such threesomes many times before. In Greek Land they were commonly known as the Fates, and were easier on the eye, far easier, quite beautiful. In the north they were called Nornir, sometimes Skaldir, monstrous and sadistic women, with raging appetites for war, men and gore. In the forested gorges of my childhood, in the distant past, they had been Scrayzthuk and had worn patchwork cloaks of the hides of deer, jackal and bear over their own bodies, bodies that had been cut with flint knives to the very bone. They, like their later apparitions, were the organisers of birth, crisis and death; they were bad news masquerading as good; favourable fortune thinly daubed on worm-infested wood.

The three before me now, common in these western lands, were the Three of Awful Boding. They were commonly found at the field of battle, or at a king's house where murder would soon occur. I had heard them called the Morrigan. They could be beautiful or corpselike, depending on their whim. It was too much to hope that they were waiting for someone other than me, but I questioned them just the same.

'Are you waiting for Urtha, High King of the Cornovidi? He's still coming home from Greek Land. He was badly hurt in combat, but is in good company; loving company.'

'Not him,' whispered Mornga, the oldest of this grisly threesome.

'Then are you waiting for the king's elder son, Kymon? He is hiding in Ghostland with his sister, Munda. They are still children. They survived the destruction of the fortress, but I don't expect them home just yet.'

'Not him, not them,' whispered the second of the Three, Mornbad. The breeze from the open door blew on them gently, and the roof creaked as they turned, but their gaze remained fixed on me.

'Then is it Cunomaglos, Urtha's foster brother and closest friend, the man who betrayed him by abandoning Taurovinda, causing the death of his wife and younger son? Urtha pursued him to Greek Land and killed him. I saw the whole combat. We are not expecting Cunomaglos home at all!'

'No, not that hound-harried wretch,' Skaald, the third of the Three, whispered. 'He prowls the edge of Ghostland, but he will always be denied.' Her blackened features were draped with long, russet hair. It stuck to the raw flesh of her breast. It was this one who continued in that same ghostly whisper. 'We are waiting for the timeless man who walks an endless path. A man of *charm*. A young man who should be old.'

Eyes like ice gazed at me without blinking from the gruesome, throttled faces. Three crows settled on the hanged women, pecking lightly at their shoulders.

'I think you've found him,' I said.

'We know,' was the reply, almost amused. The crows seemed suddenly alarmed but it was merely a gust of wind curling through the hall. Skaald whispered, 'Three are returning who are a threat to you. A fourth is already here and hiding.'

I waited for enlightenment. They waited for me to ask for more. When I proposed the question, Skaald said: 'The first is a man who needs you and will use you. He will weaken you dangerously.

'The second is a man you betrayed, though you believe otherwise. He wishes to kill you and can do so easily.

'The third is a ship that is more than a ship. She grieves and broods. She is rotting inside. She will carry you to your grave.'

The crows had become very still, watching me quietly from their raw perches, as if waiting for me to respond to these ominous visions.

I felt sure I knew to whom the first two 'awful bodings' referred, but I was puzzled by the reference to the ship. It had to be Argo, of course, the argonaut Jason's fabulous vessel on which I had sailed with him in the past. But why did she represent a danger to me? She had just helped me escape from Greek Land; she had helped me come back to this island of Alba.

She was a threat to me! *She grieves and broods. She will carry you to your grave.*

It made no sense. Argo and I were friends, or so I'd thought. I was clearly missing something.

This was an event that I would have to glimpse, in due course, but not yet. The cost to my strength of opening such foresight would be too great. For the moment I merely enquired after the fourth arrival, the one who was already in Alba, though I was sure of the answer I would get. Each of them spoke in turn.

'Fierce Eyes,' murmured Mornga.

'Your childhood friend,' whispered Mornbad.

'Your lover,' breathed Skaald, almost sneering. 'The one you lost. She still loves you, but until you open your memory to the time in the long-gone when you were together, there can be no further love between you.'

My childhood friend; the fierce-eyed girl who had become my lover, then abandoned me as she and I had been sent to walk the Path around the world, developing our powers of enchantment, forgetting everything about our pasts.

She had ended up in Colchis, established as the Priestess of the Ram, and had taken a name that continued to live in legend.

'Medea, then. Medea is already here. I understand, now. She has sent you to warn me off!'

'Medea, yes; among her many names.'

'She sent you.'

'Her gift to you.'

Her *gift*? These rank and rotting corpses? It took only a moment to realise that the gift was the 'warning off'.

'Your gift to her could be as easy as rejoining your path. Go away from this land. There will be other times for you and Medea.'

'Where is she? Is she here now?' I asked the Three, but they answered only, 'In Ghostland. Stay away from her. She must protect herself from the Warped Man, Dealing Death.'

And with that final statement, the encounter was concluded.

I had no doubt that the 'warped man' was Jason, the man who

had betrayed Medea seven centuries ago, and who, now that they were both in the same time again, sought to obliterate her from memory.

After such an intervention by either Nornir or Fates, it was considered polite to host a feast, initiate games and allow for uninhibited sexual encounter. The thought sent a chill through me as I stood in the breezy house. Nothing in me was aroused by these clotting corpses and it was a relief to find that they, too—reading my expression, no doubt—thought the idea untenable. Their strangled laughter mocked me. A moment later, the crows spread their wings, jumped towards me and chased me from the king's house.

But I sat for a long while at the edge of the untended orchard, among the cairn-covered sacred shafts into the hill, thinking of what had been said, in particular what had been said concerning Argo. Argo was the means by which I had come here, to misty, mysterious Alba, hiding out and licking my wounds. She had once been Jason's ship, and had become Jason's grave; then she had been Jason's resurrection and his new life. She had done much the same for me, though in a different manner.

As the day advanced, and the sky darkened towards a storm, I thought back over seven hundred years, searching for a memory—any memory—that would make sense of the foreboding words from the grim trio.

I remembered at once a terrible dawn in the harbour town of Iolkos, in Greek Land, where everything had begun . . .

CHAPTER TWO

—

The Blood Pact

News of the murder passed from house to house and street to street throughout the city, spreading from the palace on the hill, through the markets and suburbs until it reached the harbour, with its silent fleets and stinking quays, where gulls screeched and nets rotted in the hot sun.

'Glauce is dead! Jason's lover is dead. His betrayed wife Medea has killed the princess! A witch spell from the barbarian north. Glauce is burned to ash and bone!'

Nine of Jason's argonauts had stayed in Iolkos, after the quest for the Bloody Ram's fleece and the abduction of its guardian, Medea. As each heard the news he gathered his armour and weapons and ran through the narrow alleys, calling for the man who had been the captain of Argo, most ancient of ships, strangest of ships, and taken her to the ends of the world.

One of them, faithful, practical Tisaminas, knowing of my skills, first came to find me. I was one of the nine, and known as Antiokus at that time.

I had been making ready to leave this warm, sweet part of the world, to venture on the Path again. Seven years with Jason had finally taken its toll, though I would be sad to leave the adventurer. His lust for life appealed to me, as did his mercenary tendencies, always pushing forward, always looking for something new, ever searching for spoils and charm in all senses of that word. We were the same side of the shield, he and I, at that time at least. The other side of the shield is laziness and complacency—to conquer part of the unknown, as he had done, too often leads to the disabling condition of believing you are invincible; timeless.

Time, and the consequences of conceit, were catching up with Jason; but I still loved the man.

Tisaminas entered my room, unannounced, in a panic, his eyes wild. 'Glauce has been slain. By Medea! And she's taken the boys to her palace. Jason's sons. She intends to murder them too. She intends to destroy everything that is hers by Jason. Even us! Battle-harness and sword, Antiokus. Jason needs us.'

I had not seen this coming. I had not been blind to the growing agony and fury in the enchantress from Colchis since Jason's irresponsible courtship of the king's daughter became a cause of great gossip, hatred and considerable diplomatic adjustment; I had been blind to the certain consequences.

Following Jason's desertion of her, Medea had withdrawn behind the cool, high walls of her stark, green-and-black-marbled palace. She had closed the heavy bronze doors. The smoke from the roof holes was heady, colourful and suspicious. Only the sound of horns and cymbals told clearly of her anguish. But for six full months she had done nothing but mourn, while her two children by Jason—Kinos and Thesokorus—had played innocently in the gardens of both father's and mother's houses.

This murder came as a shock. Half-armed and half-dressed, I staggered after lithe Tisaminas, seeking Theseus. The hero, one of the original argonauts, was visiting his old friends. It would be essential to draw him to the fight as well. He had a vital way with the sword, and could help with the labyrinthine corridors of Medea's palace. We met Anthos and Argastus in the olive market. They were armoured, sharp-eyed, not quite sure what was happening around them. Then Jason himself, in the company of Anteon and Hephastos and the others, caught up with us. The red-eyed, taut-cheeked man, his face stained with tears, his hair lank, led the way up the hill to the copper-green gates that protected Medea herself.

Here for a moment he paused, wild eyes surveying the palace façade. I could smell his fear and his sweat. Medea's guards were lined up on the nearer side of a blazing wall of fire. They carried long-bladed spears and curved shields marked with the head of Medusa. Their gleaming ram's-skull masks, like crescent moons, half bright, half in darkness, were all the more sinister for the urgency of the situation. They seemed to laugh at us. Ten archers crouched behind them. From the palace beyond came the wilderness-screaming of women and the relentless, deep, three-beat rhythm of skin drums.

Jason grabbed my arm in sudden anger. 'Why didn't you see this? Antiokus! Blood of the gods, you can see Time itself! For an age on either side of this living moment. Why didn't you see what this dire-hearted witch would do?'

Did he think I had betrayed him? I had been too busy enjoying the pleasures of flesh and wine. But when I looked at him now I realised that he was capable of losing even simple reason in his anger. His head looked fit to burst with anguish and outrage.

'I wasn't looking,' I confessed uneasily. 'I should have been looking . . . '

Jason stared at me for a moment, then used his knife to scrape the dried tears from his cheeks, taking his gaze away from me. The passion and lust he had once felt for Medea had shrivelled years ago, at exactly the same time as his elder son, Thesokorus, had uttered his first words. The boy was known as the 'little bull leaper'. By his third spring the child had learned to hold himself vertical on the horns of the stone bull in Jason and Medea's courtyard. How he loved the boy! And he loved Kinos too, the 'little dreamer'; Kinos, whose childish visions were full of haunting, memorable charm, insights and part-sights into the future.

This family, with all their skills, born and gods-given, could have reshaped the heavens. They could have moved stars. They could have shaped events—had the Fates dining at their table, discussing terms.

But Medea's haunting, earthy charm had faded from the bowels of the cold-hearted man.

Even so, his passion for the pristine, prim and vacuous Glauce had seemed unlikely and out of character. He had loved the woman, I was certain, but naively, for her innocence rather than for her challenge. He was hurting deeply, but not because of Glauce's extinction; all he could think of, now, was that Medea had his sons.

And his sons were precious to him.

'She won't kill them,' he muttered as the fires roared and the guards stood, brazen, solid, facing us, waiting for our attack. 'Will she? She wouldn't dare! Hera's heart, Antiokus! They're from her own womb. She wouldn't dare put the blade to them . . . ?'

Tisaminas was eager to get to the fight. He slapped his sword three times against his shield, then once against his right thigh, deliberately grazing the skin.

'There is not a moment to lose, Jason! We must not think too much before we run at these ram-helmeted blade-fodder!'

'I know! I *know* all that!' Jason shouted at him. 'Get the boys away from her. Spare nothing and no one until you have the boys in your arms. Cut the witch to shreds if you must, but get those children from her amber-rattling clutches!'

Again he looked at me closely, pain-filled eyes as watery and bloodshot as an old man's.

'Will she? Will she kill them?'

'She is older than you think,' I said to him. 'Her heart is made of different sinew from yours. Her blood is a different hue of red when it spills from her veins. Her song of summoning brings shadows from a deeper clay below our feet.'

'That much I know. That much I found out during the nights after I brought her back from her sanctuary in Colchis.

'Mighty Zeus, strike her down,' he whispered then. 'Protecting Hera, blind the snake-sharp eyes. Strike my left arm from my shoulder if you must, but strike the woman down before she can harm my sons . . . '

With this last cry he drew his blade, struck his shield five times and with a roar of rage led the charge at the moon-masked guard.

We pushed and cleaved our way towards the palace. Argastus took an arrow in the throat, killing him instantly, but his grey shade fairly howled from his body, curling around the killer, blinding the Colchean. I was on the archer in a moment. In the shock of this shadowy assistance, all the archers quickly died beneath our swords, though Theseus went down wounded. Those men had been the main danger, and Jason left Anteon and Haphestos to finish the job in the gardens, leading Tisaminas, myself and the others to the flaming wall which Medea had caused to spring from the ground.

She stood, now, behind the fire, taunting her husband with eerie chants and laughter. She was a tall, sinister shape in a black robe that rattled with metal leaves, bone amulets and polished amber blades. Only her eyes were visible above the black veil across her face, below the fringe of gold thread that hung from her headdress.

A flaming ball was suddenly flung towards us, spitting fat as it burned. The charred flowers in its hair still held their shape. Jason screamed and held his shield before his face, as if he could deny the gruesome trophy. Then he leapt the wall of Colchean fire, pursuing the shrieking woman.

Tisaminas was pale with fear as we followed. We fought our way into the palace, and raced along the echoing, green-marbled corridors. Suddenly Medea was running ahead of us, Kinos and Thesokorus held by the hands. The boys were laughing as they ran, but their laughter was not natural. They acted as if this was all a game, but they were confused and nervous.

By trickery and confusion, Medea led us like goats to the slaughter.

She had fled to the Bull Sanctuary, not her own temple of the Ram, and as Jason led us towards the bronze-barred gate, now closed and locked by the desperate woman, so we realised our mistake.

Behind us, across the narrow passage, a stone slab fell and trapped us. Ahead of us, the towering horned effigy, before which Medea stood triumphant, split in two, revealing itself as a doorway. There, outside, was the road to the north. A cart and six horsemen were waiting, the animals impatient and frightened as their riders struggled to control them. I recognised the armoured charioteer as Cretantes, Medea's confidant and adviser from her homeland.

The boys struggled in her grasp, howling. Perhaps they were suddenly aware that this was not a game at all, and that in their mother's arms they faced a more terrible fate than in their father's, though she had led them to expect otherwise.

Jason flung himself against the bars of the sanctuary, begging the black-shrouded woman to release the screaming boys.

'Too late. Too late!' she cried from behind her black veil. '*My* blood can't save them from the ravages of *your* blood. You betrayed the ones you love, Jason. You betrayed us brutally with that woman!'

'You burned her alive!'

'Yes. And now you will freeze in *eternity*! In *gloom*! Not even your heart and the hearts of your argonauts will be sufficient meat for the dark feast of despair that lies ahead of you. Nothing will change in you, Jason. Nothing can! You are a warped man. You deal in death. If I could cut your flesh out of the boys, if I could do that and still let them live, then that is what I'd do. But I can't. So say goodbye to your sons!'

Jason's howl of pain was vulpine. He shouted, 'Antiokus! Use your magic!'

'I can't!' I cried. 'Nothing is there! This is a tomb, Jason. My talent is paralysed . . . '

He had no time for my confusion, my excuses. He flung his long sword at the woman but the throw went wide, the blade embedding itself in the god-bull's cedar pizzle.

And at that moment, Medea did the terrible deed, moving so fast I saw only the merest glint of light on the blade with which she cut the throats of the twins. She turned away from us, covering their bodies with her robes, stooping to her work with manic vigour as Jason howled again. She wrapped and tied the heads in strips of her veil, tossing them to Cretantes, who put them in pouches slung from his waist. Then Medea dragged the bodies to the horses. They were flung into the cart and covered with blankets.

A moment later, the troop had gone, leaving dust swirling into the sanctuary, with the smell and sight of innocent blood two cruel Furies taunting the argonauts, trapped in Medea's lair.

Jason slumped to his knees, fingers still gripping the gate. He had battered himself unconscious against the bars of the temple; his eyes and face were bruised, his mouth raw. One of our companions was pushing against the stone door behind us, trying to find the lever that would release us from the trap. I felt helpless: all power in magic had drained from me from the moment I entered the palace, an impotence which astonished and confused me, and I assumed had occurred because Medea had used her own sorcery to 'numb' me ready for the moment of the deaths.

Now again I felt that familiar tingle below the flesh, ability returning, saw at once how to open the door. And persuaded it to do so. We dragged Jason's body outside, through the fires and into the fresh air.

No guards were to be seen save the slain. Someone went for horses.

Tisaminas crouched down beside me, lifting Jason's battered head and wiping the blood from his brow. Jason opened his eyes, then reached out to grab me by the shoulder. 'Antiokus . . . ?' he whispered. 'Why didn't you stop her? There is more enchantment in your veins than *blood*!'

'I warned you she could be more powerful than me. I tried, Jason. With all my heart, I tried.'

My own power had been strangled. Medea had exercised her own charm upon me, stifling my inner sight and my ability with enchantment. How she had managed this was beyond me. It would be seven hundred years before I would find the answer.

Jason's look was grim, but he acknowledged my words. 'I know you did. I'm sure you did. You've been a good friend. I know you would have tried.' He groaned as he tried to move. 'Come on, help me up! Tisaminas, help me up. And fetch horses! We have to follow . . . '

'The horses are on their way,' I told him.

'She will run to the north, Antiokus. I know the way she thinks. She'll run to the coast, to the hidden harbour behind the mourning rocks. We can catch her!'

'We can certainly try,' I said, though in my heart I knew that Medea had slipped away for ever. She had always outwitted Jason.

I had not been in Iolkos on that final, fateful day when a spar from the rotting Argo, where the rotting man lay ageing and raging against Medea, fell and broke his skull. Hera found me, as she had found all the argonauts. I was walking my long path round the world, too far away in the snows of the north to return. But the others came back and lined the headlands above the harbour. They circled firebrands in farewell as the proud ship gracefully sailed into the moon and Time. Even the shade of sad Orpheus was there, allowed to return for this final farewell. And Heracles too, dark and brooding, plucked from his own manic adventures by the wily goddess, even he was there, casting his torch wistfully from the heights as the old ship passed below.

As if pursuing me, it was to the Northlands that Argo brought the hero. She sank into the depths of a lake, near Tuonela, in the bleak land called Pohjola. I always knew he was buried there. I often passed that way, out of respect for my old friend, staying for a while, trying not to hear the screams of the shade of Jason, still mourning his sons.

All this would one day change when I discovered the clever conjuration that Medea had performed for us.

PART ONE:

—

Hardship and a Long Sigh

CHAPTER THREE

—

Old Ghosts

I had been reliving the far past for half the morning, lost in my dreams, walking lost times as I walked the boundaries of the deserted fort. My reverie was abruptly interrupted by a sudden shower of rain, sleeting across the grass within the walls. It seemed to drive in through the Riannon Gate, very cold and very wet. A figure moved through the rain, insubstantial, defined by the shower, a man leading a horse by the reins, followed soon by others, entering the enclosure cautiously. And nervously.

The leader suddenly ran as if to pass me by where I now crouched in the lee of a collapsed house. His men jogged after him, their horses struggling in the downpour. I could see through their forms to the ramparts opposite; they were rain-ghosts, clad in long cloaks, leather tunics over knee-length trousers. Their horses were large and exquisitely harnessed.

The leader suddenly stopped and glanced in my direction, then walked towards me, a watery shade, gaining features. Behind him his retinue mounted up and slouched forward across their saddles, watching.

There was something familiar about him, sufficiently so for

the hair on my neck to prickle. His eyes, his bearing: they reminded me of Urtha, High King of the Cornovidi and true owner of this abandoned place. Then again, many people reminded me of Urtha: the look of such an extended family could grin at me from behind every stronghold wall.

'Are you the enchanter? The old man who walks in circles talking to himself?' He laughed as he said this.

'I walk a circular path around the world. It takes fifty years to make one circuit, sometimes longer. I talk to myself because I like what I have to say.'

'What madness would make a man do such a thing? Walking, walking.'

'The madness of my birth. It's the undertaking I was tasked with at my birth.'

'What do you achieve?'

'Achieve? Greater understanding of things that are normally confusing; more memories than I know what to do with; greater skills than I have the time to practise; but a great deal of practice in the sort of interference that can shape kingdoms.'

'I could do with a man like you,' the ghost said appreciatively, grinning as he scratched the stubble on his face. Then he peered closely. 'I was expecting someone older. You're no older than me.'

'Looks can deceive.'

'That they can. That they can indeed. Deception can kill more certainly than an iron blade. I'll remember your face; remember mine. Now, go to the river. Quickly. Someone has been following you for days. You move fast and in mysterious ways. Your help is needed.'

He was suddenly apprehensive. A horn sounded, somewhere in the distance, an eerie call, or warning. His ethereal steed tugged at the reins; his companions were anxiously staring towards the western gate, at the rear of the stronghold.

'Get out of here now,' he said to me, turning away. 'The river, by the old sanctuary—wait for her.'

He slipped into the rain, a glistening shape defined by water. 'Who are you?' I called after him, but he either didn't hear or chose not to answer. I took a deeper look at him and felt that tingle of shock, deep in the bones, as I recognised the unfocused, misty spark of one of the Unborn. I left well enough alone at that point.

I ran to the Riannon gate, the horse gate, and began to descend the causeways. Behind me I faintly heard the sound of men riding at the gallop—a raiding party surging into Taurovinda from the direction of the Land of the Shadows of Heroes.

The old sanctuary by the river was dedicated to Nantosuelta, the 'winding one', the spirit of springs and streams, wells and rivers like this wide flow that wound tightly around Taurovinda, and named for the spirit herself.

This river was more than it seemed; willow-fringed, dense with rushes, alive with movement close to the shore, it might have been any river anywhere in the island. But Nantosuelta flowed from Ghostland, the Land of the Shadows of Heroes. It separated the land of the Cornovidi in the west from the Otherworld of their ancestors; its winding course also separated the Parisii, the Durotriges and the Seutones from their own Otherworlds. To row a boat along Nantosuelta was to always row at the edge of the world of the Dead. Urtha's fortress of Taurovinda guarded five dangerous fords across the water, and the five deep valleys that led, westwards beyond the marshes, to Ghostland itself.

The sanctuary lay among the evergroves, stunted, twisted trees that reared like petrified spirits from the rocks and cairns of older temples. Weathered grey rocks, crumbling piles of stones, there was a chaos to the place, but a sense of presence, of listening, that told me that here was a sanctuary which still pulsed with life.

The rain hadn't eased. I went to the edge of the river and searched the dense greenery for the woman the rain-ghost had suggested was waiting for me.

When she finally arrived, she was not alone.

'What in the name of Llud's bastard sons have you done with my bastard son-in-law?'

The voice that challenged me from the groves was deep, angry, resonant and recognisable.

'Ambaros!'

'Merlin! Is the bastard dead? Is he coming home? Why did my daughter—the Good God grant her rest when rest comes due—why did she have to bond with a man whose dreams took him away from his duties?'

'Your son-in-law fought a good and famous combat.'

'I hope he took a head to prove it.'

'A well-oiled head. He also took a wound.'

'Mortal?'

'Watch the east. If he shows, then you have your answer. He fought well, Ambaros, and avenged your daughter.'

'I'm glad to hear it.'

Now he stepped towards me, casting aside his shield and spear, throwing back his cloak. Old and white-haired, but with eyes that were sharp as spear-points, this grand warrior, this man of Taurovinda, father of Urtha's dead wife Aylamunda, embraced me like a long lost son.

When his relief—the gesture was one of relief at finding me, that much was clear—when his relief was satisfied, he stepped back, looked me up and down and shook his head.

'Dreadful. Filthy. A dog wears better clothes. You've been in seclusion too long. There are week-old wolf-cubs forty days' ride from here, blind and helpless, who are smelling your scent and urging their mother to let them hunt you down.'

'Thank you. You've aged a lot yourself.'

'Age has less to do with it than water. Anyway, I can't get any older. You can't add white to white. I can only get stronger. When that strength goes, it will be in an instant. I'll sing loudly as my head bowls along the ground. As long as it's a clean cut, I don't care about it. I care about this land and that fortress, where the Dead are gathering having evicted us yet again. And about my grandchildren. That's why I'm here.'

'Kymon and Munda?'

'They're the only grandchildren I have, Merlin, unless the ghosts of my three dead sons have been fornicating in the world of the living! Yes. Kymon and Munda. I don't understand what is happening myself, but one of their guardians is here. One of the *modronae*. The Mothers. She's dying. So let's not waste time.'

He led me to the shelter of a slouching stone. A woman in black dress, her dark hair streaked with white, lay curled there shivering. Ambaros had covered her with a blanket. Her cheeks were so dry that she had the look of a corpse. I could hear the hollow echo of her stomach, the feeble pulse of her heart, the crow-call that was summoning her.

'She's very ill,' Ambaros said as he knelt beside her. He took her hand and massaged it, as if this act of touching might stimulate life in a body that was shedding life with every passing flight of cranes.

What could I do? Knowing Ambaros as I did, knowing of his strengths in combat and his strength of heart, his dedication to his family, I touched this dying Mother with a little strength of her own. In doing so I realised that she belonged in Ghostland, not in Urtha's world. She had crossed the divide—Nantosuelta—and now could never return.

'I remember you,' she whispered. She reached a hand to stroke my whiskered cheeks. 'You're the man who brought their father to see them. You are their father's friend.'

She must have known this already; else why pursue me from the land that sustained her to a realm that would kill her?

'I brought Urtha to see them. He and I have travelled together to Greek Land. He avenged the death of Aylamunda and his son Urien.'

'I'm glad of that,' the *modron* whispered.

Ambaros too seemed pleased, the slightest nod of his head as he watched me without expression signalling that he was content to hear of the triumph of his son-in-law.

The Mother raised her hands, palms towards me. She said, 'For a while they were safe in the borderland between the river and the land of shadows. But they are no longer safe. The Warped Man, Dealing Death, is closing in. He is searching for Urtha's children. He is hungry for them.

'Merlin! There is a storm in Ghostland that none of us can understand. Something terrible is happening. Nothing is right in that strange realm! But Urtha's children are both key and cure. You have old bones and old charm; my sister saw this when you came to the meadow with their father, before he went to Greek Land. You can take them from a broken haven to safety. Hurry. Hurry.'

Suddenly her lips pressed against mine. I felt the moisture of life on her tongue. Her eyes blazed with death. Her fingers scratched urgency through my stinking sheepskin coat. 'Leave me here,' she whispered. 'I'll make my own way back.' Then the light faded from eyes that had seen wonders. A cooling carcass curled into my arms, skin and bone glad to say goodbye to the ghost that had held this fragile doll together for the journey to find me.

I kissed her gently, this time on the brow. I closed her eyes. I folded her carefully.

Ambaros asked, 'Dead?'

'Very dead. But then, she was dead already, I realise.'

'Let's get on with it. Can you get those children out of Ghostland?'

'Will you help?'

He laughed sourly. He was appalled at the question.

I felt ashamed.

'Get me a horse,' I said to him.

'Find your own damned horse. Do you think horses grow on trees?'

'Then first help me bury this woman. She said to leave her here.'

'That is something that must be done. Under one of the cairns. The present owners won't object, and if they do, they can face me in Ghostland with their argument!'

That response was exactly what made me admire this man. In one way I truly envied Ambaros: he cut to the quick; he had no time for nonsense. In other ways I didn't envy him at all: he was old, he was tired, he was weak in heart and limb, he had a narrow view of a world that was exhaustingly complex (he was hardly alone in this, of course; he didn't walk the path that I walked). And yet, he could make sense of small affairs. For all my journeying around the wider world, all I could do was accrue memory; insight, it seemed to me, came from concentrating on the near-at-hand.

Ambaros, Urtha's father, Urtha's mentor, Urtha's scourge and challenge, the nightmare voice in Urtha's dreams, could whisper words that made sense, see strategy that made sense, understand situations where sense had taken a walk . . . but in a narrow range.

For all my broader range, I could make less sense of the world than Ambaros. I felt drawn to him, to the necessity that now drove him—to bring Kymon and Munda out of Ghostland—in a way that I had rarely experienced before.

Oh yes: Jason.

Well, it's true; when my path had crossed with young Jason's, as he rebuilt Argo before questing for the Golden Fleece and my forgotten lover Medea, yes, then I had felt a deepening of insight; my life had grown; I had learned some lessons. Gods, I had fallen under Jason's spell. I can't deny it. But a man such as Jason is one of a rare breed. It is more an honour than a dishonour to have spent or wasted time with them. In fact, honour is the wrong word. The word is privilege. Few men, few women emerge from the dry stew of human mediocrity to flavour the world in a way that can never be forgotten.

Jason did it. And if Urtha had come close, somehow I felt, even now, even at that time, that he was the genesis of something greater.

Ambaros would be forgotten, Urtha too, I expected; but they were two gusts of the wild wind that would one day create a great storm of memory, as a storm had created Alexander, Radegast, Ramses, Diana, Agamemnon, Odysseus, all of them so much more than whispers on the wind of time.

When we had laid the Mother in her shallow grave I went to the reed-fringed river and called for the small barge that had carried me back to Alba. She was a spirit echo of Argo herself, a shadow from Argo's past, loaned to me by the ship and her guardian goddess to help me escape from Greek Land.

She slipped from hiding, among drooping willow fronds on the far side of Nantosuelta, and nosed towards the shallows by the groves. Ambaros was astonished, but silently so, standing behind me, his hand absently scratching at his cheek.

The little boat was filled with furs and woollens, her prow painted yellow and carved with the features of a swan. The purple-painted glyphs that fringed the hull like a frieze suggested she had come from the island known as Krete, from a time before the sudden drowning of that land and its people, a millennium or so ago. She was just one part of the Spirit of

Argo, sufficient to have brought me here by river, stream and under the world to avoid the sea crossing.

Now I offered her the chance to leave me, to return to Argo.

'I'll stay,' her small voice whispered in my head. I thanked her. I would be riding with Ambaros to the edge of Ghostland. Would she meet me there? I might still have need of her.

She agreed.

So Ambaros and I left the river's edge, left the groves and rode away from Taurovinda, to the west, to the gorges, and to the Ford of the Last Farewell, where the Dead crossed on their way to the Otherworld.

I expected him to ask me further news about his son-in-law, but he was discreet, as was the custom, explaining that, 'News of a king, brought in the king's absence, must first be given to the king's eldest son, that's the way we do things here. If there is no son, then the news is given to his wife; if no wife, only then to the parents.' He hesitated for a moment, then glanced at me as we rode side by side. 'But I dearly needed to know if Urtha had survived his quest. I broke taboo.'

'As I said, he survived, he triumphed, though he took a savage wound. He's coming home slowly.'

Ambaros raised his hand. 'And as I said, that's enough to put my heart at peace. Thank you. The rest is for Kymon, if you find him, and after that I'll hear the full story. But now: what of Jason? Your resurrected Greeklander friend looking for his time-lost grown up sons. Did he succeed as well?'

We exchanged a glance and he smiled when he saw my questioning look. How had he known about Jason's new lease of life? It should have been obvious.

'Urtha told me what you'd done for Jason the last time you were here: bringing that ship to the surface of a lake with his body still on board. And about his sons being still alive after seven hundred years, after their mother summoned Cronos and hid them in the future.' He grinned broadly, shaking his head. 'Merlin, I've told some high tales and broad sagas in my time, I've bragged with the best of them at Beltane and winter feasts, and talked of my deeds, on several occasions, for all the night. But this story leaves me breathless.'

It had left me breathless too, when I had finally summoned

an image of what had truly occurred in the palace in Iolkos, seven centuries ago.

One nick to the throat of each boy, drawing blood as a powerful drug was passed into the flesh. The boys collapsed in moments. Pig's blood shocked our senses as it seemed to spurt from their necks. Medea stooped over their bodies and from beneath her skirts pulled heads made of wax and horsehair, wrapping them in strips of her veil. She threw them to Cretantes, beyond the open door, then summoned her strength and dragged her sleeping sons to the horses, throwing them into the cart, letting us see only their trailing legs.

So fast, so clever, so persuasive! A brilliant trick to which I had been blinded. She fled into exile, and though Jason searched the land from coast to coast and mountain to island, he found no trace of them, and ended his days a sad and furious man.

Because what she had done next had been astonishing. It was a use of her power that I would never dare to summon.

When the act was done, she had settled down to wait for time to pass . . .

'Did he find his sons?'

'He found one of them,' I answered. 'The elder, deep in Greek Land close to an ancient oracle. The young man had taken the name Orgetorix.'

Ambaros whistled with surprise. '*King of killers*? That's a strong name. Did he live up to it?'

'From what I saw of him, very much so.'

He nodded his head and smiled. 'I'm glad. So Jason has one of his boys back.'

'Therein lies a tragedy. Orgetorix had such hate in his heart, put there by his mother, that he rejected Jason, tried to kill him. I watched the whole thing. Jason was shocked and distraught. He accused me of betraying him because I hadn't told him everything I knew about his son.'

I still shuddered to think of that look in Jason's eyes as he hunched, gaping and bloody, the look of contempt for me, the vengeful look; and his words murmured as he fought to stave off death: *Dread the dawn when you wake to find me crouching over you. Dread that dawn.*

And he would be following me to Alba, now, because that was where Medea had hidden her younger son, Kinos, nicknamed Little Dreamer.

When I told Ambaros this, he laughed.

'Well, that will take a lot of searching. This may be what you call an island, but the land is vast. There are not just the Five Kingdoms. A multitude of petty kingdoms lie to the north of us, and as many to the south and to the west, beyond Ghostland. And they are all afflicted with marshes, boglands, forests, mountains, valleys and rockstrewn plains. The Lords Gog and Magog, as tall as trees, could go into hiding and never be found.'

'Little Dreamer will have left a trail,' I assured Ambaros.

His look at me was strange, though he was half-smiling.

'I am in awe of you,' he said later, as we rested for the night in a cove of rocks, sheltered by the overhanging branches of an elm to which we had tied our cloaks as a windbreak. 'In awe! And yet I feel comfortable with you, not at all afraid of what you can do with just the flick of your finger and thumb. Perhaps it's because you look younger than my own son.'

'He's battle-weary. I'm just travel-weary.'

'But where you travel, things begin to happen. It's as if that guardian of the exiles was waiting for you. How did she know you were here? How did she know when you would pass along the river, past the Ford of the Last Farewell? She tried to follow you at once, but you went into hiding. She's been searching for you ever since, and finally she found me in the settlement in the gorge, and I brought her to Taurovinda. Just as you'd arrived! Someone is stitching our lives together, I think.'

I told him about the Three of Awful Boding.

'Strange again: they never appear except to kings and their consorts. Sometimes to a king's champion.'

And of the small band of rain-ghostly men who had told me of Ambaros's presence in the groves.

'Yes, I thought we were being followed. There was a large war band as well, the sort that drove us from the fortress for the second time. Something is stirring up because of you, Merlin. Something that is putting the lives of the exiles in danger.'

I doubted very much that whatever was occurring across the

living flow of Nantosuelta had anything to do with me and told him so.

Three are returning who are a threat to you. A fourth is already here and hiding.

There would be answers, but for the moment I felt as much in the dark as he.

CHAPTER FOUR

—

Exiles in Ghostland

I waited at the Ford of the Last Farewell for a full day, with Ambaros and his small retinue of men, acquired as we passed through the camp of the exiles, the exiles, the deep valley where the survivors from Taurovinda had hidden after the raid.

When movement came on the other side it was nervous and fleeting, hesitant and illusory. But as soon as Ambaros and his men withdrew, the cloaked and cowled figure finally slipped from the woodland's edge and scurried over the rocks towards the small inlet in the bank of the river. It was hard to see her across the wide flow of Nantosuelta—that waterway separating two worlds. A haze of mist hovered over this border between realms. But I saw how her cloak rippled with colour, making her meld with her background. She was grey as she paused by an outcrop of grey weathered rock, then green and dark as she came against the far trees, then like yellow reeds as she crouched down by the water and watched me.

Her face was pale, almost featureless, save for her eyes, dark and wide as she studied me carefully.

This was another of the Mothers who guarded Kymon and

Munda. I tried to remember her. By her appearance, she was the youngest of the three.

She did not invite me to cross Nantosuelta at that moment, though I could have made the crossing in the spirit boat, which waited patiently in the high reeds, her swan-prow just showing. But the Mother and I could not speak through the separating distance, this no-man's water between worlds. So I summoned a bird. The darkness in the distance, above the deep forest of Ghostland, suggested the storm that was coming, but the crow seemed inappropriate for this urgent interchange. I summoned, instead, a skylark, the most vociferous of birds.

The lark appeared above me, circled me, singing noisily, then took my simple message across the river to the woman.

I've seen your sister. She sent me to you.

The bird flew back with her reply.

Are you the one who will guide Urtha and his children into their future?

The question took me by surprise. Into their future? For the next few seasons, perhaps; but the Mother's words contained more significance than my own limited aspirations for my friend, should he return alive.

I sent the lark to tell her: *I once came with Urtha across the river; I brought him to see his children before he went in search of vengeance against his foster brother. We came and went by a boat, not this one, but very similar. I can cross to you easily.*

The lark flew up and away, winging towards the storm-skies in the far hills. The cowled woman rose to her feet and beckoned to me, then turned and hurried back to cover.

I called for the spirit boat and she bobbed towards me. I clambered in, settling on the cushions with their old and strange designs, and she drifted across the river without difficulty, nosing gently into the soft mud of the inlet.

I was back in the hinterland of the Shadows of Heroes.

I met the *modron* in the bosk of the wood. I could hardly see her; like a clever cat, she merged with her background. But that moon-pale face smiled at me, and the pool-dark eyes welcomed me.

She asked me about her sister, who had gone to find me, and seemed unsurprised when I broke the news that she was dead. Then she talked of Urtha's children.

'They were safe here for a long while,' she whispered to me as we moved swiftly along the track. 'There are many places at the edge of this land which are safe. That's why they were brought here when they escaped the terrible raid. This is a place where we guard exiles, and have done so over the ages. They should always have been safe here, but recently there have been too many raiding bands, searching the edge. There is something deadly growing in the deep hills, spreading out, and all the signs are of danger.'

'Are they searching for the children?' I asked, panting as I followed her fleet form through the moist underwood along the twisting path.

'We have reason to think so. Their names are called out at night, though from a great distance. So far we've managed to keep our hiding place secure. But the Dead are crossing the river and settling on the Thunder Hill, making it their own.'

'I know. I've just come from there.'

I had realised the first time I had entered it that the causewayed fortress, named for thunder, was shaped around a far older sanctuary. There were mounds within its high walls, contained within the orchard groves, which echoed so faintly they must have certainly been erected over the dead of a very distant past. Interesting, then, that the Shadows of Heroes were returning there.

I was becoming curious.

My train of thought was abruptly terminated as the young Mother suddenly stopped in her tracks in alarm. I bowled into her and her small hand clutched at mine, urging me to silence. Ahead of us was a sunlit clearing. A large creature suddenly bounded across that patch of gleaming light, a boar of some size, its razor spines raised high in alarm; others followed, making no sound. Birds were disturbed above us, a nervous fluttering in the branches. Then four cloaked riders passed across the glade, slumped in the saddle, long hair framing their faces, spears held at a low angle.

They were not pursuing the animals; they seemed to be following a different spoor. In the glade they hesitated, looked around, stared hard along the track where the Mother and I crouched silently, then kicked their horses on, disappearing from sight.

After a while, the woman rose again and went cautiously forward, darting across the clearing, beckoning me to follow.

Soon, we left the wood and scrambled through the shallows of a winding stream. To one side of us was the bare ridge of a hill. To the other, an overgrown tangle of grey rocks and stunted trees, and it did not surprise me when the woman scrambled along an almost hidden path through this craggy edge, then through a deep defile, and led me to the haven where the two children lay concealed.

It was a bright meadow, encircled by a high rocky wall. Five doorways, close together, opened into the rocks, five chambers where the Mothers and the children lived. Close to the narrow entrance into this hiding place was a well, guarded by the tall wooden figures of Brigg and Nodons. The well was decked with holly and ivy and red-berried branches of thorn. The young Mother ran quickly to it, knelt down and dipped a cloth into the water, wiping her hands and face. She encouraged me to do the same. The water was scented with earth and seemed to swell at its surface, as if trying to rise above the rocks that contained it.

The moment the damp cloth touched my eyes, the charm that guarded the meadow fell away.

Ten children were playing a game with hurling sticks and a small, leather ball, laughing loudly as they clattered and tripped in pursuit of victory. Four mastiffs lay quietly watching, forepaws folded. Elsewhere, chickens pecked at the ground, and grey-skinned pigs nosed up above their sty. Several fruit trees grew in a small orchard, where another child was trying to reach for an apple. The young Mother shouted at her and she looked startled, darting away into hiding.

Not all these children were from Urtha's fortress at Taurovinda. Not all of them were from the world of Urtha and his *uthiin*, his warrior retinue. The young Mother, as if hearing my inner reflection, glanced at me with a wan smile.

'Yes, they are the forlorn. Some of them have been here a very long time. They are children who once escaped to safety across the river, but were never rescued. Two at least can go home, though how safe they will be is up to you, now.'

I asked, 'Can't I take more? I'd gladly take you all. The boat that brought me here is a friend; she won't depart until I request her to.'

'That won't be possible,' the woman answered pointedly. 'Please don't offer it to the children. They simply can't go. I'm sorry.' And she told me why, but added, 'There is one girl, a friend of Munda's . . . she has not been here long. Perhaps her.' She suddenly touched my arm. 'There are Urtha's children, over by the orchard. Always looking for magic apples. Go and stop them shaking the tree.'

She gave me a little push. I did as I was bidden.

They seemed no older than when I had first encountered them. That was the price they paid for staying in this sanctuary, at the edge of Ghostland. As I approached them, Munda recognised me and smiled broadly. Kymon frowned, looking around, no doubt hoping to see his father.

Munda was just as I remembered her, freckle-faced and auburn-haired, with little arrows painted on her cheeks. She wore a simple green dress, belted at the waist.

Kymon, by contrast, was in his little warrior's outfit, check-trousered, bare-chested, but with a short blue cloak pinned over his left shoulder with a sparkling metal clasp. Over his back was slung a small, bronzed oval shield bearing the image of a hawk riding a horse.

He stood warily apart from me, one hand resting on the small knife at his belt, the other flexing with nervous energy. His stare was very direct and reminded me of that searching gaze of Urtha's, as he tried to understand all things that were strange whilst defiantly proclaiming with his eyes that nothing strange in the world would concern him.

'What have you done with my father?' the boy asked suddenly.

'I have done nothing with him,' I answered. 'I journeyed with him, I fought with him, I watched him defeat a great enemy.'

Both children smiled, their bright eyes widening. 'He won his combat?' Kymon demanded.

'Yes.'

'Cunomaglos, that traitor, is dead?'

'Yes. A river combat in the land of the Makedonians.'

'Then where is he? Where is my father?'

'Coming home by land. Slowly. I came by boat. Swiftly. You must have patience. There is a more urgent task for the two of you. I have to take you to your grandfather, Ambaros, back across the river.'

'I am certainly ready to do *that*!' the youth declared.

His sister clapped her hands together, equally keen. But whilst her brother stood and watched me carefully, she ran over to the other children, who were still playing their game of stick-ball. She stood and talked to them, and there was the sound of excitement and laughter. A moment later they had all scattered to gather objects and plants from around the meadow, within the stone walls, and grouped again in some childish but significant ritual of parting.

Kymon played no part in this celebration. His hard gaze had softened, but he was urgent to know the details of his father's triumph. On this side of the river he was very much a child; but like his sister, like all the forlorn, he would age to his true years when he set foot upon his own land.

That was why most of the happy brood of exiles would never be able to return to the land of the living.

'Is my father wounded?' he asked unexpectedly. 'Is that why he's coming home so slowly?'

'He defeated Cunomaglos magnificently. But his wounds were very severe.'

The boy thought about this. The man shone through his sudden smile, through his eyes. 'We'll all one day die of our wounds,' he proclaimed, as if rallying a band of skirmishers. 'But we can all live with them for years!'

'I don't doubt it,' I agreed, trying to hide my amusement at his precocity. 'Don't you want to say goodbye to your friends?'

He looked coy for a moment, as if coming to a decision. 'I had a good friend. But he went away. He didn't live with us here. But come and see what we built together!'

Glancing at the Mothers, he led me through the trees to a narrow path from the enclosed meadow. 'We're not allowed to do this, really, but I always get away with it.'

He brought me to an overhang of grey stone, deep enough to allow Kymon and myself to crouch inside. On the rock above my head was a crudely chipped image of a ship, the mast more than obviously phallic. The heads of the oarsmen could be seen, little helmeted figures with bulging eyes, though the oars they held were impractically thin. There were other little figures, made from twisted grass, scattered about the place, all of them armed with twigs. And mummified animals: bats and mice.

Kymon giggled as he saw my frown. 'This is the Father Calling Place,' he said.

'Is it, indeed?'

'My friend carved the ship with a piece of granite. I come here to think of my father. I call him home. He must come by sea in the end.'

'He's closer than you think,' I informed him. 'What was your friend's name?'

'He was a ghost boy. There are lots of them in Ghostland. He talked in a strange language, but I liked him.'

'Back to the land of the living,' I informed Kymon, and led the way back to the meadow.

Munda's closest friend was a younger girl, with spiky copper hair and green eyes, who answered to the name Atanta. The *modronae* were asked if Atanta could be taken with us as well. Munda was quite desperate to have her friend with her. The Mothers left it up to me. I looked at the younger girl, who waited so earnestly for my answer, and could not fail to agree. The Mothers seemed sad, but agreed that she could go.

There was something strange about Atanta: down each of her temples ran a line of blue spots, status tattooes that contrasted with the scatter of freckles on her impish face. This design was new to me. She was not from Urtha's land, or the land of Urtha's neighbours, the Coritani, whose High King was Vortingoros. I had seen such markings before, but exactly where slipped my mind for the moment. I was concerned more for Kymon and Munda for the present.

Atanta had packed a very clever sack: she had gathered a handful of elf-shot, those small stone arrow points which the earth disgorges, and had collected a quiver of thin ash shafts to which she might fix them. She had supplied herself for the journey, and for the unknown days ahead, with admirable efficiency.

I made Kymon and Munda attend to their own supplies with equal care, but all either of them could think to bring were apples!

The young Mother would take us back to the Nantosuelta.

She seemed very frightened and I tried to persuade her that I could easily find my own way through the forest. But perhaps she was required to be our guide in this Otherworld, and what she did she did from necessity. And of course, I had not displayed my abilities with charm and enchantment; to the young woman I was a man of limited powers.

We had no sooner reached the stream, a spear's throw from the hidden sanctuary, than we were forced into cover. A long line of riders thundered along the ridge above us, heads low, cloaks flowing, the grey light glancing from their shields. They were a white-faced straggle-haired band, about thirty in number. When one of the horses slipped and brought its rider down, tumbling down the slope towards us, the rest carried on as if unconcerned. The ghostly man recovered from the fall, and dragged his complaining steed by the reins back to the ridge, remounted and continued towards the river.

It was only then that I noticed Atanta lowering one of her elf-shot throwing arrows.

'I could have stung him,' she whispered. 'I'm good with these darts.'

And without waiting for a comment, she suddenly flexed her arm and sent the little weapon soaring towards the bleak ridge on the hill. To my amazement it seemed to float upon the air, and struck the earth where the riders had passed, quivering and remaining proud where it stuck from the turf.

I was glad she had reined back her enthusiasm for a kill. She might have alerted the war band to our presence, though their neglect for their fallen friend suggested a more focused pursuit.

The spirit boat was waiting for us, hidden among rushes. The war band had passed this way, the churned earth suggested as much, but they had not noticed the craft that lay concealed at the river's edge.

'Where do they cross?' I asked the young Mother.

'At the Ford of the Miscast Spear. It would take a long time to walk there. But it seems to be their only way across from this hinterland. It's well guarded by them. They are making the crossing easier.'

I would investigate that ford at another time.

The children clambered into the small boat and nestled down excitedly. Munda and Atanta held hands and sang a quiet song together, giggling at some private joke. I took my place in the stern and the little vessel nosed her way out through the reeds and cut across the river, towards the willow-fringed bank on the other side. When I glanced back, to wave to the young Mother, she had disappeared. Perhaps she was still standing there, but her cloak and cowl were camouflaged.

A short while later, the boat nosed among the drooping branches and came to rest in the shallows. Kymon had already jumped into the water and was wading to the muddy shore. Munda, laughing, followed her brother, scrambling up the slope to the clearing. But Atanta?

She stepped on to the land, shivering as if with a winter's chill. The change in her was quite apparent: the hardening of her eyes, the set of her mouth, the tautness of her skin. A child in shape and size, she was ageing rapidly.

Quickly, she took up her pack, and with a cry of sadness, and an anguished glance at her friend, she turned away from us and ran like the hound, away among the trees and out of sight. Munda called after her, then looked up at me, hurt and questioning. She seemed stunned. 'Why did she run away?'

'Let her go!' Kymon said stiffly. The lad was standing straight and staring into his own land. After a moment his tone softened. 'I expect she has other things on her mind. Sister, we have things to do, to get back to Taurovinda.'

'But why did she run away?' Munda asked again.

What could I say to the startled and saddened girl? That Atanta even now was going through the torture of Time's catching up with her. Isolated in the Otherworld for more than a few years, she was now grown to full womanhood. Those marks on her temples, the tattoo lines, were the markings of a kingdom to the south of here, I now remembered. Atanta had been a child exile from another clan, but a clan that still existed; she would now be going home to face the reality of how the desertion of the land had affected her own family.

Both Kymon and Munda had grown and matured by a year, taller, heavier, leaner around the face. If it was less apparent in the girl, it was because the girl was younger than her brother. But Kymon showed the first signs of adulthood. The look in his eyes was iron bright, and very determined.

Neither of them had seemed to notice the transition, the spurt

of growth, though they both noticed that their clothes were
shorter than before, something that briefly puzzled them.

'We have to go back to our father's house,' he said again,
with soft but firm encouragement. His glance at me was pecu-
liar. He added, 'Because our father is still alive . . . isn't that so,
Merlin?'

'Alive when I saw him last,' I reminded the boy, and Kymon
nodded, accepting my caution.

It was some time before Ambaros found us, with three of his
entourage, all heavily armed, and spare horses, two of them
suitable for the youngsters.

Grandfather and grandchildren embraced, tearfully in
Ambaros's case. He couldn't believe how tall the children had
grown, how strong they looked. Again, I thought of Atanta, and
of the pain she must be suffering, somewhere in the woodland.

Ambaros came over to me. 'Well done, Merlin. You've
brought them safely back. By Brigg, that lad has the look of his
father. He has the look of a king.'

I agreed with the proud old man. Then Ambaros added, ques-
tioningly, 'You, on the other hand, have the look of a man with
something on his mind.'

'One of the *modronae* told me where the Shadow host
crosses the river. There's just the one place. The Ford of the
Miscast Spear.'

Ambaros scratched his white beard, his eyes suddenly bright.
He had intuited my own train of thought.

'I've heard of it. It's where those who die at peace cross to
the Land of the Shadows of Heroes; to the islands. Yes, if we
could learn how to block that ford . . . '

Did the crow fly over him at that moment? If it did, I failed to
see it.

He spoke again with his grandchildren, then despatched
them with the other horsemen back to the valley of the exiles.
He and I then rode steadily along the river, keeping to cover,
alert for sound and movement. The land was so still it might
have been what the Greeklanders called the fields of Elysia, a
bright, unspoilt place; or a land called *eden*, which would have
existed during my own life, but which I had never found on my
long travel, though I had heard tales of it.

I became so lulled with the tranquillity and emptiness of this foray through the woodlands and sunny riverside meadows, that when the arrow came out of nowhere it was several moments before I realised what was happening.

The weapon struck Ambaros squarely in the chest, piercing his bull's-leather jacket, sending him tumbling back over the haunches of his horse. He crashed to the ground, doubled up, the shaft snapping. A second arrow thudded into my saddle, and a third struck my shoulder, but didn't penetrate through my own protective clothing.

I could hear the sound of horses, and gradually the eerie war cries of a skirmishing band. I opened my eyes—I should have done it before—and the tranquillity of the land fell away. And there, before us, was the ford, heavily guarded and very busy.

In that moment I glimpsed the between-world.

They had fortified the crossing, throwing up high banks of earth on each side of Nantosuelta, constructing towers and rings of the hewn trunks of trees, on each of which crouched a menacing figure, staring down at the approach from the land of the living. There was activity in the river herself, and a great bustle of ethereal figures, human and animal.

From this hive of activity, two men were riding towards us, one with a fourth arrow nocked and ready to shoot, the other with a long spear held ready to throw. I waited for the arrow, but the horseman lowered the bow and drew his sword. Ambaros had risen to his feet and had his own light javelin ready, the other hand on the dreadful wound in his chest.

I resorted to my own tricks of defence.

The hawk that stooped and struck at the nearer of the ghost riders knocked him from the saddle. The other man charged down on Ambaros, who ducked below the sword blow and tripped the horse with his spear. Shadow warrior that he was, on our side of the river he was evidently vulnerable, and Ambaros pushed the point of his knife with finality into the gap between helmet and wood-scaled cuirass. A dead man died again. But he had left his world and he would have known the danger.

It was only then that I realised how very like a Greekland helmet was the headgear of the fallen man; and on his shield: the image of Medusa.

Ambaros struggled back into the saddle, groaning loudly. He

kicked the horse to a gallop, clinging on for his life as he rode back the way he had come.

I despatched the hawk, took a last look at the ford and the watchtowers that guarded it, curious and concerned by what I had seen, and followed the old warrior, away from danger.

The spirit boat had already gone, returning to the evergroves by Taurovinda, where she would wait either for me or for the return of Argo that the Three of Awful Boding had foreseen.

Now Ambaros faced a two-day ride to the valley. He was obstinately redoubtable. 'The breastbone is cracked,' he announced airily, 'but the heart still beats. If I ride carefully there will be no further damage.'

He wouldn't allow me access to the wound. Better to keep everything in place, he advised. The leather, the cloth, the bronze of the arrow, better not to move them until he could be properly attended to.

'Are you in great pain?' I asked him, thinking I could help ease it if he were.

'Yes. But I've been in greater pain, Merlin. Today, looking into those children's faces, I don't believe there is any pain that can truly hurt me. Did you see the *life* there? That king-in-making! That queen-in-making! What a future! My daughter's children, Merlin. Aylamunda's children. Llew's eyes, if she could only see them now! She would be so proud.'

'She may well be able to see them,' I offered, but his response was a scowl of irritation.

'How? From where *she* is forced to wander? It is Aylamunda who is in pain, Merlin, not me.'

I didn't fully understand, so made no further comment.

Despite his refusal to accept medicine, I gathered what plants I could that I knew to be effective in healing such wounds as he had received. Although he seemed strong on our first night below the stars, during the second day of our return journey he began to shake and perspire quite dramatically. I begged him to let me use a little charm. 'No. If I live or die it must be at the Good God's whim.'

I gave him water and led his horse through the winding tracks and over the ragged ground that led to the valley. By the time we entered the narrow mouth of the gorge, he was slumped over the neck of his mount; I had tied his hands around the horse to stop him falling, and applied a compress to the swelling wound.

A glimpse inside him, and I knew that it was the end for him.

I was glad to pass his dying body into the hands of his kin. They stripped him and washed him under the instruction of a druid, whose eyes blazed from the red mask of ochre with which he had covered his face and crop-haired head. He spoke the songs of the past, and invoked Sucellus the healer. Kymon stood by, solemn and contemplative, not flinching as the bronze point was finally and bloodily teased from its lodging in the old man's breastbone.

Ambaros made no sound; his watery gaze never left that of his grandson.

'There is a lot for us to do,' Kymon whispered after a while. 'And I could have done with your strength and your advice. I hope you haven't squandered your life.'

He was angry as he turned and left the healing tent. Ambaros's smile was wry and pained.

CHAPTER FIVE

—

On the Plain of MaegCatha

That night, I received a most unwelcome visit, from someone I had hoped I had left behind far away in Greek Land.

My living quarters in the Camp of Exiles were uncomfortable and spartan, a reed-layered floor below an overhang of rock that had been extended and covered with animal hides to make a passable animal shelter. The breeze curled through every gap in the stitching, and a screech owl seemed to find the top of one of the supporting poles a perfect place to make my sleep a misery. The river flowing through the gorge seemed to rush like a torrent; the new-born of the exiled clan wailed with night terrors, setting off lowing among the cattle and vigorous barking among the tethered hounds.

Restless, haunted by those shields with their glowering ikons of Medusa, I was in just the state of mind to allow the approach of the woman who was determined to cling to me.

I heard my name called; there was urgency in the summons. There are ways of crying out that alert every sense: an infant in distress; a dying man giving up the ghost; a man being murdered; a woman opening like a gate, to allow the passing of a new breath of life. And there is the cry of hurt from a woman who considers herself wronged.

'Merlin! I know you're there!'

The insistent, dreamy voice roused me from my hard bed, bringing me out into the starlit night. The hounds were restless, the horses too. I walked east along the stream until I could see the crouched figure, busy washing its hair.

As I stumbled blindly over the loose rocks to come down to the swirling pool where this wild woman lowered her head to beat the water with her saturated locks, I realised who she was. Or rather: whose dream she was.

Niiv turned suddenly to look at me, silver-eyed in the night, pale lips half-smiling, everything about her signalling recognition and playfulness.

'Not sleeping well, Merlin?'

'I was until *you* came back.'

'Did you think I would stay away?' She tut-tutted, shaking her head. 'You'll never get rid of me. I'm a very determined girl.'

'Where are you?' I asked the dream.

'I don't know exactly. Sailing towards the North Star. We have a good breeze behind us. The coastline to the east is red and rugged, covered with stones; the argonauts call it Gaul. The white cliffs of Alba are ahead of us, but not far. Argo is strong, Jason is strong, we have some fine oarsmen!' She grinned pointedly. 'We'll be back with you before you know it.'

The apparition of Niiv flung back its hair. Dark hair, dyed, and a face that was a little more gaunt, but just as elfin and pretty as when I'd known her, the girl was still in fine form. But to reach for me like this, from a ship wave-tossed and struggling off the coast of Gaul, a long way south, was a waste of her limited talents.

Before I could say a word she went on, 'You've been hiding from me.'

'I've been in hiding. Not just from you.'

'I've flown across this land ten times looking for you, but this is the first time I've found you.'

She still exasperated me with her recklessness. 'You're a fool, Niiv. Your light will extinguish like a falling star. Have you seen a big man suddenly fall over dead, for no apparent reason, his heart suddenly stopped, his head suddenly full of blood? That is your fate if you continue to be so reckless with your small talent.'

'But with my small talent and your great ability, the young and the old, the new born and the ever-living, we could be wonderful together! We were made for each other, Merlin. How many times do I have to remind you? A man like you needs a companion like me. I will take nothing from you except that which you choose to give. You have me all wrong. I love you. I want to learn from you. Why are you so frightened of me?'

The river babbled beside us. I could see the glow of moonlight on the water through the crouching girl before me. She had been ageing and dying in her desperate efforts to find me, to be close again.

I could well understand why: she was a direct descendant of a Northlands woman I had known, very intimately, over a century ago. I had been aware that that snow-bound pleasure in my past would give rise to squealing flesh and blood, a daughter; but not that the daughter would lead, at last, to Niiv, who having met me once clung to me as if I were her life.

We sow the seeds of our own despair, but even knowing this, we seem to go on sowing.

'We are related,' this *fetch*, this living ghost of Niiv reminded me unnecessarily. 'But not so closely that we cannot enjoy each other. Wait for me, Merlin. Watch for me. You misunderstood me in Greek Land, you wronged me badly. We can be so strong together.'

I remembered my last glimpse of her, as I had finally escaped from her clutches, a pale-faced figure with wind-blown fair hair, arms outstretched, a dead swan held by the neck in her right hand. She had screamed at me, letting me know just how much she had looked into my future.

She had seen events in my future that terrified me. She used her knowledge as a fisherman uses a knife to prise limpets from their granite home. She was determined to open my body and see the markings on my bones, where magic lay; and where death lurked, waiting for betrayal.

She was the one return to Alba that I dreaded. The Three of Awful Boding had kept the worst to themselves, it seemed.

* * *

The shade of the girl finally dissolved, vanishing as Niiv, on the high sea, south of Alba, grew exhausted with her dream-journey. I was glad to see her go; I was unhappy that she had at last located me, but there were other things on my mind, at the moment, and I had time to prepare for the Northlands vixen who was following my spoor.

I was more concerned with understanding the two children who had, almost without my comprehending the process, come into my charge.

Kymon had not just grown in height, he had aged in mind; he had become a determined young man. And for the first time in a long while I would have to break one of my own rules: I would influence the way he thought.

After Niiv had disappeared, I stayed by the river at the eastern end of the valley, sleeping lightly. The water was clear and cold. It murmured to me, helped me think as I dreamed. I was wide awake before dawn, and as first light streaked the starry sky I heard the sound of ponies, approaching from the caves.

Kymon and Munda rode slowly past me. I hailed them and they stopped, peering at me as I emerged from my cloak. Kymon was in his battle-harness, shield on his back.

'Merlin?'

'Where are you going?'

The boy pondered the question for a moment, then shrugged. 'To Taurovinda. Where else? It's where we live.'

'But the fortress isn't safe. I've already told you that.'

'I have to see for myself,' Kymon retorted. 'I don't expect to be welcomed by the host who live there now.'

'Nor me,' said Munda. 'Why don't you come with us, Merlin? Grandfather says you can throw hawks in people's faces.' She laughed at this thought. 'All I have is a sling.'

I was furious with them. 'Have you forgotten that you were being searched for in your hideaway? You're in danger, you little fools! I didn't spirit you away from Ghostland just to see you ride into Ghostland's clutches in Taurovinda, like two pigs to the spit!'

They were going into danger, but they took no notice of me, more amused by my dishevelled appearance than concerned by my words. They were quite determined. I would not be able to persuade them by fair means, so it was now that I did a little charmed persuasion.

'You must not try to enter the fortress!' I stated bluntly. A shadow passed over their faces.

Kymon thought for a few moments, then scratched his chin as a man scratches his beard. 'Perhaps you're right. But what about a look from the distance? From the evergroves. Perhaps the Dead won't dare enter the sacred enclosure.'

'Very well,' I agreed—did my relief show?—and fetched a horse from the stables after telling the High Woman Rianata, who was known as the Thoughtful Woman, where we were going. She gave her permission, though from the look in her eye she didn't yet fully trust me.

Kymon and Munda, slightly built and riding energetic chariot ponies, covered a great deal of ground as I lumbered along, riding the best of Ambaros's war-horses, but uncomfortable even with a canter.

This was unknown territory to Kymon, though he knew to ride east, and I led them along the wooded edge of the river, whose crossing places, between the northern lands and the south, Urtha's fortress guarded. After a day we reached the evergroves and the mounds that had been raised over the honoured dead, including Urien, Urtha's younger son. This sacred wood was still untouched by the reivers from Ghostland, and my instinct told me that it would stay that way. It would be a haven close to home. But the Dead had certainly occupied the hill, though to Kymon's eyes the stronghold looked deserted.

Munda was more aware. She led her pony to the edge of the plain, frowning as she surveyed the great rise of the fort and its winding battlements. 'The place is haunted,' she said, but Kymon just laughed. 'The ghosts our own people,' he suggested. 'Those who haven't yet gone to the Land of Shadow Heroes.'

'It doesn't feel right,' the girl insisted and glanced at me, looking for an answer. She had more intuition than her brother, I suspected; or perhaps just more sense.

'The fortress is occupied,' I agreed with her.

'By what people?' Kymon asked gruffly. 'I don't see their banners. I don't see their guards. Do you?'

This last was addressed to his sister. Munda nodded. 'They are watching us,' she advised. 'They are still strangers in our land.'

I watched her as she said this. She had gone into a daze, though it lasted only a moment.

'Now you sound like those women who guarded us!' Kymon snapped angrily. 'You are too dreamy, sister. Fill your sling and balance your javelin. We'll be back here to repair what those moondogs have done to our home!'

The last Kymon had seen of his home it had been burning fiercely, and the ground between houses, corrals, shrines and forges had been littered with the dead; and there had been no visible evidence of the skirmishers who were inflicting the destruction on the Fort of the White Hill.

The last he remembered was when Maglerd, his father's mastiff, had dragged him down, then pulled him to safety, Gelard, carrying Munda, following. Those hounds had run for all their worth, leaping the barricades, sliding down the ramparted slopes, slinking through bush and woodland, following the rivers and streams until, charged by some inner fury, some silent guide, they had brought these children to safety, ironically in the very kingdom of the Dead that had raided the fort.

'We can return and rebuild,' Kymon announced loudly again.

'The intention is admirable,' I suggested to him, 'but you are outnumbered.'

'Outnumbered by what? By dark clouds? By burned thatch roofs?' He was flushed with pride and fury.

'By the Dead. By the Unborn. They're in there now, in force.'

'I've lived in the Land of the Dead,' he said arrogantly. 'They ride proudly. But what harm can they do here?'

'Harm enough to have sacked this fort, and sent you into exile.'

'They were not the Dead,' Kymon snapped. 'They were Trinovanda, bull-stealers and slave-takers, mercenaries, disguised as the Dead!'

'How would you know?' I asked the proud youth. 'You were fallen, dazed, and dragged by hounds. How do you know who raided Taurovinda?'

'I've had time to think about it,' he said, leaning on the shield, watching me through eyes that were narrowed with inquisitiveness. 'The Trinovanda are the worst of our enemies. It makes sense to me.' Then he teased me with a look. 'Are you afraid of the Dead, Merlin?'

'Yes. I find them unpredictable.'

The answer bemused him. He glanced at Munda. 'And what about you, sister? Does this damage look like the work of wraiths, or the work of raiders?'

'Merlin is right,' Munda said softly. 'You weren't in the house when Urien died. I was. I saw the whole thing.'

For the first time, Kymon's resolve weakened. He frowned, straightened and glanced back at the silent ruins on the plain. But he would not be shaken from his goal. I heard him mutter, 'This place is ours. It's what my father would want, and what my mother would want, and what grandfather would want . . . this place is ours.'

If I'd thought for a moment that he was signalling it was time to return to the camp, I was wrong. He swung himself across the low saddle of his copper mare, then kicked the pony viciously in the flanks, whipping the reins so that the animal foamed round its bit, reared up then bolted through the edge of the grove and out into the scrub of the plain, towards the tall outer gate with its bleached skulls of bulls. He screamed as he rode, his right fist held high.

And before I could say a word, the girl had followed him, making the sound of a crow: *krah, krah, krah.* She rode, head low, small spear held across the girth of her pony. What impulse made her follow her brother like this I can only imagine.

Kymon rode furiously up and down before the Bull Gate, shouting abuse at the unseen, unseeable enemy.

'You Dead! You Unborn!' He sneered the words, several times, turning them into a rich and juicy insult, surprising from his unbroken voice. Then he added, to Munda's great amusement—she cheered as he shouted—'You bastards! You are the sons of men who ran from combat! And hid below their cowls, exposing their backsides like dogs in submission! Suckled on tits that were no more than old leather wine pouches! Suckled by mothers who never had a chance to wash their backs because they were never off them! Fostered with mange-riddled dogs and foot-rotten sheep because no king's sons would be seen *alive* with you!'

Munda rode nervously out of arrow range as this diatribe proceeded, calling, 'Enough now, brother. Save your anger for when you can get at their guts and do some cutting.'

He ignored his sister, standing up on his horse, balanced on the narrow saddle, arms spread wide. 'I will *not* be evicted from my father's house,' he screamed again, and his words started to echo from the sheer walls of Taurovinda.

Now he waved the oval shield above his head. Sunlight caught the image of the horse and hawk. I saw light reflected on ghostly eyes, high above, beyond the steep earthen walls, a line of men listening carefully to every word that this brash and dangerous youth had uttered, taunting and challenging the occupying force.

I had thought this would be the end, that he would ride back to safety, but to my amazement Kymon suddenly went into warp-spasm, still standing on his calm pony. Fists clenched to his chest, face distorted, skin as white as ash and sucked in against the flesh, he shouted the old curse, the curse of challenge.

'I will make you endure hardship and the long sigh!' he howled at the men above the gate. 'Your own blood a red plague, your women red-eyed. I will play you at the stabbing game! My face, blood-filled, rage-filled, my eyes, ice-filled, hate-filled! I will be weary after triumph, a crow that scours the ploughed ground of your flesh. My sword, the thorn that pricks the rose-bloom of your hopes and dreams, your blood the blossom, blossoming on your breast, on your shield the blossom of your brother, clotting rose, petal-scattered crimson! I will be the plucking man, your bloom at my mercy!'

This was too much for the Dead, those who remembered issuing and defending against this proud boast. A boy was challenging them; tempers could flare, even after death.

The gates were flung open and five heavy horsemen pounded towards Kymon. The spasm left the boy at once and he dropped into the saddle, kicked his pony round, whipped it with the reins and streaked back across the plain towards the evergroves. He laughed as he rode, his sister by his side, crouched low over the withers of her own mount. Slingshot whistled past them, striking into the cover of the haven where I watched, but the two of them galloped into safety, each horse stumbling and throwing its rider but without serious injury.

The pursuing host spread out in a line, horses breathing hard, hard men sitting low, watching us through masked helmets.

Kymon returned to the edge of the groves, loosened his britches and urinated on to the turf, watching the enemy with cold eyes.

Angry though he was, Kymon refused to return to the valley. We waited until dusk, then he went to the grove where Urtha's father and mother lay together, below a low cairn of stones. Kymon's grandmother, Riamunda, had been a powerful woman in the land. It was through her strength and her cunning that the land of the Cornovidi had stretched as far as it did, and had come to take in the borderland with the Otherworld itself.

There were many stories of Riamunda. She could still be seen, a silver owl with wings of hazel, flying across the fortress each midwinter, keeping an eye on events down below.

She had clearly been unable to stop the sacking of her ancestral home.

But now Kymon sang a song to her, joined by Munda, who followed his lead. It was not a song of summoning, but of courage, of intent. He drew on her sleeping soul for the inner strength to do what he had to do. The cairn was simply the grave, but his voice would echo into whatever part of Ghostland she inhabited. Ghostland was a complex realm. It had its land for queens, separate from its land for heroes.

'Grandmother,' he finally whispered, 'even if I am one against an army, your country will never come under bondage. I cannot wait for my father to return. He may never return. I am battle-eager. Send me hawks to strike from the sun and carrion birds to clean up the field. Fly low over me, and screech if I hesitate. But grandmother . . . come back to MaegCatha, and haunt the plain. I will draw comfort from your shadow.'

Two days later, as we came back to the valley and the camp of the exiles, I was saddened to see a women washing a bloody shirt in the river, thrashing the garment against exposed rocks, not really cleaning it at all, simply manifesting grief. I thought immediately that Ambaros had died, but it turned out to be the death of a child, who had fallen from the cliff while trying to snare one of the small birds which nested there. Since there was no shortage of food for this vanquished society, his intention must have been either magic or propitiation. His parents had both been killed in the last raid on Taurovinda. Now his broken body lay in its tunic on a small bier, away from the dogs, while his guardians discussed burial or a small pyre.

Ambaros was still very weak. His face had no colour to it, his breath was foul, there were shadows gathered about him. The glitter had gone from his eyes, which were moist and unfocused. That said, he was drawing a little strength from somewhere.

'Do you have any thoughts,' he asked me weakly, 'on the consequences of being slaughtered by your own ancestors?'

I told him, bleakly, that I had no insights, and my ideas would be guesses. I was as puzzled by Ghostland as was he.

'Nevertheless, I'll promise you this,' he went on. 'Whether I live or die, I'll fight to stop them crossing the river. They don't belong in this world. You can depend on me. Tell my grandchildren, will you?'

'You can tell them yourself,' I pointed out, but he laughed cynically.

'Munda, yes. But the boy reminds me of his mother. Impatient and quick to anger. And nothing angered Aylamunda more than an unnecessary death.'

I could have glanced into Ambaros's future at that moment, but I declined to do so. He was between the sky and the earth, no more than half dead, no more than half alive. He had seen nearly fifty winters. The time that nestled in those big bones and broad shoulders would either work for him or for his departure to Ghostland.

It was not my business to interfere.

Although Munda visited her grandfather, Kymon did not. Instead, the youth summoned a council, in the biggest of the enclosed caves in the valley, and requested a feast. When it was pointed out to him that the community was in mourning for the boy who had fallen from the cliff, he suggested combining the wake with the Call to Battle. This entailed eating prepared food in a different order, and seating the High Women and the warriors in a different place, but Kymon cut through this ritual with the simple exhortation that: 'I am still a youth; but I am my father's son, and I will be the first to speak. I will honour the dead boy. I will honour him at his burial. But we are not in the royal lodge, we are in a cave in the wasteland between life and death. Don't fuss about the orderliness of the dead when all that is necessary is to hear the proposal of the living.'

I imagine he had worked quite hard on that assertive and pompous little speech.

He placed the small oval shield, with its hawk and horse, at the centre of the circle of small wooden tables, and placed a cushion, a small bowl and an eating blade beside it. I knew what he was doing. There were palaces in the east where this eccentric action by one so young would have been greeted with amusement and tolerance; others where it would have been greeted with benign intolerance or even mild punishment. But so simple an action as commanding the shield centre of the circle, among the Celts as I will choose to all them, could as easily result in the summary execution of Kymon, for assuming a right in the king's absence that should have been contested, as it might in the gentle acceptance of his right to occupy this manly space simply because he was his father's son.

Munda, being who she was, had the greater right to occupy the centre space. Although I record these stories at a later time than their occurrence, I remember well how high in the society of decision-making and battle-planning were the women of Alba; it changed later, but in Urtha's day, he was the right arm of power and Aylamunda, while she had lived, had been the left. When dead, they would occupy different territories in the Land of the Shadows of Heroes, though there would be paths to draw them together as need and memory necessitated.

It was not, therefore, the surviving band of Urtha's *uthiin* who posed the danger to Kymon, but the High Women who had survived, and whose ancestors were the *modronae* who sheltered the exiled children in Ghostland.

Meat was roasted and fowl was boiled; the smell of sour bread and sweet cakes drifted fragrantly through the valley. Honey was stirred into the coarse ale, and leather flasks were filled and placed at table.

At the end of the valley, in a small hazel glade, the pit had

been dug to take the boy. He was laid there quite without ceremony, but with a little pigmeat, a sword, his cloak and memen-
toes of his parents. Kymon uttered a brief chant of forlorn hope
in a desperate world; he summoned the boy's ghost back from
the Otherworld to help at Taurovinda. The earth was piled
above the corpse, and then we went to eat.

Kymon sat silently in the centre of the ring of tables as the
uthiin, the High Women, and the Speakers for the Past, for the
Land and for Kings—the druids, in other words—settled on
their benches and began to drink. The flesh was cut from the
bone and distributed; bread passed round the table. When
everyone was eating, busying themselves with conversation and
protocol, Kymon stood, fetched meat and bread for himself and
filled a cup with water that had been drawn from the spring.

All eyes were on him, I now realised. He seemed unconcerned by the steady gaze of these rough-bearded, rough-
clothed men. He ate quietly and slowly. Two children sang for
the host, but Amalgaid, the poet, remained silent. This was not
the time to mock or celebrate the past deeds of the men here.

Suddenly, the oldest of the *uthiin* tossed the bone from his
portion on to the floor next to Kymon. The boy calmly regarded
the other man, then picked up the remnant and placed it on his
plate. A second bone came from another direction. Kymon
placed it on his plate. Then one of the elder women threw a
small, red scarf towards him. Kymon wound the fabric round
his wrist. The woman smiled at him, then murmured something
to the man who sat next to her. He frowned, but drew a small,
bronze knife and tossed it carefully in the boy's direction.
Kymon picked it up, gathered up the animal bones and stood,
the oval shield balanced before him against his body.

'If this is all you offer me to fight with, then I will fight with it.'

Two of the *uthiin* looked alarmed; they had not offered their
services to the youth, they had intended to tease him. Now one
of them stood—a man called Gorgodumnos, red-haired and
red-bearded, wearing half his battle-harness, scales of leather
over a green jacket and a bronze torc round his powerful neck.

'By what right do you take the centre?'

'I was never taught my rights in this sort of matter,' Kymon
answered loudly. 'When the slaughter happened, I was taken by
the neck and carried into Ghostland. I had only just begun to

learn. But this shield was Urtha's, the king's, my father's. He carried it when we took the fire to Herne's Grove at midwinter dusk.' He slapped the image on the front of the ceremonial shield. 'The hawk rides the horse through the worst of winter, watching for spring. I was wearing it across my back on the night I was carried to safety. I claim it as mine. There is a message for us all in this bronze and silver symbol. I offer it as the standard that will take us back to Taurovinda.'

'There is a wasteland there,' Gorgodumnos said sourly. 'When Urtha left, the druid Sciamath's ancient prophesy came true. Three wastelands. And the second wasteland is here! The realm was sacked, soiled and deserted. There is nothing there for us to return and claim.'

Kymon waved the chicken bone in the air. 'But you have pledged me your sword and spear,' he said, and there was the merest ripple of laughter at the retort.

'There is nothing to gain by going back,' Gorgodumnos insisted.

'There is everything to gain,' Kymon insisted more strongly. 'The evergroves, the orchards in the fort itself, the springs, the lives of our ancestors; the land that our children will inherit! We are all that is left of the Cornovidi for the moment. But in Ghostland, the Unborn wait to cross into the woods and fields that we have hunted and farmed for longer than I can imagine.'

'My sons lie dead and unburied, somewhere on the Plain of MaegCatha, dragged out by ghosts, but slaughtered by iron.'

Kymon hesitated for a moment, seeming to struggle for words. Then a small voice, a girl's voice, murmured, 'If you will not avenge their deaths, then there is more than one wasteland scourging the land of Cornovidi.'

Gorgodumnos glanced furiously at Munda, who had risen to her feet, behind the circle of benches. But though his face was set grim and he shook his head, he said nothing.

Next to him, his heavy-set brother, Morvodugnos, rose to his feet and placed his sword, point inwards, across the table. 'There are not enough of us to take a heavily defended fort.'

'We must gather an army,' Kymon said. 'From the Coratoni, my father's friends, from the Trinovanda, if they will accept delayed payment for their services; we can scout north for Parisii. We cannot surely be the only survivors.'

I hesitated to tell Kymon that the lands of the Coritani, to the east as far as the sea coast, were deserted as well, wooden effigies being all that remained of the knights and spearmen who had once formed such effective war bands.

A wan young man called Drendas then asked, 'Who will lead the expedition? You are the king's son, but you are too young.'

'Nevertheless,' Kymon said strongly. 'I will lead the expedition. However, I will expect wise and profound counsel from all of you. This is not a question of glory. It is not a question of cattle. It is not a question of tribute. It is not to extend our hunting territory. It is to reclaim the land inside our walls; and to banish the Dead to beyond our earth, and send the Unborn back to bide their time. I will do it for the memory of my father and mother. My sister here will show as strong a heart. We sit here at the edge of a wasteland, but Munda is right: whilst we do nothing, we are as dead as the land that was once our home.'

All but Gorgodumnos had warmed to Kymon, perhaps more for the confidence with which he had spoken than for the content of his rallying cry. And Gorgodumnos himself seemed more bemused by what was happening than angry at the proposal.

Later, Ambaros sent for me. He had been told of his grandson's address to the *uthiin* and the High Women.

He told me of several bands who had escaped from the various scenes of destruction when Taurovinda itself had been sacked. They were settled in the hills to the north, in a winding gorge to the south, and at a lake's edge in the Forest of Andiarid, the 'silver horn'.

Then Ambaros reached for my arm, his grip surprisingly strong. I could feel the beating of his heart. He was still between earth and sky, but he was increasingly urgent for life. Life comes where life is demanded. He was sucking vitality from the humid air of the valley itself!

'You know as well as I,' he said, 'that Ghostland is encroaching on us. That the war band will be facing an army of shadows. I'm proud of my children. But I believe that Urtha *will* return and if that happens . . . can you imagine what it would do to him to find *all* his family dead? Please make sure that whatever happens—whatever!—those children are protected. You can do that, can't you, Merlin?'

'It's certainly within my abilities,' I reassured him.

The grip on my arm relaxed. His eyes narrowed as he stared at the sprawl of painted animal figures that seemed to flow across the ceiling of this old home, like a herd of horned creatures and horses from some feverish dream. This was a very strange haven.

'Why, I wonder? Why are they doing it?' he mused. 'Why cross the river? I have lain here for however long, and I cannot understand why the Dead should be unhappy with their own realm . . . to me, when I watch it from Mourne Hill, even from the river's edge, I see the forests and fields of my strongest wish. I'd be happy there. If this split in my heart fails to heal, I'll be content to ride through the tracks there, hunt the forests, cross to the islands. What has made them so angry? So warlike?' His eyes met mine for a second. 'Not a question for the likes of me, I can hear you thinking. Keep your senses alert, Merlin. You see farther than anyone I know.'

'So I keep being told.'

He drifted away from me. He had achieved what he wanted, with simplicity and candour: that I was to care for the children, and not to neglect my talents when it came to understanding the blighting wasteland beyond this valley.

But now it was as if the *uthiin* had woken from a dream. The idea of a 'quest ride' set them combatively and competitively at each other. Only four of them could be spared to ride in search of recruits. So they engaged in games and a tournament to win the right to leave the camp of the exiles.

Gorgodumnos was among the winners, and Cimmenos, and a young knight called Munremur, and his foster brother Cethern. These four then trimmed their beards and tied their hair, waxed their leathers and high boots and the curves and strips of bronze that they used to protect the more vulnerable parts of their bodies. They each selected a 'full grip' of the thin-shafted throwing javelins that were useful in all conditions of battle, and the smith keened the edges of their long-bladed iron swords. Lastly, they attached charms to their leather-scaled jackets and trousers.

Amalgaid the poet was persuaded to pay them tribute in verse, though he clearly found it hard to say anything at all favourable about Gorgodumnos, who merely shrugged off the insult. 'A poet's tongue is like a bull's prick,' he said indifferently.

We waited for him to explain, but he seemed to think his meaning was clear enough and turned away.

Whatever darkness lay between them, no one referred to it. This was not the time to settle enmity between survivors of a greater threat.

Provisioned, and given the protection of Nemetona after washing at the gushing spring, they rode out in a group at dawn, slowly at first, then at the canter, their wolf-cries echoing back along the valley for half the morning before at last all was silent again.

Later, Kymon sought me out; I was curled up against a rock, close to the stream, a favourite place. He sat down beside me, cross-legged, drawing his cape around his body to protect against the night dew. His hair was unbound, though he now wore a thin torc around his neck, signalling that he was taking the role of a warrior in the coming events.

But he was less triumphal, more thoughtful.

'How can the ghost of my great-grandfather, say, shoot an arrow that can kill me?'

'On our side of Nantosuelta, the Dead are both dangerous and vulnerable.'

'So a dead man can be killed again. Do you understand the rules of the situation, Merlin? Why can we see them one moment and not the next?'

'I don't know. I'm still working it out. Besides, I thought you believed the enemy were opportunists from another clan, claiming a deserted fortress for their own, and not the Dead at all?'

He shrugged, not responding to the gentle criticism. 'I can believe in both, I suppose, though renegades are easier to comprehend. But I remember that night very clearly, when Taurovinda fell. It was so confusing. It was so . . . strange.'

I didn't interrupt him. He seemed to need to talk about the night of his mother's murder.

'I remember being fetched from my foster home by Cunomaglos, my father's foster brother and dearest friend. He told me to prepare to return to Taurovinda. My brother Urien was to come as well.

'We were training at the time, practising running barefoot, and using slingshot to bring down geese as they fled the surface of a lake. It was summer and we had made friends in our foster home. I wasn't happy to leave. But when Cunomaglos brought us home it was to find a farewell feast in preparation. Our sister Munda was too young to understand what was happening.

'My mother and grandfather Ambaros made a great fuss of us. We were given horn-hilted knives, and new woollen cloaks, and made to parade up and down before the *uthiin* horsemen. We were called "the little guardians". The whole town was singing. Urien and I made mischief. We killed one of my father's pigs, I remember, and took its bowels and lungs to the sanctuary of Sequana, where we burned them, asking her in exchange to frustrate my father's journey and send him home.

'My father was furious when he found out. I hadn't seen him for years and now he raged at my brother and myself. We had abused the protecting spirit of the kingdom; and we had broken one of his *geisa*. I didn't understand the law of taboo on the king and his family at that time, even though two had been put on my own life when I was born. On Urien too. Urien died rather than break one of his.

'We were banished for one night and one day to a small house by the tannery, where the air was foul. But our father came to us to say goodbye. He was still angry, but he told us that he was going in search of the shield of Diadara, polished bronze on a disc of oak and ash, in whose reflection could be seen the future. He knew where to find it, in a northern land. He would bring it home. Through Diadara's shield he would see the answer to a question that had been concerning him greatly. It was to do with succession, and with the holding of the kingdom after his death. He had had a far-seeing dream, and had been disturbed. While he was away we were to treat Ambaros as our father, to behave ourselves and steal neither piglet nor goose, nor chase stray cattle—everything we'd been trained for!—but instead to train in weapons and simple poetry, and to obey one rule absolutely: that whatever Munda decided in a quarrel between the two of us—Urien and me—was to be the decision we would accept.

'I wasn't happy with that instruction, but Urien was killed before Munda could find a reason to rule us.

'That was a bad night. My father had long since left on his quest. Cunomaglos, his favourite brother, was in charge of everything. But riders had arrived at the fort, weary men from the east. Ambaros was nervous. He made the children stay out of sight. That night there was a good feast, storytelling, and an exchange of news. But in the morning, Cunomaglos and most of my father's knights left the walls, riding east, riding for fortune. Grandfather Ambaros rode after them, but he returned in a fury. We had been abandoned. Cunomaglos, my father's friend, had abandoned us.

'And what then? All I know is that we were attacked at night, by a host of men who charged through our gates and set fire to our houses. I couldn't see them! I saw my mother struck down, and Urien pursued into my father's house, a great hound following at the leap. The town was in mayhem. We could see horses but not riders, torches but not the men who carried them. I could smell blood, but could not see the blades which drew it.

'Then a hound leapt for me, chewed at my clothes. I tried to kill it, but it used a massive paw to strike the sword from my hand, and then it struck me a blow. The next I knew I was in the marshes behind the hill, being dragged by the dog. Munda was in the jaws of another. For more than a day we were carried by those creatures; they swam the river before they turned and ran from us, and all I remember then is Munda whispering, "They were our own hounds: Maglerd, Gelard . . . they saved us!"'

Kymon frowned, threw a stone into the stream, then looked at me sharply. After a moment he leaned back on his elbow. 'This feels like the right time to hear what happened to my father after he went to find his brother. Will you tell me?'

'Of course.'

He propped his head on his fist and listened with complete stillness and without interruption as I sketched the river journey aboard Argo, more than the cycle of a moon rowing eastwards, to the shores of a great river dedicated to the goddess Daan, even hauling the ship overland between headwaters.

I told him how we had followed the trail of waste and

destruction of an army of Celts, perhaps fifty thousand strong, and their wagons and cattle, and riders and charioteers. This enormous force was set on raiding and plundering the Oracle at Delphi. Cunomaglos and his men were hidden somewhere in that heaving mass of warriors. It was a long search.

But in the land of the Makedonians, north of Greek Land, Urtha finally found his foster brother, riding with a cohort of Arvernii, and summoned him to combat.

'They fought waist deep in a river, close to the sea; as I remember it, Cunomaglos called for heavy iron spears, and round shields; then Urtha called for short throwing spears and slim-bladed swords. Two ferocious bouts of fighting ensued. Each man was weakened with loss of blood. But on the third encounter, Cunomaglos called for no weapons at all, only what the river could offer them. They used stones and driftwood as clubs; they wrestled and boxed. Then Cunomaglos struck your father a blow that sent him below the water, and held him down with the last of his strength.

'But suddenly the river was full of blood and broken spears! To the west, a war band of the Celts, foraging inland, had been ambushed by a force of Makedonians and were fighting across the river. The broken dead and their broken weapons came flowing through the scene of combat.

'Cunomaglos grabbed a spear and struck Urtha through the breast, but the strike was weak, though the wound was bad. Then Urtha too grabbed the jagged shaft of a throwing spear as it passed in the stream. He killed his foster brother with a single, savage thrust.

'A moment later, Maglerd, his great hound, leapt into the river and made sure that Cunomaglos stayed below the water, holding him there until his body was swept out into the dusk-dark sea.'

Kymon's eyes were alive with pride as he jumped to his feet. Munda was laughing nervously, the images disturbing to her.

'So much for the Dog Lord!' the boy said loudly. 'I am not allowed to invoke the gods, but by the strength in my hair, there is no hunter, no haunter more powerful than the betrayed! This is a story that all poets should learn by heart, Merlin! I will call it the Feat of the Shattered Spear. Will you prepare it in verse for me? It should take at least half an evening to tell.'

I reminded Kymon that I was neither druid nor poet, but assured him that I would recount the story in detail to a more qualified man. He seemed content enough with the proposal.

Within ten days our numbers had increased by twenty men, mostly of older stock, ten youths practised in warfare, and fifteen women very practised in arms and ferociously willing to set their skills against even a supernatural enemy. These recruits had come with Cimmenos and Munremur, and they brought provisions with them, and extra horses, and even four chariots, which were repaired and strengthened.

Cethern returned later with two Wolf-heads, soothsayers, usually druids who had been banished by the king. They were filthy, pale-fleshed and dressed in the grey and blue skins of feral animals. He also had in tow four slaves who had escaped from the stronghold of Ferdach, king of the Dubnonii, and had been wandering aimlessly for half a year. Their bow fingers had been removed, and their left ankles hobbled. But they demonstrated how they had learned to shoot and throw with left hand and left arm; and like the bestial Erian giants known as *fomori* they were adept at moving swiftly on one good foot. It was strange to watch, but they were quite determined to win back honour. They had been part of a band of sea-raiders from the Erian kingdom of Meath, across the western sea; they had been the only survivors. One of them was a woman, Caithach, who was related to Scaithach, legendary trainer of champions.

As for the Wolf-heads, there was something familiar about them. It is to my shame that I didn't at once recognise them for who they were. The truth was a hound, waiting to spring.

But where was Gorgodumnos in all of this?

Two days later, his horse came slowly and wearily up the stream, following its instinct. It was still saddled and bridled. There were no weapons in the sheaths. The horse's mane was black and matted with blood.

Ambaros was told the news.

The man's mood darkened. 'We have lost Gorgodumnos? Then we have lost the best of us, in many ways. His caution was one of our strengths. Kymon should certainly now take the counsel of the most experienced among us, from this valley and from the new arrivals. And tell Merlin to throw his own caution to the wind, and his farsight at Ghostland. We will need to know the strength of this invasion.'

And I'm told that he added, 'And what it hopes to achieve.'

When Kymon heard this he ordered the construction of an earth model of Taurovinda from memory, its gates, defences and the surrounding plain. The river systems were drawn in the ground. Bracken served as forest and marsh. The warlords crouched around the display to discuss tactics. They were impressed by the look of the stronghold, as if seen from the eyes of a hawk, high above.

But at the end of the day it was clear that Urtha's fortress had been so well constructed, and so well defended, that nothing short of a headlong confrontation through its five main gates would achieve anything at all. The western gate, looking out over a great area of marsh and mere and cut through jagged outcrops of dark rock, heavily swathed in tangles of thorn, was passable only to an army of ghosts, someone said.

Indeed (this man was courteously reminded) that is how Taurovinda had fallen in the first place.

Kymon became impatient with the discussion and tried again to assert his authority over the gathering of chiefs.

'Whether there are ten or a hundred of the enemy behind the walls of the fort, the problem is in the *seeing*. If they truly are the Dead, and not renegades from the south as I half suspect, then we will be fighting thin air. But Merlin can assist us. He is a man of wild talent; he told me so himself. I refuse to believe that he cannot help take the darkness from our eyes, so that we can see the enemy charging down on us. And if I understand you right, Merlin, in our land that enemy, those ghosts, are as vulnerable to us as we are to them!'

I agreed with him, and he turned away.

Outside the circle, Munda sought out my shadowy figure. Her eyes asked the question: *will* you do that for us?

If I can, I will, I tried to tell her. She seemed satisfied with the silent answer, though I suspect she was only responding to her own intuition about my limitations.

CHAPTER SIX

—

Battle-eager, Ice-hearted

It was finally agreed that the reclamation of the hill fortress of Taurovinda, either by force or unimpeded entry, would begin at dawn in two days' time. Munda immediately went in search of omens, with the permission of Rianata, the Thoughtful Woman. A guardian went with her. The *uthiin*, and men of equivalent rank from the other clans, set up contests for the right to ride in this or that position, or to take one of the few chariots that this small host now possessed.

Kymon had been training hard in what the Celts called 'the feats'. These included snatching a spear thrown by an enemy and returning it in one movement; using a shield as an offensive weapon and not just for defence; running along the pole of a chariot, standing on the yoke and casting a weapon before running back to the car; and a gymnastic display that was reminiscent of the Greeklanders in older times, a way of jumping high into the air and somersaulting backwards and forwards, with the thrust or slash of sword or spear incorporated into the movement.

Under the skilful guidance of the Erian slave, Caithach, Kymon took a final course of training in the feat of Welcoming the Blow, the ways to bend and flex the body when the strike came home, twisting so as to minimise the damage of the blade that enters the flesh, and holding and pressing to slow the deadly wound until safety has been attained.

Caithach was a sturdy, red-haired woman, easy with the display of her scarred and wounded body, and it was clear that many of the strikes should have been fatal. The worst wound was the hobbling of her left leg, but she had overcome the damage by pure will.

'It's not all about the attack,' she repeated over and over again. 'It's very much to do about returning to the fight. Like your father, at that foreign river. Hounds could have glutted themselves on the flesh Cunomaglos cut from him. But he was able to fight a third time and vanquish the Dog Lord.'

At the end of the day, Kymon finally mastered what Caithach called the Feat of the Four Points: four light spears thrown forward, backward and to the sides in a single movement. He was exhausted but triumphant, applauded by several of the *uthiin*, who scowled when the boy challenged them to demonstrate their own skills. They had once trained, of course, but they had grown lazy and sluggardly in the absence of action.

'Tomorrow!' Caithach declared in her rich brogue. 'Tomorrow we will all go through the motions.'

'Include Merlin in that,' Kymon said with a grin, as he caught his breath. 'And Munda too,' he added, looking around, puzzled. 'Where is she? She should be learning the feats.'

He shrugged the thought away and discarded his training clothes for more comfortable attire (training was undertaken in sandals, simple tunic and a weighty leather cuirass to simulate the most vigorous of battle conditions) then went to find a little meat, and to talk to frail Ambaros.

Mention of Munda reminded me that she and her guardian had been gone from the encampment for the better part of the day. I had taken her idea of searching for portents and omens as childish indulgence, since, though she was certainly intuitive, she could not have been skilled in the manner of divination and interpretation of the marks on the land that signified the imminence of events. Where had the girl got to?

The thought occurred to me that perhaps her stay in Ghostland had sharpened the horizons of her budding skill in charm, but I felt certain that the *modronae* would have made that fact known to me when they had secured my services in the rescue from the Otherworld.

How blind I was!

I followed the stream out of the valley to where it flowed into the broader river. The banks were dense with drooping willow; the river rushed noisily over a shallow, stony bed. Her guardian, no more than a girl herself, was curled up, half asleep, against a spreading oak. Somewhere, hidden from view, I could hear the sound of a girl singing.

Munda was sitting cross-legged on a rock, trailing the shaft of a thin arrow in the water. Her gaze was on the far bank where a tall woman stood, half obscured by the bushes and her dark cape. Long, luxuriant red hair framed a pale, lean face, but did not hide the vertical lines of pin-point markings on each temple.

The moment this stranger saw me she raised a hand and withdrew into the undergrowth. Munda stopped singing at once, then looked up at me, her eyes moist. There was an aura around her, a shimmering in the air; she seemed for a moment to be unreal, dreamlike.

And she uttered words that astonished me. 'Nothing is hidden,' she said, almost with a sigh. 'I see it bleached. I see it bone.'

I crouched down. Her gaze followed me, but she was focused elsewhere. Then the mood snapped, the shimmering about her body faded, she seemed to see me for the first time and smiled.

She raised the arrow with its elf-shot flint point. 'It's from Atanta,' she said. 'She sent it to me. That woman over there brought it from her. It means I'll meet Atanta again. She said once she'd always look after me.'

'I think she will,' I said to the girl, then helped her up. She was stiff with sitting for so long in one position.

'Did you see any omens?' I asked her. 'About tomorrow?'

What would she say? Was she aware that she had been possessed a few moments ago? I knew those words, I knew what they signalled. Few women are born to it, and their lives are either blighted by it, or made brilliant. It was known among the

High Women and druids as the *imbas forasnai*, the Light of Foresight. It was a small talent compared to mine, certainly, but it was sinister in that the vision was uncontrollable, unstoppable, sudden, often brutal and told at once—there was no avoiding the expression of what had been seen, no waiting for the right moment.

Many battles had been lost or won because of the sudden words 'Nothing is hidden', followed by a devastating vision.

I see it bleached. I see it bone.

She had had a glimpse of something, but did she know it? Apparently not. In answer to my question concerning omens she referred to more simple auguries.

'I saw several. Marise saw them too. She went back to the valley. Didn't you speak to her?'

'No. Tell me about the omens.'

As we walked back along the banks of the stream Munda described the encounters:

'At midday, three sparrowhawks flew together from east to west. Three sparrows were flying from west to east and the hawks took them, but parted company from each other, feasting in solitary. That was very strange. Then in the middle of the afternoon a pike flung itself from the river on to the grass, thrashing and struggling. It had a small spiny fish caught in its long jaws. The spines had pierced the roof of its mouth. The pike would die, but so would the small fish, so I took the spiny fish from those jaws, and threw both back into the water. To live again; perhaps to die again. That was also very strange.

'Then I heard Atanta calling to me. And this little arrow came over the river from her. But when I looked I could only see another Mother, like the Mothers who protected us after we were taken away by the hounds. I think Atanta has been taken below the earth, but she is telling me that she is alive and well. Those are the only omens, Merlin . . . do they mean anything to you?'

'What do they mean to you?' I asked the girl first, and she shrugged.

'Well. The three hawks taking the three sparrows: that could mean that what is together now, the gathering of the warlords, will end in separation after the fort is taken. That's a bad omen. The pike was wounded badly by the little fish, but an outside hand came to its aid. I think that says that we'll fail this time, and have to come again against the spirits. The third omen, the arrow from my friend, makes me think that everything can be seen, but what we see is not necessarily the truth. It's the pike that concerns me. Kymon is very determined to raise an army. But I think we're missing something important.'

They were Munda's omens, and not mine. But three sparrowhawks flying close together? The sign was of unity, not separation. The feeding frenzy, the battle frenzy, would be a solitary act; but the portent signified solidarity not betrayal.

She was quite canny about the pike and its stickleback prey. But then again: were the Celts the small fish? Or did the stickleback reflect the intruders from Ghostland, tentatively making a footing in our world?

I was sad for her about the loss of Atanta. There was no omen here, just a powerful friendship, now separated by a generation, imposed on Atanta on her return from the Otherworld. I could not find the words to tell Munda that her friend had both gone for ever, and yet was here for the rest of her life. As she grew older in a more natural way, Munda would find her own way to accept that reality.

'How about you, Merlin?' she asked suddenly, brightly. 'What omens have *you* noticed?'

I glanced back towards the valley, letting my face darken. 'I saw a man, out of breath, leaping twenty times over a shield, backwards and forwards, then struggling to throw five spears in the time it takes to cry "Catch these!" and being mocked each time he failed. It was a dreadful omen.'

Munda seemed alarmed. 'What does the omen mean?'

'It means your brother is learning to be a king,' I replied, 'and he has empowered a red-haired harridan to bring all fighting men and women up to scratch.'

I was thinking that tomorrow would be a hard, hard day. The breathless man in my joke was me.

'That's not an omen,' Munda laughed, meeting my discomfitted look with one of instant understanding and amusement. 'That's necessity.'

'You're right, of course. And by the way, you're to train for the day too. Necessity knows no age.'

'Nor should it. But young limbs have more spring to them.'

She suddenly broke into a run, then somersaulted three times over fallen branches of trees, bounced high off grey rocks and stood on her hands, head tilted up, watching me. From this ungainly position she spoke to me in the manner of her father.

'To be able to do this is useful. But to see clearly is the most useful thing of all. And your eyes do more than see, Merlin. So if Kymon asks too much of you when it comes to the feats, just refer him to me!'

'Why, thank you. I'll be sure to do that.'

And you, if your Foresight develops, will do it too.

She came down from the handstand, glanced quickly to where the woman had been standing, watching her, then turned and led us back to the valley.

Two mornings later, in the dark time before dawn, we were roused from sleep by the sharp note of a bull's horn, sustained and eerie. It was joined by a second, then a third. The valley erupted into startled life, and torches flared. The horns continued to sound. Birds swirled, alarmed, in the darkness. The encampment moved in force to the deepest part of the stream.

There were no sore heads, now; the ritual feast that usually preceded war had been forgone, though perhaps as much because of shortage of supplies as any notion of common sense. The various parties to this small *foedor* that would take Taurovinda again had made their own spirit preparations for the day ahead, each clan to their own hidden lord, each man and woman to the memory of their own ancestors. The final training in the necessary feats was complete—I had learned two of them, and was sore and bruised, though I could at least leap over a chariot, now, and catch a spear in mid-flight!

Now they all lined up on the two sides of the stream, forty-two in all, thirty of them men and youths, and twelve women of dour and dark demean, all leaning on their tall, oval shields, some of which were newly made and undecorated. I stood among them, holding on to a hazel staff that had been cut for me by the Speaker for the Past as a gift. We sang and chanted until the first rays of the sun peeked over the woodland to the east.

With that welcome glimmer of light, Cimmenos stepped towards the stream, lowered his shield on to the ground and washed its surface, brushing the icy water over the inlaid silver stag. He did this three times, then scooped a fourth handful of water and brushed it over his sword arm. Then Munremur washed his shield. The bronze image of the wolf sparkled for a moment, its eyes seeming to come alive. One by one, in silence, the *foedori* washed their shields and made their final, personal invocations for life either here or in the Land of the Shadows of Heroes after, and when this careful ritual had been completed they filed away, to armour themselves for the raid.

There was not one among them who was not aware that, should they die, they would at once go to a land whose spirits, their own ancestors, were now their enemies.

With Gorgodumnos lost, Cimmenos was now the leader of the raiding party, by virtue of his experience; he had fought twenty-four combats, stolen three hundred and eleven head of cattle, and shouted down seven champions without blood being drawn. He did not ask for the position of leader, but it was apparent that the High Women, the Thoughtful Woman Rianata in particular, had discussed the various merits of all the *foedori* and come to the only decision possible.

Cimmenos was a wise enough man to know that Kymon needed to be at his right hand; he was pragmatic enough to know that a skilful warrior should be at his left, and he chose Caithach, the weapons trainer. In Greek Land, or in Illyria, such a decision would have been met with a vociferous challenge. To the great credit of these forlorn and abandoned Celts, they accepted Cimmenos's decision without demur. Just as well; she was equal to any three of them.

The shields had been washed; later, the battle-harness was displayed, then stacked into two carts. The war band moved slowly out of the valley, a two-day journey ahead of them to reach the evergroves and the Thunder Hill.

We were in the old land, and the places we passed were remembered in the language of the ancestors. We marched from the valley defiles through the Pass of the Forest Brothers, south of the Hill of the Beckoning Woman, where the High Women went twice in their lives to have their mind's eyes opened. We followed a shallow river to the narrow Plain of Moon-shifting, where hares and hounds took human form once every nineteen years. And then through the valley known as the Rattle of the Chariot, where two champions had fought for eleven years without outcome, and died, still charging their ash-and-wicker-framed cars at each other. When we came to Nantosuelta, and had made a blood-offering to the river, we turned east again, and came to the ever-groves at dusk.

Here we spread out, rested the animals, rested ourselves, drank and bathed in the cool river. Then, during the night, the chariots were assembled, dressed and disguised with evergreen leaves and lashing yew-withies. Charioteers were selected, and it fell to me to be one of them. My training in the feat of chariot jumping had persuaded Cimmenos that I could master both the pair of horses and the sharp turns required of the profession.

I was relieved when Drendas, a fine spearman, asked to ride in my car. He knew that he would be in the hands of an amateur. But all I had to do was get him to the point of any combat, drop him, retire and wait for his signal to gallop in and pick him up. An important function, he assured me. And please, he asked with a grin, could I be sure not to run along the pole when the chariot was in full charge!

I gave him my assurance.

I suspect the truth is nearer to the fact that they did not want me fighting, both for my lack of weapons skill and my potential value in other directions.

After the allocation of chariots and positions, we prepared for battle.

Cimmenos was the first to armour. He had taken the wolf-crest from his iron helmet and replaced it with the crest of heron feathers that was so typical of this part of Hyperborea.

He had buckled on his heavy bull's-hide war harness over the patterned linen shirt that would stop it rubbing through to his bones; four layers thick, this covered shoulder and chest, back and kidneys. It could be slashed twenty times with the ice-forged iron of the Northlanders before it would part completely.

He had attached a bright bronze girdle to protect his midriff, a gullet shield of thin iron round his neck, and a soft, doe-skin kirtle over his blue-and-red-striped trousers. Grey goat-leather boots and pitch-blackened horse-bone greaves completed the armour. He flung his cloak around his shoulders and paraded in the Confident Manner as he yelled the exhortation to us either to win back the fort, or to make good conversation with our fathers and mothers in the Otherworld afterwards.

He was bright and strong. Dawn-light gleamed on red hair and red moustache, and reflected off the five recurved points of his *kaibulg*, the heavy bowel-hooking stabbing spear.

All totem crests had been removed from battle-helms and attached to standards: the tusked boars, the stags, the wolves, the falcons and hawks, the leaping salmon, the foxes, otters, owls and wish-hounds. There were more standards, it seemed to me, than men to carry them. All helmets were now crested with real or bronze feathers, a decoration that signified the readiness of the wearers to fly to their ancestors if they suffered one of the seven mortal blows.

Kymon emerged in his child's harness, the equal of Cimmenos's but in softer leather, and with thin, cloth-backed iron shields at his waist and heart.

Munda had armoured similarly, though she would not fight. This was a symbolic gesture only. Her small shield was inlaid in ochre with an image of Braega, the guardian of river crossings. Braega was also the warning spirit who whispered in a girl's ear during the time she was becoming a woman, though quite what she warned about was a question I had never asked; and she was also the earth spirit to whom these Celts turned at times of transition or decision.

Whether Munda's choice of shield-guard was conscious or instinctive, it was certainly apt.

Now Kymon went to the edge of Nantosuelta, with Speaker for Kings and Rianata, the Thoughtful Woman. He cried out his blood dirge with all the force of a grown man. Herons rose startled from the rushes. Birds flocked and wheeled above the drooping trees on the farther bank.

'Dawn chariots racing from the river ford
   Sun on helmet
   Sun on spear
   Sun on sword
Men scatter before the racing chariots
   Blood on the plain
   Blood on the rich tunics of the dead men
   Blood on the sword

Heads cut, proud life, proud men hang from the belts of proud
warriors
    Life goes to Earth
    Life goes to strength
    Life goes to the sword
Red on the plain, blood on the green breast of Earth
    Blood on the high walls of the fort
    Heads hanging from the high walls
The men of the stabbing game are here, strong as iron, keen as
wind, bright as sun, swift as birth, sharp as claw!'

The sun was high when we emerged in a line from the grove-
wood's edge, facing the tall-grassed Plain of MaegCatha, and
the dark, rising slopes of Taurovinda.

It was clear at once that the Shadows of Heroes had been
here in greater force since our last tentative visit. The woodland
edge was marked with the tall wooden effigies of men,
grotesquely crude, legs braced apart, arms in various positions,
each hand holding a blade or a club or a shield. All these blank-
faced idols were turned towards the groves. They were saying:
this far and no further.

Black and yellow pennants blew in the strong breeze from
the high ramparts, signifying the abundant presence of the
Dead and Unborn occupying the fortress.

And yet: once again, the main gates were open.

Without hesitation, Kymon in the lead chariot—his charioteer was the bombastic Iala, known proudly as 'the savager'—
sped through the long grass, which was whipped by the flailing
withies attached to the car's sides. He cut a furrow through the
field and positioned himself beyond slingshot range of that
open main gate. We had formed into three small squads;
Kymon's eight *foedori* followed him and spread out in an arc. I
took my chariot and squad to the north, Cethern drove his to the
south. Our *foedori* trampled down the pasture, clearing a battle
area. Nadcrantail, from Eriu, and Larene of the Parisii, used
lengths of chain, slung between them as they galloped, to
uproot the thorn and oak thicket that was springing up as the
plain was reclaimed by the Scatterer of Forests, Iernos.

We made a loud din, with voices and clashing weapons, and
waited there in the cool day, watching the clouds carefully to

make sure we would not be blinded by the sun should the sky clear suddenly. Cimmenos, on heavy horse with a retinue of six men, waited with calm aggression before the gate, challenging the Dead to come and fight.

Kymon's chariot wheeled up to mine. He had been racing the horses along a length of land on the plain, facing the eastern ramparts, a restless, angry action. The boy had made himself look fierce and let his long hair flow. 'I hate this waiting! Give us eyes to see them, Merlin. If you can't do that, tell us what *you* see.'

I see it bleached; I see it bone . . .

I shivered slightly at the memory of Munda's words. The hill was silent, but that open gate was like the entrance to a trap. I sensed the snare, but when I summoned the hawk and flew into the sky, I saw only the empty road, the deserted enclosure, the ruined houses.

The hawk wheeled. I didn't want to lose my senses for too long, but in the last moment of its shadowy existence it saw—*I saw*—the rippling in the grass behind us.

I shouted to Kymon and his spearman Iala, 'To the rear!' and wheeled the small car round to face the ambush, thirty tall men in rusting chain-link mail and tarnished helmets running at full speed through the waist-high grasses. I had seen armour like this in many lands, simple, old, heavy. These were Dead— once-great heroes, reduced to butchers. Their swords were simple, long and bright, and used with grim efficiency. They launched a sudden volley of light spears, which caught the whole rank of us off-guard. I saw several of our number thrown backwards. Kymon had urged his chariot forward, gripping the reins with one hand and stabbing furiously with his long spear with the other.

I heard Kymon shouting, 'Man against man! I will take the combat!'

But single combat to decide this issue, now, was no more than a dream.

Munremur was cut down as he charged on foot, then Iala, in Kymon's chariot, was hurled from the car by a spear through his throat. The enemy host started to close on the boy, but Drendas leapt from my car, driving his shield and spear ahead of him as he went to Kymon's defence. He was surrounded b the enemy and quickly felled and impaled, though I saw him crawl away through the grass, looking for safety. Kymon whipped the reins and turned the chariot, kicking gymnastically at a man who leapt into the car and tried to grab him. The man tumbled backwards; my own spear went into him as I turned my horses and went in pursuit of Urtha's son.

Kymon had gone into the long grass and turned, ready for the charge. His mouth frothed with fear and exhilaration. He had drawn his sword. The man called Larene, seeking to guard the king's son, had leapt into the chariot, holding his fistful of thin javelins.

Kymon hardly saw me, but when he caught my presence he shouted, 'We can take them, Merlin.'

'We cannot!' I assured him. 'The trap is baited; they are inside the hill as well, waiting for you. They will take you hostage.'

'Hah!' he screamed, not a laugh, an encouragement to his chariot horses. They bolted back to the fray. Larene performed the Feat of the Four Points, but it was a magnificent act that would end his life. I saw Kymon duck as a spray of blood coated him from eyes to waist, Larene losing his life along with his head as one of the enemy somersaulted across the chariot, cutting down in the same movement.

I see it bleached. I see it bone.

If Urtha should return alive, I would not have been able to look him in the eyes if bleached bone was what greeted him, his son's among them. Kymon had forced his chariot through the hacking zone and was whipping the horses towards the Bull Gate.

Almost at once, war-horses spilled from hiding behind the walls, flowing out on to the plain, their riders the same grey-cloaked knights who had previously pursued Kymon from his taunting stance before the high enclosure.

I saw Cimmenos and Caithach ride quickly to his aid. I chased after the boy myself.

But though a group of these horsemen encircled the raging youth, they kept at a distance; the rest of the knights formed a barrier between the general affray and the king's son. Kymon charged and wheeled, striking with all his might, but the knights kept back, containing him.

Their leader rode quickly up and down the line of men that separated the circle from the plain, his grey eyes fixed on me: he saw me clearly now. I was certain of it. I opened my ears a little and heard him whispering, 'Go away from the hill. The boy belongs with us . . .'

I recognised the voice. This was the man who had come into the fort in the rain—the man with Urtha's look about him.

By now my chariot was in full attack. A javelin struck its side, and an arrow pierced the neck of the slightly built horse who pulled on the left. If the animal was aware of its wound, it showed no sign of it. Kymon became aware of my approach. He shouted for me. Mailed men leapt at me. I used nothing but my arm to strike back at them.

Caithach, Cethern, and four others of our *foedor* had withdrawn from the fight among the stunted trees, and lined up ready to support me. The tall man on his heavy horse galloped round to block my access to the whirling, screaming boy, a boy desperate to fight, one hand on the reins, the other wielding his sword.

I thought briefly of summoning the wolf. I was no charioteer. A wolf could have leapt the ranks, grabbed Kymon and taken him to safety. I was prepared to do it, had even started to summon the charm that would enable me to run like a wolf, have the strength of that animal, and blind onlookers by seeming to appear in that form.

Kymon saved me the effort. I saw him bounce high into the air, then somersault. He did this twice, then leapt over the wall of knights, again bounced this way and that and flung his small sword with wounding effect at one of the men who were now riding down on him. The blade quivered in the rider's chest and he reared up, falling from the saddle. Bounding and leaping, Kymon flung himself into my shattered car. He grabbed my plain-faced shield, left the chariot for a moment, twirled where he stood, three times round, and sent the shield skimming across the flattened grass, striking the man who was familiar to me, knocking him from his war horse.

If the shield had been scallop-edged, blade-sharp, the man would have been cut in two by the strike! That was how fast young Kymon despatched the oval of wood and bronze.

He somersaulted back into the car, blood-drenched and wild

he had been badly cut across the chin. His eyes were brimming with tears and he shouted, 'Lost! We are lost! My father will be ashamed of me.'

'Not lost . . . just delayed. Your father will be proud!'

I turned the horses and sped us through the tall grass. Behind us, eleven only of our host came running or cantering after. Though the cloaked knights were withdrawing into the fort, making their horses walk backwards at a steady and ungainly pace, watching us, the rest of the Ghostlanders were busy at work taking grim trophy from our dead, displaying it on their spears.

Beyond the tree-line, among the groves, we were safe. But Kymon was distraught, helpless; his finest counsel, Larene, a wise young man, lay in pieces on the same ground where Kymon had been placed at his birth, to see the stars above his home, before he had been despatched to his foster father, among the Cornovidi. He stood, brooding in the shadows, staring out at the plain and the crows that were beginning to circle the killing field.

'My father will be ashamed,' he repeated softly, adding sharply, and with no room for manoeuvre: 'And don't tell me otherwise! This has been a bad day for us all.'

'Worse for the men on those spears. You're not yet bleached. You're not yet bone.'

He would not be consoled, staring grimly at the display of heads being paraded outside the Bull Gate. 'I made a mistake. It should be me gaping from those spears. Munda was right.'

Munda? Had she spoken to her brother as well? I asked Kymon what Munda had said to him.

'To bide my time. To grow stronger.' He looked round at me, desperation in his eyes. 'There will be a call for me to be offered as hostage, Merlin . . . but until Urtha returns, I can't risk that! Not that I don't have the courage. But my father will need a son when he returns from his Greek Land folly. Won't he?'

'Quite right,' is all I could say to the youth. Good gods, I had seen this slight young man perform feats that no horseman or shield man at Thermopylae had accomplished. The honourable move, if it had been the living we had been fighting, would be to now offer himself as hostage to the fort; in fact, he was too young for such a role. No king's son who had not yet finished his time of fostering could be taken hostage. Killed, yes, but not taken hostage. But all that was academic. We had fought the Dead, and to deny them their prize of the king's son was a triumph in itself.

As Kymon agonised—I let him steep in his own despair for a while, a kindly and useful abandonment it seemed to me—I went back to the plain and watched the completion of the butchering. I was surprised to see the leader of the knights trotting through the grass towards me, alone and unarmed, his round shield slung across his back, his head unprotected. He was certainly of the Unborn. He came to me in the guise-age of his middle years when, no doubt, he would be at his most adventurous. He turned right side on to me, which I thought was meant to be unchallenging.

'Who are you?' he called to me.

'Someone who is older than the bleached bones that are interred below that hill,' I answered. 'Older than the oak that was used to make its first gates or the earth that made its first walls; old enough to have walked in and out of Ghostland without noticing the difference . . .'

'Dead, then. But still alive. I had that feeling about you.'

'And you? Who are you?'

'That is a good question,' the rider said with a laugh. 'I wish I had an answer. This is my place, though; I belong here. I have dreamed of this hill. I can't wait to occupy it. The boy would have come to no harm . . . with me. Do you have a name?'

'None that I'll tell you. You? Are you named?'

'Sometimes I think I am, sometimes I think I'm not. It's the curse of being neither here nor there. I did not intend to harm the boy . . .'

'I know that.'

'The others will. They want to harm him very badly. There are more of them than us. But we are all determined to take this place. So if you want to keep your chariot-jumping prodigy in blood and brains, keep him away from here. I promise you, if he comes back I'll deal the killing blow myself. I have no choice in the matter. Keep him angry; but keep him flushed! Keep the crimson in his cheeks, not on the grass. You see it, I think; you see the consequences. You see it red. You see it crow-ravaged.'

'Who *are* you?' I shouted at this man. I opened my eyes, but the mist that separated me from Ghostland flowed across my vision. Not yet born, but a man of great power; he sat there in the saddle of his restless warhorse and searched the woods for an understanding of his own. I was aware of one thing: though we didn't know each other now, we were certainly destined to meet each other again, and in his real life.

'Who are you?' I whispered again, and from the slow shake of his head, he had heard the repeated question.

'I don't know,' he answered after a long pause. 'I'm not privileged to know. But I am certain of one thing: that there is something rotten in the heart of the realm across the river; a warped man, dealing death. He holds prisoners and makes them believe they're kings. And I want no particular part of it!'

'Then why *are* you a part of it?'

'Because I'm a prisoner who believes he is a king.'

Still he hesitated, nervous, at the edge of two worlds, between two states of mind.

Then he said, in a whisper that only I could hear, 'In my sleep I dream a name that means nothing to me. Perhaps it's mine. Perhaps not.'

'Will you tell me?'

'Pendragon. It has an odd sound to it. And you? Will you tell me yours, now?'

'Merlin,' I called. 'It's a nickname, but it's the oldest of the names I've taken.'

'It's the name I shall remember.'

Finally he turned and rode away.

I was grateful to see the back of him—his existence disturbed me—but more grateful for the information he had wittingly given me: that the rising tide that was flowing out of Ghostland was not united in its goal; dissidence and difference plagued it. We had witnessed a small incident to that effect. A brief display that had left half of our small, determined *foedor* mutilated and rotting on the Plain of MaegCatha.

PART TWO:

The Return of the King

CHAPTER SEVEN

—◆—

Sons of Llew

A fierce wind from the west had made the sea channel to Alba impassable. From a high cliff at the edge of the land of the Bolgoi, Urtha, warlord and High King of the Cornovidi, gazed over the heaving grey sea at the distant strip of white that marked a gateway into his own land. His combat wounds were healed, his strength returned.

Below him on the shingle beach a woman stood at the water's edge. The wind streamed through her yellow hair and would have whipped the green cloak from her body had she not been holding it so tightly against the storm. Behind her, the two boats that would take them across the channel were drawn up almost to the cliffs, pegged down and covered. They had had to barter two of their four horses to get the use of the boats. Their owners, youthful and surly men of the Atrebates, were used to crossing to the Island of Mists, trading wine and bronze, sometimes meat, sometimes hostages. But they would not risk this high sea.

The woman was a Scythian huntress, Ullanna, daughter of King Androgon, and had been used in her time to warmer conditions and more fragrant oceans. She turned where she stood in the freezing spray and looked harshly up at the man crouched on the cliff above her. Seagulls swirled and screeched; her voice carried through the noise of surf and gull.

'This is a grim sea. This is a desolate stretch of water. There is no warmth in it at all.'

'I've seen it brighter. I've seen it calmer,' Urtha shouted back down. 'But it's not here to please you. It's here to guard that island and its kingdoms, including mine!'

'This is a dreadful wind. It's blowing through my bones!'

'The good thing about winds,' Urtha replied through his cupped hands, 'is that they blow themselves out.'

Ullanna's eyes narrowed as she stared up at the king on the cliff. 'You're in a fine mood despite this storm.'

'I should be. I'm on the boundary of my homeland at last. Too far south, I'll admit to that. But home is in sight.'

'Only when the wind drops,' the Scythian reminded him, her voice almost carried away in the gale.

'Nothing lasts, however strong.'

'Nothing? Not even love?' she bellowed back, folding her arms and cocking her head.

'Can't hear you!' Urtha shouted down with a smile.

He drew away from the cliff's edge and followed the rough track to the small village which had given them hospitality and the offer of the boats, one for Urtha, his retinue and the two hounds, the other for the horses and chariot. Cathabach and Manandoun, Urtha's *uthiin*, were crouched by the fire. Their cloaks were slung from the rafters to make a windbreak. There was fresh straw and horse-blankets on the ground.

'A real palace,' Cathabach muttered as Urtha entered. It was a crude community, behind a wind-broken enclosing wall, and Urtha had chosen an animal shelter as his camp rather than share the delights of the communal round-house.

Cathabach was slowly turning the spitted carcass of a chicken over the wood fire. It was warm, at least, in this grim house. 'Someone doesn't want you home,' he went on dryly. 'Wrong river, wrong weather.'

He was alluding to the fact that Urtha, with reckless and false confidence, had guided them along the wrong tributary some days ago; instead of reaching the muddy estuary of the river inhabited by Soma, flowing into the sea close to its narrow strait with Alba, they had travelled along broad and beautiful Sequana, far to the south, and had spent the best part of seven days in dangerous territory reaching this cliff-lined beach, in sight of the island.

'After the journey we've just made,' Urtha said, looking hungrily at the food, 'nothing will stop me. Not even the bastards who live beyond the white cliffs of my own country.'

Manadoun muttered grimly, 'It's not those bastards who worry me. All they do is shout at the sea and show off at the river crossings. It's the bastards to the north: the Trinovanda. They collect heads like most of us collect eggs; they gather hostages as we would gather forage. And their forests are the stalking ground of some very strange gods.'

'Nothing as strange as we've seen in recent seasons,' Urtha reminded him. 'Wouldn't you agree?'

Manandoun shrugged. He was tired; they were all tired. The journey from Makedonia had been arduous and long. Urtha had been between life and death for a good part of it, the wounds in his body healing slowly. But now that he was healed, he seemed to have boundless energy.

His knights were weary, though. They were impatient to be home, and apprehensive: they held no real hope of finding anything other than wasteland. They both knew their families were dead. But they also knew that two of the king's children were alive. They were Urtha's *uthiin*, and honour bound to bring the king safely home.

'We should steal the boats the moment we've made the crossing,' Manandoun grumbled on. 'Sail them north along the coast.'

Cathabach shook his head in disbelief. 'Do you know how many ships have foundered north of here? The land comes up suddenly from the bed of the sea, a sucking sand that swallows them down, like a fish gulping a fly! I've heard their masts can be seen at low tide, the rigging slapping against the broken wood. Screaming men are tied to the masts by weed and wrack. Where did you learn to navigate?'

'When did you get so superstitious?' Manandoun asked dryly. 'Oh yes. I forgot. You were once a druid. Well, the sucking sand is just legend. The creatures of the Trinovandan forest are old and dangerous. Not legend at all.'

The two men looked at Urtha, who smiled. 'To get to the point,' he said, 'I don't fancy the sea journey north, sucking sands or no. Nor the forests, stalking boars and mad-eyed hounds or no. So I agree with Manandoun: we'll certainly steal the boats when we get to the other side. And then we'll navigate the river channels, west and north until we're at the borders of our own realm. It will have its own dangers, of course. But we have a good hunter in Ullanna, and she has a nose and an eye for direction.'

Manandoun and Cathabach exchanged a meaningful glance.

Urtha said quietly, 'Explain that look between you.'

Manandoun said, 'The look meant only that I'm not sure of Ullanna's sense of direction on the sea. But if you trust her skills, that's good enough for me.'

Cathabach said, 'The look meant only that I doubt Ullanna is familiar with our land, Alba, its forests, valleys, rivers, mountains, plains, clans, dangers and delights. But if you trust her skills, that's good enough for me. You perhaps know something we don't.'

'I don't trust her skills,' Urtha said bluntly, ignoring the sour tone in the other man's voice. 'But we've brought that chariot, two horses and the four of us on a journey of two seasons and over more hills and dales, and plains, and woodland edges than I can imagine: from north of Greek Land, over those snow peaks, those ice peaks, those frozen rivers, and then that boar-rich forest, and the angry tribes, and the refugees from the wasteland; and my own mistake at the river junction which brought us too far south. In all of that, you, Manandoun, watched at our back and you, Cathabach, watched at our front. And I hunted, to get back my strength. And Ullanna, whom I love—I'll not hide the fact, I love her!—Ullanna kept our horses cleaned and fed; she kept the chariot greased and mobile; she sniffed wind, rain, spoor and blossom. She plucked food in mid-flight for us. She, like you, did her part in getting us here. All of that said, I agree with you. Once in Alba, she'll be as lost as all of us.'

'It's on the matter of the way you live with the Scythian woman that I've been meaning to speak to you,' Cathabach murmured.

'Yes. I've had the feeling since we crossed the mountains north of Makedonia that you had a thorn speared in your chest.'

Cathabach went pale at the insult, his green eyes narrowing with hostility. 'Aylamunda, your wife, is dead, but has not been given the honour and tribute due to her. It is unsanctionable that you share your blanket with the Scythian! My heart is heavy as I say this, but you are in breach of the code of kings! Until Aylamunda's living spirit has been sent on its journey to the Island of Women, you should be in what the Eberianii call "the condition of the long face and the howling heart".'

'We call it "mourning", old friend, and I *am* in mourning. I just don't have time to howl.'

'It defies the law that you love the Scythian—'

'Ullanna! Daughter of King Androgon, descendant of Atalanta.'

'The *Scythian*! It defies our law that you *pillow-talk* with her. You will bring hardship and a long sigh on the clan unless you pay proper tribute to the mother of your children. Ambaros's daughter. Your consort in arms and wisdom. You have not washed at the spring. You have not made the shield to protect her. You have not walked for the three days of remembering. You have not sung the Three Noble Strains.'

'I intend to do all of it,' Urtha said calmly. 'The Good God knows, I miss Aylamunda.'

'You don't show it!'

'That is discourteous.'

'It is you who behaves with discourtesy.'

For a moment the two men sat and stared at the ground between them, each regretting his angry words. Then Urtha asked, 'Cathabach—what should I do if my favourite horse dies suddenly?'

'Follow the law. Then take and train a new horse.'

'What if the horse is killed during battle?'

Cathabach shook his head, understanding the king's simple meaning. 'Of *course* you'll find a new mount on the field. This comparison is unworthy. Of me and of Ullanna . . . '

'The *Scythian*?' Urtha goaded. 'Need defines worthiness, Cathabach. Need decides strategy. The law is all very well when all is in its place. I was not in the kingdom of my ancestors when Ullanna stepped into my life. I *will* honour Aylamunda. Cathabach, old friend—I *ache* to do it. Lord of Forests, hear my pledge!'

Manandoun said bluntly, 'I don't know what all the fuss is about. If Ullanna's warmth keeps the king a king, we will all triumph at the end of the day. We can follow west, and we have an idea of north! Gods! Ullanna is skilled at finding trails and tracks. As long as we head in the general direction of Taurovinda, we're bound to fetch up somewhere close to home.'

Though the high winds faded away during the night, and the sea calmed, Urtha's optimism proved unfounded. A dense fog formed over the ocean and the land, sitting still and silent. Urtha and Manandoun walked along the shingle beach to where the men of the village waited by the two ships. Their beards and hair glistened with damp.

'Can we row in this?' Urtha asked, but they shook their heads. The Prowler of the Sea, whom they called Kraaknor, sent this fog whenever his daughters rose from the sea bed to swim. Their backs were covered in sand, and any ship that struck them would be held fast and dragged down.

Manandoun was sceptical, but Urtha suspected that the sand banks might have shifted in the storm, and the villagers were exercising a very real caution.

Besides which, it would be very easy to get turned round in this low visibility. Lode-stone metal, which would help steer a straight course, was not among the possessions of either Urtha's *uthiin* or their Atrebatian hosts.

Those hosts were growing restless too. They were not happy with the exchange arrangements for the risk of their lives crossing the channel: two horses which Urtha was confident he could replace on the other side. They had their eyes on the solidly built, iron-rimmed chariot that Urtha had been given in Makedonia, after his combat. They had asked twice, in the courteous fashion, and been bluntly refused. They had offered to take the *uthiin* north along the coast, thus avoiding the Trinovanda, but they had been refused. Urtha and Manandoun kept their swords unthreateningly across their hips, and not their thighs, though they had loosened the fastenings of their heavy woollen cloaks.

But if tensions were beginning to rise on the beach, shortly after dawn they were dispelled when the low call of a horn droned through the sea fog from the south.

A slow drum beat and the swish of oars told of a ship pulling cautiously along the coast. Urtha went down to the surf, letting the sluggish waves roll over his boots. Manandoun at his shoulder, he peered hard through the mist. If someone was navigating the channel, they must have a direction finder; the two small boats, with their passengers, might then row in convoy.

The ship passed them by, the strike of the drum slow and relentless, the creaking of boards and ropes in rhythm with the dip and rise of the oars on the still water. Urtha was about to hail the vessel when one of the villagers stopped him

'They are almost certainly coastal raiders,' he said urgently. 'This weather is their preying weather. They count distance by oar strikes. Watch: they'll pull into the mouth of the river when they've navigated the sand flats.'

Urtha followed along the beach to where the cliffs dropped away and the muddy estuary of the small river was lined with wooden jetties. The drum beat had stopped; only the gentle rush of the waves against the shallow moorings and the reed beds could be heard. The fog shifted, thinning one moment then closing in.

And the ship appeared, drifting lazily across the mouth of the river, the eyes of the man who stood by the massive figurehead at the stern and the woman who was braced at the high prow looking to the land, searching hard.

Urtha recognised the ship at once: the narrow, sinister painted eyes on the hull at its prow, the carved image of the Northland's Forest Lady, Mielikki, the protecting goddess of the vessel, her face leering forward across the deck, her long, straggling hair appearing to blow in a strong wind. Shields of all descriptions were slung from its rails. Ten oars rested gently in the swell on the landward side. A low, sleek, beautiful ship, a ship from another age.

Argo.

Urtha met Jason's gaze, the big man, the dark-bearded man

who stood in black cloak and copper-sheened Greek Land helmet below the face of the growling wooden goddess. But Jason appeared not to see him. The woman at the prow, her cloak brightly patterned with gold and crimson chevrons, her hair a loose flow of auburn-tinged black, called out something in her own language, and the drum took up the strike again, and the oars dipped and heaved.

Urtha recognised Niiv, the Northlands enchantress who had so taunted and charmed Merlin on their long journey to Delphi.

Who else was aboard Argo, Urtha wondered. Which other of those argonauts? Certainly, if there were twenty rowers, ten each side, then Jason must have made new recruits along the way. Was that giant Dacian aboard? Rubobostes? With his ship-dragging horse, Ruvio? And perhaps Merlin too was hunkered down at his rowing bench, the young man who used his gifts of enchantment as Urtha used his skills with weapons: with cautious, controlled facility. Merlin, ageless but kept youthful by his own reluctance to practise his skills. Merlin, who had recognised something in Urtha of Alba, just as the High King of the Cornovidi had intuited a fateful interweaving of his life with the unwashed, lice-ridden creature on that occasion—how many years ago was it now?—when the charmed man had been given winter quarters in the same tent as the warlord and his *uthiin*.

On the eerie ship, Niiv suddenly made a birdlike call, a strange sound that seemed to echo up the river, between the low chalk cliffs. Urtha felt his body chill, the hair on his neck prickle. Had she seen him? Or was she in that same trance, the journey-trance, which had once allowed her to guide Argo to the narrow, shallow headwaters of the great river Reinus?

Hull-shields glistening, guardian spirit brooding darkly, the Greekland ship moved away into the fog, turning out towards the grey sea, to make the silent crossing to Alba.

Urtha realised that Manandoun was calling to him. The older man was pale-faced with irritation. Urtha realised that he had been in a dream.

'That's Argo!' the red-bearded man was saying. 'Our own ship. Our old ship . . . why aren't we following?'

Manandoun had hailed the vessel several times; Urtha had heard nothing of this. The men of the village stood silently and grimly in the mist, but one of them spoke up. 'I've seen ships like that before. They're of the older world; spirit ships, sent by the Prowler to entice us into deadly waters.'

'Nonsense!' Manandoun snarled. 'It's no ghost ship. But even if it was, we once sailed on her. Those are our friends!'

There was a ripple of cynical laughter. 'They didn't seem to know you.'

Ignoring them, Manandoun said, 'Urtha! We can still find the drum beat if we launch now. We can follow her. Why else would Jason be returning to Alba if not to find you? He has no other business there. Has he?'

'He has the business of his second son. The boy called "little dreamer". Don't you remember what Merlin told him? The prophesy from the oracle at Arkamon? Jason's second son has been hidden between "sea-swept walls".'

'An island!' Manandoun stated. ' "Sea-swept walls"? An island. Is that what you're saying? But it could be *any* island! This is not the only island in the world as we know it, Urtha.'

'True enough. It just seems strange that Argo should come back to the west.'

Manandoun was insistent. 'Follow, then!'

But their hosts, this small tribe of the clan of the Atrebates, would not sanction such a crossing under such conditions.

Gloomily, Urtha led the way back through the dense sea-fog to the grim quarters within the village.

Not long after, however, the sound of a two-horse chariot, being recklessly driven by two screaming, delighted youths, penetrated the choking blanket of mist. Urtha rose slowly to his feet as he heard the rattling of chariot wheels, the lash of the whip, the complaint of the horses. Curious, he went out on to the top of the cliffs. Beside him, his *uthiin*, Manandoun and Cathabach, scoured the fog with their sharp eyes and sharp ears, pointing to where, beyond their sight, the chariot was being driven.

'I know those voices,' Cathabach muttered. 'Why do I know those voices?' The mist had condensed on his red beard and dripped from the points of his moustaches.

'I know them too,' Ullanna called from below the animal shelter. 'Those twins from our time on Argo! The Cymbrii. They went on to Delphi with Jason after we'd left the quest.'

Urtha recognised them as well. 'Yes. Conan. Gwyrion. Those irresponsible sons of the Bright God Llew.'

'I don't like the sound of it,' Cathabach said. He had thrown back his heavy woollen cloak and rested his hand lightly on the ivory pommel of his sword. But Manandoun added, 'If it's a chariot, and they're looking for us, then we'll get to Taurovinda faster! One chariot between four has been very crowded.'

Cathabach shook his head. 'Chariots can't cross the sea. And there's little enough room in those boats as it is.'

'Be quiet,' Urtha said. 'What in the name of Kernos are they doing?'

Golden light flashed through the fog. The chariot streaked past, out of sight, from west to east, made a sharp turn—the whip cracked, a voice cried, 'Too sharp! Too sharp! The axle will break.'

'Breathe the fresh air, brother, leave the driving to me!'

There was boyish laughter. Again, the mist was penetrated by a blinding flash of gold and the earth thundered as the chariot streaked towards the cliff.

Urtha ran in the same direction, suddenly alarmed. 'The land ends! The land ends! Turn, you fools, turn now!'

From the sudden whinnying panic of the chariot horses, the terrified screams of the charioteers and the grinding, smashing sound of the car being thrown end over end, it was clear that the fatal fall had been avoided by a damaging last minute turn. Whether they had heard the cry of warning, or simply seen the end of the land where it dropped to the wide shingle beach below, was of no importance.

Cathabach led the way to the edge at a run. The two young men were dazed and dishevelled. They were pushing the chariot the right way up and inspecting the damage.

'Have you no eyes?' one of them was demanding of the other. 'Couldn't you see the cliff?'

'I drive, brother! You watch our backs and when danger threatens, you throw spears. That's your job. At least the wheels are intact.'

They looked up as Cathabach marched towards them. They were almost identical; long golden hair reaching to their shoulders, bright, shaven faces, bronze circlets round their brows and their dress that of princes, richly coloured; they each wore a short cloak, pinned at the breast, and bore the solemn face of the Sun Lord on their tunics.

'Cathabach!' one of them cried in delight. 'What a welcome sight you are. We'd thought you long lost. Help us get the chariot into shelter; it needs repair.'

Speechless with fury, Cathabach came up to the boys—the driver was Conan, the spear thrower Gwyrion—and knocked their heads together.

Conan looked furious and began to reach for his sword. Cathabach's withering gaze made him ease the gesture. Gwyrion kept searching for blood, rubbing hard at his temple.

'You pair of mindless fools!' the warrior priest shouted at them. 'Do you think chariots grow on trees?'

The twins stared at him blankly. 'I understand that they're *made* from trees,' Conan offered.

'A chariot is a precious thing. How can you use it so recklessly?'

'We're in a hurry to return to Alba.' They exchanged nervous glances. Cathabach was immediately suspicious. 'Why? Whose chariot is this?'

'We obtained it from Nodons,' Gwyrion explained. 'Some old sanctuary. It was lying around in a corner. Somewhere in Divodurum.'

'Nodons? Sanctuary? Obtained? What are you telling me?'

'We stole it from Nodons. From his sanctuary. At Divodurum,' Conan amended.

For a moment, watching this interchange, Urtha thought his friend the druid would burst into fire, like a willow effigy on midwinter's eve. Whatever Cathabach was thinking, he managed not to express it. Gwyrion said, as if intuiting the older man's thinking, 'It's what we do best.'

'What is what you do best?'

'Stealing chariots,' Conan explained.

'We were born for it!' his brother emphasised. 'That's all I know. Speaking only for myself, when the time comes to go into battle, I want to be driving the best chariot in the land, and have the best spearman at my side. Preferably not *this* unbalanced idiot. We were born for it. But chariots break up when you practise with them . . . '

'Exactly,' said Conan. 'Especially when *you* hold the ponies. Which is why we must keep stealing them.'

'We've stolen the best,' Gwyrion agreed. 'We even stole our father's! Llew's golden chariot, with its yokes of polished cedar and wheel rims of mother of pearl.'

'Unfortunately, we crashed it,' Conan confessed uneasily, then, brightening, 'This is his cousin's, though. Nodons. A very great man, it has to be said.'

Gwyrion frowned critically. 'Though his chariot has poor cushions, not enough goose-down, and its turning curve could be improved. But there's no doubt about it, it's still a fine car!'

'And will be again, when we repair the damage,' Conan said reassuringly.

Cutting through this, Cathabach roared, 'And Nodons? The good god Nodons, the silver-handed protector of limbs in combat, the good healer, the Cloud-maker . . . does he know about the loss of his chariot?'

Conan laughed nervously. 'Well, yes. It's the only one he had. I suspect he's missed it by now. Which is why we're in a hurry to get back to Alba. To lie low for a while.'

'You may be the flesh and blood sons of a god,' Cathabach said solemnly and carefully, 'but I swear I shall put a *geis* on each of you if you behave recklessly again before we get back to Taurovinda. You will be forbidden the luxury of riding on the feat-days or into battle.'

'Only a druid can pronounce such things,' Conan sneered at the older man.

Cathabach pulled open his shirt to reveal the nineteen cuts of the moon and the four spirals of the seasons. 'I *was* a druid; and I will be again. A *geis* has condemned me to carry a sword for ten years.' He leaned close to Conan, staring him straight in the eyes. 'And time's almost up.'

Conan scratched his temple, his face echoing his curious concern. 'You're a complicated man,' he said.

'We're all complicated men,' Cathabach replied cryptically.

The reckless youths had broken the axle of their splendid chariot, and lamed one of the ponies, though not seriously. And

despite his threat, Cathabach's fury was merely oil off two
already oiled heads. Each of the twins was furious enough with
the other for shifting his weight when he should have been
crouching! They couldn't agree on whose wrong step in the car
had caused the accident. But when the chariot had turned over,
as they had failed to see the thorn roots that ridged the approach
to the sheer chalk cliff, they had damaged the fine gold-inlaid
image of the man who had built the car in the first place:
Nodons!

It was bad enough that their god-father, Llew, the Bright
Father, Lord of Light and no stranger to head-hunting, was after
their blood for stealing his chariot, years ago. Llew's flame-
haired cousin would now be asking for tribute, recompense, and
possibly bloody-necked trophy.

Their only hope—they had decided, in their brotherly argument—was to cross back to their own land as fast as possible.
Better the vengeance you knew than the vengeance of a
stranger. Fathers were always a soft touch when a son's humil-
ity could be convincingly displayed. And they could make a gift
of Nodons' chariot, and leave it up to their father to tussle with
the ethics of that gift.

So they were in an agitated but cheerful mood when Urtha and
Manandoun approached them in the camp. The two youths were
ready to carry their broken chariot down to the beach. They were
quite convinced that they could repair it sufficiently to make a
dash at the ocean, and cross the sea, riding on top of the waves.

Urtha had other ideas.

'Answer me this: what happened in Greek Land? What happened to Jason and Merlin?'

Gwyrion looked perplexed. Conan simply shook his head,
staring at the king. 'Jason? He died searching for his eldest son.
He went into the oracle at Delphi, during the battle, and never
came back.'

'You didn't wait for him? Or look for him?'

Gwyrion threw out his hands, the sign of innocence in the
face of what he imagined was an accusation from Urtha. 'He
was dead. Argo's protecting goddess told us as much. We were
guarding the ship's heart. You and Jason had cut the heart from
the ship—that grim figurehead—and we carried it on a cart
overland. Don't you remember?'

'I do remember.'

'We sat with her, that scowling face in wood, while the battle raged in the valley where the sanctuary was being looted. Conan went off to gather weapons from the dead, and while he was absent, Jason's friend Merlin came to me on the hillside above the slaughter.' He struggled to remember the events of that encounter during the chaos in the valley of the oracle of Delphi. 'He uncovered the figurehead of Mielikki and prayed to it. Something like: "Mielikki. Argo! Spirit of the Ship. I need to go to Dodona, where a part of you was cut to build you." Something like that.

'After that, he went into that vacant-eyed state. When he was using enchantment. He walked away, down the hill, and the land swallowed him up. Conan came back and we waited for a day or more. Then the goddess herself came to us. The Northlands goddess. She was veiled in white, and in her youthful form. She said: "It's all over. Merlin is gone. Jason is gone. There is nothing more for you to do. You must find your own way home." Who were we to argue? We caught horses that had been abandoned with the deaths of their riders, and did as we were told. That whole time in Delphi was a disaster. The place had been abandoned long before we reached it.'

'You took the goddess's words to mean that Merlin and Jason were dead.'

Conan shrugged. 'Yes. The quest for Delphi had been dedicated to slaughter and plunder, we all knew that. As far as we knew, you had died of your wounds as well after fighting Cunomaglos.'

Urtha exchanged a long glance with Manandoun. 'Jason is alive,' he said. 'And Niiv. They are on Argo, heading back to Alba. And I cannot believe that Merlin would have been so foolish as to allow himself to die, despite the violence of events at Delphi. I wonder if he was on the ship?'

Manandoun was staring into the fog. 'There is something happening over there, and we should be a part of it. It's your land, after all. I'll persuade Cathabach to break taboo and finger one of his nineteen cuts. If he calls on Teutates, perhaps we can summon a storm to blow this veil away . . . '

Persuading Cathabach would not be necessary, however.

Ullanna suddenly emerged out of the mist, wet and shivering. She had been exercising the dogs, which is to say, she had been looking for game, but without success.

'Where are my hounds?' Urtha asked as she reached to draw a little warmth from inside the king's cloak.

'By the sea, staring into this gods-forsaken fog, sniffing their island and howling for it. I swear they can smell the place!'

It took a moment only to realise the implication of this: that in Maglerd and Gelard they had their guides to Alba, however blind the channel!

'Take all the horses. Leave the chariot for our hosts. We'll take both boats, with or without their agreement.'

'The chariot must be taken,' Conan insisted loftily.

'The chariot stays,' Urtha retorted. 'It's too bulky. Leave it with your mark of apology for Nodons. And the gold on its panels will be good compensation for the boats. To remind you of your own words, you'll steal another before too long.'

Even so, the Cymbrii purloined the wheels, slinging them across their backs like shields. Good wheels were rare; the wheels of Nodons' chariot were the rarest of all.

On the beach, as the longer of the two sea vessels was hauled across the hard shingle to the surging waves, Manandoun observed quietly, 'It could be, of course, that the hounds can smell their mistress: Niiv. You put them under her control, if you remember. They continued to obey her long after she had been abandoned by Merlin, and made an outcast.'

Urtha hauled, his face reddening with the strain as they plunged the craft into the water.

'As long as we get across, friend Manandoun,' was all he said to that. 'Now, get the horses aboard and on their sides. While the sea is this calm we have a chance of rowing the distance. Quickly.' He glanced apprehensively towards the village, invisible in the fog. 'If I knew which gods looked after Merlin, I'd invoke them to have him come to me. But I don't, so we must keep our wits and wiles about us at all times. Maglerd! Gelard! Aboard!'

CHAPTER EIGHT

Rough Crossing

They had crossed the sea-channel in heavy fog; now a storm lashed Argo as she fought her way along the island coast, in sight of the steep, grey cliffs, searching for a haven. Billowing waves crashed across the deck and down into the hold, where the argonauts huddled, braced against the violent movement of the ship. Rubobostes, the brawny Dacian, was secured by ropes to the mast as he clung to the steering oar, heaving it with strength and experience as he helped the vessel stay at a distance from the surf and the shore. The sail had started to tear along the cross beam and Jason, in the stern, cloaked and sodden, watched the parting in the canvas as it moved towards destruction.

Clinging to the rising curve of the high prow, the small figure of the Northlands enchantress Niiv lay sprawled, dark hair matted, her sharp sight keenly scanning the cliffs for the tell-tale sign of a drop to a cove.

For the first time in this voyage, Jason felt the dull ache of despair. He could not afford to be cast, wrecked and ruined, against the wrong shore. This island was vast, and the way to its heart would be along one of the five rivers carved into the land by forces more powerful, even, than his own gods of old.

'Goddess! Aid us! I *must* make land. My son is there!'

He turned to face the grim-visaged carving of Mielikki. The figure leered from the stern, stretching out across the deck. Its hair seemed to stream in the strong wind. The eyes were narrow, demonic, the mouth turned down in contempt. Where once Hera's divinity had smiled rose-lipped and kind-eyed at the men on Argo, now this monstrous Northlands witch was the small ship's guide. Hera had been warmed by sun and sweetened with wine and olives. The Lady of the Forest was a shadow from the dark woods and snows, where for half the year only the moon was in the heavens to bring pallid, pellucid light to the frozen world below.

Rubobostes' voice was one more howl against the screech of wind and rain. 'The sea will have us! I cannot hold this oar! Jason, we must take our chances on the beach!'

'No! Hold the bearing. Hold until the oar breaks!'

'My back will break before the oar. I am being bent in half by the billows!'

'Hold longer!'

Jason put his hands on the sinister birchwood face above him. The eyes seemed to move to watch him, mocking. Mielikki hated this man. She had not spoken to him since Greek Land. Olympian Hera's love for Jason, her divine protection, had been replaced by loathing, by reluctant obedience to the captain's orders.

'A haven from the storm. I beg you, Lady! Make the cliffs break open, or the wind drop.'

'I can do neither,' the goddess murmured. 'But I will hold that big man's spine in one piece. He is a better man than you, Rottenbones. And I will help my daughter in the prow.'

Argo plunged and rolled, the mast creaked ominously and the sail tore so badly that it now began to flap uselessly. In the shallow hold, the drenched and sallow argonauts, recruited from five lands on the long voyage to Alba, shouted for their lives, echoing the Dacian's demand to be put ashore. Above the vessel, a wide-winged sea-eagle swooped and hovered against the storm, watching the deck below as if there was easy prey to be had from the fragile craft.

Then Niiv cried out, her voice almost lost on the wind. 'An inlet! The cliffs are dropping!'

She watched Jason through the rain, pointing to the north. The land seemed to recede from them, the sure sign of a river's outlet to the sea. Rubobostes heaved on the steering oar, screaming with the effort. A wave broke across the vessel, knocking Jason to the gunwales, but he slipped back across the galley, summoned two of his sailors and struck through the sheets, letting the canvas sail flap loose, letting the Dacian do the work, letting the frail craft nose on the roaring gale and the hurling tide towards the broad grey beach, where the land opened its arms.

A while later they were in a haven, sea anchor dropped, rocking on the swell but protected from the main force of the storm. Later still, the wind eased, the clouds moved on, the sky brightened. The hull of Argo steamed. Her crew stripped and squeezed the salt water from their clothes, then baled out the hull and secured bales, ropes and barrels that had come loose in the storm. There was laughter and mischief from several as they took up their positions on the benches, slotting oars into place for the river journey to follow.

Six of dark and grim demean, however, stayed at their benches, slumped forward, exhausted, ignored by the others.

Rubobostes too had slumped to sleep, more than exhausted by his efforts of the last half day. Jason stood by Mielikki, his gaze on the dark-haired girl who crouched, watching back, at the other end of the ship. After a while he stepped down below the deck and beckoned to her. Reluctantly, she crept along the vessel and joined him at the threshold to Argo's spirit.

'What do you want?'

'She talked to me. For the first time since we've left Greek Land, she talked to me. The two of you are like a pair of Harpies.'

Niiv tugged her hair across her left shoulder and began to twist it, squeezing out the wet. She said nothing. After a moment Jason reached out and took the braid in his two hands, twisting carefully, as if helping her, his face close to the girl's. 'She talked to me.'

'Who?'

'Who do you think? The wooden witch!'

'You should be more respectful.'

'God's eyes! I've promised the she-goat to take her north again! What else can I do? She is making this journey too difficult.'

As he spoke, Jason folded the braid. Niiv had let her hands drop. The hair tugged at her scalp, pulling at the roots. When Jason saw pain he gave the sodden lock a final twist, pulling at the skin, threatening.

'Why is she suddenly talking to me? You're her virgin daughter, her little lass. You whisper in the night. I'm not afraid of either of you, but I need to know. There! My heart is open to you. I need to know.'

Niiv licked her lips suggestively, bright eyes glaring through the pain of her twisted locks in this old man's grasp. 'I can do you harm.'

'I know you can.'

'I can do you *great* harm.'

'I'm aware of it.'

'I can change the way you see the world.'

'I know. You and a thousand like you. A little enchantment and you think you can own the world you see.'

'Mocking me will only make it worse for you.'

'You like to think so. But experience tells me that it won't.'

'I can do you *harm*!' she snarled again.

Jason drew her closer. 'But you won't. I know you won't. I can read your thinking as easily as I can tell which way a bird will fly in winter!'

'Not all birds fly with the flock.'

'Easy prey for hawks, then.' He released his grip and took on a more approachable posture, crouching before her. 'I know that no love is lost between us.'

'It certainly isn't.'

'I know I once tried to kill you. I wouldn't try that now. It was a mistake. I learned my lesson.'

Niiv laughed in his face, almost surprised by this apology. 'It's taken you long enough to tell me. You'll understand if I doubt you.'

'I'd expect nothing else. You've been a good navigator. I've said little, but without you at the prow and that giant man over there'—he glanced at Rubobostes—'we could not have reached Alba. I know that. Mielikki, the spirit in this ship, abandoned me in Greek Land. But for what reason? The question haunts me.'

Niiv smiled, rubbing her hands together to get them warm. She was amused, perhaps by the thought that a 'question' could haunt this man who was seven centuries out of his time, and pursued by the ghosts of his previous life.

'Why should it matter? You don't need the goddess, just a good strong sail, good oarsmen and a keen pair of eyes. All of that has brought you to Alba. Leave the Lady in peace.'

There was something in the way she said this, a touch of anxiety, that intrigued Jason. It took him a moment only to realise what it was. 'She's weak. She has been too long from home, too far from home. She's ill! Now I understand.'

Niiv met his gaze, evenly and without expression, saying nothing. But as Jason turned to stare at the jutting figurehead, rising from the spirit of the ship below, so Mielikki herself whispered to him: 'Not ill; not weak; but divided. A part of me is in the heart of this island, an older boat, with an older man. We are all coming together again, Jason. The second part of the play is about to begin.'

The wind had begun to rise, the sky lowering. The argonauts, refreshed and repaired, were anxious, now, to get away from the swell and the seagulls that surged and swooped about their ship.

Jason stood and faced Mielikki, pushing the lank grey hair back from his face. 'You mean Merlin! Merlin is already here! And he travelled on one of your ancient echoes. Your hidden ships. That is why you have been so quiet.'

'He has been here for a long while. He sailed by a shorter route than you. And he has been living both inside and outside of Time. We are all coming together again, Jason. We are being drawn together. The winds are rising. And Merlin is at the heart of the storm.'

Jason was furious. He remembered the long land journey, north through Makedonia and the snow-blasted valleys, through the dark forests to the river Daan, where the hull of Argo had been hidden, all the while dragging her 'spirit', this wretched head, the birchwood presence that guarded the heart of the ship. To have met with Rubobostes again had helped. His unnatural horse, Ruvio, lying peacefully in the hull, had helped haul the wagon and saved them time. But then they had sailed east, to the Bythnian Sea; and south through those treacherous straits where rocks clashed and whirlpools reached in spouts to the clouds themselves. They had fought against storms and raiders as they sailed to the south of his homeland, Greek Land, and along the rocky coasts of Sicilia and Gaul, then the hostile seas of Eberia. Finally they had turned north again and entered the cold sea-mists of the western isles, where every cliff-top was alight with burning effigies, and the howling of war-trumpets was like the dying of a legion of the damned.

But Merlin had come here by a shorter route! Through the underworld, no doubt. At Argo's pleasure!

'I built you!' he shouted at the goddess. 'Not once, but twice! This is *my* ship!'

'This ship was built a long time before you came to the world,' was Mielikki's murmured retort. 'All you did, like those before you, was shape her for your own needs. Your possession of her is temporary. And she is not complete. The enchanter Merlin sails in a small echo of Argo, an older part of her. She aches to have that part returned. But only when Merlin is ready to release it. If you lay claim to it, you must argue it out with Merlin.'

Jason's black mood lightened as the skies brightened, the storm passing across the channel. He caught the watching glimmer in Niiv's eyes and crossed the deck to join her. She huddled slightly, arms folded inside her cloak, watching the man suspiciously but with the hint of a smile.

'We both need him,' Jason said. 'I'm aware of that.'

'Who?'

'Merlin, of course. Don't play the innocent. We can search for him together. But now that we're in Alba . . .'

She gave a little laugh of surprise. 'What? Work together? But Jason, you want him dead. I want him alive.'

'Who has told you that I want him dead?'

'You! In the moaning in your sleep. He hurt you badly.'

'He betrayed me. He was an old friend. He helped me back to life. He helped me find Thesokorus, my elder boy. But he kept things back from me. He knew Medea was close to me, protecting her son, yet he said nothing. When I finally met Thesokorus, he did this to me . . .'

Jason pulled up his saturated linen shirt to reveal the jagged, swollen scar of Thesokorus's sword blow. Niiv had already seen the wound, discreetly, while Jason had slept, but she still feigned shock.

'Merlin did that to you?'

'*Thesokorus* did this to me. He is no longer my son. But Little Dreamer is on this island, and I will find *him*, or die trying.' Jason covered his belly again, leaning forward, his gaze canny and amused. 'As well you know. You know all my needs! Don't think I haven't felt your fingers in the night. You probe men's skin and bones for their secrets like every charmer in the world. That's why we should work together: you to learn from him, me to follow him to Kinos, little Kinos. And when you've learned, and I've followed and found: then we can all discuss the matter of Medea and betrayal, and what compensation is due.'

'You'll kill him.'

'Not necessarily,' Jason said carefully. 'I'll listen to what you have to say . . .'

Niiv said nothing. She gave a little shrug of her shoulders, a small signal of agreement, perhaps, or a signal of her willingness to think about the offer.

Truth to tell—this much was obvious to the circling seaeagle—there was still so much she didn't know or understand.

A Ligurian, his face tattooed with curling snakes, stood up and called to Jason in his own language, but made gestures that were clear enough: let's get on before the rain comes again. These are good rowing conditions.

Jason raised his hands in agreement. The rough crew began to sing, a rousing melody learned from the Sicilians on board, a coarse song that always made them laugh as they shouted out the last stanza of every verse.

They had their minds on adventure, and on spoil. Jason had played up the availability of talismans, new weapons and armour and the beauty of women on the isle of Alba. This crew had been easy to recruit, but he didn't trust a single man among them, save for the six of dark demeanour.

Niiv was nervous too. Only Rubobostes' protective bulk and Jason's authority had saved her from violation on two occasions, though both those men had ended up mysteriously without speech and been put ashore on a high rocky headland, far to the south.

Now Argo moved almost effortlessly through the water, drawn ahead by the steady rhythm of the oars, silent and serene as the river channel narrowed and the forest crowded closer to the edge. Niiv was still in position in the tall prow, calling out the hazards of gravel banks and floating logs. Standing in front of the oarsmen, Rubobostes used his brawny arms to signal port and starboard. Jason had trained his rough crew well. Argo drew smoothly against the flow, winding her way into the heart of the land.

CHAPTER NINE

———

Wolf Stalking

It was Urtha's two great hounds who first sensed the wolf, slinking through the undergrowth at the edge of the camp. First Maglerd, then Gelard—old names for old dogs—rose slowly to their feet from where they had been sprawled by the crackling fire. Hackles rose, heads dropped and two low, warning growls roused Ullanna from her half-slumber. She reached quickly for her bow, used it to tap on Urtha's foot below his cloak. The voices of the hounds rose and fell; their bodies had started to shake. Where their dual gaze was fixed, bright, lupine eyes watched back. The maw glistened. The lean head turned right and left, taking in the sprawl of sleeping figures and the guttering flames, and was then withdrawn.

Maglerd made ready to begin the chase, but Urtha called softly, 'Easy, dog. Good dog. Easy, Maglerd.'

The wolf stalked the edge of the camp for a while, then silently disappeared.

The hounds settled uneasily by the fire.

Ullanna shook her head quizzically. 'Why did you stop me? I could have got two shots off before it disappeared.'

'It was just a wolf,' Urtha said, frowning. 'It wouldn't have hurt us. Besides . . . it didn't disturb the horses. Don't you think that's strange?'

The Scythian glanced at the two silent horses, tethered close by, asleep on their feet. Urtha was right. Their calm was uncharacteristic.

'More than a wolf, then. Is that what you're saying?'

The king drew his red cloak around his shoulders. His face was still dark with thought. 'Yes. I think so. I was dreaming when you woke me. I was dreaming of Kymon and Munda. They were calling a warning as they ran towards me. And behind them, watching me through the dream, was our friend from the Northlands, that young-old man with all the charm . . . '

'Merlin?'

'Friend Merlin. Yes. I didn't call on him. I didn't know how to do it. He's found us on his own. Maybe he'd found us before.'

They looked back at the undergrowth where the wolf had appeared, then—remembering Merlin's trick of inhabiting birds—glanced up at the night sky, searching for a hawk. There was nothing there but the movement of clouds and the occasional glitter of a star.

'There is something wrong,' Urtha murmured.

'You keep saying that,' Ullanna teased gently. 'It's beginning to be unnerving. We know there's something wrong. The Desertion of your land. The wasteland. It's why we went to Makedonia, to kill the man who had left your home unguarded.'

'They are warning me about something else,' Urtha insisted. 'Why else be in my dreams?'

'I believe strongly in dreams,' the huntress agreed, adding pointedly as she rubbed sleep from her eyes, 'but I also believe that dreams *break* in unexpected ways. They don't always signal the truth. Don't anticipate trouble before you've reached the Hill.'

Urtha looked around him at the dark wood, then smiled at Ullanna. 'You're right. But may Quick Forest Father clear our track to that Hill, as you call it, and bring me there safely.'

And with that brief, concerned invocation, he hunkered down into his cloak, to stare silently at the fire until that last hour before dawn, when the first preparations for the next day's journey would be made.

* * *

This is what it has come to. A king who exiled himself from his own land and is creeping back to his home as a beaten dog crawls back to the stink-pit behind its master's house. How did it come to this? I couldn't have made it any worse! No one has that much talent.

Oh, Aylamunda! Why did you listen to my dreams? Why didn't you take a quern and knock some corn-sense into the chaff inside my head? I miss you so much. I will find where you lie and kiss you to the Beautiful Island. I promise you.

Forgive me for loving Ullanna. She saved my life. She will never be you. Cathabach would have me pinned down with hazel pegs in a shallow pool and drowned for loving her, but I know you would understand. Take the next step after a blow, strike back, worry about the shaking legs when there is no further threat. You were my battle cry. You always will be.

Why did I go in search of the shield of Diadara? What mad spring hare drove me to such springtime madness? Such quests are the quests of fools. I should not have left the stronghold on the whim of a druid's henbane-scented ecstasy. I might have more easily found Dagda's Cup, that great iron cauldron of rebirth, simmering with the souls of the chosen, ready to be plucked from the stew and returned to life. Sometimes I think I can smell the flavourings! Nightshade and rosehip, a son, a daughter, earth and stone . . .

'Urtha? Are you dreaming?'

Ullanna had reached out to rest a hand on his arm. She looked concerned. 'You've been murmuring and sighing.'

'I was thinking of what I've wasted. The time, the lives. Look what I've come to: a king with a retinue of two critical men, one of them half druid; two capricious Otherworldly twins, the god-sons of Llew, not a god to take lightly, one chariot, four horses, one tent, cushions that apparently have an insufficiency of goose-down, and several stinking blankets.' He turned to look at the woman and smiled as he saw her brow, raised and ready to object to her omission from the list. 'Thank the healing hand of Nodons for you.'

'At last,' she joked. 'I was about to give you a *reason* to invoke the hand of the healer. It's not so bad. We're not far from home . . . ' She sat up suddenly, shaking her head. 'That sounds so strange, and yet so right. I begin to think of your country as my home. And I've hardly been there. Well, home is where you cross your spears against the door, as we say in Scythia.'

The wolf prowled, the warlord's mastiffs howled, but the quick, grey interloper kept at his distance, and the king kept his dogs on the leash of his commanding voice. Maglerd and Gelard were old dogs, named for even older gods, and they knew enough to trust their master.

But they hated the lupine stink that occasionally carried on the air.

Soon it had gone, however, and the *foedor* made its way past the totem stones and grotesque wooden carvings of horses, slung from oak boughs, that marked the entrance, through this forest, to the land of the Coritani. Here loud-laughing, heavy drinking Vortingoros had once been High King, with fifteen chieftains paying him tribute. He had owned five bulls and a hundred horses; he made claim to a tenth part of a thousand cattle. The pig forage in his forest was so hearty that he could claim a fifth part of each sow slaughtered and that portion would feed the four hundred in his fort in a single feast.

Or so he liked to claim.

But Vortingoros, like his knights, had disappeared with the Desertion of the land, that blighting shadow. Only effigies in polished oak and elm had been left, crouching figures, fully armed, littering the valleys and the woodlands, each carved to resemble the man who had been drawn away by whatever gathering had culled the men of the Coritani.

Two days later Urtha led the small band between the towering effigies of boar, bull and crane, on their stork-thin legs, that rose above the winding road where it entered his own forested realm from the east. The river was close by. Sun-wheels, fashioned from willow and hazel, blocked the narrow paths. The chariot creaked and rattled over the rough ground, avoiding the obstacles, the two Cymbrii, carrying Nodons' wheels, riding in front of it. The hounds sniffed and growled, aware that ahead of them, pulling back as they advanced, the scrawny wolf was still an insistent observer of their progress.

A day after that the whole character of the river changed. It felt heavier, more silent, its edges crowded and brooding with low hanging trees. The dogs were almost uncontrollable in their excitement. They tugged at the leash, nosing the undergrowth as if for the first time in ages they were in the presence of familiar scents.

The Cymbrii cantered through the woodland, following the maze of paths that led westwards. And eventually Conan came back, eyes bright, long hair filled with leaf matter.

'There's a plain ahead of us,' he said with a teasing grin. 'A hill rises on the other side of it, with some sort of structure on its top. A bit ramshackle, like an animal shelter. Does that mean anything at all to you?'

'I think it might,' Urtha replied.

Then Gwyrion returned from scouting, almost falling from his horse as he reined in, eyes wild, smile broad. 'Ahead, by the river, is a place with tomb-mounds and tall stones, and secret groves, and a wolf crouching on top of the highest of the mounds, watching in this direction . . . does any of that mean anything at all to you?'

'I think it does,' Urtha said. 'Lend me that horse, will you?'

Gwyrion dismounted happily. Urtha rode, bent low below the branches, until he came to the first of the groves. He reached out to touch the nearest of the tall grey stones that rose from their nests of briar; pressed on, through the clearings close to the rushing flow of Nantosuelta, until he saw the crouching wolf, black-cloaked and dark-haired, eyes glittering as it watched the king's approach.

The wolf slowly stood, casting off the cloak.

'You took your time,' I called to Urtha. 'I hope you've brought some good wine from the south.'

'Merlin! I knew it was you. When did you start watching us?'

'In that sea-fog. I'd been beginning to give up on you.'

'Well, here I am. Home again.'

I ran down the slope of the tomb. Urtha dismounted and we met and embraced, relief making us laugh, lost for words.

'Time to get things back to normal,' he said quietly, then frowned as he saw the look on my face.

'That will not be as easy as it sounds,' I said to him, but he stopped me there, perhaps not willing to hear the worst until he had celebrated the best: the return.

CHAPTER TEN

—

Dark of the Moon

Urtha would not hear of riding on, past his own fortress, to the hidden valley of the exiles where Ambaros and the others had taken refuge. He stood at the edge of the woods, staring through the line of idols that marked this Ghostland territorial claim, out across the thicketed plain. He shouted insults at the enemy, very much in the manner of his own son a few days in the past, and called on Segomonas, the Mighty Victor, and Rigonemetis, King of the Sacred Groves, to turn the favours of the Crow and the Raven to his advantage, and away from those who now possessed the stronghold.

As his anger grew into rage, he swung his heavy body on to his new horse, my welcome gift to him, and entreated me to follow him, and the two of us rode through the long grass towards the closed gates. No one from the fortress came out to challenge us, though we were certainly watched. When we came to the scatter of corpses he rode solemnly around each sprawling, twisted body. He didn't know them all, and their faces were impossible to recognise now that the birds had feasted, but he spoke to each one, and reassured the fallen men that they would soon find 'an earthen cloak' with due ritual, song, and proper remembrance.

But not just yet, he apologised.

I asked him why he needed to leave these sad dead in the grass where they had fallen, but his answer was a grim smile and a curious look, as if to say: you, above all, should understand.

'Those woods and groves are our home now; that is where we'll camp, among our memories. The dead won't mind.'

I hesitated to point out to the newly returned king that some of the dead amid whose tombs we would find shelter were probably among the enemy army. The time to explain would come when it was ready.

Urtha was saddened to learn of Ambaros's dreadful wound. He sent the two Cymbrii to fetch him—they had attached Nodons' wheels to a newly furbished chariot they had found in the evergroves, left there after Kymon's failed assault—and the twins rose to the challenge with vigour, whipping the ponies so that they raced along the edge of the Plain of MaegCatha and were past Taurovinda before the Shadow Knights could emerge and confront them.

We now began the task of erecting a short palisade wall along the edge of the wood, with a single gate to the plain. This was a token, a signal to the occupants of the fortress that we were digging in for the duration. In due course, with more help, we would extend the wall and make more comfortable lodgings; but for the moment we pitched our single tent, open to the river, and dedicated it to Taranis, the Thunderer.

At the end of the first day, as dusk closed over the land and torches began to flare on the stepped walls of the fortress, Urtha led his two *uthiin* on horse out on to the plain and to the line of warning statues. They used ropes to haul the rough-hewn carvings down. Two at a time, ten were dragged about the plain at the gallop, cutting through the thistle and thorn, sweeping down the long grass before being returned to the evergroves and butchered.

The gates to Taurovinda remained closed against this defiance.

It was Urtha's intention to make a pyre of them, to set a fire to the memory of Aylamunda. Scarred and silent, the wooden idols were nothing more than firewood, now.

Towards the end of the second day, sudden flights of birds to the west had us running for our weapons. A small band was approaching, cautiously and nervously. In the dusk, it was hard to make out their banners, but the sudden thunder of a golden-wheeled chariot, and a boy's cry of delight, announced that the arrivals were Kymon and Munda, with the rest of the community from the camp of the exiles.

The children were in the chariot, with Conan, grinning and stripped to the waist, at the reins. He turned the ponies and swept through the gate in the rough wall, then through the trees. The horses snorted and sweated.

Kymon jumped down, wearing his short cloak and dagger. Munda in a swirling dress, her hair braided, rushed to where her father stood and jumped into his arms. She was taller than he remembered and the big man heaved and groaned as he kissed the top of her head.

'When did you spring so high?' he said to her. 'And look at your brother!'

Kymon approached, his eyes glowing, but his demeanour tight with shame. Urtha put his arm round the boy's shoulder.

'I made a terrible mistake,' Kymon said grimly.

'Yes you did,' his father agreed. Then he tugged the boy's hair and grinned fiercely. 'To be added to the world of mistakes we've all made in our lives, giving fighting fodder to the Good God's cauldron! But we'll learn from it, as we always do. Lord of Oak! I can't believe how tall you've both grown. Your mother is pushing you to completion; she's impatient to see the cycle renewed.'

'What cycle?' Kymon asked innocently, and Urtha laughed. I noticed that Munda was amused too. I wondered if the High Women had also sensed the Light of Foresight emerging in the girl, and had begun their gentle instruction accordingly.

The tents and enclosures were quickly erected. A flight of swans, beating east along the course of the river, had Ullanna jumping in her skins, ready for the hunt, but Urtha stifled her enthusiasm. Munda had been eyeing the raunchy Scythian with some curiosity and a little disdain. Now Urtha introduced her to his children.

This happened down at the edge of the river, in the belly of one of its more serpentine curves. It was not my business to interfere or pry in this private moment, but I watched from a distance, half expecting Kymon to remonstrate with his father, as Cathabach had done whilst they had waited for the fog to clear.

It was the girl who seemed troubled, however. She seemed to be shaking. After her initial exuberance, she appeared to have lost all jollity and could not meet her father's eyes.

The smells of cooking and the appalling sound of singing from the retinue had come to invade the peace of this sacred place. If raiders surprised us now, we would be easy prey.

Ullanna left the family group, noticed me and came quickly over. She glanced at the fires and the festival and asked me why I was keeping so aloof.

'Watching you,' I answered truthfully. 'Like everyone, I need to take the returns one step at a time.'

'Munda reminds me of Niiv,' the Scythian said, frowning slightly. 'She neither likes me nor dislikes me. But she sees a shadow from me that disturbs her.' Ullanna met my careful gaze. 'She said: nothing is hidden. And as soon as she'd said those words, she drew away from me. What did she mean? Nothing is hidden?'

'She has what the Hibernians call *imbas forasnai*. It means quite simply that she gets vivid glimpses of the future. The Light of Foresight. The talent is still raw in her, but she saw the killing field out there, on the plain, the bleaching bones left when her brother failed his first feat.'

'Then what is it that is not hidden?' the woman asked, crouching down before me. She was pale in the soft light of the moon, her marked face shadowed and concerned.

'All women with this foresight use those words. It's a tradition as ingrained as waking and sleeping. *Nothing is hidden*. Meaning: I can glimpse unborn days in my dreams! Munda has seen something about you that has made her uneasy.'

Ullanna pondered this, then asked, 'What should I do? Persist with her? If she's seen my death I'm not concerned. I'm not afraid to greet the eighth horse; I'm not afraid of riding the long-grass plain with my father and mother. If she has seen my death, should I ask her to tell me? I'd like her to be content with me, and not apprehensive.'

The 'eighth horse' was a fully harnessed horse without a rider. In Ullanna's part of the world, the steed was led by the seven champions who came to collect the dead.

'She's lost a mother. You are not her mother. She must certainly be aware of the closeness between you and her father, though. She may be resentful. Why should it be more than that?'

'It *is* more than that,' Ullanna murmured. 'She feels something else. I wish I knew what.'

And with a quick shrug of her shoulders, she stood and turned away.

Urtha posted two pickets at the edge of the wood, watching the dark fort, but the phantoms who occupied the hill would not come against us in this sacred ground, I was certain of that now.

After we'd eaten, Amalgaid the poet had declaimed a few verses in Urtha's honour, then wittily and gently criticised the king's son's impetuous actions on the Plain of the Battle Crow before celebrating the valour of the men and women who had ridden under his banner. Now we huddled round the king to listen to his account of the journey to and from Makedonia. Kymon listened with the greatest interest, often glancing round at me quizzically and stating, 'That's not how Merlin told it.'

In our days in the camp of the exiles I had given a fairly honest account of what had happened.

Uncharacteristically, Urtha was underplaying his role in events. But as soon as he realised that Kymon was searching for some real meat and drink in the adventure, he summoned the spirit of the storyteller and the iron brightened, the horses broke into a sweat, and the air in the extended tent became crimson.

He spared no detail when it came to the combat between himself and his foster brother, Cunomaglos.

'He had hidden among the great army, almost lost in the legions of men who were riding south, to the oracle at Delphi. But the hounds knew his stink. They followed him for days; I followed the hounds. Merlin was with me. One day Maglerd began to bark very loudly. A man turned in the saddle and looked at me. When a dog whimpers with fear, its face changes. When a man sees his death, his face becomes a fearful dog. The Dog Lord was a frightened skull, a man who saw not a brother coming towards him, but a determined flight of ravens. It cheered me to see it.

'The warlord Brennos, who commanded this great host of men—a fine king, a fine leader—set the place for the combat at a narrow river, close to the sea. I was armed and advised by Cathabach here, Cunomaglos by the betraying Lexomodos. We exchanged the Three Unavoidable Embraces—you must always do that, Kymon . . . '

'I know, father,' the boy said. 'For a past shared, for kind words shared, and for a future when we will ride side by side in Ghostland.'

'Always. No matter what the grievance. You too, Munda, if you take up iron and shield against another for vengeance.'

'I'll remember,' the girl whispered. 'I doubt I'll need iron, though. The horns of the moon will cut throats on my behalf.'

'Will they, indeed?' Urtha eyed her curiously for a moment, frowning, then continued: 'First we fought with heavy stabbing spears and shields made of oak covered with calf skin, with studded bronze rims and animal-head bosses. After a morning's striking at the bastard I was hungry, so I filled my belly with his raw flesh, then washed the blood from my mouth with fresh river water.'

Here we go, I thought to myself. From sublime truth to ridiculous fantasy.

'We went into a second day,' Urtha continued. 'This time we used heavy-bladed swords with ivory hilts and small, light shields of ash covered with goatskin and decorated with silver herons. I was like a salmon, leaping from the water, leaping over his head, striking down at him while he prodded at me like a child poking at apples on a high tree. I made the twenty leaps of Gryffe! One breath and twenty jumps over that screaming man's armoured head, and with each leap I shaved his beard. You would have been proud of me!

'Nevertheless, the dog was a difficult foe; he was always a strong man. We went into the third day. The choice of weapons was his. Do you know what he chose?'

'The two spears that fly back to your hands!' Kymon shouted, forgetting, in his excitement, what I had already told him. 'And the singing shields with the sharp scalloped edges that can be thrown like discs.'

Urtha shook his head, his face registering an echo of the astonishment he had felt at the time.

'He chose "that which the river can give us". No weapons at all, but rocks, water and the strength of our arms!'

Kymon remembered, now, and clapped his hands together as he listened.

'A small man's weight in muscle and bone had been cut from each of us,' Urtha said grimly. 'And so we were not at our best. But we wrestled like the famous champion Ferdia at the Ford of the Cheating Blow. I performed the Feat of the Seven Falls, tossing that bastard over my head seven times in the instant it takes an owl to swoop and take a mouse.'

Kymon turned quickly to look at me, his eyes filled with passion and excitement. 'You didn't tell me *this* part, Merlin!'

I raised my palms apologetically. 'Must have slipped my mind.'

Urtha lifted his arms for dramatic effect. The roaring fire cast light and shadows on his face. His own eyes glowed. Even Munda was leaning forward expectantly.

'But do you know what was happening further up the river? A band of knights, riding with Brennos, encountered an army of Makedonians, fearsome fighters, heavily armoured, their ears cut off so that they couldn't hear the screams of their friends as they died, their eyes blinkered like a temperamental pony's so that they could see no more than the man ahead of them in battle, their neck muscles twisted, tied and knotted so that they would be unable to turn and run. There was a great slaughter. The dead came down the river, still clutching their spears and slashing swords; shields floated past with the severed hands still attached. Heads with their teeth chattering and their eyes rolling, begging for help.

'My back was to this sudden wealth of armoury. Cunomaglos—may his eyes never fail, that the crow may constantly feed on them!—that bastard dog snatched a spear and did this to me!'

He parted his shirt and showed the scar of the terrible wound. 'He pushed the blade through my father's treasured breastplate . . .'

Now he pulled a golden lunula from his small sack; the gold halfmoon was pierced in its centre. 'A hundred generations have passed this treasure from father to son. It saved my life.

When I finally ride away, it will be through this small gate to Avawn, in the realm of the Shadow Heroes.'

He poked his finger through the gash, then continued.

'I struck back at the dog. Was it friendly spear or enemy spear I used? I have no idea. The blade sank into his neck. Cunomaglos sank into the water. Maglerd jumped upon the body and held it down until it flowed out to the sea. Then that fine hound dragged the whole corpse back from the ocean and nestled it in the rocks, licking the weed and brine from its face to clean it up. I was too weak to do anything myself, but friend Manandoun did the worthy deed, and has allowed me to bring you this special gift . . . '

He reached again to the leather sack and pulled out a small skin bag. Kymon clapped his hands in anticipation. Munda covered her mouth with her hands. Manandoun was grinning with amusement as he watched his friend's son.

'This is for you,' Urtha said. 'My thanks for what you tried to do, out on the Plain of the Battle Crow.'

The smell of decay and sweet oil wafted through the air. Urtha was holding the grisly head of Cunomaglos, its hair and beard lank with the drenching fluids. The eyes half stared at the boy. The mouth gaped and dribbled as if in despair.

Kymon said anxiously, 'You honoured him?'

Heads preserved in this way were generally to be respected.

'I didn't honour him,' Urtha said grimly. 'I *collected* him. I've denied him the road. This bastard will live in darkness for all eternity. Find a stone-hole and wedge him in, face down. Seal the hole with clay and mud. I want to know he'll be screaming in a thousand times a thousand years, as you and I hunt the forests of the Beautiful Island.'

He returned the trophy to its bag, tied it and tossed it to the waiting boy, who caught it, shook it angrily, then punched it fiercely.

'I like this gift!' he proclaimed to the rest of us. 'And I know just where to bury it.'

Urtha then looked at Munda. He reached into his bag for the final item, producing a small straw doll, clothed in red dress and with a small patterned shawl, pinned at the shoulder with a tiny, gleaming silver brooch. 'I found this in a deserted town, in the foothills of snow-capped mountains. I thought of you when I saw it, but I see now that you're older than the games it can play.'

'I'd like the doll,' Munda said. 'I have several of them already.' Her father gave it to her. But she was clearly disappointed and Urtha noticed the fact. He hesitated only a moment before picking up the pierced, golden lunula and placing it on the ground before him. 'I'm going to give you each a better gift.' This was my father's as you know; there was a time when a hundred names could have been attached to it. The men who remembered those names are dead, now.'

The druid, Speaker for Kings, coughed pointedly at that, but Urtha ignored him.

'It saved me from being separated from the two of you. Now I'll make it hold you together . . . '

And before anyone could say a word he had drawn his polished, wide-bladed sword from its chevron-patterned sheath where it lay on the floor beside him, and hacked the lunula in two with a single blow, splitting it through the hole that had been made by Cunomaglos's spear.

'There! Half each. Take whichever half you want.'

'The left side,' Munda said quickly. 'The dark of the moon side.'

Kymon picked up the left side of the precious object and passed it to the girl.

'I like this gift better than the first,' he said. 'I'll pin my half on to my shield. Its brightness will confuse my enemy. What about you, sister?'

'I'll dream about it before I do anything with it,' the girl said with quiet confidence.

Urtha watched them with pride. He said one thing more, before moving on to other matters. 'After I'm gone, remember: the two halves belong together. They may be separated now, but no matter what happens, they must be joined together before you place my cold flesh in the final hill.'

'I will build that tomb right here, where we sit!' Kymon announced, to his father's amusement. 'But not for years yet, I hope.'

'I hope so too.'

The celebration and reunion lasted late into the night, more sober than might have been expected, because of the lack of either wine or the sweetened, strong drink that kings and their retinues favoured, but no less riotous for all that. Around the bright fire, among the tombs of their ancestors, the misery and mystery of the second wasteland was briefly put aside.

Tomorrow, preparations would be made to mark the funeral of Urtha's queen, Aylamunda. With her body having been dragged away during the sacking of Taurovinda, carrion-lost and rotten in the forest, there would be long and detailed discussion concerning the manner in which she might be suitably honoured.

The sound of a girl's singing drew me from shallow sleep the following dawn. It was Munda, of course. She had not been to sleep at all. She had spent the night sitting in the tight curve of the river, holding the fragment of her father's lunula, catching moon and starlight and whispering to herself. Now she was singing about swans.

A light mist hung in the trees and over the river, which flowed almost silently past. Munda looked up at my approach, though she kept singing in that thin, reedy voice. As I stooped to splash water in my face, she stopped the song, watching me.

'The swans are coming. Can you hear them, Merlin? They're coming along the river from the sea. Can you hear them?'

'Not yet. Can you?'

'A strange wing beat,' she said, and looked away to the east.

The birds emerged from the mist, twenty or thirty of them, flying low and silently but for the rhythmic sighing of air, the wings rising and falling as if in a slow dream as they passed up the river and over our heads, the long necks craning down as they peered at us before they disappeared.

One came back, black feathers cresting the white wings, eyes golden bright; it beat past me just above the water, then rose, picked up speed and flew back towards the east.

'She was watching you,' Munda said, her voice slightly hoarse, perhaps because she was tired, perhaps because she was surprised. Her innocent face was bright with that sudden understanding as she stared up at me.

I had been noticed. I had been found.

CHAPTER ELEVEN ·

—

Morndun

The return of the king had been celebrated. Now Urtha began the ritual mourning for his lost wife, Aylamunda. He used powdered chalk to whiten his beard, face and arms and began the ritual of the Three Noble Strains: a day to lament her in song; a day to celebrate her memory with song and laughter; and a day to call for a guide from the Otherworld, to find her spirit and take it safely and asleep to the appropriate realm of Shadow Hero Land.

Ullanna understood very clearly that it would be wrong for her—Urtha's new love—to remain in this sanctuary of the ancestors at this time, and she took provisions and a strong, grey pony and, accompanied by the Cymbrii in their speedy, flashy chariot, crossed the river to the north, and went to find stray cattle and pigs. Kymon and Munda wore the white of lament with their father, and spent the day among the round stones and cairns of the evergroves, walking the track from the river that wound through the groves three times before passing on, unseen for the moment, across the Plain of MaegCatha to the Bull Gate of Taurovinda.

They were joined for this tearful time by one of the High

Women, Rianata, and the old priest, the Speaker for the Past, in his cloak of white bull's hide and his collar of blue and white feathers.

Urtha asked if I would like to join them, but the skin-and-feather man looked disapproving. I seemed to have known his type all my life. A man of prodigious memory, deep insight and complex thinking, and a vigorous defender of tradition, he would have a small ability to see through the veil of Time, but darkly. Even Niiv would have been more perspicacious. These rough priests had been born with little, and achieved their dream-sight by dedication and training rather than innate ability.

Still, in this rough land their crude methods would probably be sufficient to arouse the sleeping spirits, and make them ready to accept another among them. I decided to keep my distance, though Urtha urged me not to stray too far.

Aylamunda was lost, not just her body—dragged away during the sacking of the fort—but her ghost. She was wandering. And such wandering, to the Celts, was a terrible thing. She would have to be called back, and deciding the means to do this would involve a great deal of discussion.

That discussion dominated the second day, though not before broken-breasted Ambaros had stood, holding strongly on to a spear, and delivered a fond testimonial to his daughter. His legs would barely support him; his face was drawn and ashen, the flesh shrinking on his skull. I watched him with sympathy. I realised, now, that he was keeping himself alive for the moment of his daughter's funeral. No event that might come later mattered so much as the ending of her wandering.

Cathabach, the once-priest, found me later by the river's edge. Perhaps he had come at Urtha's behest, perhaps on his own initiative, I don't know. His hair was tied in an elaborate topknot and he had marked his face and arms with protective blue symbols.

'Could you fly and find her?' he asked me bluntly. 'It's a big request; it may be beyond your ability. This is the sort of death that we find very difficult to honour properly. Aylamunda may be watching us from that glade over there, or she may be halfway round the world below, confused and frightened. Bringing her home will not be easy. Not for this small tribe.'

He looked at me carefully. He had nothing to hide and he knew it.

'Tomorrow, we must call for her guide. Knowing where in the darkness she is wandering would help greatly.'

'What a wilderness this is,' I commented, and the warrior laughed, understanding exactly what I meant: that everyone was lost!

'My own feeling,' he said after a moment, 'is that she is following Tauraun, the white bull with the red ears and the eyes of Taranis the Thunderer marked in brown on its flanks. The Donn. The Roaring Bull, whose stamping of the earth threw up the great fortress itself. But that's just a feeling. I'm still in taboo when it comes to knowing.'

Now I understood the sound of bull-roaring I had heard when I had first returned to the deserted stronghold. The ancient spirit of the hill was awakening in response to the changes in its occupation. There was a great deal of Time locked away below the orchard groves and ramshackle houses inside the ruined enclosure.

I told Cathabach that it would be pointless flying as a hawk, running as a hound, or swimming as the salmon in search of Aylamunda. I would have to travel in the ghostly form of Morndun. The action was difficult to do and costly to an enchanter's health. This enchanter, at least. I had used the ghost in Greek Land, not long ago, and the deep scars of that journey still ached.

Cathabach said he understood. 'Ten masks with ten charms,' he said, referring to my talents in enchantment. 'Is that right?'

'Yes. I make no secret of it.'

'Ghosts and creatures, and the moon, and Sorrow, and Memory, and there is one for the child in the land, and one to see the shadows of forgotten forests. Is that right?'

'Yes. All of them.'

'Memory would interest me; and to see forgotten forests, that too. We must talk about this another time.' He tugged his rough beard as he looked at me, curious about the masks, curious about my origins. 'Are there no other masks through which you might see the dead queen?'

Moondream, I thought to myself. Perhaps Moondream, the facility to see the woman in the land. But I had never used it to look for a ghost, merely to summon and invoke the feminine presence in the earth.

'It will have to be Morndun,' I told Cathabach. 'I'm willing to try. But I'll have to wait until night. And I'll need help.'

'To make the mask?'

'The mask is in the mind. It's a long time since I carved tree bark for my living. I need someone to watch me.'

He touched a finger to his brow, a gesture of thanks. 'If you need company, I'll be glad to join you. Within a year I'll cast off the *geis* and start training in dreamwalking again.'

I told him that I welcomed his offer. I added that he would learn nothing from what might occur, since he would see nothing but my motionless body. But there was a certain comfort in knowing that my undefended carcass, its mind absent, would be under the constant surveillance of a friend.

We were hailed by the watch at the gate. It was late afternoon and the light was going, the sky a rolling swirl of storm clouds, the wind becoming fierce. Urtha remained inside, but Manandoun and several others picked up their spears and ran quickly to the palisade.

The grass of the plain rippled in the wind. The high ramparts of the fortress were dark, the streaming banners of the invader like threshing snakes on their poles, brightly coloured, designed like hideous grinning animals. Two men walked towards us, one of them bent under the weight of a pack, the other striding ahead, tall staff in hand. I could see the flash of his eyes. Both strangers seemed grey: grizzle-bearded, grey-haired, grey-cloaked.

Then I recognised them as the Wolf-heads who had earlier passed through the valley of the exiles.

Twenty paces from the gate they dropped to their haunches, watching us nervously, and asked for food and shelter. Manandoun shrugged, allowed them to enter. They came into the camp, looking around, and made for the nearest fire.

When the moon was high, adding an edge of silver to the clouds above us, I walked downriver with Cathabach, to the end of the evergroves, and took a small boat across the water. On the other side of Nantosuelta, beyond the landing, was a broad area of silent marsh, crowded with thickets of willow, alder and hornbeam, and mossy banks enclosing reed-fringed pools, some of them deep, some shallow, all dangerous.

This was the Pressing Down place, the place of sacred execution, and Cathabach was reluctant to enter it, though he had done so once in his life, to participate in the ceremonial despatch of a young prince, an abandoned hostage from the Videlici who gave his life in exchange for the fertile marriage of a noble couple within Urtha's clan.

A raised walkway led out into the thickets, above the saturated and reedy earth. There were platforms hidden in the gloom, each with its votive idol, each above a wet pool, where the final rites had been practised before the gruesome slaughter of the chosen victim. The marshes were still screaming with those who had been staked out, face down, pinned into the mud and slowly drowned, some for the return of the sun, some to pacify the howling spirits of encroaching winter; some because they had broken one of their *geisa*, their birth taboos.

'Why here?' Cathabach whispered uncomfortably, rubbing his fingers over one of the images on his right forearm.

'A need for the dead,' I said. 'I need a vehicle.'

'You'll have your choice of those. But these aren't ordinary dead, Merlin. They no longer belong to us.'

He watched me, wondering if I knew to what he referred: that the corpses in the marsh were the property of gods, the earth, or the night-stalking warlord Araun, who gathered the spirits of those who had betrayed their own lives. These were mostly adulterers, matricides, hostages from other clans who had been deserted and men who had shirked battle-combat.

'Besides all that,' he added, 'this place has been used from before our clan ever came here. There are some very old corpses in those pools.'

'I'm just going to . . . ' how could I put it to the anxious man? '*borrow* one. For a while. I'll take the consequences.'

'You certainly will,' the once-druid said emphatically. 'I resign my charge of watching over you against anything other than a worldly man with an iron sword.'

'I ask for no more,' I reassured the wan-faced warrior-priest.

The raised wooden walkway on which we crouched was as corrupt as the battlements of the hill fort, battered by winter, weakened by rain, half sinking into the mire. I walked out along it with the greatest care. It branched twice, running into the willow groves, but I kept always to the left. Behind me, Cathabach had lit a torch. Its small flickering glow was comforting in this stinking, silent darkness.

The platform I finally reached had also been ravaged by the winds, but there was enough planking left to sit upon. Around me, in the darkness, creatures moved and scurried, splashed and chattered. They had come to think of this killing ground as their own again. The tarred and leathered coracles were all half submerged, the homes of eels and rats. The willows loomed eerily in the slender light, drooping giants, the fronds of their branches gathering in the bones of three thousand years of water sacrifice.

I have written elsewhere about the painful and frightening process by which Morndun is called, and the dead can be addressed and used as guides. The last time I had resorted to this particularly unpleasant form of travel had been by the Daan river, before the great assault on Delphi, in Greek Land. I was still haunted and hounded in my sleep by the sights and voices I had aroused during that desperate mission.

I felt sick, now, as I summoned the dead.

They struggled. The first thing I felt was their tussle against the ropes and hazel pegs that had forced them into the mire. Most were rotten, bones dissolved, only the grimace of their jaws remaining. Still they screamed, the shadows of their souls, the thin shards of light left in the bleached bones, fighting to return.

I needed someone more complete.

I felt the flexing of a wronged man, his hands bound behind him, his throat opened by the blade, his lungs packed with mud.

He thrashed like a small fish out of water, several feet below the reeds. He turned on to his back, sat up, pushed and strained to reach the surface, and distantly I saw the reed-bed shift and part as he managed to struggle into a kneeling position, sunken eyes blinking to grab the moonlight, leathery skin holding his bones together.

He was neat and trimmed, his beard cut elegantly, his nails manicured, the patterns on his body those of a noble man, a prince.

I was not ready for this! he raged in my head. *I was betrayed. I was tricked. My nine years had not been served!*

Nine years and the king is drowned, I remembered, though

that was a practice from many generations before Urtha's. So this man was more than a prince; he was a young king who had been selected for midwinter sacrifice before his time. His anger was tangible, terrible, persuasive . . . useful.

'I need your help,' I whispered to him.

My brother has caused me to be put in this place. He rides with the priests at moonrise; he sheds blood on the tall stones with them. He has betrayed me.

How could I tell him that that betrayal had been long since forgotten? As he lay in anger in the mire, his brother was staked down somewhere else, a victim, almost certainly, of his presumption. I had not been there to witness it, of course; but I had witnessed such betrayals on many occasions.

'I need your help,' I repeated. His form rose to its feet, shambling in the murky darkness, glistening with water, hunched with anger.

A voice behind me rasped, *I will help you if you take me to my children.*

I turned quickly. The lank-haired, corrupted figure of a woman leaned towards me, clinging to the edge of the platform. Hollows in her skull still sparkled faintly with the thread of life. The rope around her neck, biting into the sinews of her throat, did not constrict the ghostly voice. Behind her, a tall man swayed, watching me, hoping. His arms were bound behind him. The shaft of hazel wood that had been driven through his neck to fix him in the marsh stuck from his gizzard like a broken spear.

I will help, he whispered. *Can you free me? I came here as hostage. I was used as a slave. I was killed on a whim.*

'There is nothing I can do for you.'

When the dead come awake, it is best to be blunt with them. They had little understanding of the realities of Time, and of how they could do nothing to change past events. Sometimes, of course, Time allowed for resurrection. That was why Jason was again in the world. But such extravagances were rare.

I realised I was getting impatient with the thought of more of these rotting memories surfacing to moan at me. The leather-faced prince, his body preserved remarkably where he had been buried a thousand years ago, was exactly what I needed.

I sent the others back to the mud, kicking the woman away

from where she gripped the oak platform. As she sank back she wailed at me, but I hardened my heart as I had hardened it for ten thousand years.

Cut me loose, the princely leatherskin demanded.

'When you've helped me.'

I'm tied to this place, he whispered.

'You are a threshold I need to cross,' I replied. 'I am looking for a woman, dead and wandering. She will have been walking in circles, so she can't be too far away.'

The leatherskin was silent. I let him brood for a while. His mind was sludge, but there was a sharp point of memory that assisted his decision: that since he could never leave this place, there could be no real reward for him for helping me, not in terms of resurrection. But I had insight, memory, and one valuable gift to give him. He murmured: *I will tell you my name. You will repeat that name. Make a mark somewhere that shows my name. Make it so that I cannot be forgotten. I must not be forgotten. Will you do this?*

'I will make every effort to make sure your name is never forgotten. First help me find the spirit of a woman, a queen in her country, called Aylamunda.'

He had been walking towards me through the mire. Now I saw the gold band around his brow and the red and blue chevrons down the left side of his neck.

A Trojan? Here, in Alba?

Do you recognise me?

'The siege of your city was a millennium ago. The story is told across the known world: the persistence of the Greeklanders, the savagery of your champion Hector, the cunning of the Greek commander Odysseus. Only a few of you escaped. How long did you wander?'

Half my life. A sword blow from Achilles opened my skull to the air. I lost my wits; but when I healed and became strong again I raised a small army of mercenaries and sailed west. I came to this fabled island. The island of mists and the dead. My ship was burned and buried below the citadel I founded. Does it still exist, I wonder? I set out to explore the land, but I strayed too far north, out of safety, and it was my fate to fall into the wrong hands. Do you recognise me now?

A citadel on Alba, founded by a Trojan? I knew of it. On a

wide river in the south, dedicated to Llew. The stronghold had long since been swallowed by the earth.

'Brutus. You fled with the noble Aeneas . . .'

Aeneas. Aeneas. A good friend. I lost sight of him when I lost my wits. What was his fate, I wonder.

To be renowned across the southern world, I thought to myself, to found a dynasty, but I blocked those thoughts from this probing corpse. Brutus, ill-fated founder of a now ruined fortress on the shores of the river Taemisis, had brought knowledge and skill to this mist-shrouded island, but had been rewarded with a ritual death when he had strayed to the stone sanctuary that had long been built on the willow banks of Nantosuelta.

Remember my name, Brutus's ghostly whisper urged. *And mark the place of my burial.*

'I shall,' I promised him.

He struggled against the ropes that bound his arms, then turned and stepped through the reeds, back to his resting place. He called to me to follow, and I stepped as Morndun, the ghost in the land, into the darkness of the world where the restless and uprooted wandered.

This was a night world, a realm of gloom, similar to the underworlds of the Greeklanders and Scythians. Nothing Elysian here, just full-leafed trees, swirling pools and crumbling rocks. There was movement everywhere, but it slipped, shade-like, into the dark clefts of cliffs and encompassing paths of the forest.

I walked until my limbs ached, skirting the wide, silent meres and crossing the sluggish, icy streams that drained the moonless hills. The spirit of Brutus walked behind me in silence, ghost-limbs freed from their bondage, reaching out occasionally to tug at my clothes, to make me stop and stare at the lumbering shape of an animal, or the forlorn figure of a woman.

He had seen the red-eared bull on many occasions. It had often crossed the crystal flow of Nantosuelta, sometimes alone, sometimes led by a small band of white-haired, silver-armoured riders.

I tried to keep track of time in this bleak, lightless world, but the measure was hard. There was no rest, no sleep, no food, no drink. It was exactly what I had expected: a wandering, a steady walk through shallow valleys and round whispering woods. Perhaps two days and nights, perhaps three, walking a circle, a small reflection of the Path I walked all my life.

And we found the bull.

It was walking steadily to the south, head lowered, huge horns scything the long grass, towering above me in the night. The ground vibrated like distant thunder with each step it took. Its massive white body was covered with bushes and stunted trees, gnarled growths from its heaving flanks, tangled up with the flailing ropes that bound the shrouded remains of sacrificial victims. They lolled and dangled like children's puppets as the beast moved on its ponderous way. Behind it, arms crossed over their chests, a straggling group of ten or twelve people followed, heads lowered like the bull's. These were those of the lost and forgotten who had died during a time when the Donn was stepping through the land, and had followed the beast.

When I called for Aylamunda, one of the forlorn figures raised its head and looked towards me. Bright eyes in a sad face met my own, a hand quickly brushed away the lank, greying hair. She wouldn't have recognised me. We had never met. But there was the merest flicker of hope in her snow-white features, as if she was aware that her time of wandering would now come to an end.

The Donn suddenly stopped in its tracks, shaking its shoulders and stroking the ground with its left hoof. Its huge head turned to look at me, breath misting from its nostrils, the sound of its breathing like a massive pair of bellows in Wayland's forge. It lumbered round, approached me, lowered its head until the miasma of its breath enveloped me. Eyes the size of shields blinked, blocking out my ethereal reflection.

Then the head went up and it bellowed, turned back along its path, back towards the river where it flowed through this Stygian limbo.

I was shaking, both with relief and with the effort of this search. I loathed travelling in Morndun; it was exactly like walking with Death. But I had persevered, and now with Brutus still behind me I followed the bull until we returned to the place where the Trojan had met his end. The bull and Aylamunda and the others went on towards the roots of the fortress, soon lost to my view.

I crossed back to the night world of Urtha's land and whispered to the shifting reeds, where Brutus had returned, 'I'll keep my promise,' as I stretched my stiff and aching limbs.

It was almost dawn. I could hear Cathabach calling for me from the far end of the walkway into the marsh, where he waited for me. There was no anxiety or urgency in his voice. He had probably called to me all the time I had been away, keeping the connection between us.

I stumbled back to where he crouched, hunched in his cloak on dry ground. He greeted me with a smile of relief and a small skin of cool, honeyed ale. He offered no food. The meat and oatcake he had brought for me had proved too tempting during his vigil, even though I had been gone for only one night, as it turned out. It was not important. He seemed very satisfied with what I had seen during my journey. What I had learned meant that he could now complete the funeral arrangements in the most appropriate manner.

'Her spirit is home. And the boat is being built,' he added cryptically. 'The processional way is ready. The pyre will be ready shortly.'

We went back to the groves.

CHAPTER TWELVE

—

The Thunder Feat

As far as anyone from Taurovinda was aware, the double ring of stones on the rise of ground overlooking the river had been standing for all time. A ceremonial way, now hidden below the long grass, had wound across the Plain of MaegCatha from the Bull Gate of the hill fort to the stones; a shorter path then led from the sanctuary to the river itself. The stones had been encircled, now, by a high fence of willow, though their decorated tops showed above the barricade, and the fence was open to the water.

In remote times past, the procession of the dead had begun on the hill and made its way to the river, passing through the rings, first resting in the heart of the circle before the butchery of the corpse and the ritual washing of the knives. The ceremonies that celebrated the first budding of spring, or the ripening of corn in autumn, had begun at the river and danced to the summit of the hill, where the marriages of man with earth and woman with tree had been consummated.

Now, however, the funeral procession would begin at the banks of Nantosuelta, where a crudely fashioned, shallow boat was moored, moving side to side in the flow like a sluggish fish.

This flimsy craft had been filled with branches, bright flowers, yellowing leaves and ornately ribboned and tied bundles of grass, on which were placed the two halves of Urtha's lunula. It took a moment for me to realise that these bundles were shaped into the figure of a woman, lying in repose on the colourful bed of nature, her head at the stern of the ritual ship, the golden half moon on her chest.

A small hand sneaked into my own. Munda looked up at me, smiling.

'I can hear her singing,' she said. 'Or is it a dream?'

'I don't know,' I confessed. 'But she is close to you, now. She'll soon go to her proper place, across the river.'

The girl cocked her head, struggling with a thought, then asked the question. 'You're very old,' she began.

'Yes, I am.'

'Did you ever love anybody?'

'Yes,' I admitted, wondering where this was leading.

'What did you do when they died? You don't seem to belong anywhere. How did you bury them? How do you visit them?'

I didn't know how to answer her. There had been so many short encounters in my life: I had left so many women behind; I had seen a few die, and grieved for them, some greatly so. But I made a point of never returning to where I had known such affection. It was too hard to stare at the time-ruined remains of a place that once I had known well.

The only real love I had known was still half in shadow, and hiding in the land of shadows. Medea, the enchantress of Colchis, Jason's once-wife. She was close to me again, afraid, uncertain, defensive and defiant, I was sure.

She would have had aged: unlike me, she had used her Time-given powers to protect herself and the sons she loved. But she would still be beautiful.

'You're crying,' the girl beside me whispered. Her hand tightened on mine. 'Don't cry. I've seen it for you, Merlin. Nothing is hidden—I've seen it constant; I've seen it joyful. Not yet, but one day in time to come. Everything will be all right.'

For a moment I was too stunned to react. Then I gripped her by the shoulders and shook her gently but forcefully. 'Never do that!' I admonished her. 'It's a dangerous thing, to see into a friend's future.'

'I couldn't help it!' she said in alarm, eyes widening as she looked up at me. 'I didn't *look* for it. The sights just come. Why is that wrong?'

It would have taken too long to explain. As she had said the words I had been powerfully and unwelcomely reminded of Niiv, the Northlands enchantress, waving a dead swan at me, shouting defiantly: *I have seen you wear forests like a cloak.*

Niiv had prowled and probed my future and used her knowledge in a sinister and devious way. Now she was coming back to Alba. Urtha had seen her in the sea-mist; and the swans were confirmation!

I was uneasy to say the least.

The last thing I needed was a *brace* of visionaries prying ahead into my time on the earth.

I reassured the girl and left her sitting by the prow of the boat, singing quietly as she stared at the grass effigy.

Ullanna and her entourage—now extended—rode noisily and colourfully from the north later that day, arriving at the other side of the river, driving before them over thirty head of whites and browns, plump cattle that had grazed widely in the years of the Desertion. They had two deer slung on a white pony, and had found five wild horses, which kicked and reared as they were led to the water's edge and penned in crude corrals. Seven new men were in the troop, leather-armoured, without helmets, heavily armed and coarse-feathered. But they seemed in awe of Ullanna and obeyed her every direction.

The Scythian woman could see that the funeral had not yet occurred. She raised a hand to me, in greeting and farewell, then kicked away again, towards the woodland, Conan and Gwyrion with her, always anxious for more hectic adventure. The rest of the troop set up camp across the river, to watch over their plunder and wait for the invitation to cross to the groves and discuss payment for their services.

Night embraced the land; the horns of the moon were fattening. It was low in the west, its gleam illuminating the dark ridges of the wooded hills and the rise of Taurovinda.

Drums began a low, steady beat. Horns sounded harshly
Metal tambours rattled. Pipes wailed.

The groves became alive with torchlight. The curl of the rive
seemed set on fire. The boat was hauled to the shore and eigh
men lifted it to their shoulders. Torches burned on prow and
stern. The men walked slowly, stepping side to side at a stead
pace, up the slope to where the stones waited. A hooded an
masked figure walked ahead of them, using his staff to mark th
rhythm of their progress.

The funeral boat was carried through the gate in the willow
fence, to the heart of the grey stone ring. The drumbea
stopped, the wailing horns and rattling tambours were silenced
The boat was lowered to the ground. Nothing could be heard
but the crackle of fire.

The long silence ended with the ringing of a small bronz
bell. The drums struck a single thunderous beat and the boa
was hoisted again.

Now the horns sounded their droning music in harmony, and
the shrill pipes played a lament of singular beauty, punctuated
by the dramatic striking of the calf-skin drums. The processio
moved beyond the stones and through the groves, then out on t
the plain. It snaked its way through the long grass, following th
ancient ceremonial way, still marked by the humped backs o
fallen stones.

This winding route across the plain was a reflection of th
river journey that the spirit of Aylamunda had made to arrive a
her birth. She would go back to death with Tauraun, the Thun
der Bull.

Three times the procession stopped in dead silence, the boa
lowered to the ground, the masked man who led the line o
mourners standing facing them. The sky swirled with moonli
cloud; horses at the back of the column whiskered nervously
the grass rolled and rustled in the breeze.

Then again the sound of the bell, the strike of drum, and th
boat was up. The horns wailed, deep and forlorn, as the ste
began again.

In this way we arrived before the rising slope of the hill, and
the heavy Bull Gate that marked the first entrance to the forti
fied enclosure.

Were the Shadows of Heroes watching from those fortifica

tions? Only their banners, streaming black and silver in the night, told me they were there.

All sound drained from the air. The horses were kicked forward, dragging the broken totems of Ghostland, grim-carved trees that were stacked in a low pile. The boat was gently placed on top of the fallen symbols of the Dead, a challenge to them. Urtha gently removed the broken lunula from the 'corpse'. Hazel faggots were pushed below the trunks and quickly lit; flames licked high into the night. As the boat caught, and the grass effigy began to burn, the horns and drums sounded again.

Urtha stood before the pyre. He was in his battle-harness. The fire gleamed on his helmet and cuirass, and on the narrow blades of the heavy-shafted ash spear he held in his right hand. He stared at the fire, but I thought *through* the fire, his eyes focused on the dark ramparts of his citadel.

He began to shout; the shout was a chant, though the words were lost to me against the noise of the horns, but I heard the name Tauraun repeated; the great Donn was being summoned.

I had thought that the creature would emerge from the forest behind us, to walk steadily across the plain, and several times I glanced that way, curious as to how it would make itself manifest in the real world. In fact, it rose through the hill, something I should have expected, considering the name of the fortress.

The earth shook below our feet and the pile of burning trunks slipped, scattering a whirlwind of bright sparks into the night sky. The moon itself seemed to brighten and thicken, the clouds forming a swirling storm pattern above the ramparts.

Urtha's voice rose in aggression and volume. I suddenly heard the words he was using, and thrilled to recognise a language far older than the lilting tongue of these Hyperboreans. The words he used were a dialect of the language of my own time, fatal and vital in their use of charms and enchantment, the pacifying, celebrating and summoning chants for the first and greatest forms of life on the earth itself.

'Ka-scaragath, raa-Dauroch, Cuum Cawlaud, Nuath-Raydunfray, Odonn Tauraun . . .'

Winter-scavenging Wolf, Green-faced wildwood Hunter, Oldest Owl, Silver-hoofed, velvet-bannered Stag, Brown burnished, sun-draped Bull . . .

But of all of these praised, Tauraun alone was called; Urtha offered his life and his grandchildren's lives to the Great Bull in service after death for the span of two bull-lives, two generations of man himself.

Tauraun had answered the call.

The sun began to rise inside the fortress. Two wide, curved horns rose behind the highest ramparts. The sun glowed between them. The air filled with the stink of the creature's breath. Behind those highest walls, the gates of the citadel were opened and the forces of the Land of Shadow Heroes rode in fear and disarray from the stronghold they had won by stealth and defended with vigour. They suddenly poured out of the gate at the bottom of the steep embankments, spreading left and right, a force of one hundred or more. Again the earth was shaken as the Great Bull pounded its hooves above them, its broad, dark face peering out across the plain, the sun-disc swirling like fire between its horns.

The army of the Dead and Unborn lowered lances and drew swords and charged in a line against us. A horse was galloped up to Urtha and he jumped into its high-backed saddle, taking the reins from Manandoun. Cathabach and others galloped in front of the pyre, weapons gleaming, their faces bright with the pleasure of imminent combat. Kymon, harnessed and helmeted, was among them.

But there were not enough of us!

Then the shaking of the earth took on a different rhythm. I turned in time to see the charge of an army of horsemen from the forest at the edge of the plain, a wild, screaming ride of armed and bare-headed men, spreading out to circle round the base of the hill. At the same time, Conan pulled up in the gold-wheeled chariot beside me. 'Jump in! Grab a spear!' he shouted, sweat streaming from his face. 'Quickly!'

I did as I was bidden. Javelins split the air, a sword crashed down through the wicker frame, remaining embedded there. Conan had whipped the ponies into the centre of the fray. My spear was wrenched from my hand and thrown back at me, but I used the jumping feat to avoid it and snatch it back.

'Well *done*!' my driver cried with enthusiasm. 'My brother will soon be looking for another partner! I like the way you jump!'

'Where did those riders come from?'

'A trick up Urtha's sleeve!' was all the response I got, except that he added, 'Cornovidians! We met them on the way back here!'

We had galloped through the fray. Now Conan turned the chariot and tore around the edge of the struggle, screaming like a Fury. Manandoun and Urtha fell in on horse behind us, then Cathabach, then Ullanna and her recruits. We rode in an encircling column, striking down to the left, leaping over the bodies of men and fallen horses. The horsemen from the forest streamed into the muddle, some jumping down to fight on foot below the stamping hooves of the Dead. Conan was screaming and laughing as he whipped his ponies, giving them their head. His hair streamed, long and golden. His torso, ridged with muscle, gleamed with sweat. The man was possessed!

I had thought we were a small party finding the right moment to re-enter the battle, but Conan suddenly turned the chariot towards the Bull Gate, a sudden charge, the king and his retinue alongside us now, acting according to a plan that took us through the gate and up the winding street, between the stockaded walls, and again into the heart of Taurovinda.

Triumphant cries, and delighted screams, accompanied our entrance into Urtha's home. Then sudden silence.

At the far end of the enclosure towered the shimmering image of the bull Tauraun, its legs braced apart, the sun-disc faint, now, like a starlit wheel spinning between its horns. The breath from its nostrils steamed in the suddenly frigid air. It watched us through huge eyes, but made no move towards us. Standing quite still between its front legs, watching us as he leaned on a radiant, oval shield, was a tall man with long yellow hair and beard.

When the ponies that drew Conan's chariot reared nervously it was not because they were afraid of the gigantic creature that faced them, but because their driver had been startled by the apparition of the figure below its maw.

The young man, until now so cheerful and reckless, had become ashen and tense with fear. 'Get down, Merlin,' he said quietly. 'Get down! Quickly!'

When I hesitated, he reached a hand to push at me, his eyes not straying from the lounging, golden figure at the far end of the fort.

I could still hear the battle-screams of men and horses and the ringing of iron. Urtha was shouting with triumph. More horsemen, bloodied and lathering, came riding through the inner gate, dismounting and running to the battlements to tear down the streaming banners of the fallen kings of Ghostland. I heard someone cry that the Ghostlanders were fleeing back through the marshes to the river.

Then Gwyrion came riding through the gate, Munda on the saddle behind him clinging on to his arms. His horse, too, reared up as he saw the Bull and its sun-haired master. The girl fell to the ground and Gwyrion slipped down from the saddle and helped her up, apologising profusely.

Though there was mayhem and shouting all around us, Cathabach and wise Manandoun watched in silence, aware that the young Cymbrii were in trouble.

Conan glanced at me, almost tearful. 'Well, Merlin,' he said, 'it's been a long journey, and more fun than pain. I wish I'd got to know you better.'

'What's happening?' I asked him, but he simply smiled and shrugged.

'Reckoning time.'

The man between the bull's legs had raised his spear and was using it to beckon the boys. I began to grasp a truth that should have been obvious.

'We stole his chariot,' Conan said forlornly. 'Remember? It was decorated in gold that had been spun by a Greek Land god called Haephestus, and had iron worked into its wicker frame to make it stronger than a stone wall. That man there was very proud of his chariot. Very angry when we stole it, even though he'd stolen it himself in the first place. Alas, we managed to crash it in a race, though only because the other team cheated: swords attached to their wheels. Bastards! Anyway, I don't think this bit of copper-varnished wicker will satisfy him, even with its gold-rimmed wheels.'

'Who is he?'

'My god-father,' Conan muttered sadly. 'Who else? The great god Llew himself. That's his Sun Bull. He always arrives with it when it surfaces from the dark. We won't get out of this one lightly. He has other bright sons to cherish, more obedient ones—little arse-lickers!—so he'll certainly have our heads. Goodbye, Merlin.'

Gwyrion, looking equally anguished, smiled wanly at me as he came over, then stepped into the car, gripping the rail. 'Fun while it lasted, though,' Conan shouted at me with a last burst of youthful bravado. 'And you *will* make a great chariot-warrior!'

Then he gave the ponies their heads and the small chariot was drawn towards the waiting man. The great god Llew stepped into the car and took the reins, turning his back on his sons. Their faces became silver in hue, in contrast to his radiant gold. Frozen, unsmiling and unfocused, gripping the rails with both hands, shadows in their father's angry eyes, they seemed to watch the end of their mortal adventure with sadness.

With a powerful lash of his whip, Llew turned the panicking horses and rode the chariot below the body of the Bull, soon disappearing into the gloom of the hill. The Bull gave a mighty shake of its head, suddenly coming alive again, and turned, to lumber back into the darkness, descending into shadow, and continue its slow walk through the underworld.

But it had done its job. Though we had lost two youthful friends, Aylamunda's ghost was now alive again, and she was in her proper place in the most appropriate land among the Shadows of Heroes. And Urtha had reclaimed his fortress. Already, the massive gates were closed, and the banners and standards of Ghostland were being nailed to a 'mocking tree', made from dead wood hewn from hazel and ash. This would be hung over the north wall, permanently out of sight of the passage of the sun.

I joined Urtha on the wall. The Shadow Knights had dispersed, taking their fallen with them. But if the king was triumphant, he expressed it in subdued manner.

'We won't have seen the last of them,' he said quietly. 'Don't you agree, Merlin? They won't give up this easily. They're extending their realm. Though why they should be doing that is beyond me for the moment.'

Behind us, the small army of warriors and their families were spreading out through the streets, laying claim to the houses and planning the rebuilding. It would be a lengthy task.

I recognised, among them, the standards of the Coritani.

It seemed that Urtha, when he had passed through the territory of the High King of the Coritani, had found it reoccupied by the men who had lived there before. They had returned ahead of him from the chaotic adventure that had led an army of the clans into Makedonia and Greek Land. Nosing as I was, in the form of a wolf, I had not seen this encounter. Urtha, alerted to the problems with Taurovinda, had won the respect of these men, and their agreement to assist in his own land. He had kept them in the forest, out of sight and silent. He had not known what to expect in his home citadel, but in the event the Shadow Knights, made mortal in this world, had been outnumbered.

How he would now pay his mercenaries for their continued service was a bridge to be crossed in due time; they would certainly stay for the cycle of a moon. After that they would start to claim cattle and horses.

PART THREE

—

The Light of Foresight

CHAPTER THIRTEEN

—

Taurovinda

Urtha had claimed back his ancestral fortress of Taurovinda, savaged and stolen from him years before. He had reclaimed his stronghold with boldness and imagination, harnessing the slender forces of arms, men and the supernatural to great effect. He told me almost at once that he had been inspired by the fire and fury of his small son, Kymon; he might otherwise have delayed, seeking the best strategy for what had seemed to him a task that would lead to at least one failure, if not more. He had anticipated a long struggle and had won in glorious, rousing triumph, seduced by youthful recklessness.

Yes, Kymon, the spirit of the king, had been the kick to his flank; only later would he tell me that when he had heard my account of the forlorn figure of Aylamunda, moving behind the Bull on her way to a greater happiness, he had glimpsed her himself, and been filled with such insensate rage that he came close to storming the citadel himself, alone, naked and unarmed. He had seen her as clearly as I had seen her, a glimpse of the darkness below, a glimpse of the woman he had loved with passion. If he suspected that I had in any way *seeded* that momentary sight in his mind's eye, he kept the thought to himself.

Love does not perish when the body dies. And in Ullanna, Urtha had a new companion—herself the survivor of a tragic separation—who understood the nature of the gash in the muscle of Urtha's heart. With this Scythian woman by his side, he bragged, he could conquer the Land of the Shadows of Heroes itself!

This thought was idle when he expressed it to me, still in the sweat of victory, but he was aware that Ghostland would need a great deal more subjugation before Taurovinda could again open its gates to the Plain of MaegCatha.

Indeed, there was a great deal to be done, and beginning at dawn of the day following the night of the attack, Urtha and Ambaros, still frail from his wounds, tried to bring a sense of order to the chaos.

The druids, the Speakers for the Past, for Kings and for the Land, keepers of ritual, began to walk the perimeters of both the fortress and the woodland at its heart, the groves and sheltered shafts where offerings had been deposited in the deep of the earth for the last few centuries. They were joined in their task by the High Women, although the women fussed at the wells and in particular at the apple orchards—if apple is the correct word for the small, sour fruit that these people held in such high esteem.

The two Wolf-heads, the itinerant soothsayers who had appeared in the gorge when Kymon had been gathering his forces, were as dirty, grey and unkempt as ever, and stank of the animal oils in their skin clothing. But they were experts at carving, it was discovered, and took it upon themselves to cut away the burned wood from the tall statues that were gathered at the heart of the fortress forest, remaking the faces and using dyes and ochres to bring back the life to them.

I had expected that Munda would involve herself in these sacred duties, but she was nowhere to be seen; up to her own private tricks and trade, no doubt.

Her brother Kymon, however, was very much in evidence. He walked alongside his father, saying nothing, seeing all. He was the heir apparent and his sense of grief and anguish at having failed in his own attempts to retake Taurovinda had rapidly been consigned to a votive shaft in his own mind. He had failed; he had learned a lesson; and that was that! No time to look back, only to look forward, and Taurovinda, the citadel that would one day be his domain, had to be protected against an enemy who were more like gusts of wind than warriors: hard to see and hard to fight, but strong only where the shelter against them was flimsy.

The mercenaries recruited from the Coritani, horsemen and spearmen allied to the warchief Vortingoros, were adept and swift in their abilities in construction. Vortingoros had furnished this small army as Urtha had passed through his land, as repayment for a bond of honour that had fallen due when the two men had been in battle against a northern clan. The force of fresh and eager men swiftly dismantled many of the burned and broken houses, pulling up the roof poles and setting about building two long hostels, one on each flank of the stronghold, living quarters and feasting areas, sufficient for the host of men and women who were now in occupation.

The king's lodge would be left alone for a while, at Urtha's specific order. It had not been burned, though was badly ransacked and the roof broken through. But it could be lived in, and counsel could be held there. This was not a gesture of magnanimity on Urtha's part, simply practical. His priority was to erect good quarters for his new army, good living space for the survivors of his own clan.

Meanwhile, four forges were re-established close to the well and were soon in hot production, repairing weapons and armour, fashioning the tools that would be needed for the general rebuilding itself.

Out on the Plain of MaegCatha the carrion birds had come to feast. Some picked at the eyes and throats of those of Urtha's people who had fallen in the battle; it would be a while before the remains could be taken from the field. Others, spectral birds, white-plumed, red-eyed, strangely slow in their searching flight as if they hopped and flew through water, feasted on the fast-corrupting sprawl of those who had died from Ghostland. Grey faces, bodies clad in rusted iron, arms uplifted in despair greeted the talons and hooked bills of these feeders on the twice-dead.

It was a grim sight. It was not possible to survey it without feeling subdued by the display of coiling guts and arching backs, blood-blackened grinning mouths widened by the sword.

Standing close to Urtha on the ramparts, I overheard Ullanna say to him, 'I don't understand. Why did they come out of the Otherworld? What can they have hoped to achieve in this drab and dreary land? They had lived life to the full, they had died in battle, they had a new life in a country where all was kind to them, where they would meet their sons and daughters in due time. Why cross back to this godforsaken plain?'

Urtha hesitated a long time before he answered. 'Why does a wild horse run towards a thorn thicket?'

She frowned. 'Well, perhaps because it's being pursued. Men are pursuing it. Or perhaps wolves. It finds a way to escape.'

'Why does a wide-eyed calf run into the maw of a wicker-walled trap, to be captured and marked, led away and slaughtered?'

'Because it's being driven. Men are driving it.'

'So: either escaping or being driven to do the deed.'

Ullanna laughed and leaned on the warlord's shoulder. 'I see what *you're* driving at! But we're not the best qualified to answer the question.' She glanced at me as she spoke. 'What about you, Merlin? Do you have an insight for us?'

'A glimmer of one,' I answered, and she acknowledged my words with a little nod of the head.

I had already spoken to Urtha about my suspicions concerning the Shadows of Heroes, that they were a divided host of Dead and Unborn, and that though he certainly had allies among their ranks, distinguishing friend from foe would take some time. What I couldn't address was the reason for the division, though my suspicions on that front were growing as well. I would need to go back across the river, and journey more deeply into Ghostland than the small sanctuary where the children, dislocated from their own world, had been nurtured and protected by the *modronae*.

Behind us, in one of the open spaces, Kymon was riding a grey pony in tighter and tighter circles, getting the animal used to his feet, his weight, his use of the reins. He looked very much the small man in control. Then his father asked, 'Where is

Munda? I haven't seen the girl since we entered the fortress last night.'

Both he and Ullanna looked at me, as if I might have known her whereabouts, but the last I'd seen of the girl she was walking towards the far end of the hill, where the apparition of the great Donn had faded, and the reckless Cymbrii had disappeared.

Suddenly Urtha was in a panic. He jumped from the walkway inside the wall, calling loudly for his daughter. Kymon stopped in the middle of his circling, shook his head when asked if he had seen his sister.

An awful sense of fear swept across the newly claimed citadel. The striking of iron in the forges hesitated; the babble of laughter and shouting eased to an eerie silence. Only Urtha's voice calling for Munda broke the stillness.

The girl's voice called back as if from a dream, becoming stronger, sharper, finally as real as the girl herself. She was beyond the fortress forest, standing quite still. I could see her and she could see me. Across the distance, she smiled at me.

Urtha, relieved not angry, spent time with her.

When later he returned to his duties of supervision and building, Munda sought me out. I was scratching double spirals on stones to turn, marked side down, around the edge of the shallow spring that rose in Taurovinda. The deep well, behind its stone wall, was supervised only by women. The girl sat down beside me and ran a small, pale finger along my small, shallow scratching, the two spirals, running alongside each other, connected at the middle.

'I know this.'

'I'm beginning to realise that you know a great deal. What does the spiral say to you?'

'It's Time. Time starts young, here, at the outside, and grows old, here, at the centre, then winds back upon itself to become young again.'

I was astonished. She caught my look of curious surprise and shrugged. 'It's easy. As we go forward through Time, deeper into it, so we pass ourselves going back. Time reflects the seasons, growing older then renewing. Simple. Can you see across the divide? Can you see yourself going back?'

'Where did you learn this?' I asked her, ignoring her impertinent inquiry. (It was very costly to see into that other Time, where the world moved back to its start. I'd never risked it. I could see no possible use for it.)

'I have a good dream teacher,' she replied. 'I like her. She makes me laugh. In the dream, it's always snowing and we skate on icy lakes and eat fat fishes, grilled over wood fires. She's nice.'

My head reeled with her words.

If you have read my account of the resurrection of Jason, in the land of the Pohjoli, before he and I ventured into Greek Land, you will understand why my blood turned to ice at that moment. Munda's 'dream teacher' could surely be no other than Niiv, the northern enchantress, daughter of Mielikki, the Forest Lady who was also the protecting goddess of Argo.

'What's her name?' I asked carefully, and shuddered as Munda whispered, 'Niif. She's very pretty, and she gets very angry . . .'

I remembered that!

Niiv was killing herself, using her talent without care or consideration for the fact that she would age very rapidly if she experimented so powerfully! She was as determined as Medea in this. If I felt a moment's concern for the young woman from the north, the mood was soon replaced by anxiety for myself.

Yes, I knew that Niiv was making her way back to me, aboard Argo, taunting Jason. She had visited me in the valley of the exiles and taunted me in turn! But Munda's words made it clear that Niiv had been closer to me more often than I'd realised. She had been in the groves by the river, whispering to Munda in her dreams . . . Perhaps she had been in Ghostland, before the girl had caught up with the interrupted breath of her life, quickly ageing as we'd crossed the river.

Perhaps, indeed, Niiv had been spying on me from the moment I'd left Greek Land, aboard the shadow of Argo herself. Niiv was determined to exist permanently in my life.

I gently asked Munda when her dream teacher, the pretty girl, had first started to talk to her. She answered, 'After we came back. After my friend Atanta went away.'

'Not when you were playing with Atanta before we crossed the river?'

'No. I don't think so. When Atanta went away I was very
ad.'

'I remember. I'm sorry you were sad.'

'But Niif came and told me that all old friends will eventu-
lly find each other. Sometimes they get taken for different
asks, and sometimes they forget that they need each other. But
n time, everyone who is joined at the heart comes back for the
inal embrace. Do you believe that, Merlin?'

'I believe that Niif believes it,' I commented, trying not to
,ound sour.

'But you don't?'

'I believe it slightly. One day I'm sure you'll find your friend
again.'

She smiled, looking wistful. 'And you'll find the forest that
you'll wear as a cloak. I hope I see you in that cloak of forests!'

The girl's words spilled from her lips as innocent as leverets
spilling from a hare's womb. Full of potential magic, full of
significance, full of taboo.

Her expression darkened for a moment, before she added in a
distant whisper, 'But I see it grey, I see it running . . . '

She would not elaborate on the cold image.

The day had grown bright; the wind was strong but fresh. The
air was fragrant with charring wood from the busy forges and
the smouldering herbs from the fortress orchard grove, now
being concealed again behind high wicker walls. The sound of
drumming and singing drifted from the same direction. A shaft
was being dug ready to take the trunk of a tree and the cleaned
bones of a sacrificed horse. Since there had been no captives
taken in the battle, their shades having dissolved into night and
their dead unusable according to Cathabach, who knew about
these things, a horse would have to be offered. It was a white
and grey mare. She was already bridled and braided, and some
of the children were decorating her with flowers and grasses
under the watchful eyes of two mothers.

Several other horses had been culled, those with broken
limbs and deep wounds, and their flesh removed, to be prepared
as food.

By the well, the High Women had managed to summon
something in human shape that shimmered and shifted in the
air. They were busy rubbing the petals of yellow meadow flow-

ers between their palms and holding their hands towards th
elemental emanation from the earth. They were testing the eff
cacy of the old invocations, and the reliability of the source
water. They seemed pleased with what they were seeing.
manifestation of Nodons, god of healing, I was told discreet
by Manandoun.

There was the murmur of joy in the air.

All was returning to normal in Taurovinda.

Munda's revelations weighed heavily on me for the rest of th
day. I began to feel stifled in Taurovinda, trapped by the hig
walls, the bustle of people and animals and the choking smell
From the western ramparts I could look out across the marshe
and forest to the distant hills that bordered the Land of th
Shadows of Heroes, and I could feel the cool, fresh wind th
blew from those hidden valleys.

There was someone there I badly needed to see again; and
mystery I would have to solve if I was to escape the bond I nov
felt to Urtha.

Where was Argo's spirit boat? I called for her and sh
answered. She was lying in a shallow creek, some way awa
upriver. Hidden by tall reeds and drooping willows, she ha
been sleeping quietly, waiting for the moment when either Arg
would come and find her, or I loosened my tie with her, allow
ing her to slip out of Alba, across the grey sea, to find th
mother ship herself.

Now she nudged from the reeds, turned into the current (
saw this in my mind's eye, just briefly, before I withdrew fron
the contact) and began to make her way to the stone sanctuar
by Nantosuelta, where we had camped before the battle. Sh
would take a little while to get here.

At dusk, the host of the Coritani settled down at two lon;
tables, to talk, eat and drink, two fierce fires burning betwee
the benches. In the king's house, Urtha and the survivors of hi
own clan invited the chiefs of the Coritani and myself to spraw
and eat, and listen to stories for a while, mostly of the quest t
Delphi, until the Speaker for the Past stepped into the centre o
the ring and proceeded to rededicate the royal lodge to its right
ful owner.

This process took until the high of the night, an interminab!

incantation of tribal history, clan raids, cattle raids, strange births, falling stars, wild warriors, cunning women who had ruled in the past, foolish men who given away all that their fathers had gained.

I was impressed with the phenomenal feat of memory shown by this clip-bearded, cropped-haired man of fifty years or so. His eyes never left the limbless tree that rose at the centre of the house, though he walked around it several times during his long description of the past generations of Taurovinda. Once in a while he struck the tree with a bone blade. At one point he urinated against the trunk, to the sound of rhythmic hand clapping from the gathered host. All part of the renewal process, apparently.

Then the Speaker for Kings listed the dynasty that had preceded Urtha, from his grandfather, a man called Mordiergos, down to Durandond, the founder of this stronghold in Alba. Then, at seven generations, the name was that of a woman— Margomarnat—and then women's names went far back, High Queens of the fallen citadel on the other side of the sea. The final names might have been from a time before Jason had been born in Greek Land. Each was mentioned in terms of her children, her girlhood, her first feat as ruler of the people, and the warlock who served her. The recital went on for ever, it seemed, but no one who listened seemed in the slightest bored.

When he too was finished, with the fire still burning high, several of the men around me began to brag about their deeds, laughing and sneering at each other, throwing dirt and scraps of food to signal their disbelief.

I'd seen this too often before and left them to it, bade Urtha a good night, and found shelter where I could sit and think and summon my strength.

I had intended to leave at first light, but the druid known as Speaker for the Land began to call from above the Bull Gate. He was waving a staff of hazel rods, twisted together, a *collcrac*, and making a sound like a crow in between calls in a language that I suspected was an ancient dialect of Urtha's own tongue, now obscure to all but these men of memory.

It seemed the time was now propitious to bring in the bodies and limbs of the dead of our two hosts, from this attack and from Kymon's failed assault. The gates were opened and twenty men rode down to the plain. Urtha called for me to come and help, bringing me a horse. I clambered into its rough saddle and followed. 'We bring in what we can,' he called to me. 'Do you have the stomach for it, Merlin?'

I laughed sourly. I had once watched Medea chop her brother into pieces whilst the boy screamed, casting the fragments into the sea to delay her father, a man raging at what he believed to be her abduction by Jason.

Yes, I imagined I had the stomach for it.

The crows had already gathered again. Urtha's great hounds chased them off, leaping among the slow-flying carrion eaters and bringing them down, shaking their feathers and their lives across the field. I gathered up swords and shields, a few fragments of limbs. Urtha pulled the decaying body of Munremur across the withers of his own mount and returned slowly and sombrely to the *nemeton* at his stronghold's heart. There, the wicker gates were pulled open by the druids and the bodies carried in, laid out on benches. The limbs of the newly dead were stiff, but would relax before long.

When all the dead were inside the grove, the wicker gates were closed again. Before the rampart gates were shut and sealed, I had slipped down the road to the plain, following the ceremonial way back to the river. I had made the briefest farewell to Ambaros, who was very understanding. But Urtha was dismayed by my disappearance and rode out from the fort, thundering down the safe track, yelping and shouting my name like some newly blooded youth. I ran ahead of him, faster and faster. He had a small javelin held high above his head. Had the man gone mad?

Bursting through the underbrush that bordered the river, frantically searching the stream for my small boat, Urtha circled round ahead of me, bare-chested, hair hanging free, galloping through the shallows and riding into the tree line. The javelin thudded into the trunk next to me, quivering, the grey feathers tied in a plume around its shaft shaking like a frightened bird.

'You were a guest in my house. And you leave without telling me?'

I had offended Urtha's sense of courtesy. I suppose I should have known.

'I need to leave. I told Ambaros. I didn't leave without a word of goodbye.'

He was not pacified. 'Yes. Ambaros told me. But Kymon and Munda are deeply fond of you, the girl in particular. When they find out, they'll be distraught. You should have spoken to them.'

'I spoke to Munda yesterday,' I told him. 'Your daughter is growing strong. She has the Light of Foresight. She began to develop it in Ghostland, and I intend to find how and why. That's why I'm leaving.'

He seemed genuinely disappointed and I reassured him that he had not seen the last of me.

'But I've only just found you again!' he complained bitterly. His hand rested on the pommel of his sword as he sat, staring down at me. 'I trust you more than those men of oak. I trusted you from the moment you stepped into my tent, away in the Northland. And what am I to tell the Coritanian host? They're eager to get back to their own fortress in case Ghostland attacks it next. I've assured them that you're the greatest man of oak I've ever known, the wisest Speaker for the Future. It's one of the reasons they are staying to assist at Taurovinda.'

'Then you lied to them.'

'I thought you *were* staying.'

'I'm no man of oak. I'm a man of the Path. I've forgotten a thousand times more than your druids can remember, prodigious though their memory is.'

'You're going the wrong way for the Shadowlands,' he insisted.

'I have a small boat to take me there.'

He laughed. 'The river is flowing to the sea. Ghostland is upstream. And you're not that good an oarsman, as I remember from Argo.'

'This boat has a mind of its own,' I said and he frowned.

Urtha had challenged me. Now he shrugged, kicking his warhorse towards me, reaching out a hand to say goodbye as he passed, his eyes hard again.

'Well, take care of yourself across in that place. I'm certain they haven't finished with us. This is just the beginning.'

'Indeed. Stay on your guard,' I agreed with him. He was certainly right about the danger from Ghostland.

'And the javelin is for you. The feathers were shed by one of

the carrion eaters that fed on the enemy. I made it myself. It has
a king's blessing! You'll know what to do or not to do with it,
expect.'

I had to wait for her until dusk, but I should have foreseen that
She slid through the water towards me, bathed in moonlight
rocking as she cut effortlessly against the current, the river
sparkling silver where it broke against her prow.

I waded out to her and hauled myself inside, nestling down
on the fur rugs, drawing them around my shoulders. I clutched
the spear, thinking about Urtha, his simple, noble gestures
wondering if he might indeed have invested the simple weapon
with any meaning by tying on the feathers from the otherworldly ravens.

In this way I entered a dreamless condition, the detached state
of thought that a ship like Argo, or this little offspring, will
always demand if she is to sail against nature. I was aware of the
stars and spent the time making a careful study of how some of
them had moved in all the millennia I had studied them. Some
moved speedily; some seemed to fade and come strong again,
like the glaring moon. Most seemed to move as slowly as a boul-
der inches down a river, a change of celestial position scarcely
visible unless seen at intervals of several hundred years.

There was wonder and intrigue in that roof of fire, but I
doubted that even if I sacrificed my life I could reach as far as
to touch one. The moon, perhaps, but the risk was great. Who
could guess what elemental forces guarded her face from the
probing fingers of the men who recorded her, and acted in con-
junction with her moods.

The boat rocked and was still, tipping slightly towards the land.
'We're there,' she whispered. 'I'm tired. I'll slip downstream
to rest until you call. This is where you met the Mother. The
Ford of the Last Farewell. This is where I crossed with your
children. But I fear the others have been taken. I sense only
desertion and damage.'

I watched while she slipped away. A thin mist hung over the
river. On the far bank, several deer were grazing. A flight of
cranes beat their way towards me, passing overhead, flying from
the land of the living to the land of the dead as if without concern. I made a mental note of that, then turned to follow them.

CHAPTER FOURTEEN

—

Moondream

The spirit of Argo had seen truly. When I came to the enclosed valley with its high rock walls, its woods and meadows where the children of royalty from Urtha's world had once been hidden, I found only desertion and the signs of struggle. The place had been abandoned many years ago. Time had worked a different trick on this sad communal home.

The brittle white bones of a horse, still with shreds of leather on its carcass, suggested that the attack had not been totally one-sided. Ragged strips of clothing, caught on branches and rotting below the overhanging rocks, were a grim suggestion that the conflict had been violent.

How long after I had taken Kymon and Munda and their friend Atanta to safety, I wondered, had this deed been done? However recently, Time had warped to shift the event backwards in the cycle of the years.

I was sad but not surprised. A small terrain of woods, meadows and crags, separated from the world of fortresses but not fully enveloped by the Otherworld which loomed large to the west, this hinterland was both a refuge and a dangerously unknown region. In this, it was like hinterlands everywhere around the Path. The children of kings had found safety here for a while, no doubt because of the protective presence of the timeless *modronae*, who had weaved their simple spell of isolation around their charges for many centuries. That the weave would one day be torn was inevitable. The hinterland was a place of crossings. It was no-man's land but vulnerable.

It was also all-time land, as I had discovered previously. Hidden in its forests and winding gorges were connections, through caves, pools or stone sanctuaries, to all the hinterlands of the world; they overlapped. I could as easily enter the misty fringes of Tartarus or Tuonela from the edge of Ghostland as I could come to these woods from those distant borders of distant underworlds. Those regions were timeless too. I had been born in such a place and, in one sense, that birthplace existed everywhere. It certainly had a presence here, somewhere near. I had been close to it before, and I was certain that Medea, too, would have visited that old pool and waterfall, and the bristling woodland that contained it; the place where she and I had grown up in the long, long gone.

I alerted my senses. A smell, a taste, sometimes a sound, can take you back to childhood in a very powerful way. I moved further away from the river, towards the shimmering mountains in the heart of the realm; sniffing the air for the scent of water.

After a while I became aware that I was being stalked. The watcher was not behind me but ahead of me, drawing back from me as I approached.

Emerging from woodland into a glade, a silvered hound loped across my path, turning to raise its hackles and growl in a threatening way before bounding off into the darkness.

A falcon swooped on me, its wing striking the top of my head.

Somewhere, a woman cried for her lost love.

A child giggled, peering from the underbrush, sticking out its tongue, pelting me with acorns.

Then suddenly the whole woodland seemed to shift and twist around me. I was on a track, caught in shafting sunlight. When I turned, the towering trees turned with me. I turned a full circle, and, like a strange cloak, the forest swirled about me and was still. When I walked, the forest followed.

It was very quiet, then; my heart raced, my senses quickened.

There was no birdsong, no furtive animal movement in the tangle of brush. Just silence. Again I walked forward and again the wood flowed with me. I was half man, half tree, blood and sap.

And then, ahead of me, a spinney of thorn and hazel gathered itself like a robe around a human figure, and shifted away.

I gave chase, running as best I could despite the dizzying effect of this distorting forest.

That it was Medea hiding in the spinney I was certain. We were close to one of the places that echoed our birthland. These manifestations, of hound and falcon, the child, the lamenting woman, were echoes of the training in disguise and insight that had been our feats of learning as we had grown to full childhood, over many hundreds of years. Ten masks for ten powers, known as *rajathuks*. We were in the guise of Skogen, the shadow of forgotten forests.

I wondered whether we were being watched, Medea and I, even as we played our game of chase, even as I tried to come close to a woman I had once loved, and then forgotten for a long, long time. Everything about the landscape I could see suggested we were back in the place of our birth, far south of the Ford of the Last Farewell.

Medea sent a stag to buck against my bark, a giant creature, almost bronze in its strength and sheen, its antlers gouging me as it bucked and kicked and bruised me. Then she despatched hornets to swarm in my branches, agonising, distracting. She was trying to shake me off; but in her own inimitable, teasing way.

She had been a precocious and irritating companion in my childhood, forever tricking me, forever playing jokes on me. It was part of her charm, in both senses of the word.

Spine-backed boars, snarling and stinking, a whole family of them rushed into my roots and began to chew and paw the ground. Painful!

That was when I heard her laughter, saw the flash of human eyes from the hazel foliage, and saw her melt away into the deeper woodland.

Both fun and fear, then. I turned quickly. The sudden movement sent the swine spinning away, landing heavily on their sides, angry and confused. The runts yelped and scattered.

I could smell water, now, and hear the susurration of the fall. I came to it all at once, a wide pool backed by a high cliff from which the crystal water tumbled noisily. There was an island in the middle of the pool and the spinney shivered and shook as it stood on that muddy rise of ground, shaking the water from its branches.

I nestled down on the bank and waited for her to make her move.

She sent a dove to nestle in my branches. 'Stay away from me. Why are you following me? This place is all I have, now that Jason has discovered my elder son. Kinos is my life, now, and he lives, hidden, at its heart. He lives in constant fear of the Warped Man, Dealing Death. I am trying to protect him. It's a mother's job. Why, if you loved me, do you try to destroy all that I have left?'

I was angry that she would think I was trying to hurt her. I was frightened of her, certainly. She had used up her years in the development of skills that would certainly outweigh mine. She could have squashed me on the spot, I imagined.

But in my mind's eye I could see her, remember her. I could smell her freshness, her breath; I could remember her laughter, her love. And I remembered the dreadful time, those long years in the past, when she had been sent away from me. Such loneliness I would never know again. I had killed that ability—to feel alone and lost—as one of my first acts of charm.

Even so, she haunted me again, and my heart was raging with memory and need.

I summoned a skylark, enticed him into my branches, took over its tiny spirit and sent it back with my reply.

'I don't want to hurt you. I want to find you again. I have a good friend in Urtha, the High King, back there in the fortress. Something in this land is threatening him. You can help me find what it is and stop it in its tracks.'

I was being deceitful. I already had a good idea what that evil presence was.

Medea answered with a crow. I'd guessed she would. The bird had killed the lark, carrying the savaged bird back to me and letting it drop.

'Liar! Liar! You mean me harm. You are still indebted to Jason. You will help him in whatever he asks.'

'Jason had a great influence on me,' I replied through the

same sharp-eyed bird. 'He had a great effect on you as well. Jason is one of those few men who can make even enchanters dance to his tune. But Jason will kill me if he finds me. He hates me, now. I thought you knew that.'

'Why does he hate you? You brought him back to life.'

'I kept the fact of your presence in this new world from him. He'd had no idea you had waited through time to find your sons again. And I made it difficult for him to find Thesokorus, the Bull Leaper. When they met, Thesokorus tried to kill him, near Dodona, left him for dead. It was a great shock to Jason and he has taken the pain of that wound and turned it into hate for me. All he has left, now, is to find Kinos, the Little Dreamer.'

'And so he's coming here. Because you told him where Kinos was hiding. That's your way of not hurting me?'

'You told him yourself, Medea. When you came into the oracle at Arkamon, and saw Thesokorus for the first time in seven hundred years. You told your first boy where his brother could be found. "Between sea-swept walls; he rules in the world, but doesn't know it." Those were your words. I know, because I was listening to you from the shadows.'

She was silent for a long time, then the crow flew back.

'And so you told Jason.'

'He was my friend. I helped him as best I could. Now I'm frightened of him. Powerful gods still keep their eyes on him. I don't think I'm his match.'

This time there was no reply. Dusk began to close around us. The crescent moon rose above the cliff top and the spill of water that rushed into the pool.

The sound of the waterfall must have lulled me to sleep. I was tired anyway, from the journey and from the effort of maintaining the illusion of the *rajathuk*.

When I woke, suddenly, wet hands on my face, she was next to me. Our little cloaks of forest had merged. To prying eyes we appeared as no more than a patch of tanglewood; but within the bosom of the copse, Medea stood before me, half in, half out of the thick trunk of hazel that commanded the spinney.

Her eyes were dark and fierce. Fierce Eyes. As I remembered her.

Her face, once sensuous, was now intriguing; her body, once

voluptuous, now lean, still desirable. Hers was a beauty that had not faded with age or time. The tumble of her hair was more conspicuous for its rich copper than its swan.

She eyed me up and down, as I stood, naked and aroused before her, still so young because I had rationed my charm and enchantment skills, keeping the marrow in my bones soft and succulent. But she could see through the flesh to the forlorn man behind the eyes.

'You've missed so much, Merlin. You could have aged gracefully, and become very skilled, old in years and wise.'

'Think how much talent I have left that I can exploit.'

She laughed at me. 'Like a tree struck by lightning: a sudden fire, bright as the sun, a glorious fire. And nothing remaining but a charred stump. That will be your fate. For all your plans to live for ever.'

Is that what she thought motivated me? To live until the stars fell? To live until the moon was finally swallowed by the sun? To live until the earth gave vent to birds large enough to carry men to the vault of the heavens? All of these things would come to pass, but these were not my reasons for staying young, intriguing though it would be to witness such events.

She suddenly stepped from the tree, a soft-fleshed dryad embracing me as I shivered naked before her. Her hands cupped me and stroked me, her thumb teasing me hard again as she brushed my lips with hers, watching me through half-opened eyes.

'I remember this.'

'I remember it too. Any moment now you're going to—'

She performed the deed and I yelped with surprise. Medea laughed, cocked her head, and looked down as she played with her old friend.

'You stink,' she said bluntly, detumescing words, instantly effective. 'Let's swim in the pool. We're not alone, you know.'

The whole woodland seemed to rustle with laughter. Yes, I'd thought we were not alone. But that didn't matter, now. The eyes that watched us were tired with watching and waiting for our return from the Path. They would indulge us a while longer, I was sure of that.

She took my hand and placed it on her breast, just briefly, a reminder of the past, and a reminder of her age. She was watching me for a reaction, but the touch of her—so long denied me—was more exciting than I could put into words. She was everything I had ever wanted. She was the thrill of it all, even after ten thousand years.

She saw this and was pleased, and gripping the young-old man again firmly in her left hand she led me, running, to the pool, dragging me painfully into the cold water.

We swam below the fall. It was deep there, deeper than I could dive in my normal guise. An enveloping blackness and a feeling of being pulled into the depths discouraged all exploration. This pool was a *hollowing*, one of those ways under and through the world, connecting all the hinterlands of the earth. We would have to be careful not to swim too far.

Such considerations were of secondary importance for the moment. Two children played in the pool, darting below the surface like otters, wrestling and boxing in the deeps then hiding behind the fall or among the rocky coves around its inner edge. The laughter was bright. There is nothing quite as wonderful and hopeless as sex in cool water when the mood is playful and teasing. Nothing is achieved except for an enhanced and memorable intimacy of touch. It is one of the great, simple pleasures.

On the bank, stretched out on our clothing, Medea opened her arms to me in more conventional manner. Our mouths were hungry for each other. Her fingers pinched and pulled, stroked and squeezed. The young-old man shook off the cold, armoured up as if for war, but went willingly to summer quarters.

We swam again in the morning, after which Medea went in search of a honeycomb. She had a nose for such things, and returned successfully, and not pursued by angry bees. We could both suspend our hunger for long periods of time, but the treat was welcome. The sun was bright and the day warm and still.

She was like a girl again.

'This is the deepest I have been,' she said. 'From the top of the fall you can see a long way towards the mountains. Ghost-land is vast.'

We were still in the hinterland, still half in and half out of Time.

She became excited at the thought of finding the small valley where we had lived. Its memory would be close to this pool, where we had so often swum, but the tracks through the woodland were tricky here. When we had washed the sticky honey from our fingers and chins we set off through the trees, looking for the narrow, arched mouth of the chasm.

Soon we heard the clattering of wood. An eerie breeze blew towards us.

The masks were slung across the gap, weather-stained and rotten, but each still recognisable. The wind blew them together. They turned and twisted on their ties, light flashing through the empty eyes.

We chanted their names together, Medea and I, as we had been taught to chant them in the days of learning.

Falkenna, spirit of the falcon . . . Cunhaval, spirit of the hound . . . Moondream, memory of the woman in the land . . . Sinisalo, the child in the land. . . .

At their centre dangled Hollower, ringed eyes and grinning mouth still green with the dye that had daubed the mask. He was the trickster who could take you through the hidden spaces of the earth. Or send you on your way to death. As Medea passed below this gate of masks, she touched a finger to her lips and touched the finger to the grinning mouth of Hollower.

'Why did you do that?' I asked her.

'Best to keep him happy,' she replied as if nothing could have been more obvious.

I did the same, just for security's sake, but it was not Hollower who caught my attention as I entered that narrow cleft in the rock, but the strange mask that related to the telling of stories, the memory in the land, the memory of people. I remembered that this teacher had been called Gaberlungi, though the name was strange. The druid in Urtha's fortress known as Speaker for the Land was a recent reflection of this tradition, though far less mysterious than the shy and watchful Gaberlungi herself.

I think I understand why the storyteller whispered to me as I passed. She was perhaps setting in motion the events that led me to write these words, these accounts. Of all those children who were sent to walk the Path, each was to fulfil a different function. Mine, I surmised briefly, was to leave a record that could transcend the telling of tales. This would be a record to be read.

Although I write many centuries later, I remember distinctly entertaining that particular train of thought as Medea led me back to the riverside and caves of our childhood. And she herself, what role for her? At the time I remember thinking that she was the spirit of Sinisalo, that eternal child that protects children.

She had dedicated her life, after Jason, to just that effort, after all.

We came to the river. The caves in the cliffs were protected from the elements by thick skins slung from holes painstakingly drilled through the overhanging rock. I could smell cooking, and the putrid odour of hides being tanned. I heard distant laughter, the angry shouting of a woman, the squealing of a piglet, the syncopated beat of several skin drums. All of these were the haunting sounds of the past, recreated from memory, almost real but elusive.

Laughing, excited, she led the way from cave to cave. 'Oh, Merlin, this is just as I remember it! Look! Here's where the animals were skinned and paunched. Here's where that old man carved the shapes on bone and antler, all the amulets we took away with us!'

She plunged into one cave, squealing with fondly remembered recognition. 'My dolls! My dolls!'

I followed her into the gloom. Furs and skins had been fixed to the cold walls of the cavernous space; the floor was deep with rushes and straw, furs on the top for sitting. A pile of bearskins marked her bed; there were four beds in the area, and three small wooden dolls, funny painted faces, arms made from thin, flexible withies, were sitting on the pillow.

Medea picked up each of them and kissed it, then placed it down again. She muttered words over them, moving her body so that I couldn't see exactly what she was doing to these scruffy little puppets.

'You slept there,' she said, pointing to the deepest part of the cave.

I'd already seen the pile of grasses, the goat's-skin cover, the bare rock wall sloping over the bed, the faint red marks of imaginary creatures that I'd finger-painted over the years, practising the summoning art. How strange those animals looked, how unreal. Had I managed to summon such beasts, the valley would have been in greater danger than from a stampede of wild horses along the shallow river.

This was a cold place, coldly recalled; there was the flesh of reality here, but the gnawing sense of dream. I was uncomfortable and left this reflection of my childhood home, following the woman who had been my friend and torment in those tender years.

Medea and I sat by the water for a long time. She reached for my hand, held it tightly, tears in her eyes.

'So long ago. How far we've come. How sad it is to be so far from home.'

I found her sudden melancholy upsetting, perhaps because I didn't share it.

I said to her: 'Until I came to this sea-girdled land, with Urtha and Jason, I had forgotten everything of this time in my life. When so many friends come and go in what seems to be the blink of an eye, there seems to be no point in living for anything but the next adventure.'

'I thought the same,' she said. 'Until Colchis. When my path took me through Colchis, generations before it was the great city that you remember from the raid in Argo, I realised I had found a second home. Everything in the signs and in the spirit world told me that I would one day be happy there, and when the city grew, and when the king Aeëtes came of age, grew older than me, and adopted me as his daughter, for a while I was in paradise. I was Priestess of the Ram. I'd been the priestess of many things in my time. A python, a bull, an eagle. I knew what to do.' She laughed. 'I killed and burned a lot of rams. The stink of charred mutton still haunts me! Then Jason came and everything I had hoped for in a woman's life happened in a brief, startling, wonderful few days. Have you ever felt love, Merlin?'

'I've loved and indulged my way through ten thousand years. In and among the adventuring. I rather like it.'

'True love, I mean.'

'Only for you, you tell me; and even that seems far away.'

Why did I lie?

'Our love was designed,' she said soothingly, kissing my hand as she spoke, still distracted by her memories. 'We were made to love each other before we were parted from each other. Inasmuch as we live almost for ever, we are immortal. But mortal love? That man, that Jason. So different from the adventurers who sailed the seas and roamed the lands. He is touched by the gods, by something deeper than an ordinary human soul. So when I loved him, I loved him with fire. And when he betrayed me, I hated him with fury. I still do. He broke my heart. I could have killed him. I decided to steal his most precious loves: his sons. And I did it very well indeed, I think you'll agree. But then, they were *my* most precious loves as well.'

She seemed so calm as she talked about it. Previously, in the underworld, on our way to Greek Land, she had raged at me. Spite and spittle, like a viper's venom, had blinded me as she'd condemned me for being Jason's friend.

This was a more reasonable Medea, a reflective and saddened woman.

I took a chance and addressed the subject that divided us.

'After all this time, isn't it possible to forgive a man who, as we both agree, is both strong and weak, a mortal man? Even if he is a "warped man"? Why not let him find Little Dreamer? He will die shortly. Kinos will live on, but not for ever. You will outlive your sons. Your own future is as empty of children as Jason's has been for seven hundred years.'

Too late I remembered that Medea too had lived in isolation over seven centuries, and in greater pain than Jason.

I braced myself for Fierce Eyes' fury, but she rolled on to me, pressed a finger to my lips and whispered, 'I'll think about it. There's time enough to think about it. For the moment, do you remember this?'

I hadn't. Struggling to release myself from her painful, pleasurable grip, we rolled into the water and came up spluttering and laughing.

I loved this place. The sun filled the narrow gorge for most of the day. Flights of birds settled in the trees, on the water, and we snared them, creating ceremonies of sacrifice with each small carcass that we plucked and spitted, roasted over a small fire. We invented strange gods and stranger rituals. The world seemed unreal; the days were magic in that sense which indicates a state of existence almost unbelievable in its softness, its fruitfulness, its simple pleasures.

Medea was adept at finding fruits, roots and herbs. I set lures for fish and hunted the woods. We explored the hidden parts of this hinterland, and sometimes climbed to the high cliffs and stared at the mist-laden mountains at the heart of the Realm of Shadow Heroes.

There was an ocean there, Medea told me, and islands of every description, few of them habitable. How she knew this I didn't ask.

'And Little Dreamer is secreted away among them,' I suggested.

She looked at me with a half-smile. 'Little Dreamer has built his own home. He turned out to be very good at building homes. It's well defended, though he's always vulnerable.'

She would say no more to me on the subject.

Those few days were idyllic. It had been a long time since I had laughed so much. The stews that Medea created were strange and wonderful. A little touch of this, a little taste of that. It hardly mattered. I saw only the young woman in the old flesh, felt forgotten pleasure in the renewed pursuit of satisfaction.

All I failed in was the fishing. I could never lure one of the plump, silvery creatures that grazed so calmly at the surface on insects and weed. They would not jump into my trap.

I could have made them do so, of course, but that would have been against the spirit of this reconciliation with my childhood friend; my lover; my new ally.

One evening as we lay lazily by the river, she suddenly straddled my body, pressing her hands down on my shoulders. Her gaze was earnest.

'If I promise to let Jason see his son . . . will you promise to keep the man as far away from me as is humanly possible? *Merlinly* possible?' she added with a little laugh.

The question puzzled me. 'Of course. It's not you he wants, it's Kinos.'

'He'd like my head on his spear.'

'Mine too. But to see his son again, if that were possible . . . '

'Everything is possible,' she said cryptically. 'But I must have assurances.'

'To the extent that I can reassure you, then I reassure you! The man hasn't long to live anyway. He must be fifty if he's a day. I give him ten years at the most.'

'He's touched by the gods,' Medea whispered, frowning. 'I'd put nothing past his gods. Hera loved him. Bitch! If she's still in the underworld, she can yank out his twine, stretch him for centuries.'

'His gods played games with fate; they were tricky, always

sparring among themselves. Heracles apart, I've never known them grant extra mortality to their children. "Children" is how they saw the people of Greek Land.'

Medea laughed. 'I know. I spent years among them remember?'

She gave me a quick kiss, and with the words, 'I could stay here a thousand years, but there are things to do,' she stood and disappeared down the valley.

I too could have stayed there a thousand years. This was sublimely lazy living. Back at Taurovinda, the tasks of rebuilding and regenerating the clan would be proceeding apace. Jason was still far away, struggling through the complex of rivers that wound through Alba, searching for the heartland where he believed his son to be hidden.

There was certainly time to relax with Medea.

Over the next few days, however, the *rajathuks* visited me in a disturbing way. I was hunting, for example, when the giant hound Cunhaval leapt upon me from the cover of an ash grove, pinning me to the ground, snarling as it tried to bite my throat. I was still carrying Urtha's spear, and wedged the weapon between the animal's jaws. It left deep bite marks. The eyes in the creature were insensate and red. I was terrified for a moment, but as I went to open up my charms, to despatch it with finality, it drew back, still growling. I used the spear to whack its haunches, but it followed me for the rest of the day, snarling at me from the cover of the wood.

One midnight, I woke to find Falkenna on my chest, wings spread, curved beak pecking at my flesh. It flew up to the moon as I woke and struck at it, and Medea put soothing lotions on the gashes in my body.

The encounter had been dreamlike, disturbing. Again, as with the hound, I felt I was being told something.

Moondream came to me in my sleep. She was voluptuous, naked, her face half in moonglow, half in moondark, shining, tilted eyes watching me with concern.

'Wake up, wake up,' she whispered, leaning to kiss me. I reached for her, held her plump breasts, felt her tongue on my mouth. 'Merlin, dear Merlin, it's time to wake. Wake up now.'

'Lie down on me.'

'Wake up. Look around you. That's all I have to say.'

'Don't go!' I urged the dream spirit, but with a final embrace she returned to the river, sank down into the midnight water and drifted, half bright, half shadow, away to the east.

The next day I asked Medea if she too had been visited and plagued by the *rajathuks*.

'No,' she said simply, then looked at me thoughtfully. She pushed me down where I sat, rolled on to me and said, 'I have a question.'

'Ask away.'

'If I promise to let Jason see his son, will you promise to keep him as far away from me as is humanly possible?'

The question took me by surprise. I remember wondering if she was drunk, or half asleep.

'You know I will. I've already said I will. We've had this conversation before.'

She reared up above me, looking startled. Her eyes hardened, then went vague. The grip of her hands on my shoulders weakened. I could see the sky through her pale face. She became insubstantial.

Wake up! Wake up! Moondream's ghostly words came back to haunt me.

When I shook Medea from my lap, there was nothing to shake. The illusion dissipated like mist in hot summer air.

I focused my inner sight and almost cried out with shock. There was no sunlight, only a dank day, a cool drizzle making the rocks glisten. The caves were gaping mouths; inside, nothing but the ledges that had been formed to take the sleepers. No dolls, no leather, no furs, nothing to enhance memory. The river was low, weed-covered and sluggish. The grass on its bank was flattened where a single body had lain and dreamed; there was no sign of a second shape.

I had been alone. Tricked. Seduced into spending time in this backwoods. How much time, I wondered, and when I let my inner sight find out the truth I felt both foolish and incensed.

A whole season! Twenty times as long as I'd believed I'd been here. In the meantime, Urtha would have been giving me up for dead or as a deserter, and Jason was coming closer, driven by desire, defying death.

What Medea had been doing was anybody's guess.

I felt sick in my stomach and sick at heart. I ran back towards the river that separated Ghostland from Urtha's realm. I couldn't help thinking of cunning Odysseus, hero of the war against the Trojans, a man who'd worn his wits like armour yet who had been delayed from returning home by the beautiful Calypso, lulled into a false sense of ease and security, unaware of the rampant passage of time.

How could I have let this happen? How, having once listened firsthand to that brave man's tale of woe, could I have failed to remember his advice: to always strap on the battle-harness of wile and guile when facing an enemy who smiles and offers peace?

And when—and this was the question that dogged me, snarling, like Cunhaval—when had the truth ended and the lie begun? Her compromise on Jason? Her passion for me? Our rediscovered fondness for each other? *Trickey or truth*? I'm sure I screamed out loud as I ran back towards Argo's small spirit, waiting for me in the shade of willows at the water's edge

Medea!

From loving her, I was now terrified of her. She had eaten me, chewed me up, laughing, no doubt, as she'd spat me out into the scummy river, a fool, seduced by need and memory.

If I had seen her at that moment, Urtha's spear would have flown through her breast with my throw and passed on down the valley.

I fairly raced to the Winding One, Nantosuelta, calling for my little shade of Argo as I ran. A biting wind blew up, below looming grey clouds. There was rain in the air, and the skies wheeled with flocks of dark birds.

Then her voice whispered to me: *Stay back from the river. There is danger at the river. Stay back.*

Was this another trick? I kept running, weaving through the windlashed woodland. Again, her voice whispered: *Be careful. Danger is closer than you think.*

I had to believe that this was no trick, but my friend urgently warning me off. I slowed my pace and cautiously approached the enclosed meadow where the children had played. The grass in the meadow had grown high. On the other side, the narrow defile that led towards the river was murmuring with the sound of voices.

I drew back into the cover of a rock overhang. The voices grew louder, then abruptly fell silent. Whoever was approaching had seen the open space and stopped talking.

A few moments later three figures emerged from the defile, spreading out swiftly and crouching down, half concealed below the high grass.

'This is the place,' a woman's voice said, her accent strong. 'This is the place I came to in my dream. But it's abandoned. No one has been here for years.'

'I don't trust it,' a man replied gruffly. 'Rubobostes! Bring the others.'

Five more figures slipped into the open, crouching down, light catching their blades and the decorations on their oval shields. Three were from among the group of grim demeanour that I had glimpsed as Argo had reached on the coast of Alba.

Dark-haired, big-limbed Rubobostes towered above the grass, his rough eyes scouring the field for danger. I had assumed no mortal man could enter even the hinterland, so either I was wrong, or Rubobostes was indeed Otherworldly, a part of myth, as I had long suspected.

'This *is* the place,' the young woman repeated. I sensed the way she probed the glade; she was suspicious; she sensed danger; but she could not identify the source of her concern.

Ah, Niiv! So much to learn despite the fact that she had used her gifts for enchantment to excess and with relish.

I had hidden myself from her the moment I'd recognised her, cowled and caped though she was, her hair now black, her face striped with disguising mud. She wouldn't spot me, and it took very little effort to divert her attention.

Jason, mortal man, touched by the gods, was another matter. He wasn't looking for me; but his eyes saw beyond simple defences, even though he often failed to recognise what he was seeing. He was a warrior, a mercenary, and his wits were so sharp that he could outwit charm itself, as long as he didn't think too hard about what he was doing. I might be transparent to him, though it would take him moments to recognise me.

'There is nothing here. Just grass and memories,' Niiv whispered to Jason.

'Are you sure?' the cautious man asked.

'I hear echoes of a raid; I hear screams and sorrow; this all happened a long time ago.'

Slowly, the argonauts rose to their feet, shields still to the fore, swords held behind their backs ready for a quick strike. Then they began to approach me, moving through the grass silently, spreading out in a line. Niiv seemed to be watching the sky. Jason seemed focused on my concealing rock. Rubobostes was frowning, glancing left and right, unnerved by something that not even I could see.

They rose out of the grass like a sudden flight of birds, ten or so armoured men, all on horseback, the animals kicking the air as they struggled from their hiding places. They seemed to emerge from the earth itself. The argonauts shouted with one voice, raising shields, bringing swords to the front. Niiv fled back towards the defile. Rubobostes ran forward to stand side by side with Jason as the Ghostlanders rode down on their prey.

Their helmets were high-crested, copper-tinged, the faces blank. The riders were all bare-armed, chests and backs protected with leather battle-harness, waist protected by brightly coloured tunic, shins with strips of leather as greaves. They carried thin, wide-bladed stabbing spears.

They looked like Greeklanders!

Iron on iron, iron on leather, the clang and thud of the skirmish was frantic, noisy and bloody. A woman's voice screamed from the Ghostland host. One of the horsemen, the leader I surmised from the flash of gold on his helmet, rode around Jason, hacking down at him with a long, leaf-bladed sword, grim and determined as he tried to cut his way to Jason's head. I heard him grunting the words, 'You are *not* the one! You are *not* the one! Are you the one? No! You are *not*!'

This was a strange encounter.

Jason moved as if in a dream, his face blank, effortlessly parrying the cutting, slashing blows, but making no effort to slice at the exposed legs of either rider or horse, neither using his shield for offence, nor pushing forward, only cowering below the assault, anticipating the direction of the attack and responding to it. The rider hesitated only once, glancing in my direction, before returning to his singular task.

Two of Jason's men were cut down, two of the grim-faced, but they crawled back towards the defile before collapsing quietly. Then Rubobostes took one of the horses by its front legs, upturned the beast, crushing its rider, and swung its heavy carcass in a wide arc, unnerving the nearer warriors, including Jason's determined opponent, though that particular horseman was already in nervous retreat. Sword held out before him, point towards Jason, he was making his mount step awkwardly backward through the long grass. His words, hissed like a wildcat at bay, were suddenly meaningless, but full of fear and fury. Whatever he had suddenly seen, it had upset him.

The Dacian's brawny intervention gave Jason and the others time to withdraw into the defile. Rubobostes bounded after them, his shield held defensively behind his head and upper body as three javelins thudded into the hide-covered oval of oak.

As quickly as the attack had happened, the horsemen, all but the leader, streamed away through the grass, becoming tenuous in form as they wound through the orchard, before kicking into a canter and turning inland, towards the mountain fastnesses. Two of their number lay silent in the meadow.

The singular rider came slowly over to where I crouched in cover. His body dripped with the sweat of the effort he'd made to cut down Jason. There was blood on his chin; he'd bitten through his lip. Dark, cold eyes stared at me searchingly through the gold-flecked Greekland helmet, skull-like and gleaming as it moved this way and that, the rider scanning the overhang.

I noticed that on the left cheek guard was the image of a ship; on the right, the image of a ram. And on the brow: the unmistakable image of Medusa.

'This is my place,' the young man whispered in the ancient Greekland tongue. 'You're in my place. That's the Father Calling Place.'

His words were spoken without expression. Then he turned his horse and suddenly, with no further glance at me, sped away across the field, following his troop. I looked up at the overhang of rock and saw for the first time a ship, a phallus, a hound, and several little stick men carved on the grey surface. But this was not the Father Calling Place to which Kymon had taken me, when I came to collect the royal children. Could it have been Munda's?

I had no energy to think. I was still stunned by the sight of the vicious attack on Jason; still cold with the recognition of that screaming, feral, female voice. It had been Medea's, of course. I had not seen where she was hiding. Indeed, she may have been one of the riders. She was trying to end Jason's quest there and then, but had been frustrated by the big-boned Dacian, the Heracles of the new argonauts, who had pitched brawn against the supernatural and won the day.

As I have said before, this hinterland was a strange place, equally alien to Ghostland as to the mortal realm. There were no true rules here, no true paths to guide the inadvertent traveller. This was unknown territory.

Time passed. I stayed in the cover of the rocks, gathering my wits.

After dark, Rubobostes came cautiously back to the meadow in the valley, a torch held high above his head, as if he were nevertheless unafraid to advertise his approach. The shadowy, slinking figure of Niiv crept after him. He gathered the two wounded argonauts in his fist, holding them by the hands— their eyes were open and alive, but they remained quite silent— and dragged them back to the river.

Niiv stayed, standing boldly above the grass, her eyes glinting like a lynx's.

'I know you're here,' she whispered. 'I can smell you. I knew you'd be here. Why don't you show yourself, Merlin? You know you want to.'

I stayed exactly where I was. The wind murmured through the defile, and the breeze chased across my skin like a ghostly finger.

'I know you've been watching me,' she called softly. 'I was keenly aware of you watching me: first from your crow eyes; then from your gull eyes. Did you think I didn't notice? I noticed! I watched you too, Merlin. First from my swan eyes; then from my spirit eyes, do you remember? Don't try to deny it!' she added with a little laugh. 'You and I have *eyes* for each other!

'I want you so much. You have no idea how much I want you. I would do nothing to harm you. When I first met you, I fell for you. We could be so strong together. I'll walk your path with you. It's not about *spells* and *trickery*—I don't want to steal your magic. Just your heart! I forgive you for what you did with Medea.'

With that ambiguous last comment, she turned and scampered back along the valley, following the fading torch wielded by the Dacian. Had she been spying on me even here, when I was beguiled by Medea? Or was she referring to something that had happened a long time in the past? Where *had* the girl been prying?

Shortly after this disturbing encounter, I walked cautiously to the defile, followed along its narrow passage. When sinuous Nantosuelta came in sight, I could see pure, beautiful Argo moored against the bank, held strong against the powerful river. Her sail was furled, though the mast was still upright. Her colours were enchanting, the emblems and shades of her original crew painted on her hull as good luck and good voyage.

Caped figures crouched on the shore of the inlet around a blazing fire. Rubobostes was standing guard, a small pile of spears at his feet, a large axe in his hand, his gaze restlessly shifting between the river and the defile where I crouched. I could see neither Niiv nor Jason. Mielikki, the goddess in the ship, scowled from her painted effigy in the stern, icy features, highlighted by flame, reaching forward as if she struggled to draw herself from the wood.

The land across the river, the entrance to Urtha's realm, was enfolded in night and mist. I needed to return there. And to do that, I needed Argo.

I distracted the watchful Rubobostes with a cat's cry, close behind him, and slipped past the ship to the reed-bed where the small boat should have been secured. She had been waiting for me, whispered that I should *get in quickly*, and as I hunkered down on the damp furs in her bilges she rocked away from the shore. I was startled to see a figure crouched before me, featureless for the moment. The boat passed like owl-shadow to the farther bank and spilled me out into the shallows.

Then, turning stern-on, the hard face of the Forest Lady suddenly loomed greyly at me; the icy breath of Pohjola, in the far north, chilled my skin. Those slanting, fate-filled eyes blinked at me, but the thin lips stretched into a smile I'd known before. Mielikki, goddess of the northern woods, was very fond of me.

'Well, Merlin, it's time to leave you. I'm glad you found your way back here; I'm glad you found your feet again, after Delphi and that hot, unpleasant land.'

Ah, Greek Land! How much I missed that heat, that fragrance, that dryness. But for this snow-wasted beauty, this stalker of ice-sheened birch forest; those sun-drenched climes had been a curse. I sympathised and thanked the guardian spirit of sleek-keeled Argo.

She blew me a mocking, knowing kiss, adding, 'Niiv will not let you go.'

'I know. I'll be on my guard.'

She said, 'I am her protector. What you do to avoid her is up to you. What you do to dissuade her is up to you. But if you try to harm her . . .'

To illustrate the implied threat, a *voytazi* of bull-like proportions loomed out of the water and snapped its gigantic jaws in front of my face before sinking back, gloating, into the shallows.

'I will not harm her,' I promised Mielikki. 'But I will match beguilement with beguilement. And I will not stand in the way of her death.'

Mielikki scowled; moonlight flashed on her teeth. Her eyes went blank with anger, but she accepted my words.

'Your life is in her,' she reminded me. 'I can still smell the love in the lodge where you filled and thrilled her ancestor, generations ago when you visited Pohjola; I can still smell the sick on your breath as you tried to drown that woman, only to come to your senses; I can still taste the salt in your tears as you watched her child born, great-mother-to-be of your little Niiv. Like salt in diluted water, she is still potent with your own charm, so just remember: what you do to her you do to yourself!'

As the little boat slipped away, Mielikki's features becoming young and lean and beautiful as she smiled from the stern, I called, 'She wants to strip the magic from my bones.'

'You'd better fatten up, then,' the goddess laughed.

'She will gnaw me like a jackal, given half a chance. I shan't let her do that, no matter what you say to me.'

'It will be a long struggle for you,' the goddess whispered back. 'Whoever ages first will be the loser!'

THE IRON GRAIL

lost sends was personal survive, aggressive and ab-
after entered flow. A cause through the way

CHAPTER FIFTEEN

—

Under Siege

The little boat, the comforting companion, slipped away
from the shore and was drawn into Argo, timber into timber, old time into the present. I felt sad to see her go, but I knew
that Argo would be glad to have her back. Jason loomed darkly
at the stern, peering across Nantosuelta, flint eyes seeking the
shadow of the man he half suspected was watching him. Then
he gave the order and Argo was cast free of the bank. Nantosuelta took her and shifted her to the side closer to life and the
living; the oars rose and dipped; my old friend Rubobostes
grunted the rhythm as he took charge of the steering oar, and in
the prow the small, sleek dark shape of Niiv hunched like some
cat, ready to pounce, staying still, as still as death, waiting for
her moment.

Argo passed from sight along the river between the worlds
and I was forced to contemplate the more pressing reality: how
to return to Taurovinda before Jason and his mercenary crew
reached the stronghold.

I had reckoned without Mielikki. She must have slowed
progress down the river, perhaps because she was more sympathetic to me, a timeless creature like herself, than to Jason,

whose agenda was personal, private, aggressive and abusive. In any event, after several days of running through the valleys, the forests and the narrow passes standing between Taurovinda and Ghostland, I finally saw the looming hill, with its fires and banners and totem figures rising above the high ramparts, the clear signal that Urtha was still in control of his home.

Taurovinda, however, was under siege.

I had been passed, during my journey, by a long column of what I believed to be the Unborn; they rode heavy horses and were cloaked in plain colours, reds and greens, rather than the elaborate patterns of the dead. Their swords were sheathed in gold-inlaid scabbards, and they carried single, thick-shafted lances rather than the clutch of slim javelins with which Urtha and his predecessors had become adept.

Their shields were narrow ovals, very plain, and carried at the horse's flank rather than slung over the warrior's back. I was learning enough about Ghostland to be able to recognise a squadron of the future warlords of the realm.

Though I had hidden from them as they'd passed, they conveyed no sense of danger.

Then a band of Dead, twenty or so, stripped and stained with colour, rattling with bronze and bone rings on their upper arms, ears and ankles, had scampered past on foot, pursued by the shadows of ravens, a flock keeping an eye on the men upon whose appetites it would feed. Cruel and crude, this band seemed to exist in a world of hidden sense, aware of me though not seeing me, passing through the forest like moisture on a cool wind. Almost as soon as they had come into view they had slipped away, but I was able to follow them for days; they left a trail of wildwood slaughter.

Somewhere in the besieging armies both Unborn and Dead had drawn into cover, encircling the hill, blocking all the paths and passages save for that which led from Nantosuelta, the winding track along which the wicker boats were carried bearing the corpses of the deceased.

This was my way back to Urtha, as indeed it would be the way into Taurovinda for Jason when Argo finally berthed at the rough wooden harbour.

Willow men, and hazel men and yew men and oak men encircled the hill in five ranks; sometimes elaborately constructed, mostly just two branches crossed and hung with human skin, these gaunt, grim idols would stop even scavengers from passing out of the fortress. In the long grass, the Dead moved like shadows. I circled them and came to the river. There were hundreds in the field, most of them curled up in sleep. Each breeze, each gust of wind was a passing ghost. The air was rank with decay. From the corner of my eye I could see the gleam of metal, the flash of plumage on a helmet. Tall horses and small ponies scampered in the half-light of near existence. When I opened my ears to the truth, there was the sound of laughter and battle practice, the crackle of fires, the baying of hounds.

These invaders from the Otherworld were intent on winning back Taurovinda; there was no doubt about that. They had left their own world and brought a little bit of Ghostland to surround the Thunder Hill.

But why? What could they hope to gain from possession of such a fortress?

Urtha's defences were the closed gates, sacred fire and the images of men constructed out of parts of the Dead. No doubt he had had advice from the Wolf-heads and the Speakers. They seemed to be effective against the enemy. The Shadows of Heroes were vulnerable here, as I have pointed out before.

I was on the point of beginning my walk through the ranks of the Dead when I heard a girl's voice, singing. For a moment I failed to recognise it, despite its familiarity, but when the soft song stopped and I heard the whispered words *I see it green, I see it bronze* I realised that Munda was somewhere close.

I called for her, but the strange singing continued. The sound led me to her and I found the girl crouched in the jaws of two grey rocks, staring out across Nantosuelta, her eyes locked in Foresight, blind to the world of the river.

I stepped inside her vision and she turned slowly to look at me; there was light in her eyes; she recognised me and smiled. There was no sound of the river, here, no sound of the wind.

'Merlin,' she whispered; she looked away. She said, 'The warped man is very close. He will deal death. I see it, Merlin, but his face is so strange: it is both young and old. He is truly warped.'

'That's because he is out of his own time,' I explained to the girl.

'Is he? That accounts for it: I see him lost, I see him void; I see him angry; I see him crying.'

I shook my head. 'The man has no tears left. He didn't cry when his eldest son rejected him at the end of a blade.'

'I see no sons, only brothers. Two angry men with two pale ghosts who wear their faces.'

Munda never ceased to astonish me, though that may reflect only my sense of her as being very young. The young can see the spirit world with great facility, but it is a narrow vision, hindered by lack of life. Not so Urtha's daughter! She had seen Jason's two sons with their tenuous companions: each brother, separated in the world when their mother had hidden them in the future, had been given the echo of his sibling, to keep him happy, to stop him grieving. Thesokorus was in far-off Greek Land, an echo of Kinos dogging his tracks. Munda had seen them nevertheless. I was very impressed.

'Come out of the *imbas forasnai*,' I said to her softly, and she shivered, drew in a deep breath and at once came back to the world of stones, trees and autumn breezes.

'Merlin! Merlin!' she cried with genuine delight, clapping her hands to my face and jumping up to embrace me. 'Where have you been? You've been gone so long! We've all missed you.'

'I've been across the river.'

'We're under siege,' she said darkly. 'Only a few of us can get through the army. We follow the old track . . . '

I smiled. 'I'd guessed as much.'

'But my father is furious with you for abandoning him! He'll have some harsh words for you! But the sooner bruised, the sooner healed, so come on, come on.'

And with that, the girl grabbed my hand and dragged me after her, away from Nantosuelta and through the spirit-ridden Plain of MaegCatha.

Urtha saw me coming. He sent men through the fires that blocked the winding approaches to open the gates. Munda, her grip on my hand like a tiny claw, dragged me through bull, stag, wolf, man and horse and almost flung me towards the welcoming cordon of chariots and grinning warriors, Urtha and Ullanna prominent among them.

Save that Urtha and Ullanna were not smiling.

Urtha grabbed his daughter by the shoulder, furious. 'Where have you been? How did you leave the fortress? What have I told you? Do not leave the bounds!'

'I can't see in this place,' she said. 'It's too confining.'

'Too confining? We'll see about confining. You have been forbidden to leave the walls. How many times have you done this before?'

Munda stared brazenly at her father. 'I cannot *see* in this place. I have to go to the one who winds around us.'

'You seem to be seeing me without difficulty.'

'Not that sort of seeing! Let me go.'

But her father was too angry. Two High Women were summoned and Munda was marched, objecting, to the house where those guardians lived. She had broken her father's law; she had endangered Taurovinda; that much was clear from the reaction of the High Women and the Speakers.

As she was dragged away she continued to shout angrily: 'You don't understand! If I can't see clearly, I can't help you!'

Urtha ignored her. He strode towards me, glaring at me before indicating the ramparts. I followed him to one of the towers where we could see the sprawl of the plain below, and the shimmering host who penned us in.

'Where have you been? A quarter of a year, you bastard! A whole season! Look what's happened to us in the meantime.'

'I fell under a spell.'

He laughed sourly. 'You fell under a woman! I know your tastes, Merlin. I spent time with you in the Northlands, remember? And on the way to Delphi. And I saw the way that skimpy creature Niiv dangled from your shoulders.'

'It wasn't quite like that.'

'You were lovers, don't deny it.'

'I do deny it. The woman is after my secrets, not my kisses.'

'What took you so long?' he asked angrily, punching me hard on the arm. 'Look at this host of men! Of ghosts! Of heroes! My ancestors are there. Probably the sons of my sons! They haunt us and taunt us, they pin us down. Only the druids can get to the river without interruption . . . and my daughter, apparently! We're starving, depleted, and the bastards won't engage us in single combat. And so I ask again: where in the name of Sucellus have you *been*?'

It took me a moment to summon the words; Urtha was clearly in a foul mood. 'With a woman,' I said.

'Hah!'

'But not just any woman.'

'Well?'

'Medea. She has run me ragged just as these heroes have run you down. We've both spent the last season under siege, only you knew it and I didn't! She tricked me, Urtha. But it has opened my eyes.'

'You and my damned daughter! Always complaining you they can't *see* properly! What am I to do with you?'

'A drink would be very welcome. And meat. And cheese, and a small bowl of olives? And less of that glaring, baleful eye.'

Urtha smiled behind his long, dark moustache, his eyes crinkling with amusement. 'A drink? We have Nantosuelta's wine in abundance!'

He meant river water. Surely they'd managed to ferment *something* in this place: from apples, from grass, from thorn berries, haws or rose hips? It occurred to me that even if they had, they'd have drunk it all by now.

'As for meat, with luck I'll be able to oblige,' he went on. 'Here it comes now. Stand by at the gates!' he added with a shout across the wall.

In the evergroves by Nantosuelta there was a sudden glint of light on armour, a swift movement out on to the Plain of Maeg-Catha and three riders came hurtling along the winding way, one with the flopping carcass of a doe tied across the withers of his mount.

From the grass of the plain, ghost riders erupted just as they had risen to tackle Jason in the hinterland. A long column raced alongside the three hunters, the air shimmering, almost drawing the human riders away from the track they followed. The three kept low, kicking the flanks of their mounts and beating left and right with long rods tied about with strips of coloured cloth, pierced at the ends with the curves of an animal's bone. The ribs of a bull, I later learned; and the flapping rags were strips that had been taken from the bodies of the Dead. As a renegade wolf can be scared away by the grinning skull of its own kind, so the spirit riders shied away from the smell of their Other-worldly kin.

The Bull Gate was flung open and the three hunters galloped through to safety.

It was then that I asked Urtha about the rods. Ullanna answered me: 'Charm sticks,' she said. 'I asked myself what *you* would suggest if we were to get our hunters back safely. And I'd seen something similar used when my father went to the oracle at Airan Kurga, in my own country. The passage to the oracle is dangerous because of the wandering lost, the dishonoured. They are beaten back by their own bones.'

'A little bit of this and a little bit of that,' I said, impressed, and she gave a little bow.

'It's often the best way. The Wolf-heads helped. They've had a long journey of survival. They're charmless in one sense, but they have a good knowledge of the powers of enchantment.'

I had returned to a restless, unhappy citadel. The host from King Vortingoros's Coritani, who had agreed a short spell as mercenary help, were now frustrated and confused by their extended stay. They were concerned for their families. They had seen that it was possible to escape from Taurovinda, through the shadowy siege-works, and only Urtha's charismatic leadership had kept them rooted to the Thunder Hill.

Urtha's powers of persuasion were wearing thin, however, as were supplies, and the co-operation in the manner of entertainment and games. Mock fights and challenges, combats and races, were increasingly turning lethal as tempers frayed and hearts became increasingly forlorn.

There was a good supply of food, however; Urtha had made sure of that. And as pacification on this particular day, and partly to welcome me back, the new kill was paunched and its liver grilled at a feast given for the men of rank among the mercenaries. Fourteen of us sat at the low benches, Ullanna included, Cathabach, and the Thoughtful Woman Rianata, who would need to hear my account of Ghostland. Urtha's hall was richly coloured again; weapons hung from roof beams, shields gleamed on walls, and cloaks were spread between them to help cut out the draughts and sounds of the melancholy nights. The house was once more encircled by a deep ditch and thorn stockade, hung with the colours of the Cornovidi and the ancestral colours of the Tectosages.

The king's feisty son Kymon was not present; Munda's wailing objection to her incarceration could be clearly heard at times. The girl was furious.

As strips of deer flesh were beaten flat to make them tender, then held above the burning fire, so the conversation lightened and the spirits rose. There was a little apple cider, sharp and strong, pear wine, and a drink made from fermented milk, which was disgusting but which delighted the Scythian woman, whose concoction it was. She sat next to Urtha and made rude remarks about him, and even ruder ones about the bull-breasted, red-bearded Morvodugnos, brother of Gorgodumnos, to both men's apparent amusement.

I was given a slice of the deer's tongue, a chieftain's cut, Urtha's way of saying welcome, and perhaps: I was angry that you went away so long, but that's that, it's done. Now to work!

Urtha described how the first signs of the siege of Taurovinda had been at the return of a hunting party similar to the one I had witnessed running the gauntlet today. 'Morvodugnos and two others had gone on a recruiting mission, east as usual, since that is where most of the returning spearmen are showing up as they creep back from the conquest of Greek Land.'

Conquest? That disorderly if massive raid through Makedonia to Delphi and its oracle? This story had sweetened in the telling!

'They came across a king's son, Conary, of the Clan Thulach, with his retinue of knights and three slaves, captured from Makedonia as they'd returned. The Makedonians are good fighters and have given their bond to fight as mercenaries for seven years in return for their release to find their own way home. They're an unhappy trio, as you can imagine, but we need all the help we can get.'

I felt sorry for the three men, brought to this hostile climate and its earthy fortresses.

Urtha went on, 'This band had followed the river as far as the forest. When they saw our high towers in the distance they broke into a canter across the plain, sing-shouting to us to let us know they were coming.

'The Shadows of Heroes must have been waiting in the long

grass. Forty or fifty of them just rose up on horseback and attacked them. I was watching from the tower on the Riannon Gate. Those marauders appeared to ride up out of the ground, as if from hidden tunnels. Conary was struck by seven darts each as thin as a thorn, as long as an arrow, and died in agony out there on the plain. All in his retinue were wounded; the Makedonians were luckier. They seemed to pass through unscathed, though they too sustained glancing blows. It was a bloody troop that streamed into Taurovinda; one of the slaves had picked up the body of Conary, and we later buried him by Nantosuelta's well. I will arrange for his body to be taken home as soon as this siege is finished.

'Where had they come from, I imagine you will ask? It was impossible to tell, Merlin. But over the following days the whole plain, and the marshes to the west, became filled with the shades of the Dead and the Unborn. When it rains you can see them, like water ghosts, hovering in the saturated grass, gesturing towards us, or riding around us, either "counting coup", or trying to kill us.'

I remembered that from my first return to the deserted hill.

'Can you tell one from the other, a dead man from an unborn hero?' I asked, but Urtha shook his head.

'If their armour is familiar, perhaps they are from the past. If they ride those very large horses, and their armour seems strange, then from a time to come. Perhaps.'

Morvodugnos raised his meat knife to get my attention. 'One thing I've noticed: some of the host on the plain are very active, attacking our riders, when the moon is new, before the silver has grown bright. Others, quite different—those who seem strange to us—ride more when the moon is approaching full face, when the silver gleams brightest.'

'I have seen that too,' said the Thoughtful Woman, Rianata, quietly. She was watching me carefully. 'The host who surround this place are not at one with each other. There are struggles and arguments. I have seen it. There is much coming and going among the bands. There is a sprawling spirit hall to the east, close to the forest. That is where the High Lord resides. That is where the conflicts are acted out among the host, on the plain before it.'

Cathabach clapped his hands together, striking them three

times. 'I've seen it too. The hall is protected by shades of creatures that are only half human. The High Lord's banners bear the emblems of no kingdom or chiefdom that I have ever seen.'

Which was not saying much.

'But what do they want with Taurovinda?' Ullanna asked, shaking her head as she chewed both meat and the question.

'What indeed?' Urtha echoed. 'I'd hoped that Merlin might have some insight. Merlin?'

'If I do,' I replied truthfully at the time, 'it's very *much* in; very much out of sight.'

But my understanding of the Shadows of Heroes had grown a little with this suggestion that each presence from Ghostland was influenced by a different time in the regular darkening of the moon. It made sense: the moon, through her springs and groves on the land below her, exerted many influences on the living. She showed her dark and doleful face to the Dead and her comforting white breast to the Yet-to-be-Born. She was certainly playing a role in events.

I gave an account of my journey into the hinterland, hiding nothing of my vulnerability under the spell cast by Medea. Urtha seemed excited at the thought of Jason's return—I imagine he was thinking of boosting the numbers of his warrior host—but less than intrigued by the thought of the artful northern enchantress Niiv's returning to our company.

Brawny Morvodugnos suddenly climbed to his feet, adjusting his short scarlet cloak and sheathing his meat knife. He frowned at me, his heavy face filled with a sudden concern. Firelight made his red hair seem to writhe with life.

'If my brother, Gorgodumnos, is dead, as I believe him to be . . . then he is among the Dead, in Ghostland. He was a fine man, a fine fighter, a little short of temper, a little long in vengeance, intolerant of taking prisoners, keen to claim trophy, sometimes harsh in his actions when it came to claiming cattle from across territorial boundaries, not one to take an insult lightly, or even a compliment, but a fine man none the less. As those of you who knew him will remember, he was the best among us at five of the twelve winter feats: the feat of the twelve thunderous drums, the feat of the five shields ringed with bronze and gold, the feat of the ten somersaulting knights, the feat of the six brightly decorated goose eggs, and the feat of the eleven significant whistles. Who else in this house can claim as much?'

There was a general murmur of agreement that Gorgodumnos had been good at his feats.

Manandoun whispered to me, 'For all of that, the one feat he never mastered was the one feat we all learned first, and to perfection: the feat of the nine whirling women.'

'You whirl nine women? To what end?'

'One woman: nine whirls,' Manandoun said with a significant frown, as if the feat should have been obvious. I realised, then, that he was not talking about dancing.

Morvodugnos came to the point. 'If he has ridden in the company of Riannon and Avernos, across the river and into the Realm of Heroes . . .'

If he has been killed . . .

' . . . then he could now be part of that haunting host, out there among the long grass and twisted thorn of MaegCatha. Will he attack us? Will he attack his own brother? What am I to do if we face each other, sword to sword, open breast to open breast? What is the consequence for Gorgodumnos if I deliver the breath-denying thrust? What for me if he delivers the mournful blow?'

Morvodugnos's question brought home yet again the strange and sinister situation in which the defenders of this stronghold found themselves: they were at war with their ancestors . . . and with their unborn offspring. What Morvodugnos had done was to bring that discomfort right to the heart of the king's hall. For months each man and woman in this place must have been scouring the field of the Battle Crow, searching among the shadowy figures camped on the plain for some sight, some glimpse of a husband or son or father whom they had buried with dignity and honour. And in searching the field in this way, they would certainly have lived in private dread of seeing that once-loved coming towards them, sword drawn, perhaps, or bow stretched, spear held high . . . the mournful deed, as Morvodugnos would have put it, clear in their mannerisms if not in their hearts.

The Thoughtful Woman rescued the silence that followed Morvodugnos's plaintive question.

'There is no dishonour in turning away from a brother or

father that you recognise. Leave the field. From what I have seen, these Shadows of Heroes are weak in our land, weaker than us. Remember the scatter of bones we left when we took back the Thunder Hill? Whoever it is that has led this invasion across the Winding One, those we once loved, those who will love us in memory in their own time to come, are here against their will. The Warped Man Dealing Death has caused this to happen. There have been such men before; and there will be such men again. But they are only ever in this land one at a time. Some are good. Remember Cuhuloon, that great man of Ierna, that man of Twelve Feats and the famous warp-spasm in combat. Yes, some are good. And some are evil. This one is evil. And Munda, the girl who has the Light of Foresight, has already seen that he is close.'

As if she had heard her name invoked, from somewhere in the distance Urtha's daughter began to screech her annoyance at being separated and incarcerated.

I couldn't take my gaze away from Rianata. She met that gaze steadily.

There have been such men before; and there will be such men again.

This woman had once possessed the *imbas forasnai*, I was sure of it. It had gone from her, now; such foresight is doomed to fade. She had her memory, deep and detailed; she had her insight, in need of constant testing. Munda might become her protégée; the girl would certainly walk the same path.

What could Ghostland want with Taurovinda? The answer, perhaps, lay in the past of the fortress, a subject that the Speaker for the Past now addressed.

I listened to him carefully; he was eloquent, descriptive, passionate, but it soon became apparent that he was talking simply by rote, verses learned and remembered, without any deeper understanding or vision; these were words that had been passed down across the centuries. Two centuries, in fact: the time that had passed since the vanquished Teutoborgan kings had first come to this sprawling hill, in the heart of Alba, and fought in combat to agree which of them would claim the steep slopes and rich woodland for his own.

Durandond and his wife Evian had won the day. Three of

their four companion exiled families had moved south; one had journeyed to the north. New kingdoms were quickly established; but this Thunder Hill had been the first place of gathering, the place of the first Council of the Exiles, and the first to be protected.

Later, the five kingdoms would again be involved in bloody war and bloody mayhem, this time against each other.

I knew of Durandond and men like him; my path, my eternal walk around around the world, took me through the centre of those forested lands and open pastures where the aristocratic ancestors of Urtha and his kind had once presided over estates that were devoted to the support of luxury and the indulgence of an elite. That elite had had no concept of honour beyond its own set of castes: the well-born, the knights, the holy ones, and the High Women, the true rulers of those vast estates.

I remembered seeing the bodies of the favoured knights of the High Women, dead after battle, folded up in full armour in great golden vases. The lids of these extravagant coffins were sealed with pitch before being buried in deep shafts, covered with shards of marble and granite, sealed with oak, and decorated with flowers of the field.

The betrayers of those of noble birth were similarly confined—but alive, and in barrels made of wood; dropped into deep pits and covered with dank earth.

The five dynasties had been weakened by a series of minor wars against invaders from the east, including the Cimmerians and Scythians, and by a devastating invasion from Greek Land, an army that had marched across four lands and through two ranges of mountains. They had taken booty and deposited much of the treasure in the oracle at Delphi.

But it was their own greed that led to the fall of the kingdoms, ravished by the people they had used and suppressed.

What might those exiled rulers have brought with them that could make Taurovinda so attractive to the spirits of the Dead? Surely not the corpses of Durandond and Evian, even if they lay in a gilt-edged chariot?

I had tried to see into the hill, and though their shaft, like all the shafts, was clear to the inner eye, there was nothing else visible, save for the spiralling flow of water that fed the springs in the stronghold, crystal wine drawn from Nantosuelta. If anything else lay below our feet, it was hidden even from me.

The feast ended; the guests dispersed. Urtha indicated that I should take up my old lodgings in his hall and I accepted. I was exhausted.

I was roused from sleep by a small hand on my mouth, a child gazing at me earnestly. She whispered, 'Delight! Delight! I see a swan; I see her flying . . . My swan has come back to me!'

And at that moment the warning wail of a horn on one of the watchtowers brought the fortress alive again.

CHAPTER SIXTEEN

—

Stolen Ghosts

One of the armies on the Plain of MaegCatha had managed to breach the western gates, a night host that now
stormed into Taurovinda, horsemen and chariots wreaking mayhem as they thrust towards the *nemeton*, the sacred orchard. They
carried no torches. Entering the walls they had at once become
substantial and vulnerable to iron, and the Coritani, called from
their hostel, were tackling the invaders with an equal fury.

The chariots wheeled in a circle, javelins flew and arrows
hissed through the night air. I saw Ullanna run into the fray,
clad only in her riding trousers and her bronze-scaled cuirass.
She dropped to one knee and began to shoot arrow after arrow
at the invader, turning with each shot, devastatingly accurate by
the spill and spin of bodies from their mounts.

Horn calls from the east told of a similar attack there. The
high walls of Taurovinda became alive with torches and the
flash of arms.

I kept a cautious distance, intervening only once: when an
axe, thrown from horseback, struck Ullanna and sent her
sprawling. The rider was straddling her in a moment, axe
retrieved and raised to split her skull.

Almost without thinking I summoned a giant, rabid wolf, set it on the man, watched as it bore him to the ground and began to worry at his neck. Ullanna scrambled to her feet, looked round in alarm, failed to see me and returned quickly to the task of shooting, exhausting her quiver and running, head down, for cover again.

I released the wolf from the dead man, but the beast stayed! I watched in surprise, then alarm, as it carried its prey through the mêlée and through the gate, down the winding road and out towards the willow marshes, no doubt to enjoy a feast of liver.

Who had taken over my charm?

Delight! A swan is flying . . .

Munda's words shrieked with laughter at me. Niiv was here! She had managed to scurry through the affray and enter Taurovinda, and was here, close to me, watching me, stealing my powers even as I closed them down.

Riders thundered past me, chariots squealed and overturned. Manandoun and his guard loomed before me, swords drawn and shields discarded, ready for the hard fight: Manandoun saw me and urged me out of the way.

'Have you seen that girl? The Northlands girl?' I screamed at him. He was already summoning the blood rage, his face suffused, his eyes beginning to glow. But my words attracted his attention for a heartbeat, and he pointed behind him.

'Yes. She has dyed her hair black and is wearing swan's down on her shoulders. She was running to the *nemeton*. Never mind her,' he added fiercely. 'The Riannon gate is holding. Come and bring your skills here, Merlin! Conjure an army to sweep them back to their graves!'

He laughed, knowing that my response would be inactivity. He knew me well, this old friend of Urtha's. He performed the War Feat of the Foot and the Sword, then, and became possessed of the fury that would allow him instant access to Ghostland if his breath should be stolen.

The Coritani mercenaries, despite their complaints about the lack of payment for their services, had held the western quarter of the stronghold, though they had paid a brutal price, battered and beheaded by the desperate Dead.

I circled the orchard, ascending the ladder to the eastern

wall, to look out across the widest stretch of the plain. It was alive with fire and movement. The struggle below me was implied by the press of torches, the warrior bands pushing towards the Bull Gate—they had breached the Bull Gate!— fighting to bring down the second of the totem barriers on the causeway, but failing.

Distantly, a line of men on horseback stood silently before the tents that we had come to believe to be the royal enclosure.

They watched us from behind black, Greek Land helmets, lances held low, shields slung across their backs. White-winged hawks fluttered and struggled from tethers on the left arms of this small band of knights. Oddly, I sensed they were disturbed. One of them was struggling to control his mount, though the animal's restlessness seemed to stem from its rider's nervousness. He kept looking towards the river. His helmet flashed with gold.

Bright fire blossomed by Nantosuelta. I could see the top of the mast of a small ship, and had no doubt at all that Argo had tied up at the mooring.

There was something strange in the air, though, an ethereal glow, a shifting of space between the fortress and the ever-groves.

Then, on the night air, came the unmistakable scent of the Northlands enchantress; I would know that perfume anywhere. I turned quickly, expecting to find her right behind me, but she was still in hiding. In the orchard, Manandoun had said, and when I walked the perimeter, outside the tightly woven wicker wall that enclosed the sanctuary, I soon found the gap—no larger than a fox would make—where the girl had forced her entry.

She was lurking on the other side, hunched up, holding her breath, waiting for me to come through. Instead, I pushed the broken wall back into position, blocking the hole. I heard her little grunt of annoyance. A moment later the wall buckled outwards, bent under a fierce blow. A second strike, then the wall split open and the fierce-eyed, dark-haired girl stood there, furious with me for a moment, then running to me.

'Merlin! Don't avoid me! I need you!'

'That must have hurt,' I said to her, indicating the wall. I took her hands; the knuckles were skinned and raw. But she hadn't had the physical strength to make that breach alone.

'You keep using your power for such trivial things,' I said wearily. It was true. She was wasting her young life. It was so important to harness and conserve what powers of enchantment one possessed, especially such small charm as was held by so insignificant a charmer as Niiv.

'It doesn't matter,' she said. She clung to my arm. 'Jason is here. The ship . . . ' her voice dropped to a whisper, 'the ship delayed us. I knew what she was doing. But he's here now. He thinks you will know where Little Dreamer has been hidden. He says he's lost one son, but he will not lose the other. If you help him, perhaps he won't kill you!'

'He won't kill me.'

'He will! He can! He thinks you're in league with Medea.'

I almost laughed at that, but the pain of Medea's own deceit still tore at me.

Niiv held me tightly. She was shaking. 'Keep me close,' she whispered. 'I promise not to look into your future again. I promise to keep my nose out of your business.'

'In the same way as you just sent my wolf out of the fort?'

'I'm sorry,' she said. 'I couldn't resist it. I only meant to tease you; to let you know I was here.'

She was dangerous. She was not in the least bit vulnerable. She was not in the least bit truthful. But I remembered the words of a Cimmerian chieftain I had once known: keep the untrustworthy in clear view.

I had no time to ruminate further. The screech of battle at the western gate had dropped to a murmur. Horns sounded from the Riannon gate and there was a general movement of men towards the wall overlooking Nantosuelta. Ullanna bounded past, clutching her bow and empty quiver, hair streaming. She glanced nervously at Niiv, then at me, and shouted, 'They're withdrawing. What's happening?'

From a watchtower, Urtha's voice boomed loudly: 'Merlin! Argo! Quickly!'

I had a sense of what those three words meant and climbed the ladder to the ramparts, Niiv keeping close behind me. If I laughed as I looked out on to the plain it was with surprise and admiration for the ancient, clever ship.

The night host was in disarray. The winding ceremonial path, from Nantosuelta to the fortress, was now a gleaming river!

Argo sailed that twisting waterway, her oars rising and falling to the steady beat of the drum. Rubobostes was making the strike. Jason stood in the prow, staring up at the hill, searching the small faces above him in the night for features he knew. If our eyes met, it was for an instant only.

Niiv was breathless. 'Mielikki! My mistress! She's made the river reach to the gates!'

But it was not Mielikki who had created this living dream, I suspected, but clever Argo herself, the Spirit of the Ship, older even than me. She had, in my recent experience, sailed up rivulets no wider than a fallen tree. She could bend the world of water to her whim. She was an enchantress in hull, mast, prow and stern; the oars that drove her were legs and wings, fins and fingers, taking her where she wished.

She also knew what she was doing. As she moved serenely along the path that was now a river, so the Shadows of Heroes gathered in their clans, picked up their weapons, and rode or ran from the Plain of MaegCatha. They were alarmed and disorientated. There was confusion in their ranks, and dismay as well.

They fled to the south, away from Nantosuelta, pouring into the marshes and the tangled groves of willow that covered the western land for as far as the eye could see. Watching carefully, I noticed that the brutal army of the Dead rode in one direction while that of the Unborn, on their heavier horses and in their strange armour, took a different route.

Only the white-hawked elite remained.

When the plain was clear they released their birds of prey, swung shields to the fore, kicked their grey ponies and galloped towards Argo as she came slowly on. Jason turned to face this band, reaching for a sword. At the last moment, as they closed upon the ship, all but the leader peeled away, following the flight of their comrades to the south. This one man cast his javelin. It took true flight, striking Jason where he stood, knocking him back, almost over the side of the ship. But he had been prepared for this, his breast protected by a thick layer of leather and wood. He wrenched the spear from his armour and as his attacker, screaming fury, reared and turned on his frantic steed, so he flung the weapon back. It hit the rider in the side. Again the weapon was tugged from the wound, this time held aloft in defiance.

'You are not the one!' I heard the young man scream again in the language of old Greek Land. 'Not the one! Not the one!'

Four chariots, torches streaming from their sides, had sped from the Bull Gate, sending a spray of water from the illusory river that now flowed through it, and turned to pursue this shadow knight from the field of the Battle Crow.

He outdistanced them easily.

Argo slowed but kept moving. The oars were shipped. Jason jumped to the bank, throwing his cloak back across his shoulders. Rubobostes, too, leapt for dry land, then the dark-featured argonauts gathered their shields from the hull and clambered from the vessel. Argo, however, kept moving. She breached the gate and was swallowed by the hill, sliding into the earth below our feet as easily as dawn mist is swallowed by the forest.

Everything was suddenly very still.

Niiv was shaking. She clutched my shoulders as she huddled behind me, staring down at the scene below. 'Tell him what he wants to know,' she urged me.

The narrow focus of her thinking did not surprise me. I asked her if she had just seen what had happened.

'Yes. Jason has found you. Argo has worked her special magic. Merlin, you're in danger!'

Taurovinda had been under siege for months. The oppressing forces had disappeared like will-o'-wisp the moment Argo had opened the old river to the hill. What had frightened them? A ship? A man? What could have had the effect of breaking the deadlock? What had sent the night host fleeing back to Ghost-land?

'You are disturbed,' the girl said, clawing at me. I smacked her fingers away. Jason was leading his men into the lower enclosure, escorted by two chariots. The harsh sounding of the horns and the harmonised singing of women was the music of welcome. Urtha, wearing the grey-fur cloak of the High King, called to me. He had descended from the tower and waited for me below, his proud son Kymon by his side.

'What in the name of the Good God is going on, Merlin?' he shouted.

'Time will tell.'

'Open your eyes! I need to know!'

Niiv laughed. 'Everybody needs Merlin. Merlin can see into hills!'

I didn't like that. She was right: in moments of crisis it was always assumed that I could turn a trick, fake a wolf, magic a spear, glimpse a secret. And sometimes I could, and sometimes I couldn't, but all of these things cost me, and I was not prepared to bear that cost unless I chose to do so. Urtha's tone had made my blood pulse with anger, and Niiv—wretched nymph—had sensed that human failing. I did not want her under my skin. I certainly didn't want her fingers feeling along the carvings on my bones, touching the secrets of my birth.

I had to judge this moment carefully. Urtha's frustration was understandable. He simply couldn't comprehend why the host that had almost worn him down had so suddenly withdrawn. He was both elated and angry, relieved and confused. As indeed was I. But I couldn't have him thinking that I was there to perform at his whim. I'd thought we had established that on the long quest to Delphi.

He needed a reminder.

But when I stalked up to him, ready for the argument, he put a hand on my shoulder. Xymon has just told me that Jason is a danger to you. Don't worry, old friend; no lank-haired, grizzle-bearded Greeklander is going to insult a favoured guest of mine within these walls. But what is happening here?'

'If I knew, I would tell you. If I knew a way to see the truth, I would try to see it. But there are cloaks around us, Urtha, cloaks that confuse our sights and senses.'

I watched his face. He thought hard for a moment, frowned, then suggested, 'We are being beguiled? Not everything is as it seems?'

'I couldn't have put it better myself.'

He jumped to a conclusion with which I could not argue. 'Your fierce-eyed fuck: Medea.'

'My lover of old,' I corrected more pleasantly. 'She certainly has a finger in this storm of strangeness. But Jason's arrival has set up a storm of its own. It's to our advantage at the moment, but you'll have to give me time to understand what's happening.'

Urtha grunted. He looked down at his son; son looked up at father. Their expressions were the same: hard, accepting, slightly disdainful. Like echoes, they shrugged and looked back at me.

'In the meantime,' Urtha began, but he paused as he saw my suddenly weary look. 'What?'

'A feast, are you going to say? A feast of welcome?'

He was astonished. 'At this time of the night? Has the moon kissed your mind?'

'Thank the Good God for that, at least.'

I felt relieved for the small family of boar that were confined on the southern flank of Taurovinda. I'd started to believe that the Comovidi did nothing but fight and feast.

'The feast of welcome will be at dusk tomorrow,' Urtha concluded. 'In the meantime, I must make sure you're safe. And that Jason and his men are properly lodged. Shall I take this carrion-eater off your hands?' He looked hard at Niiv, who sheltered behind me. 'I hope you know what you're doing,' Urtha added.

I don't.

The Riannon Gate was opened at that moment, and by torch-light the thunder-faced argonauts entered the Thunder Hill.

I watched them from cover. As I had noticed from my seabird flight (an age in the past, it seemed now) there was something very sinister, very wrong, about several of the cloaked men who stalked in behind Jason. Rubobostes was as I remembered him, save for the fact that he looked weary and hungry. Four others looked around sharply as they came through the gate into the welcoming enclosure, as if searching for opportunity, though more likely they were looking for signs that they could sleep for a while in comfort.

The other six were drawn and haunted, shadow-eyed, olive-skinned, only half alive. The six of grim demeanour.

It was the work of a moment to glimpse their thoughts and realise what Jason had done. One of them sensed my presence and glanced angrily towards me. I stepped into the darkest shadow possible, one thought on my mind. *How had Jason managed this? Not alone; someone had helped him. Athene's sweet breath, please not Niiv, not the silly, prowling, predatory girl . . . She couldn't have willingly brought herself this close to death!*

Niiv sensed my sudden alarm and tried to slip away. I grabbed her wrist, tugging her close. 'If this is your work, you little fool, you've lost everything. Everything!'

'Not mine. I swear. I knew who they were. But I had nothing to do with it.'

'Then how did he manage it? How?'

'I don't know.'

I let go of her and she scurried off into the night, a small creature seeking safety.

Urtha greeted Jason with formal hospitality. His house was Jason's house; there was room on the floor for all his men for the rest of the night.

Jason acknowledged the gesture, then asked, 'Is he here?'

'Yes. And like you, he's a guest under my roof. I keep a peaceful house, friend Jason. If you try to kill him, I'll have you killed.'

'Plainly spoken, Lord Urtha. You may rest assured. I have no intention of killing him.'

He looked around in the torchlit night, and soon his gaze found mine. He stared at me for a few moments, then turned away. I heard him say to Urtha, 'A few old friends of Merlin's are here as well. He has a lot in common with them.'

'That is a subject for a later discussion. For the moment, I'm intrigued to know why the sight of Argo has sent our enemy scurrying back to their grave-mounds.'

I shared Urtha's puzzlement. Unable to rest, unwilling to sleep in the king's hall alongside Jason, I prowled the battlements until the moment dawn began to break across the forest to the east of MaegCatha. All sign of the Ghostlanders had gone; it was hard to realise that a force of three hundred or more had been encamped there for the better part of a season.

Though they had seemed to abandon their tents, those temporary dwellings, too, had been swallowed by the earth.

A heavy footfall on the ladder behind me announced the arrival of Rubobostes. He had snatched a little sleep and a little food and was looking better. I reached out to help the brawny Dacian on to the platform inside the palisade and the hand that gripped mine was like an iron vice.

'You would have made a fine match for Heracles,' I told him.

'I'd have liked to have known him. He was famous in my

land. He carved a valley through a hill with his bare hands. The river that rose there still flows to the sea. We call it by a name that means "The famous man's urine".'

'I'm sure you do.'

'I'm glad to see you again, Merlin.'

'I'm glad to see you as well, though I saw you in the hinterland. How did you get across the river? Argo, I suppose.'

'Mielikki opened the way. It's a strange thing: when we were exploring that strange edge-land I could swear that I heard your voice. We were attacked by a squadron of riders, one of them a very angry, very furious young man.'

I told him I'd been there, witnessing the assault from across the meadow. 'And what happened to your horse? Ruvio?'

Rubobostes' mount had been a creature of supernatural strength. Man and beast might well have been created together.

'We've left him close to Ghostland; strategically placed. He was exhausted from the journey and there are several wild mares at the edge of the forest, and good grazing. When Ruvio looks at me in a certain way, I never argue. I gave him his head and by now the bellies of those mares are filling up with little stallions; they'll be greatly useful in times to come.'

The sun suddenly sparked into fire above the trees. Rubobostes went quiet for a moment, going through his sacred dawn ritual with a haste that narrowly bordered on the blasphemous. It occurred to me, briefly, that I would have liked a ritual of my own, but if I'd ever had one it was long forgotten. When the sun rose in this way, bright, clear, suddenly sharp, it opened a thousand memories for me, all of them profane.

'Before the others rise,' the Dacian said quietly, when he had finished, 'there are six old friends who never sleep and who would like to see you. The druid has let them enter the apple grove. He's too frightened of them to refuse.'

I glanced towards the *nemeton* behind its high wicker walls. The Speaker for the Past stood before the gate, his hazel staff clutched in both hands as if he was guarding his precious orchard from anything else that might want to sully its precious soil. He looked dark-eyed and deeply unhappy.

'How did Jason raise them?' I asked the Dacian quickly, but Rubobostes shrugged his broad shoulders.

'He'd raised them before he found me again. I was on my

way home, after that big fight in Makedonia, on the way to Delphi, remember? But I changed my mind. I'd got the taste for adventure again, Merlin! And as I think you found out for yourself, it's nothing if not adventurous around that cold-hearted Greeklander. I found him and his new retinue riding north through the foothills, close to the river Daan, where we'd hidden Argo before heading for Makedonia. The six were with him. All I know is that he had called on a promise they'd made to him. Apparently, you were there at the time. Some sort of bond of honour made when Argo sailed for the golden ram's fleece.'

The Dacian's words surprised me, though I wasn't shocked. I'd spent a great deal of time with Jason on that famous voyage of Argo, seven centuries in the past. He'd made many deals to achieve his ends. I began to understand what might have happened.

Advising Rubobostes that, though he was weary with travel, he might be well employed echoing the procreative activities of his horse, since Urtha would need a strong retinue in his later years, I left him for a more difficult meeting.

He looked bemused for a moment, then called after me, 'Just to be clear: you're not suggesting I mate with horses?'

'Of course not.'

'But the women here all look so fierce! Even the unmarried ones.'

'The gentle sound of a harp, a love song . . . very soothing, very pleasing.'

'Thank you,' he said sarcastically. 'I can't sing and I can't play the harp. Thank you.'

The druid scowled as I approached him. He had limed his short hair and it rose in a series of curved spikes across his head, emphasising the gaunt anger of his shrivelled face. He was wearing a dark cloak, tied at the left shoulder, and he had smeared the garment with clay. He now held his hazel staff like a spear, pointed towards me. He was very upset indeed, and clearly considered himself to be in danger.

'There are six dead men in the orchard,' he growled. 'Stay away.'

'We're fighting a war against the Dead,' I reminded him. 'And these six are on our own side.'

'They are not dead like the Dead. The Dead are still alive! Shadows of Heroes. These dead *are* dead. Reluctantly resurrected! They don't belong here.'

'Then why did you let them into the orchard?'

'Better there, in Nantosuelta's reach, than out here; more chance of descending into the earth, out of harm's way. And that ship is down there, in the heart of the hill. They belong with the ship. Who are they, Merlin?'

'I don't know yet. I know that they are six of Jason's argonauts; six of the old crew. Let me pass. You're in no danger from them. I'll lay my life on that.'

'My life doesn't matter,' Speaker for the Past murmured angrily. 'This fortress matters; only this place.'

He stood aside, but as I stepped into the orchard he ran the tip of his staff down my back. A little charm, a crude thing, both protective and spying, touched my bones. I let it rest there. I trusted this man and it would be a good thing if he could see what I knew, and learn that his fort was not under threat from these Six of Reluctant Resurrection.

They had scattered through the grove. Each of them had found a place to stand in the early morning gloom of the sanctuary, but as I entered the orchard they turned to listen and look. I went to the grass-and-flower-covered stone mound that marked the deep shaft to the tomb of Durandond and his queen. One of the old argonauts drew close. He removed his helmet to expose his face. Though his eyes were haunted, there was also the shadow of pleasure there, and hunger; hunger to understand, perhaps, or hunger to hear a greeting from an old acquaintance.

'Tisaminas. How well I remember you. You stayed with Jason until his death. You were the best of them, the most courageous.'

The haunted expression in the strong, grey face didn't change. 'Was I? Does it matter? I saw him die in Iolkos. But they all came back when Argo sailed away with his body. All the crew. Do you remember how they lined the cliffs above the harbour? They cast their torches into the sea. It was a moment of wonder. The moon swallowed the beautiful ship. Yet here he is again. And you! Antiokus. Antiokus. How can you still be alive and warm?'

Antiokus was the name by which I'd been known on Argo.

I saluted the old man, then took his hands in mine. They were cool, not cold; he was strong in this resurrection, not frail; Jason had somehow launched life back into the bloodstream of his corpse.

'You always knew that I was from a different time, a different age,' I reminded him.

'Did I? I've forgotten.'

'Who else is here? Who else among the six of you?'

'Hylas; Cepheus of Arcadia; Lynceus of Arene and Leodocus of Argos, both wounded; and Atalanta.'

If I were to use the language of the Celts, this would have been one of the Seven Shocking Revelations of my life. I had been shocked before; no doubt I would be shocked again; but I will not deny that though the mention of Hylas—Heracles' young servant, lover and spear-carrier, and a helpful friend to me during my first difficult days on Argo—had sent a surge of anguish through my stony heart, the mention of Atalanta was more distressing.

Hylas had become tired to the point of desperation with Heracles and his ego. Jason had conspired with the other argonauts to hide him from the monstrous man, pretending he had been taken by water nymphs, seduced and drowned when we'd put ashore on our way to Colchis. Heracles had destroyed the lake where he believed his favourite boy had been killed, before stalking off to other adventures. Hylas had sneaked back on to Argo, departed from us at the mouth of the river Acheron, and I'd hoped had gone on to have a long and less demanding life. It would be difficult to greet him again.

Atalanta, however, was another matter. I have not mentioned her before because, truth to tell, she kept herself to herself when she sailed for the fleece. She was not given to easy conversation, and though she took her pleasure with several of us, as we all did with each other in those lonely times on the wide sea, she did not share the spirit of the ship; she had her own tasks to perform. She was good company and a good hunter, and she had sea-sense and a woman's nose for impending trouble that had served us well on that voyage.

When she went ashore and decided to stay ashore, before we reached Colchis, she was missed for a long time.

I had known her briefly, and not very well. But I knew the woman who had descended from her: Ullanna, Urtha's new consort. Ullanna: Scythian and strong, and living in admiration of her legendary ancestor.

This would be a difficult introduction.

Wise Tisaminas had read my concern, perhaps. He said, 'We are a strong band, even though we are out of Time. We are here because of Jason, because of our promises to him. We can be kept apart from the others. When Little Dreamer is in his arms, we can all go home. No need to look so concerned, Antiokus.'

'Where is home for you, Tisaminas? How did Jason persuade you away from it?'

The old man looked at me and almost smiled, but the weight of his displacement from his land dragged at the muscles of his once handsome face. 'Home is a wide plain, with olive groves, fresh water, wine flavoured with resin and the occasional visit of my ancestors, none of them so old that they wish to stay long, none of them so young that they have to make an effort to sit and talk and drink and eat with me.'

'Is that what you wished for in life?'

'Doesn't everybody?'

'I don't know, Tisaminas. I'm one of the visitors.'

'So you are. I remember now. But that can change; if your future is to be as long as your past, you can build a tower to the moon. In my day, I'd heard that there were people in the east who were planning to do just such a thing.'

'They didn't succeed.' I was able to tell him. 'The builders came from lands too far apart. Too many languages; too many foremen; too much bargaining; too much cheap mortar trying to keep the whole thing together; too soft.'

'It collapsed?'

'They always collapse.'

'Nothing changes.'

'Not even you, even though you've been dragged abruptly from your grave.'

'Don't call it a grave, Antiokus. Graves are where the bodies go.'

'But this *is* your body. Isn't it?' I pinched his cool flesh.

'On loan.'

'Tell me about the terms of the loan.'

His answer was a whisper, his face darkening even further, brow-furrowed and frightened, as if the answer to my question was a curse in itself. 'Kolossoi. Kolossoi.'

It took just a moment for me to realise the significance of what he was saying. Everything I knew about Jason at that moment became meaningless. Cold fury burst in my breast. I had not realised how truly that man had been a mercenary, how much he had *gathered*! I had not known the man at all. I felt stunned and betrayed. But where had he hidden the spoils of his greed?

'I can help you,' I said angrily to Tisaminas. This shade of my old friend seemed to recognise my intention and begged me not to. He seemed alarmed by my urgency.

'Not yet. Not yet. The consequences are unforeseen. We gave him kolossoi willingly. You must realise that. We had no comprehension of what he could do with it if he so wished. But I understand that it is his right by our agreement.'

'He's a bastard. He tricked you.'

Tisaminas tried to calm me. 'He gave kolossoi to us in exchange. We never felt the need to use it. We discarded it long ago. We did it willingly.'

'Listen to me! Last night I summoned a wolf to protect one of Jason's more recent argonauts, a woman called Ullanna. That act, the enchantment, cost me very little. Perhaps one more grey hair, a minute off my life. I use my talents sparingly. But every so often I use them rashly and with pleasure. Something in me makes me do this. I never question the impulse. And I want to do it now. Tisaminas! I can help you, all of you. You don't belong here, and you don't deserve this callous summoning; Jason has betrayed you. He accused me of betraying *him*. The man is greedy, selfish, lost in instinct; he's a wolf, chewing at the corpse of his remembered life, a scavenger on everything still living that reminds him of that life. To kill him would cost me dearly. I'll age. I'll get gout in winter! But I'll kill him for you, and gladly. Just tell me where he has hidden the kolossoi. I can do nothing without knowing that.'

A voice behind me murmured, 'Do you think if we knew the answer to your question we'd still be here?'

As I turned, so Atalanta kissed my cheek, cool lips on a

fevered face; a gentle touch of affection, calming rage. I returned the embrace.

She had not lived to old age. Whatever had killed her had taken her in the prime of life. Gaunt though she was, she was beautiful; and from her eyes, Ullanna watched me; it is always the eyes that tell of the unbroken bond. There is something in the look from eyes that passes down the centuries.

Behind her stood Hylas. I recognised him at once. He too had failed to pass his middle years; no painful rigor of his bones, then; the gods of his age had been fickle and capricious; no doubt they had punished him for his desertion of their beloved Heracles. He was still in good shape, though more brawny in limb than when I'd known him, and the lines of distress, inflicted by the grotesque demands of his lion-skinned master, had smoothed away.

Hylas said, 'You must have loved us very much when you sailed on Argo to offer such a sacrifice now. It will age you.'

'I didn't know you knew. About the cost in years to me of performing magic.'

'The girl on the ship talked to me about it. The Northlander. She loves you, Antiokus. She talks about you in whispers. She whispers to me about her feelings.'

A chill hand clasped my heart. Niiv had clearly penetrated the shade-cloak of this youngish man. She could seduce the dead! Good gods, I'd have to keep her close! I realised at that moment that I could never let her get away from me. Whatever her shaman father had bequeathed to her, on his death in the far north, it was more than I'd realised. She was akin to a rose, growing strongly, reaching for the sun: beautiful, spreading untamed, not always in blossom, but always extending suckers to snare the unwary.

It was upsetting, to say the least, to be reunited with these friends from the past, friends whose deaths or departures I had mourned at the time before coming to terms with their absence. That crew aboard Argo, in the long-gone, when the seas had been full of challenge and a misty shore spoke more of the unknown than of the known, had been as close to a family as I had ever come, since beginning my walk around the world.

They had felt something similar. The confines of a ship create an intimacy of spirit that transcends clan, tribe and family.

Everything is shared just as everything is risked. That we sympathised with Hylas over his overbearing master, Heracles, was simply testimony to the essential democracy that formed on such a tiny world within the world of Ocean.

But of these sad resurrections, it was Tisaminas whose presence upset me most. I had liked him very much, and he had been the most faithful of the argonauts to Jason, staying in Iolkos long after we had all dispersed, looking after the ageing, rotting man, keeping him in food and simple comforts, being the listening ear that could cope with Jason's tirades of anger and grief against Medea, and at the loss of his sons.

Tisaminas should not have been here.

This was a rotten move of Jason's. He had used the kolossoi, given to him in friendship to signify Tisaminas's willingness to take up arms for Jason in the living world, as a means to crew his new ship on this selfish mission with the easy option of arms and limbs. For Tisaminas, this meant an absence not from his life after death, but from his life during life. I knew enough of the gift-bringing that was represented by kolossoi to know that for every day Tisaminas spent in the living world as a ghost, he had been shorn of vitality when he had been alive and with his family; and he had had a big family, four sons and two daughters, a clan that would have been a great burden to many in Iolkos at that time. Fortunately, one of his sons grew vines and one of his daughters had entered the Temple of Pallas Athena. A parent's problems are often solved by such a combination of produce and promise.

The last thing I asked Tisaminas was how long he had been on Argo, this time round.

'Half a year,' he said. 'Looking back, I can see where I was absent. My wife was distraught; she took a lover! My eldest son tried to kill me. I even tried to kill myself in the harbour of Iolkos. I felt like a shadow of myself. I slept like a cat. I remembered nothing from day to day. A man who lives his life in the arms of wine-swilling Bacchus could not have felt more estranged from the world than I did at that time.' His gaze was full of pain. 'But it lasted more than half a year . . . '

How strange: to think that Tisaminas's life several centuries in the past was now dependent on my dealings with Jason. This is what the Dacians called a *conundrum*; a knotty problem.

'Old friend, what has been taken cannot be returned; I'll send you home as soon as I can. While you are here, you are still alive in Iolkos, but in a stupor, and there is a celebration to be had when you appear to return from the living dead.'

'That celebration is a distant memory,' Tisaminas said with a wan smile. 'But I did enjoy it. I raised a cup to you. I didn't understand why.'

'We are shaping the past. It's easier than shaping the future. Your shade was aware, even if you weren't.'

'The consequences, though . . . '

'Leave them to me. I play a very good game of consequences.'

He seemed relieved to hear my words.

That night, five spectral figures slipped past the guard at the rear gate. Tall men in long cloaks, their hair loose, carrying only sword and scabbard, they sought me out. I recognised the man who dreamed himself Pendragon. His eyes caught the silver of the moon as he greeted me quietly. For a moment, again, I thought I was looking at a reflection of Urtha.

'This has been a wonderful day,' he said to me. 'The Sea Prophecy has come true. The Old Ship came.'

'The Sea Prophecy?'

'One of the Five Uncertain Prophecies made by a man called Sciamath, an enchanter, now lost to us.'

Sciamath again, the man whose cloak was a whirling flow of forests, a seer of ancient days. An enigmatic figure who clearly worked his visions in the Otherworld as well as in the territory of kings. I had not known he was lost.

'The prophecy?'

'That an Old Ship with a crew of ghosts would release us to pursue our dreams again. We have been slaves to the Dead for too long. The siege of this place is ended. This is our moment! This is goodbye, Merlin. I had thought we could investigate the world together, but the time is not right. On the other side of that winding river there will now be a reckoning, of no concern to you. I will see *you* on another day!'

The five warlords, the five Unborn kings, held their richly patterned scabbards towards me in salute, then turned and slipped from the fortress, silent and unseen, to take war across the river.

CHAPTER SEVENTEEN

—

Light of Foresight

A squad of men, armed with Ullanna's contrived charm-sticks, had gone out on to MaegCatha Plain, beating the grass and brush in the manner of children beating to disturb wild fowl and woodcocks for the waiting archers. Nothing on the plain that was now in hiding, and might be induced to fly for freedom, would be edible, however.

Still mindful of Jason's last bitter words to me, as he had lain 'mortally' wounded by his own eldest son in the shadow of the oracle of Dodona, I went in search of the man, to confront him on the matter of his own trickery. The guard at the king's enclosure recognised me and allowed me past, but I entered a long house that was barren of any life save the fire and its tenders, the two hounds which were catching up with sleep, though each raised a languorous head to study me as I came into the place, and the Ligurian argonaut, who was sick and curled up on a low bench.

'Where's Jason?' I asked the man. Smoke swirled in the main room, and light picked out the details of shields and weapons, scattered around, ready for use. Gold filigree flashed from several of the banners hanging from the rafters.

'Looking for son. Looking for stinking sorcerer bastard who know son,' the sick man grunted before pulling his cloak over his head.

Looking for me, then.

But I ignored the gesture of reconciliation in the Argonaut's voice. I could have prowled for him as the hound, or scanned with an eagle's eye from the low cloud above the hill, but I had a strong feeling that the old Greeklander was close; and sure enough, as I entered the antechamber from Urtha's main hall, stepping into the claustrophobic gloom of the place where shields and spears were stored, I felt the prick of a knife below my right ear, a point painfully made.

'Where's Little Dreamer?' was Jason's question. The knife point was as insistent as Niiv's groping, and as futile.

'Somewhere in this land,' I replied.

'I know he's somewhere in this land. "Between sea-swept walls, where he rules but doesn't know it." The words of the oracle at Arkamon. I haven't forgotten.'

'This is the land between sea-swept walls. The island of Alba.'

'Island? It goes on for ever. This is no gods-protected island! I've been sailing its rivers for moon after moon. I'll never find the boy unless I can narrow down the search.'

He used the blade like an oyster knife, turning it as if he could prise open the bone below my ear. I paraphrased the words of Achilles, when surprised unarmed by his mortal enemy Hector as he made an offering to Athene in a grove outside Troy. Feeling the prick of the sword against his spine he had said, 'Push in the blade or sheathe it. I don't negotiate with metal, only *men* with metal.'

Hector was subdued, and later that day died by Achilles' own sunblessed hand.

Jason laughed at my small conceit. 'The very words Daedalus used to King Minos, when his first maze had failed to hold his half-creature son, the Minotaur, and the king was about to kill him. You know your history!'

Daedalus? Perhaps I'd been misinformed.

But I ignored the gesture of reconciliation in the argonaut's voice. The blade still hurt, and my blood still beat furiously with the thought of Tisaminas, shade-dragged and vacant because of the mercenary whim of this once-great man.

'Where have you hidden the kolossoi?'

He grabbed me by the shoulder and flung me round. He looked old and hard, angry and dead at the same time. A rank odour seeped from his mouth and there was that liquid look to his eyes, which might have been illness or the imminence of old age. His hair, loose and grey, hung like an oily blanket around a weathered face that might have been carved from stone.

'Never mind the kolossoi! Kinos is all that matters. His bitch-mother has hidden him here. I haven't the years to scour every damp valley and every stinking marsh for the lad. But you, you, Antiokus, you are the key! I know you know where he is. You are too meddlesome not to have found out. Where is he?'

'Where are the kolossoi?'

'Why?' he screamed at me. 'Why? What in the name of the gods does it matter about such tokens?'

'It matters to me. It matters to Tisaminas and the others.'

'They are *dead*. They have no understanding. Once they mattered. Now, they don't matter at all! Except that they're strong.'

'They matter to me.'

'They're out of Elysia, they'll return to Elysia.'

'They're hurting.'

A rage engulfed the old man. His fist slammed into my cheek and my knees buckled as my head spun from the blow. He shouted, 'No!' as he struck me. I never let my gaze leave his. He did not want to confront the truth of what I had told him. He kept his hands on my jacket, hauling me back to my feet. I was as dizzy with the foul miasma from his lungs as with the addling of my senses from the pugnacious response to my insistent questions.

I could have ended this so quickly, but this man had once been my friend. I wondered, even as he leered at me, whether a demon was riding on his shoulders. Nothing was visible; madness ruled the day.

'Is he here?' Jason breathed, his teeth bared. 'Kinos! The boy who could dream for all of Greek Land. Is he here? Tell me, you bastard! Tell me and I'll never trouble you again.'

'Where are the kolossoi?'

'Forget the fucking kolossoi! Antiokus . . . I know you too well; I know you will have found the scent of the boy! Just tell me where he is and you can go away, settle down in a small meadow, grow belladonna and beans and every midwinter go into a trance and fart your way to the stars! It's a simple thing I ask. I no longer want to kill you. I did then, I don't now. It's a *simple* thing I ask. Kinos! Where did that bitch hide him? Kinos. Simple question. Simple answer. Leave the rest to me.'

'Kolossoi.'

He clearly didn't understand. 'Why?' he breathed in exasperation. 'What is so important? They died seven hundred years ago. I'm just using them to row the ship. It's a big ship. I need strong arms on the oars. I don't intend to keep them around. They were my friends, they are the only friends I've got! I'm not disturbing them, Antiokus—'

'But you are!'

'How? They've been in their graves for seven centuries.'

'They are alive. The kolossoi take from their life. Seven centuries ago, these men—Atalanta too—are the living dead.'

He tried to wrap his thoughts around the statement. Shaking his head, he said only, 'What was done then is done.'

'Not at all. Your actions now can easily affect the lives of your six resurrected dead in their living past. How they will be remembered depends on when you give back the kolossoi. You had no right to use them; they were intended for use in your argonauts' lifetimes. Once they were dead, you should have cast them away.'

He smoothed my clothing, looked thoughtful. 'I wasn't aware you knew so much about our little tokens.'

'Your *little tokens* have been the stock in trade of sorcerers for ten thousand years. Under different names, and in different forms, but of course I know about the Gift of the Greeklanders! Where have you hidden them?'

'Where is Kinos hiding?'

I could hear the approach of men along the path that led to the king's house. One of the women, tending the fire, had gone for help at the sound of raised voices.

I decided to let Jason know how close he had been to his son. I told him that he had been within slingshot range of the boy who was now a man. I told him that he had exchanged blows with him.

'Blows? When?'

'When you crossed the river. The horseman who tried to kill you.'

You are not the one. You are not the one.

Jason was taken by surprise. 'That aggressive bastard could not have been Kinos. He would have recognised me. I always wore a beard . . . the grey in the beard would not have stopped him recognising me.'

'He remembers you differently. He is a grown man. Your other son was a grown man. What sort of reception did you get from him? Ask the flesh of your belly! Don't expect a welcome feast until he is sure of who you are.'

My words affected Jason, a moment of concern, the lines around his eyes crowding together. Even so, he whispered, 'You *do* know where he is . . . '

Behind him, Urtha and Manandoun entered the gloomy room, hands resting purposefully on the decorated ivory hilts of their swords. Manandoun asked sharply, 'Can we help?'

'Thank you. No.'

Urtha reminded Jason of what he had said the night before. 'I will not have a contest between you at the moment. You are both guests in my house.'

'There is no contest,' Jason said, then turned and bowed his head to the king. 'I have just learned that I have seen my son without recognising him; and that he saw me without recognising his father. I have just learned that Merlin can help me, and I plead for that help; I pledge no hostility while I am in your fort.'

'Except to the enemy, I hope,' Urtha suggested.

The two men turned and left us. Jason's face, again creased with thought, caught the light from the door as it was opened and closed, a brief glance towards me. 'I don't know where the kolossoi are to be found. I lost them as soon as Argo came along this river. Ask the ship. She's more a friend of yours than she is of mine.'

If I could have sucked the truth from the sap of his brain, I'd have done so, there and then. But Jason was closed to me. He always had been. Besides, something in his manner suggested he was not lying.

*   *   *

A kolossoi is both a simple and a complex thing; an object; magical and personal, each one quite unique since each one is constructed out of the life and dreams of the man or woman who offers it as the token of help to a friend or brother or parent or son.

In the Northlands they call them *sampaa*. In the hill country beyond Colchis, they are *korkonu*. In many countries their power has been misunderstood and they have, and had, become simple objects, amulets and talismans: trinkets, sparkles, dew drops on the meadow, nothing more.

In the long-gone, in the murk and magic of the forested, formidable world into which I was born, I had known them by a name, but since the name itself has power, I cannot write it, even mark it, even sign it.

My own ancient 'kolossoi' is well hidden. Not even Medea will find it.

The kolossoi of these old Achaeans, Greeklanders, call them what you will, were hideous, portable, and almost hypnotic if looked at for too long. I doubt that Jason had even glanced at them when he had dug them up from where he'd hidden them. He would have used the shield trick, made famous by Perseus in his encounter with the mother Gorgon, Medusa, whose direct look at a man could literally petrify him. The shield would have been of polished bronze or silver in which he would have viewed the reflection of the artefacts he sought as he reached for them, a simple diversion of light that would have sapped the power of the objects for a moment, long enough for him to cover them in a leather bag; or box them; or conceal them under a cloak if they were large and beginning to grow after having been disturbed. And some kolossoi were indeed *colossal*.

Those of Jason's friends would have been of the smaller kind.

I had an idea of what had happened to them, but Argo, if Mielikki would let me pass into the Spirit of the Ship, would certainly be able to tell me. Though that certainty, of course, was not a reason to believe that she would divulge the hiding place.

Argo had hidden below the Thunder Hill, somewhere along the intricate channels of the river, Nantosuelta, which coursed through Taurovinda in a series of helical veins, much as the blood, I believe, flows through the limbs and bellies of men: controlled and urgent. The hill was a world of its own, opened by shafts from the surface, seething with a spiralling network of water coming up from below.

The most obvious place to descend and find the ship was through the well dedicated to Nodons, close to the western gate.

A stone maze, the height of a tall man, protected the well, though its centre could be seen from the higher fortifications. This was protective not so much against men as against the supernatural. The maze around Nodon's Well was simple, a winding double track, no blind ends, and somehow I still got lost.

When I reached the pool, below its thatched and flowered roof, the three women who drew from it were hardly able to suppress their laughter. They each had a tree under which they sat: a blackthorn, a rowan, an aspen.

'Have you come to drink, wash or watch?' blackthorn asked me. By watch she meant ask for a favour from Nodons, which would mean the depositing of an offering into the deep well.

'To descend,' I said. 'And without interference from you, if you don't mind.'

They looked at me blankly, then with amusement tempered with surprise as I stripped, piling my clothing neatly in a niche in the stone wall.

I slipped into the pool, arms above my head, and let the tug of the earth draw me down. I summoned *silvering*, the spirit of the fish. My chest ceased to ache, my vision cleared, if water entered my lungs I was not aware of it. I could hold this state for half the morning before the urgency of the human flesh would drive me to seek air again.

The well descended, then levelled out, rising again through the earth, water caught between sharp rock walls; then it plunged again and soon I felt the powerful grip of Nantosuelta drawing me into her arms. This was another maze, a water maze; I swam through the hill, deeper and deeper, pushing against the rocky tunnels, squeezing through crevices hardly wide enough for a fish, let alone a large-limbed man. Sometimes bent double to follow the flow, sometimes plunged into a wide underground chamber, at last I slipped across slimy, smooth rocks into the river herself.

Light here was dimly phosphorescent, a green and yellow glow from the walls and roof. The hill above this place rumbled and moaned, shuddered and breathed, as if it were a beast, slumbering unhappily.

Everywhere there were signs of the connection between Taurovinda and the Sun Bull, from dried dung, voluminous and rock hard, to the scattered skulls and horns of smaller representations of the beast. Every outcrop of phosphorescent rock in this underground river system seemed to be the calcified head of such a creature.

More numerous were the boats, the small boats which had carried the honoured dead from the hill to the river over so many centuries. They lay on the rocks, or drifted sluggishly in the flow, tethered by leather cords. They were empty, of course, and some were very rotten, though they spoke of many ages in the carvings and tracings on their simple hulls.

In the world above, rites and ceremonies were played out month after month in the groves, sanctuaries and sacred ways, while everywhere else life went on as normal, with due acknowledgement to the secret language of the underworld. I wonder how surprised those priests and kings would have been to know what vestiges of their ceremonies were accumulating below their foundations.

It would not have happened in any other fortress. I had now seen all I needed to see to grasp the greater significance of Taurovinda.

But where was Argo? She would be moored somewhere in these caverns.

I could do worse than call for her, it seemed to me, so call for her I did, and after a while she answered. I slipped and slid along the rocks until, gently illuminated in the strange phosphorescence, I saw her prow.

Mielikki watched me sternly as I climbed into her hull and went to crouch below the figurehead, naked, shivering, hoping that Argo would open her spirit to me.

A gust of warm summer air; a lynx peered at me, then turned and bounded away towards a thin stand of trees, aspens, shaking in the breeze. I crossed the threshold, stepping into the summer landscape. Mielikki sat close by on a rocky outcrop, dressed in a thin, white dress, youthful and pleasant to look at, except for her eyes, which narrowed at their edges in that way the Northlanders call *pookish*.

'Thank you for returning the little boat,' she said. 'Argo is glad to have her back. A wound has been healed.'

'That little boat has been my friend and my comfort. I know it left a wound in the great ship. I'm grateful for the loan. I would like to thank Argo herself.'

Mielikki scowled; the breeze took on an icy edge, a flurry of snow, the growl of a cat hidden in the undergrowth. The summer landscape returned, but now there was a fierceness in the protecting goddess. 'No thanks for me? I intervened for you in Dodona. I persuaded Argo to lend you the little boat and take you away from Jason. No thanks for me?'

Without thinking I simply told the truth: 'When I fled from Greek Land, I was thinking of nothing.'

'Nothing but yourself.'

'I was confused. I live through centuries. Understanding friendship is not made easier by watching friends die old and corrupt while you still live as a vigorous man. I draw back from friendship. Several times in my life I have formed a close bond with someone. Jason was one such. Those bonds mean a great deal to me, and when Jason confronted me at Dodona, threatened to kill me, dismissed me as just another betraying bastard . . .'

I couldn't finish. A rage of anxiety and grief rose to form, like thunderclouds, in my skull. I felt bleak.

Mielikki said the words I couldn't bring myself to say. 'You felt lost.'

'I felt lost.'

'Do you still feel lost?'

What a question. Did she understand how taunting that question was? Lost? Nobody on the earth above me would be alive forty years from now. I would lose them all. Jason included, since he had now been abandoned by Argo.

But *lost*?

If I am to record the truth of the matter it is that I live for these small whirlpools of action and desire, quest and conviction, loss and grief, that occasionally spiral through the world as I know it, little whirlwinds of passion in a dull, dull landscape.

No. I was no longer lost.

'Where do I find Argo?'

Mielikki laughed. 'She is all around you, Merlin. Look around you.'

I turned slowly, looking between the stands of wide-branched oaks, blind for a moment before I understood.

'This is the wood from which she was first built,' I murmured.

'Carved,' Mielikki amended. 'Argo began her life as a canoe, a primitive craft hacked out by one man's hand. He rowed her to some strange places in the wilderness before she passed on to her second captain. Only those captains, the men who built and built *on* Argo, can talk to her directly. But tell me your question and I'm sure she'll answer you.'

Mielikki sat on the rock, the lynx rolling on its back at her feet, batting at small bees with its paws, a playful cat despite its ferocious growl. She reminded me of the Pythia who sat before the cavernous oracle at Delphi, the intermediary between men and the gods. Perhaps this was one of the first oracles.

'Jason stole the lives of six of his argonauts; small tokens; kolossoi. Men are in limbo because of his action, and he claims he has lost them. He said that Argo would know.'

The woodland shivered. A shadow passed around the small glade. The lynx sat bolt upright, alarmed and suspicious. Mielikki reached a reassuring hand and stroked its head. Her pale face was thoughtful and I knew she was listening to the voice of old Argo herself. This girl, the protecting goddess of the ship in her summer form, was so pretty compared to the figurehead on the vessel. It was hard to remember what ice-raging violence could suddenly storm from her.

'She knows the small lives,' she said suddenly. 'Jason brought the kolossoi to this place and hid them close by. But though Argo loves Jason, as she loved all her captains, she could see that he was using them badly. They are quite safe. She has hidden them elsewhere, across the Winding One, and when Jason has shed his cloak of fury, she will fetch them back and give them back to the men and the woman who have lost them. This will not take long. She knows that she will have to sail across the Winding One. But she will not make the longer journey into the Realm of Shadows, to pacify the Warped Man, Dealing Death. She is too tired. These last years have been arduous for the ship as much as for her crew. When she is rested, Merlin, come with us, and she will tell you where to find the small lives. You will then be their guardians.'

I questioned her more, but she simply smiled and stroked her cat.

Dealing with gods and oracles is a frustrating affair. Whether by riddle or omission, they never can bring themselves to tell you everything they know.

Argo had hidden the kolossoi in Ghostland. That much was clear. And that she 'knew' she would soon be sailing across Nantosuelta suggested she was aware that Kinos, Little Dreamer, lived there now. Jason had half suspected as much; he had already put a tentative step into that Otherworld, but had abandoned the landing, crossed back and come to Taurovinda.

The reason was obvious: the Realm of the Shadows of Heroes was a far more complex land than Alba itself. He needed a guide.

Medea knew the whereabouts of Kinos. And he knew that I was drawn to Medea by a bond of forgotten love. I could almost hear the tugging of the ropes inside his head, raising and lowering sail, signalling his direction. Follow him, find her; follow her, find my son.

I was still crouched on the slippery rocks of the underground river, feet resting against the ship's cold hull, when Mielikki whispered, 'Something is disturbed above! Something is wrong! Go up, Merlin. Go up now. Hurry!'

The cause of the disturbance was Urtha's daughter.

Munda's protestations at her incarceration in the women's hostel had become increasingly anguished. Her voice, raised and furious, sounded through the citadel; animals were disturbed and children amused; but when the fury had turned to wailing there was a marked increase in concern among the wiser in the enclosure.

The girl was no longer angry. She was in pain. Her voice was an animal howl, distressed and primal. When Ullanna commented that she sounded like a woman in labour, Rianata, the Thoughtful Woman, reacted like a hare bolting from its form.

'Eyes of Riannon! What have I done? How could I have been so blind?'

She returned later and urged Urtha to call a council. 'The girl will have something to say to us all. A representative of all who live here must be present. Hurry! She is not in our world. She will lose her wits if we don't bring her to a sounding place. She will have something to tell us.'

'What sounding place?' Ullanna asked, concerned.

'The king's hall. Make a circle. Tell all present to maintain absolute silence until the frenzy takes her. Poor girl. Poor girl. I should have seen it coming.'

And this is exactly what was done. Twenty men and women made a circle in the royal lodge, seated on hard benches. In the lower parts of the room others, Jason included, sat cross-legged and curious. A fire blazed some way away from us, but torches gave a clearer light, a shadowy light, picking out the gold and bronze of the buckles and brooches of the men present, and the brightness of colour in the hair and on the faces and arms of the women.

When Munda came into the hall she was feral. She flung herself down on the hard floor, scratched at the surface, her head waving from side to side, her copper locks glinting. She was murmuring words, but in a slurred way. I was not alone in the room in discerning the endlessly repeated statement: I hide nothing.

That Munda was already inside the ageless cloak of *imbas forasnai* was obvious—to me at least; the glow was there, that glimmering of the skin, the shimmering aura that covered her from head to foot; her eyes were empty, depthless. What was she seeing? Her tongue flicked between her lips, tasting the air of future worlds.

Suddenly she was calm. She rose to her feet, facing her father, hands held up before her at chest height, palms out, fingers spread. She was trembling like a fledgling thrush, dropped from its nest.

'I am Munda. Daughter of the king. Sister of the king-to-be. I hide nothing. Listen to me, and despair at your actions.'

In her child's voice, sometimes strong, she said:

'I see a lost man, a twisted man,
A lordly man.
His eyes are the colour of hazel,
He is lean of limb, easy on the eye, dark hair curls to his
shoulders,
his laughter a delight.
His belt is stained with crimson.
His sword is a scythe, reaping. There is no meaning in his killing.
Bronze is thirsty, as strong as iron in the warped man's grasp.
This man means doom for two of you,
Two whom I see now.
I hide nothing.

'His stronghold is a green place,
A place of verdant stone, vibrant, shining.
A vast sea crashes against the shore.
A host is camped there, blood-blinded,
Siege-wearied, year-lost, men-lost.
Your ship beached among them!
This encounter means doom for two of you, one a woman.
I hide nothing!
I can hide *nothing*!

'Islands like bright jewels float in the ocean.
They lead the way to the crooked king,
On the Island of the Three Brothers.
I see a father-calling place, hidden in the stronghold,
A man and a boy in each other's arms,
Tears and laughter, snakes and dreams.
And the rest is void.'

As she finished speaking, the girl doubled up in apparent
pain, falling to the ground, thrashing wildly, her open mouth
flecked with foam, though no sound emerged from her. Rianata
and Manandoun held her limbs until the seizure eased. Munda
was suddenly aware of her surroundings again, sitting up and
tugging at her long hair. She looked at me with the expression
of someone emerging from a deep sleep, wits slowly returning.

'That was a strange dream,' she said.

'We've shared it,' her father answered. 'I was wrong to shut you away. Foresight was struggling from you.'

'I dreamed of wild dogs stripped of their pelts, and a wailing man tormented by spirits. And a boy who has built animals from pieces of bronze. All living on islands.'

Urtha glanced at me, frowning. These facts had not been in the declamation. Rianata intercepted the look. 'She will have dreamed more than Foresight will speak. But what she saw will fade quickly. You must remember every word she says. This girl has *travelled*! She is remarkable, Urtha. It will be years before she has her first rush of blood, but she has had her first rush of vision. She is already in Setlocenia's embrace.'

Setlocenia was a goddess of long life and long sight, Manandoun whispered to me.

'Why are you talking about me like this?' Munda demanded as she stood, looking round at the circle of impressed faces.

'Because you are ahead of your time,' her guardian informed her. She smiled at that and sought out her brother in the circle of seated men, giving him a look that said: so there!

Kymon straightened up on the wooden bench where he sat beside his father, and folded his arms, as if to say: but look where I'm positioned in the ranks!

Siblings competing, children at play, though the cloak of age was slowly spreading around them.

'I am hungry for this,' Munda said.

'Don't be too hungry,' Rianata countered. 'Fine taste comes with discernment; discernment is learned with patience.'

Now Jason rose to his feet in the shadows at the back of the hall. 'If a guest may ask a question?' he said in Urtha's language, broken but clear enough, continuing when Urtha encouraged him to do so: 'The only ship I know in this place is my own ship, Argo, and the girl has seen it beached in the middle of a war. Is there any way I can get a clearer picture? Is there some god, or elemental, or High Woman, who can help her with the detail? I would be grateful for the detail. I am more than prepared to honour a god with sacrifice, or be provoked by an elemental, or obey the whim of a High Woman. I need the detail. Is there a way?'

There was not, and he was told so, Cathabach adding: '*Imbas forasnai* is a glimpse of things to come, and is often misleading.

We are now in *dur viath*: the constantly dividing path. And we must pick our ways carefully. The girl's foreseeing is the likeliest course of events, but if we choose insightfully we can avoid doom.'

Jason looked at me for a moment, as if I might translate the incomprehensible statement. I simply shook my head. There was a moment of old fondness in that glance before he turned away.

The gathering broke up and Munda was taken back to the women's house, but this time as a friend of the lodge, not its prisoner. She had already assumed the wild look I always associated with such precocious prophetesses, her hair taking on new life, her eyes sparkling, her body movements like a bird's, sudden, careful, checking from the corner of her eye. It is from the corner of the eye that glimpses of other worlds can be garnered.

And she was very aware of me.

Cathabach declared that his *geis* was ended. After ten years carrying sword and shield, he would return to the way of oak. There was a question that he had not served the full ten years. He went to the women's lodge and lay with the Thoughtful Woman. When she examined what had come from him, she pronounced that there was indeed wood sap in the fluid.

Now Urtha verified the end of the period of taboo. He accepted the old warrior's sword and blunted its edge, then knelt across its shaft and began to bend it. Cathabach himself completed the bending until the blade was turned back on itself, ready to be cast into the river.

Truth to tell, several of those present knew that Cathabach had been casting off his *geis* for several seasons. It had begun in Greek Land, on the blood-quest after Cunomaglos, during the march on Delphi. When Urtha, wounded, had decided to return to Alba, Cathabach and Manandoun had been distraught at breaking their pledge to Jason, to accompany him in search of his son. Such a promise counted strongly among these men of bulls and iron.

Jason, away chasing after his eldest son, had come to them—I had brought him there, in dream form—and the bond of allegiance was ended. Cathabach had seen the trick; if Manandoun had known of my intervention, he was too wise to have ever mentioned it. But Cathabach had known, which meant that even then he was shedding metal—his warrior's arms—accumulating feather for his cloak, and tree-bark for his mask.

Cathabach now painted his body with woad, a purple dye used to tattoo the skin. He was already much marked. The new symbol was obscure in form, but served to make the connection between air, earth and water, the links severed in his ten year tenure as iron-gripped scourge of his chieftain's enemies.

It was a short ceremony, conducted inside the low wall around the well. Only Urtha, Manandoun and myself were present, apart from the three women who tended to the water and 'Nodons' Cloak', the flower and foliage that was fitted, entwined and draped about the stones around the deep pool.

Naked, Cathabach made an impressive sight, his hard body a whirl and confusion of images in blue and purple, a few in crimson, many of them more fabulous than real. It would have taken me days and nights to read him, longer than it would take to read a similar amount of the carved glyphs on the stones of the sanctuaries in Aegypt. Not just one life was pricked into this man's flesh; an eternity of knowledge was recorded there. And Cathabach knew that it was beyond knowing; his sly look at me, as he saw me examining his skin, suggested that he, too, knew that the pair of us carried the past in or on our bodies.

He would not have disputed that my own secret history, etched on the living bone itself, was more powerful than his; but we were men alike, and what he lacked in depth of charm he certainly had in experience, since he had lived a life to the full whilst I had kept full life at arm's length.

'How many times have you seen a little ritual like this?' he asked me sourly, noticing the way I stared at him. He was assuming I was cynical of this passing rite in a passing year in the passing of time and people.

But I answered him quite truthfully. 'Many times. But only occasionally when it has a meaning that is profound.'

He reached to the metal pail, with its water from the pool, and splashed his face and back, holding his wet hands before him, examining the contours of his palms.

'This well is profound,' he said. 'And it is ageless, endless. It reminds me of you. And of kings. Urtha is the moon that waxes this month. Next month, another moon. You are the morning and evening star that follows in its gleam. I think, Merlin, that you will be the last man alive to drink from this well. In the meantime: be a friend to the kings who follow Urtha.'

Now there was a solemn chant as Cathabach rekindled the life in each picture on his skin, made the count of nineteen by cutting the nineteen lines symbolising the phases of the moon, then dropped a short green tunic over his torso before wrapping a black cloak with rust-red embroidered edges around his shoulders, pinning it at the heart with a eagle's-head brooch of silver and amber. He used shears to cut his long, greying locks to a finger's length that could be limed and stiffened.

He shaved the beard from his face then left the fortress to spend a day and a night in one of the groves by the winding river. He carried a sack of dead birds with him. In his seclusion he would stitch the feathers of eagle, blackbird, lark and crane into the cloak. The feathers of the crane were the most potent. They would ensure the constant protection of Guranos, stalking god of water, land and air. After this he would be able to eat crane flesh, forbidden to all but druids.

Inside the orchard, the old argonauts were restless and unhappy. Word of Munda's startling prophecy had reached them—how, I wondered—and they were disturbed at the thought of 'doom' taking them before their kolossoi could be returned. Atalanta in particular was agitated. 'Is it true? Is it true?' she asked, her gaze gaunt and beautiful as she searched mine for an answer.

My reply—that nothing was certain—confused her. It took a moment to realise her question was about Ullanna, not the prediction of a woman's death. Was it true that a descendant of hers was in Taurovinda?

I told her the truth. I also indicated the immense span of time and generations that separated the two women, the two hunters, ghost and echo.

Atalanta shivered. Tisaminas stood close by, his look at me one of warning. I wondered if his concern was that Atalanta, should she meet her distant kin, might take a memory of that meeting back to her life and her family, if her kolossoi was found and this nightmare extraction from Time was ended.

Instinct suggested that the living Atalanta, her spirit stolen, her life in suspension, would awake as if from a dream; a strange dream, of a woman from an age too far ahead to imagine, perhaps. It would be comforting, half real, more a delight than a burden.

I would arrange the meeting. I would ensure it was kept private. It would be important for Ullanna not to say too much about the history she knew. There is a dark and uncontrollable sorcery in such meetings across Time, for those who are not equipped to control it.

CHAPTER EIGHTEEN

—

Persuasion

It was Cathabach who came to me to consult on the nature of Ghostland, though I knew he represented Urtha. I had overheard several quiet discussions between the king and his retinue on the subject of the Otherworld's unprecedented and vigorous attempts at conquest. It made no sense to the men of Taurovinda, to whom the Otherworld was the place of ultimate contentment, not a realm that was restless to the point of wishing to extend its boundaries.

'If they raid for our cattle,' I heard Morvodugnos say, 'I'll know that nothing I was taught in my foster home was true, since the bull meat in Ghostland is supposed to be equally tender from shoulder cut to rump, and requires only a hot word to cook it. Our cattle would not impress.'

'If they raid for our pigs,' Drendas agreed, 'I'll doubt all my beliefs and find another land to die in, since the pigs in the Land of the Shadows of Heroes shed their plump hams when pursued, only to grow new ones, milkier and sweeter than before. Our pigs would not impress.'

'They are not raiding for bullocks, swine or horses,' Manandoun pointed out, 'since we have no stock to boast about. They are raiding for the land itself—for this high ground in particular.'

'We must take the fight to them,' Urtha said thoughtfully. 'To wait for them to attack again would suggest we are weak, and we can't have that.'

'We *are* weak,' Manandoun reminded the king, but Urtha rapped his sheathed sword on the round shield beside him.

'An old ship and a handful of vagabonds sent that enemy scurrying back to their tombs,' he continued. 'We need to know why, when they are so numerous, an old Greekland goat can scare them as a full-faced moon rouses fear in hounds.'

The old Greekland goat was not present at this council.

Manandoun's voice was calm and firm. 'You are the warchief of this citadel, and High King of the seven clans who pay you tribute. And so far you have always listened carefully to my advice.'

'I'm listening now,' Urtha agreed, 'though I know you disapprove of my proposal.'

'Good. That you're listening. Because what you propose is madness. Your own experience tells us that a man can enter the hinterland on the other side of the Winding One. But no man alive can enter the land of the Dead and Unborn. If it had ever been done, a bard somewhere would be drunk on ale and fat to bursting with boar flesh on the story!'

'There may be reasons why no one has ever told the story. There may be a taboo on such accounts. Is that it? Or do you have more advice for me?'

'More. Even if you enter the Otherworld, as we know from Merlin's experience, the days and seasons run differently there. You might succeed in returning only to the future ruin of this fortress.'

Urtha pondered the idea. 'That may explain why there are no stories of men returning from an adventure among the Heroes. They are still waiting to come back and tell the tale.'

'An excellent point, Lord Urtha, profoundly made. To take a host of men to Ghostland would be to defy the gods to whom we pay tribute; and a senseless act into the bargain.'

'Nevertheless, if I can find a way to do it, that is what I shall do. The fight to the enemy! I have an instinct for strategy, Manandoun, mostly learned from the Greeklanders.'

Manandoun laughed in amazement, though there was a sour tone to his humour. 'Your words are the words of a man who will certainly be remembered for his deeds.'

'To be remembered for courageous deeds is one of the Five Delights for our Children.'

'The word "foolhardy" was the one I had in mind.'

Cathabach called me to the orchard. He had constructed a simple bower in a circle of fruit trees, a thatch-covered sleeping area with a low bench on each side. We sat opposite each other in the gloom, his speckled cloak spread between us. Furtive movement around us suggested the restless prowling of the resurrected argonauts, perhaps listening. In any case, Cathabach was uneasy and irritated with his unwelcome guests. He had protected himself with iron bracelets on his arms and a necklace of iron nails that hung below the fine torc of woven gold that gripped his throat.

'Urtha wishes to attack those in Ghostland who ruined his fortress. The idea is unfeasible. Manandoun and myself will persuade him of the fact. But who among us *might* enter the Otherworld? To know our limitations is essential; to know our power over the Dead would be an advantage. The Old Divide is not as strong as it was.'

The druid's comment was made with a meaningful look at me. He had come close to grasping one of the peculiarities of Taurovinda, I suspected; perhaps *the* peculiarity.

'Not as strong as it was—when?' I prompted.

'When the stronghold was built. When the Winding One was deeper, wider, impossible to ford, by horse, by foot, by the shining chariot of the harsh god Llew, even if driven by his reckless sons.'

He had sensed the cause, but misread the signs. All his life the signs had been there to see, to question, to suggest the answer. Nantosuelta was indeed the reason for the weakness of the Old Divide, but greater gods than Cathabach's had had a hand in the plot. Shaping had happened: the shaping of a land. I would show him what he had missed.

I led him to the river, among the evergroves. I pointed out that the ceremonial way was slightly dipped, hollowed out in the plain. Searching in the earth I pulled up rounded stones, not slingshot—water-rolled. We walked east along the nearer bank until the woods crowded to the water, stretching inland. A short distance further and the bank became shallow, wide, indented: I plunged into the gloom, following a wide depression, rock-strewn, its edges a tangle of the roots of willow and hazel. The place was damp—occasionally there were sluggish pools of water, insect-ridden, ferny, greened with slime. It was humid here. The hollow path wound through the forest, and suddenly widened into a glade of white willow, tanglethorn and trembling, silvery aspen. Two huge rocks rose on either side, mossy, green and glimmering in the sparse sunlight.

Cathabach stared at them in amazement. When the light intensified, casting shadows, the impression of a three-faced head could be seen on each rock, though fronds of ferns grew from the eyes like eerie emanations.

'I know this place!' the druid breathed. 'This is the Ford of the Single Leap. It is legendary. It was lost in the far past, stolen by the god Brugos, guardian of deep water crossings, whose challenge to leap from rock to rock across the river was accepted by the youth Peradayne. Peradayne had been born lame. He used a long spear to propel himself across, and since Brugos couldn't punish him for winning the challenge, he hid the ford for ever, denying Peradayne the chance to leap back.'

'This *is* that ford,' I confirmed.

Cathabach shook his head, though there was a look of wonder and comprehension in his gaze. 'The Ford of the Single Leap separated the realm of kings from the Otherworld. These rocks were either side of the Winding One. This is an old river course. I see it, now. Where we entered the forest along this path, a spring sometimes rises, in very dry summers. The place is called "The Dry Woman's Sudden Rush".'

'Then you understand the significance of Taurovinda.'

'Yes,' Cathabach said solemnly, laying his cloak of feathers on the thorny ground above the dead river. 'It was once a part of the Realm of the Shadows of Heroes. Perhaps the very stronghold from which they watched the passing of seasons in the world of the living. There is a story about that place as well. "The Hill of Cloud and Air". It was sometimes seen, sometimes invisible, searched for, never found. The strangeness of the tale, however, is that the champions who seek the vanished hill are adventurers from Ghostland, and their terrible and tragic stories come to us through the dreams of visionaries such as Urtha's daughter.'

There is a country at the east of the world, a place of hills and deserts, rocky oases and briefly flowering fields, where rivers change their course in the span of two winters. They move like snakes, following favoured routes through the shifting land. The same river can flow through five or six different beds, but only ever one at a time—the rest are infertile and dry. No one can explain the reason for this fickle behaviour. On those rivers' whims, men who should have died have lived, and families that have settled to farm have died.

Rivers in Alba were never so capricious, and Cathabach's understanding of the force of change was all the more remarkable. But he had a pragmatic point to make.

'Why now? Why after all these generations does Ghostland attack us now? Taurovinda was a hill before it was a citadel, but it was a hill in the world of warriors and priests. Ghostland has waited a long time since Nantosuelta cut off its eastern territory.' Cathabach tied his cloak around his shoulders and gathered several rocks, mosses and small flowers from the Dry Woman's bed. 'But Urtha will not be able to penetrate beyond the hinterland. His notion is still flawed.'

We left the dank woodland before discussing Urtha's determination to take the challenge into the Realm of the Shadow Heroes further, in the comfort of a shady glade at Nantosuelta's edge.

The land as far as the Plain of MaegCatha served as a form of hinterland for the Dead and the Unborn, explaining their ability to enter it. On both sides of Nantosuelta, where she formed the boundary between the two worlds, they were vulnerable to iron blade, arrow and spear. Their second death would despatch them straight to Ifuren, an underworld of icy lakes and dull gloom, a grim extension of the world where I had found Aylamunda attached to the protecting Bull which journeyed down below, guarding such hapless spirits as Urtha's wife. No such beast-helpers wandered through Ifuren, however.

As for 'mortal' entry into the Land of the Shadows of Heroes, I was certain that of the present inhabitants of Taurovinda, only a few—those estranged from Time itself—could safely make the journey, though they too would be vulnerable to *dismurthon* (second death) once across the Old Divide. Thus: an expedition could be mounted with Jason and his six blighted comrades; Rubobostes was less mortal than he seemed, far more 'god-favoured'; and Niiv was so drenched with enchantment that I had no fears for her own successful passage—inwards, at least. Munda's gushing prophecy gnawed slightly: doom for two of you, one a woman.

I could go, and certainly would, even without Argo. My help would be needed in locating the kolossoi of the ill-used Greeklanders.

The two sons of Llew, Conan and Gwyrion, would have been useful, but they had stolen one too many of their father and his cousin's chariots.

Ten was not enough to take the battle to the enemy. Urtha would need the old ship. Argo might wrap her wooden walls around a few mortal men-of-feats, but her protective powers were surely limited. She was tired. Essentially, Manandoun was right: Urtha's feverish enthusiasm was a child's whistle being shrilled in the wind.

Again I descended through the well, again to the amusement of the three women who supervised its decoration and ritual.

I found Argo in a winter mood, silent and frosty. I told her of my discussion with Cathabach, of Urtha's dangerous proposal to make a raid into Ghostland, an impossible act almost certainly unless he had greater help than I could give him. I asked her if she would consider making one last journey.

Such a journey would be madness, she replied. And she was tired of Jason. It was time for her to move on to other seas, other captains. For the moment, she would spend time where she was. And she urged me not to enter Ghostland.

'I am more familiar with such places than you, despite your great age and long journey. Your path has been defined with great precision. Mine has not. You will possibly lose your skills, your powers, in that place. Be warned.'

I pleaded again, but she didn't answer. I couldn't even see Mielikki. Argo's voice was a cold whisper.

Then she said, 'This is the second time you have come down to me; and the second time there is a disturbance on the land above. Go up again.'

The day was well advanced when I returned to the surface, and I found a very different mood. The three women at the well were shrouded in green, kneeling in a neat, sorrowful row on one side of the shaft. Facing them, also kneeling, was Cathabach, wearing a cloak of black fur into which hundreds of yellow and white feathers had been stitched. His face was black with dye. His body was naked below the cloak.

One of the women raised a hand towards me, warning me off. She moved her fingers dismissively: go away. Leave us alone.

What was happening?

A group of riders thundered past the well, cloaks flying. One of them spotted me, wheeled round and shouted, 'So there you are! Urtha is looking for you. The girl has been taken by those wolves!'

'What wolves?' I shouted.

'Those who are the likes of you,' he answered suspiciously.

When I found Urtha he was in distress, hair lank, face striped with clay, breast bared below the torn shirt. Ullanna, his comforting partner, had imitated the grieving ritual of the Celts and was similarly dishevelled, though less obviously in pain. Manandoun, armoured, stood behind them, watching carefully.

'Why is it that every time I need you I can't find you?' the chieftain thundered at me. Rubobostes held him back, gently and persuasively, otherwise—from the red heat in the man's eyes—Urtha, I believe, would have struck me. He shrugged the big Dacian away, shook his head, gathered his garment about his flesh.

'Go after her, Merlin. For the Good God's sake, go after her. They were dead after all, those two Wolf-heads, and they've gone like the wolves they are.'

How long had I been below the hill?

I asked quickly, 'When did this happen?'

'Too long ago! They outran us. Wolves are swifter than horses, but you can summon the wolf and catch them. I know you can.'

'This is a device to have us desert the fort,' Manandoun urged, but his words were ignored.

A second group of riders came galloping in through the Riannon Gate, weary and dishevelled, one of them waving his hand as if to say: no luck.

I saw Niiv lurking in the shadows; she was beckoning to me. Urtha raged at me, but his words faded from my consciousness. Rubobostes was saying something, and Ullanna watched me through hooded eyes, her lips moving, her words lost to me. I looked back at the tiresome girl.

What do you want?

I can help. I know what happened. I looked into their heads.

Of course you did, I thought with no satisfaction; too curious by half, Niiv had sacrificed more days of her life to try to understand a situation that still, as far as I was concerned, was confusing. I had the beginning of an idea of what had occurred, but the girl was now useful.

Urtha was outraged as I walked away, but I sent calming signals. I couldn't see Jason or his other argonauts. This eastern sector of Taurovinda was seething with Urtha's anxiety at the loss of his daughter.

I stepped into the shadow of a house where Niiv sat, knees drawn up, hands clasped around them, eyes bright below the dark, dyed hair.

'They were Urtha's own druids,' she said. 'They look very different, now. Do you remember when Urtha was searching for the shield of future time? In my own land?'

I remembered very clearly: a frozen lake, a snow-shrouded land, winter woods and endless night. We had huddled in an inadequate tent, Urtha, his *uthiin* retinue, and his two druids, the men who had sent him on the quest for the shield of Diadara on the basis of their interpretation of his dreams. The shield in which he could see the future of his kingdom.

Fed up and furious with them, persuaded that the shield, if it existed at all, was hidden elsewhere, he had banished them to the wolf-haunted forest. He had not expected them to survive the journey home. The land was fierce, their talents as sooth-sayers and priests severely limited.

He had reckoned without *fortuna*, as capricious a spirit of men's fates as any of the Three of Awful Boding. The elemental often attached itself to famous men on distant quests. In Greek Land it was known as *tukhea*, 'the chancer', and could well have been haunting those woods around the lake since Jason had sunk there, with Argo wrapped around him as his coffin. *Tukhea* may have been aboard as well.

That, in fact, made a great deal of sense: a lonely elemental, displaced from its own land, at long last finding not just the vehicle of its escape from the forest—there would have been many opportunities to attach to the human traffic through the area—but the correct occasion: abandoned men, lost men, men in a precarious situation; men who would now need to take their chances!

Niiv was glowing, her mouth glistening, her hands shaking as she reached to take me by the arms and tell me what she'd seen, a child bursting with pride at knowing a terrible truth, eager to gossip.

'They walked south for days, after Urtha sent them from his quarters by the lake. Their fingers turned black with the cold. Their skin cracked like thin sheets of ice. They cursed Urtha and Cathabach, scratched the marks of their *red doom*—that's what they called it, *red doom*—scratched those strange signs on trees and rocks, and drew them in snow fields. They were *very* angry. But the snow was being disturbed by the tracks of someone else, they could see this. They were being followed. They offered . . . bits . . . ' she grimaced as she recalled what she'd seen, 'bits of their bodies. For help. It was horrible to watch. But the spirit that followed them helped them home. It showed them a way under!'

'What way under?' I asked her impulsively.

'I don't know what you call them, but you used one once to reach Greek Land. Ways through the underworld. Ways through to the Otherworld. Ways to pass across lands without being seen. Ways home.'

She had a triumphant look about her. I could almost hear the cauldron bubbling, the words screaming to be heard: you and I together, Merlin. What a force we'd be. Your age and knowledge, my youthfulness and energy, a couple in love who could shape mountains: make forests flow around us like cloaks of green.

Her triumphant look, however, was because though she had

told me the truth, she had disguised it, and did not expect me to guess it. She was teasing me again. But it was so apparent, now.

The druids, guided by the elemental *fortuna*, had found their way home, but risen to the earth again in Ghostland! And that would have been a very difficult circumstance for them, to say the least.

'So they came up in the Otherworld,' I mused.

She frowned, outraged. 'I didn't say that! Why do you say that? Have you been looking inside me? You always tell me not to *do* that!'

I was surprised by her outburst. 'You mentioned the Otherworld. Ghostland is close. *Fortuna* is a tricky elemental. Just the sort of trick it would play.'

'*Fortuna*?'

'*Tukhea*, then.'

'How do you *know*?' she wailed, eyes wide, angry. 'You've been looking inside me!'

'It had to be a chancer from Greek Land. An elemental. There are five I know of from Greek Land but only *tukhea* sits on a man's shoulders and walks with him through the world. The others just lurk, waiting in caves and woods and such. They dish out luck the way these High Kings dish out slices of a cooked pig's haunch.'

'Reluctantly.'

'Not at all. Randomly, perhaps. But also when appropriate.'

'You know too much.'

'I'm old. And experienced. Your own words.'

'I never *used* such words,' she objected furiously and correctly; I had only been imagining the workings of her mind.

But she added, 'It's true, though. You know too much. There are no surprises left for you.'

'There certainly are. You were a surprise.'

'Yes,' she said cannily. 'Because I was born as something different from what I became. Yes. I can understand why you are cautious of me.

'Mielikki, your guardian, would not be pleased to hear you revealing your birthmarks quite so easily.'

'My birthmarks?' Your secrets.

'No. I won't. You have secrets from me; I'll have secrets from you.'

'That's another birthmark. Shown to me as easily as if you'd lifted your skirts and beckoned to me. Say nothing, Niiv. Be like Manandoun. Wise counsel is best kept with open eyes and closed mouth.'

'That sort of saying is as old as the hills.'

'Older than mountains. And I don't argue with mountains when I'm in a hurry to go somewhere.'

'So you don't want to know what happened here.'

'I do. I do very much. What you now know affects others. Niiv: you need to protect yourself from yourself, but if you can't help prying, then there's no point in hiding the truth.'

She crossed her arms, staring at me coldly, rocking back on her haunches; thinking hard. 'Is that one of your own birthmarks?'

'Yes it is,' I lied. 'A little given for a little taken.'

'You think I'm naive. You think I have no judgement.'

'I think you're naive. I think your judgement is forming. Slowly. I think you're dangerous. That last *is* a birthmark. Now: what happened to Munda? Quickly. I have to find a wolf and go out hunting, when all I really want to do is sit and think.'

Though the Wolf-heads had transformed into the fleet animals that had become their *fedishi* (chosen shapes) after death, since they were carrying Munda, flesh and crimson blood, white bone and grey Pallor, they could not travel fast though they had certainly travelled faster than the hounds that Urtha had set on their trail.

I had a good chance of intercepting them before they reached Nantosuelta; they would, I imagined, make for the Ford of the Miscast Spear; that of the Last Farewell would deny them a crossing. A third ford in the area, that of the famous Overwhelming Gift, would also have denied them, since they were anything but heroes.

I summoned the wolf again; and armed with what Niiv had gone on to tell me, I ran in the hope of rescuing Munda.

I caught up with them in the forest, not far from the river, but far enough to force them to confront the chase, turning to stand their ground. The girl was huddled below the broken bough of an oak. The two wolves slavered and snarled at me, legs braced apart, forming a defensive line on the far side of the small, overgrown glade. I challenged them at once: *I should have recognised you earlier. It's to my shame that I didn't. Give the girl back. Urtha has suffered enough losses.*

They bayed; laughter. *He sent us on a long trail in a wilderness of ice. It's not in our hearts to forgive him for that.*

Then attack the man, not his daughter.

If we were attacking the man, what better way to do it than to steal his child?

You made the long journey home. You must have learned a great deal.

We made a long journey, the wolf replied. *It did not bring us home.*

I was about to continue the argument when, to my astonishment, Munda made a gesture of impatience, throwing a large stone at one of the wolves. For a heartbeat I thought she was urging me to stop talking and reach for her. But her words gave the lie to that naive judgement.

'Hurry,' she shouted. 'Get rid of it! We have to cross before my father gets here and catches us. Hurry!'

The Wolf-heads drew back a little as I lurched forward, shocked by the girl's words. I realised then that she hadn't recognised me. Of course! From her point of view her two companions were merely being stalked by a wolf.

One of them said to me, *Little Dreamer wants to play with her again. Her brother doesn't want to play. He sent us to fetch her, and the girl is travelling willingly. She will come to no harm, not for the rest of her life; a very long life in the palace that Little Dreamer has built.*

Again, there was a sense of wry humour in the words.

A moment later one of the Wolf-heads leapt at me, and in the moment of the struggle, as we thrashed in the long grass, the other had bolted to the girl, who flung herself on its back, hair flying, clinging to the unkempt but sleek animal as it loped away, and they were gone.

When I travel as the wolf, or any other animal, I am a shadow inside the beast; I had claws and jaws and found the strength to rip my assailant. The *fedishi* faded as he died; he was the older of the two druids, as I'd suspected, but he gave me a look through his beard that suggested he was at peace. Then I realised that he had bitten through a ligament in my arm. The look on his maw was one of triumph. In the fury of the encounter I had not felt the wound.

Munda was now beyond me. In a short while she would cross back to Ghostland, believing that she belonged there and was welcome there, a dreadful misapprehension.

How was I to break this news to Urtha? I thought long and hard as I limped home, shedding the wolf when I came to the marshes, west of the dark hill, tying a strip of the softened bark of a white willow, around the wounded arm.

What could I now say to the man?

Urtha was waiting for me in his hall, in a grim but less distressed mood. Kymon and Ullanna were doing their best to comfort him; his retinue sat around the room in half battle-harness, talking quietly.

He could tell at once that I'd failed. He'd also sent his best riders on the fastest horses, but clearly, he surmised, their chase would also be fruitless.

I told him truthfully what the Wolf-heads had told me, that she was going to play with the boy, Little Dreamer; that she would be safe. I didn't mention her strange words: hurry, before my father catches us. I didn't believe it was the girl talking. I judged that to repeat the instruction would only hurt the chieftain more.

'And what of Argo? Will she help us cross? Cathabach has told me you've been to ask her.'

'She's thinking about it,' I replied carefully. 'She's a weary ship, and weary of Jason.'

He said nothing for a moment, then sighed, resolve hardening. 'Well, then we must find another way to get into Ghostland.'

One of the women from the well was waiting outside the king's enclosure, cloak wrapped around her, hood drawn over her head. Cathabach wanted to see me urgently, she told me. He was in the orchard.

I found the man waiting in his cloak of feathers, standing in his arched and thatched bower at the heart of the *nemeton*. The argonauts who sheltered in the apple grove were not in sight, already in dusk's shadows.

I told him what Munda had revealed to me. He seemed surprised but not shocked. He asked me what Argo's response had
been to my request. My answer made him sigh.

'It would have been hard enough persuading Urtha out of his
foolish idea of a raid into Ghostland. Now it will be impossible.
But for Urtha it *will* be impossible . . . '

His hesitation suggested he required a response and I agreed
with him. 'Impossible for him unless he has protection.'

'But not impossible for him to go there?'

'As we discussed, it's not the getting in, it's the getting out.'

Cathabach touched fingers to the new marks on his chest and
cheeks. 'I've prepared myself for his loss. When the king dies,
his son rules, unless challenged. When a king is lost, the Speakers for Past, Land and Kings must guard the land for seven
years. I am the new Speaker for Kings. The older man who had
that honour has now retired from the ritual, and will be sent into
his shaft in this orchard in due course. Not yet.'

Why was Cathabach telling me this? He got to the point. 'A
land without a king is a land that is vulnerable, as you have seen
all too clearly. That cannot happen again. Merlin . . . I have
seen you summon the shade of a man from his lake burial of
generations ago. And if such things as kolossoi exist, temporary
life, out of Time, then is it possible that you could reach into the
depths of your enchantment and find a way of drawing such a
spirit from Urtha: sending it in his place, guarding it, protecting
it, bringing it home to be with the king again? Is there any way
at all that Urtha can be sheltered with charm, with shadows,
with the veneer of a ghost, to allow him to undertake the journey there and back in safety?'

Again he touched the cuts on his body, the dye still soaking
into his skin. His gaze at me was strong and steady. 'If there is
to be a price to pay for it, a life to pay for it, then again it is the
Speaker for Kings who must pay that price. The older man can
be reinstated, to pass on the list and the achievements of our
ancestors.'

I was impressed by the man's courage. He had been Urtha's
closest friend in the retinue of the *uthiin*, the elite knights who
rode with the king; he would always have given his life before
the king's in battle. Most men would. This more calculated
offer of sacrifice was a rare quality in my experience. Catha-

bach had clearly arranged the hierarchical structure of Tauro
vinda to protect both figurehead and memory.

'There are two ways in which it might be done,' I told him
'Neither would call for your death. One of them would be a
demanding piece of sorcery on my part. And I will willingly
practise it. I have a great reserve of energy; it's time I put it to
use.'

I was almost as surprised by my words as Cathabach wa
pleased with them. I had spent millennia guarding against the
wasting consequence of using my skills. The next few genera
tions would be very different for me, though that was just the
shadow of a self-prophecy at the time.

'And the other way?' the Speaker for Kings asked.

'She's thinking about it. Argo. She's tired, but she might be
prepared to give protection to a king. Lets wait and see what she
does.'

As I left the orchard I heard a brief burst of laughter, two women
sharing a moment of amusement. Sitting cross-legged, close to
the wicker wall of the sanctuary, Atalanta and Ullanna were
examining Ullanna's bow and arrows. Each wore a heavy cloak
but the hoods were thrown back and they had tied their hair iden
tically in a loose braid hanging from the right. Small clay cups
and a half-emptied pigskin of fermented milk lay between them
Their conversation was soft, a struggle to understand each other
dialect, but with much miming, much humour.

When they realised I was watching them they glanced at me
and each, with affection, blew me a kiss. But they were making
a point: go away, this is private.

I wonder what they talked about? Ullanna would have
learned a great deal, the detail in the legends she had been
taught as a child. Atalanta, no doubt, was being fed the stuff of
dreams.

Ullanna was very subdued and very sad when I next saw her
returning to the enclosure around the king's house. But it was a
dreamy sort of sadness, as if she knew she had been granted a
very special gift an enriching and wonderful gift, but the time
for gifts was now finished.

PART FOUR

Argo in the Otherworld

One equal temper of heroic hearts,
Made weak by time and fate, but strong in will
To strive, to seek, to find, and not to yield.

from *Ulysses*, by Alfred Lord Tennyson

CHAPTER NINETEEN

——

Shadows of Heroes

I was woken by the touch of winter on my nose. The air was frigid. The dew on the ground had crystallised; breath frosted. A winter's dawn painted the sky with star-speckled magenta. Horses whickered and dogs shivered. Across the town, people rose into the chill, astonished at this intrusion of ice into the summer.

The whole of the ceremonial way from hill to river was crusted with white. The evergroves were in their winter wrap. Nantosuelta had frozen upstream for as far as the eye could see.

Sitting aslant on the frozen surface was Argo; she leaned, ready to be pulled upright. The eye on her bow seemed to watch, from the distance, with amusement.

Rubobostes was amazed. Urtha was swearing, tightly wrapped in his heavy cloak as he stared at this winter landscape in astonishment. He was less distressed, now; more angry and determined. But Jason laughed.

'She says yes,' he murmured, wiping the gathering ice from his long beard.

'Who says yes?' Urtha demanded.

'The old ship. She's agreed. Don't you think so . . . Antiokus?'

I acknowledged his words. Jason added, 'You must have spoken to her well. But she has decided to make us work for our journey, Lord Urtha. She won't make it easy for us.'

'Your ship has done this? Turned warmth into winter?'

Jason acknowledged the king's complaint. 'You'll work for your battle, it seems.'

'We'll have battle enough without your ship testing us,' the Celt complained. Jason laughed so loudly it came close to insulting Urtha. The two men glared at each other, then lowered their lances. As the old Greeklander turned away, I swear he commented unflatteringly on the trustworthiness of goddesses.

I may be wrong.

It was of no importance to me. I was delighted to see my friend back from her much-needed rest. I knew exactly what Argo was doing: exhausted, she had none the less consented to a further adventure; but homesick, she had created the landscape that most comforted her. Argo, Urtha needed to be reminded, was not at this time the ship of the warm, wine-dark sea of Aegaea. Mielikki, the Forest Lady of the North, now shaped her taste, and snow and ice, and the menace of *voytazi*, were what excited her. Elemental *voytazi*, indeed, struck at the ice on the river, causing it to buckle and crack, the mean, pike-faced heads chattering and grinning as these fish creatures, summoned from the deep, came to sniff the air of their temporary domain.

They could consume a man in moments. More impressively, they could hold a man below the water for a year, keeping him alive until they were ready to feed on his flesh.

To each goddess her own helpers; her own hounds; her own terrors. I had thought that beautiful, gentle Hera, daughter of Cronos, had had only benign helpers when she had guided Argo and Jason to the Golden Fleece; but her terrors, when she revealed them, were appalling, though no account of them has survived in the records of that famous voyage, save for my own.

What we needed now was Ruvio, the Dacian's magisterial horse. Rubobostes and a small retinue rode west to find the creature, and later in the day returned, following the galloping stallion, who raced three times around the fort before coming to a head-shuddering stop before the outer gates. Five mares had galloped with him, red flanks shining, black manes flowing. Their breath frosted voluminously in the winter air. They were Otherworldly by their look, sleek and graceful, all of them pulsing with the beginning of new life, Ruvio's seed at work in their wombs.

'Can we take them too?' Ullanna asked me in a whisper.

'Not on Argo. But I imagine they'll wait for Ruvio at Nantosuelta's ford of farewell. They'll follow us into Ghostland if they can.

'Good,' the Scythian said practically. 'They'll be useful. One more string to our bow.'

I laughed out loud. I liked the expression. It was novel. She often coined pithy images such as this. But her mood darkened when she was told she was to stay behind.

Kymon was stalking the length and breadth of Taurovinda in a deep sulk, his hand resting on his sword, his face more grim than the argonauts in the orchard. He too, was not to accompany his father on the expedition, and he was not happy about the fact. He and Manandoun were to take charge of the fortress, to entertain their guests, show hospitality to strangers and defend against intruders.

The boy was still ashamed of his failure, before his father's return. Anxiety and irritation fought for control in the youthful, flushed features. He wanted the chase, but Urtha was adamant.

'I trust no men but you and Manandoun to guard the hill. You are both experienced men. Manandoun has insight and resolve. You have vision and determination. If you stay here, then this is one old man who'll not worry about his home.'

'Very well,' Kymon agreed. 'But next time there is an expedition, I expect to be taken along.'

'I agree,' said Urtha. 'Now go and make a plan for defending what will one day be your own citadel.'

Ullanna was to remain as well. This had been negotiated with Argo—she had called me to her—who was prepared, as I'd suggested, to protect the king but no other from the 'mortal' world.

Cathabach was required to stay behind for the same reasons, though his position, now, would in any event have required him to do so.

Argo had further promised, however, that our small crew would be sufficient to search for Munda and Jason's son.

Niiv had finished instructing on the method of turning Argo

into a sledge. The ship sat upright on the ice, braced by the thin trunks of trees felled for the purpose, draped with the harnessing that would be attached to Ruvio. Argo seemed placid, almost amused. Ice formed on her hull, stretching stiffly from the shields below her rails.

She seemed to call: come on then, let's get this done with.

Supernatural though she was, she perhaps had no idea of the strange journey that awaited her, awaited us all.

Supplies were loaded aboard; Cathabach marvelled at the edge of the winter world that Argo had created. 'If she decides to stop playing the game and the ice melts, the ship will founder with all that strapped-on wood.'

His caution was understandable, but Niiv grinned and reassured him. 'She will make us take the strain for a while. Her intention is not to drown us. You can watch our progress in that well of deep water.'

Some time in the next day or so I was summoned to take my place on the ship. Ruvio stamped and snorted. The frozen river stretched out of sight ahead of us. Shivering men and women sat on the benches, cloak-wrapped and gaunt. Farewells had been brief and few—but there had been tears in Ullanna's eyes on two different occasions. Atalanta was very aware of the sky and the woodland, and the steep-sided fortress. She was absorbing the sights and sounds of this world, remembering for her dreams, with the hunger of a starving child.

Rubobostes, who was used to taking command of the steering oar at the stern, now stood at the bridle of his wonderful horse. At the signal from Jason he urged the beast forward, and after a few moments of straining and heavy breathing the animal got the measure of Argo; the ship lurched, skidded slightly, then began to slide. Niiv cheered loudly. On the shore, the gathered horsemen followed us for a while, before striking off across more amenable terrain, to wait for us at the Ford of the Last Farewell. They would not be able to enter the Otherworld, and they knew it. But Urtha wanted them with him at that point in case the Heroes had learned of the expedition, and had sent their own army to face us.

The river and forest froze ahead of us for as far as the eye could see, melting behind us in an eerie transformation from stark white to lush, drooping green. We were drawn into bleak winter, snow falling constantly, the ice below us creaking and threatening to break. Two arrow flights away, behind us, summer bloomed, waving us goodbye.

Ruvio slipped and struggled as he took the strain, but was soon into his stride, and Argo travelled fast across the ice. When the breeze shifted, Jason order the sail unfurled; it caught the wind, the ship skidded for a moment, and then continued on its journey in the fashion of a chariot racing through water, great sprays of ice and snow slicing into the winter trees that crowded the river, knocking herons from their feet and sending dark birds circling skywards in shock. Mielikki seemed to grin from her position in the stern, enjoying the game.

Ruvio, released from the burden of hauling, galloped beside us, the sweat from his flanks and the breath from his nostrils forming a shimmering, misty cloak around him.

Less than two days later we were approaching the final curve in Nantosuelta before the Ford of the Last Farewell. And at this point, Argo and Mielikki decided that the game was over. Argo was rested; the point had been made (that though she was not always at a captain's beck and call, she would keep a promise). The winter melted away, along with the ice, but slowly, giving the argonauts time to swing over the sides of the ship and untie the wooden rollers that had converted the hull into a sledge. She sank into the river, lurching alarmingly, and Ruvio swam to the shore, released from his harness.

It was an altogether different ship that now glided peacefully and silently round the curving stream, until the tall stones that guarded the ford came into view, and the shallow banks, and the inlet on the far side, with its rocky gully leading into the hinterland.

The stream that flowed through the gully was narrow. I had expected that Argo would wait until nightfall, then make us all fall comatose while she negotiated the impossible waterway with the aid of a little ancient magic. She had done this before, on our way to Greek Land. But I was wrong. She sent Hylas to the place of exiles, on her whispered and private instruction. He returned later, depressed and weary, and took his place silently.

Argo moved on into shallower water, below denser canopy,

dazzled by sunlight, drifting in silence. The argonauts sat quietly at their benches, heads turned to watch the way ahead, all curious as to where Argo would take the turn into the world of the Dead.

After a while I was summoned to Mielikki. Crouched at the threshold of the Spirit of the Ship, she confided: the *kolossoi* are not where I concealed them. Someone has taken them. If they had been there, Hylas would have heard the cries of his own.

We approached the Ford of the Miscast Spear. The structures on each side of the river were in ruins, the bridge that had been spanning the water collapsed into a series of untidy wooden columns. The retreat of the Dead and the Unborn from Taurovinda had been very thorough, it seemed.

Close by, a river flowed into Nantosuelta from the west, pouring sluggishly through high gravel banks, capped with sheer cliffs of thorn-cloaked limestone. There was a small cheer, almost an ironic gesture from the argonauts, as the ship nosed round, leaving the Winding One and encouraging her crew to take up their oars and begin the journey inwards.

To the steady beat of the drum we rowed into an echoing ravine, so narrow at the top that on occasion the branches of the trees at its edge closed off the sky. The water was icy and translucent; below us, sparkling granite boulders formed its bed. Each strike of the oars seemed to reverberate from the sheer rock walls that contained us. Stones slipped and tumbled into the stream. The sun flashed down at us, turning gloom to moments of startling and luxuriant green.

It surprised me that I could react so strongly to this beauty. I had seen such gorges a thousand times before. I was becoming 'human', I suspected. Argo's warning to me was coming true. My strength with charm was diminishing as we entered his Otherworld.

Rubobostes held the oar. I beat the drum. Ruvio nestled in the shallow hold, breathing hard, perhaps missing his harem, now abandoned behind us, since there was no path below these overarching walls.

Niiv stood at the prow, as ever, searching the way ahead. Jason and Urtha, side by side in the stern, each resting an arm on the figurehead of the Northland Lady, were impassive, though the very nature of their statue-like demeanour suggested the anxiety they felt. I watched Urtha carefully. He alone among us might be vulnerable to the warp and shift of time in the Otherworld.

When Argo rounded a bend in the river and began to approach two tall, craggy rocks, rising from the water like jagged shards of bone, Jason screamed the order to *back oar, back oar!* Memory of the clashing rocks, when we had journeyed to Colchis, was vivid. Ships destroyed, smashed to splinters by the restless pounding of the unnatural pinnacles. We had used a dove, at that time, to test whether the rocks were awake or asleep. On this voyage we had no such willing bird, and I could not summon one, even though I tried. This came as no surprise to me, though it was of concern. From the moment we had entered the ravine my abilities in charm had begun to wane.

Now Hylas rose from his bench, casting off his cloak. He had always been a good swimmer. Though his face was grey, he had a bright look to him; he plunged over the side of the ship and swam strongly upstream. When he had passed through the rocks he turned and waved, then drifted back towards us, floating on his back, face to the dappled sky catching the shafting light. He seemed at peace, and for a moment I thought he might have died, rejoicing in a moment of freedom from the curse of life to slip back into his grave. But he suddenly rose in the water, swimming to keep position, his face alarmed. He beckoned us towards him urgently.

Jason shouted at me to sound the strike. The oars rose and dipped; I beat the drum hard and fast and Argo began to plough the river. Everyone aboard, even those not rowing, screamed as the oars were shipped and the vessel raced between the rocks, cracking against one of them, scraping the river bed with a noise like breaking wooden beams, though the granite boulders did not manage to pierce the hull.

A line was thrown for Hylas and he was hauled aboard. The rowers took Argo out of the shallows between the rocks and someone cheered, but was then silent.

Hylas was pointing back the way we had come. Jason was breathing heavily. He was not alone in being able to read the words that had been carved on the smooth face of each of the pinnacles.

'Symbols,' Niiv said unnecessarily. 'There are symbols carved there.'

Deeply and massively engraved, stained with orange lichen, greened with ferny growth from the winter-cracked stone, the two messages, one on each rock, were chiselled in a language that Jason had once spoken: on the right hand stone was the inscription: IT IS NOT AS IT SEEMS. On the left we could read: WHAT WE ARE IN ETERNITY SHAPES OUR LIVES.

When the crew had been informed of the cryptic meaning behind the epigrams, Rubobostes observed, 'This is just a gut feeling, but I suspect that if it's true that things are not as they seem, then we are in for a few tricks.'

'Well done,' Jason replied, and Rubobostes glanced at me with a glowering look that asked: was that sarcasm?

I was more intrigued by the other carving. I was in the company of Six-in-their-Shrouds whose life in eternity was very much shaping their life in the past. But the words meant more than this, I was sure. That they were in Jason's language was highly suggestive; indeed, significant.

As Rubobostes was aware, sometimes a strong feeling nags in the gut.

Atalanta called, 'A storm is coming!'

The sky darkened and the river began to pattern with waves as the wind gusted increasingly strongly from the west. The air chilled and we returned to our stations, taking Argo deeper into Ghostland.

Soon the high ravine dropped away and the river widened, flowing through heavily forested hills. Then the land seemed to dissolve into colourful fields and tight woods, and though rain drummed on the turf, and cloud chased cloud across the greensward, we could see that this was the beginning of a place of idyll. Horses pranced and cantered in small herds, and their manes and flanks were shaved and shaped to designate ownership. Only their owners were absent. As the ship struck onwards we saw, too, the misty heights of citadels and strongholds. Wood smoke, the scents of cooking, the aroma of stews and roasts, wafted past us, but not even Niiv, with her far sight and her tricky nature, could see the homes from which these delights emanated.

We were in Ghostland, and were probably being watched; but there was no reason why we should be able to see the watchers.

We pulled to the shore as a dusk of intense beauty settled on the land; where the sun descended beyond distant peaks, the sky burned, literally burned, flames rising in languid strands from the edge of the disc, tongues of fire, Atalanta called them. They seemed to shed stars, which rose and settled above us.

During the night that followed we heard riders and horns, the baying of hounds and the clash of arms, but could see nothing but the vaguest of shadows, and those only glimpsed from the edge of vision. But at dawn the first of two strange incidents occurred, events that should have signalled the nature of change in the Realm of the Shadows of Heroes.

Rubobostes shook me awake. The argonauts were all rising from their blankets, peering across the creek at the forest edge. 'Something coming this way,' the big man hissed. It was unlike Rubobostes to show fear, but nervous alarm creased every part of his bearded face.

For a moment I heard only the rumble of thunder; but it was not thunder.

A flock of strange deer burst frantically from the woods, led by four stags of great age and size. Forty or fifty of the slender animals, their coats a brilliant scarlet, their rumps turquoise, their feet white, bounded into the water, leaping through the stream towards us, dividing to pass Argo, drawn up on the bank. Gracefully, taking strides that seemed impossibly long, they passed behind us. Other creatures were hot on their tails: foxes the size of hounds, hounds like ponies, and swirling flights of bright-eyed, richly coloured birds, some passing over us so closely that their wing-tips struck us.

This had happened in instants, this sudden burst of fear-filled life. And as the last of the flock—ravens, green-winged and red-beaked—left the woods, so a gleaming maw opened and snapped, catching the tail feathers of a straggler and drawing it back out of sight.

Copper sheen brightened the woodland edge; two narrow eyes blinked from behind shuttered lids; fire flickered briefly from some part of the creature's gigantic body, and metal creaked for a moment as it turned, taking its pitifully small catch back into cover.

'What in the name of all the gods was that?' Jason asked loudly, looking, as usual, in my direction. 'Anyone's gods will do. That was a vision from Hades.'

Urtha said, 'No such creature should be walking Ghostland. The scarlet deer we know about, and the other creatures; we have seen them from the Ford of the Last Farewell. But not the hunter. It belongs elsewhere. It must have strayed here.'

'Yes,' Jason concurred, repeating, 'from Hades.'

'From *someone's* Hades,' I suggested.

If we had been lulled into a sense of calm idyll, as we had rowed, now our skin crawled and our muscles tensed; the stroke was fast, the drum almost unnecessary. Argo slipped to the water and we rowed to the haze-shrouded hills beyond which the sun had descended with such a spectacular display of fire, aware that the air was suddenly fragrant with the smells of the sea.

'An ocean!' Niiv suddenly called from the prow. 'I see islands!'

'An ocean? Here?' Urtha demanded.

As he rose from his bench, the rhythm of the oars was broken and Argo lurched violently. The warlord stumbled to where Niiv lay sprawled in her black cloak, tethered to the rails. He peered into the distance, then noticed the swoop and swirl of seagulls far ahead, their skirling screams just audible. 'We've come too far west,' he shouted. 'This sea leads nowhere; it's the grey void. The islands that grow there are unreachable by boat, everyone knows that for a fact. Even Maeldun, the greatest of the seafarers of antiquity, failed. Only his song came back, and only part of his song at that!'

Jason called to his co-captain. 'Settle down. If that's a void, then what are the mountains we can see? This is an inland ocean. I know all about inland oceans!'

'Those mountains could be clouds!'

'Those mountains are where we're heading,' Jason retorted with authority. 'If they turn out to be clouds, it doesn't matter— we'll be flying on wings of charm before tomorrow's dusk. Don't you agree, Niiv?'

The girl shuddered, but nodded her head. 'We don't want to go there; all my instincts tell me so. But Jason is right. This ocean is a true part of the world within the world. The mountains are at Ocean's End. The other sea, the grey void, lies further west.'

Just as the river had widened, now it narrowed again, between rust-coloured cliffs and shores that were rich with stunted, sharp-leaved oaks and grey-trunked trees with dark fruits that twisted from the ground as if effort had been made to pull them up like weeds and failed, but left them bent and weary.

Jason was at home at once: the gnarly growths were olives; the trees gathered heat and stillness; shimmered in stillness; indeed, the air here was scented with the warmth of southern seas. The more grim of the argonauts among us brightened, recognising the mellow fragrance and sharp tangs of herbs and fruits unknown in the grass-and-greenwood-rich landscape surrounding Taurovinda.

This was the second strangeness pointing the finger at what would be waiting for us. If Jason was aware of it, he kept his own counsel, not even favouring me with a knowing glance, though he must have guessed that I had seen the same signs.

We had rowed upstream for several days; now the current began to pull us and the oars were employed to guide us carefully, to slow us where the river rushed into the ocean. Gulls followed in our wake. A school of dolphins decided to chase Argo as she followed her new coast. They breached the surface in chattering delight, playful and inquisitive. They were as black and gleaming as obsidian, with stripes of scarlet and cream on their flanks, the colours of rowan, the 'quickening' tree; their eyes, so watchful and intelligent, were ringed with turquoise and pale green. These were no creatures of the natural world.

Perhaps they thought we were what Ullanna would call 'after-lifers', and on our way to our chosen island—it was their function in the south to accompany the dead in such a way—and when they realised that at least two of our company were trying to harpoon them they broke from their friendly task, still chattering as they dispersed, but angry at the insult, quick to find safer waters.

'It's as well we didn't kill any of them,' Jason shouted. 'To do so would have brought bad luck to us. They are sacred creatures.'

From the corner of my eye I noticed Rubobostes hurriedly cutting a taut line at the stern, afterwards behaving as if nothing had happened.

'Breakers!' came Niiv's cry from the prow. There were rocks here, stretching out like fingers. The sail was hauled up, braced to catch the good breeze, drawing us away from the cliffs, leaning against the gusts and waves, taking us into deeper waters.

Now Jason was in his true element. He knew that we should have followed the line of the shore, but not far from us, visible through the heave and spray of this quickening sea, was a steep-sided island, promisingly green and with the sparkle of white that suggested habitation.

Oar, sail and steering oar all combined to set Argo on a firm course, and in a matter of half a day we had come into the stillness of wind shadow, dropping the sail and drifting quietly in the lee of a promontory, searching for a landing place.

The beach, when we found it, was narrow and sandy, backed by cliffs and covered in footprints. Niiv waded ashore and ran among the tracks, calling out: 'They are all the same. One man running frantically. Mostly in wild circles,' she added.

A stream tumbled from the wooded heights behind the beach, spilling through a narrow gully into the ocean. Massive chunks of fallen rock hid parts of the shore from our view. And from somewhere out of sight came an unearthly wailing, five deep and different tones, blowing without change, though not all at the same time; the sound was a gusting cacophony, like bagpipes being started up, a terrible, groaning drone, the melody not yet installed. Or was it? There was something haunting about what I was hearing.

This was the island of the wailing man, I realised! Munda had seen it from the corner of her eye, as she'd been bathed in the Light of Foresight. And though my talents in enchantment had been stifled on crossing into Ghostland, my intuition remained unaffected. I remembered an old friend, an expert with the pipes, a songster and storyteller, a 'chancer' as his people would have called him, and a brave man.

If I was right, an Hibernian called Elkavar was lurking somewhere close. Was it possible? He had certainly intended to come this way after sailing with Jason and myself on our last journey to Delphi.

Elkavar had been born to find passages through the underworld: it was his function in legend, and like Atalanta and Rubobostes he was a being of legend. Alas, Elkavar had been given everything he needed . . . save for a reliable sense of direction! And this Otherworldly island was exactly the sort of desperate place that he would have stumbled into by mistake and his own impatience.

We found the carved pipes, five hollowed trees, positioned
and shaped to catch the gusting ocean wind. They blew their
mournful racket, so loud when the wind was strong that the
reverberation knocked us back. Jason and Urtha stared up at the
towering structure in amazement. They were monumental ver-
sions of the strange pipes our old friend had carried!

Niiv, clever little thing, jumped up and down, clapping her
hands.

She too had recognised the calling sign of the piper. Our
spirits soared.

It was Niiv's intuition that persuaded Jason to stay on the
island. Disappointed with what he saw to be a smaller place
than he'd imagined from a distance, he was all for filling our
flasks and barrels with the fresh water, then putting off towards
the mainland to the west. He was convinced that his son would
be found in 'royal premises'.

*He lives between sea-swept walls. He rules in his world,
though he doesn't know it.*

But if Elkavar was indeed hiding on the island, he could be
of great use to us.

Urtha elected to stay with the ship. Jason elected to search
for the young Hibernian. Niiv stayed behind, reluctantly, along
with Tisaminas and pale Leodocus. Rubobostes, Hylas, Atalanta and Jason came with me, following the path that ran
beside the rushing stream, and crossing over the cliffs to find
the plateau of wooded land within.

The other argonauts were sent to scout and hunt for supplies.

A sweeter blast of music suddenly drifted on the air, a fresh
melody, slightly mournful, a brief snatch of some longer song.
Then silence, then a scream of rage. I laughed out loud. I hadn't
recognised the rage. But the music was unmistakable, that combination of vivacity and longing.

We broke cover to find ourselves in a wide clearing, circled
by three tombs, grassy and steep-sided mounds. There was a
strong smell of earth, the whiff of dank caves, the hint of burnt
bone. In the centre of the clearing was a grey stone house with
many windows in its high walls, and a sloping roof, thinly
thatched, more open to the elements than closed against them.
Here there was the sickly smell of rotting meat.

Jason was about to stride towards the building when a series of brief, almost musical howls, sounding from within the walls, stopped him in his tracks. Again, the pipes were played, a melody of eerie beauty, something old and strange that affected Atalanta as much as it moved the old Greek Land goat.

At once, the low entrances to the mounds bustled with activity. Then, faster than a mortal eye could see, shapes darted from under earth and into the house. Manic laughter was accompanied by the shrieks and fury of the piper; the droning tones were now those of a set of pipes being rent, torn and broken. As these taunting elementals fled back to their mounds, one of them paused, so briefly that only I—and Niiv perhaps—caught a glimpse of it. She, used to *voytazi* and other elementals of the lakes and woods, was unperturbed by the astonishing appearance of this fleet tormentor. I had seen such corpselike creatures before as well. They were designed by some rough nature to terrify the vulnerable, not the knowing. Nature in dreadful disguise, but vulnerable itself, I suspected.

Jason was breathing hard, alert in every sense, brow furrowed. 'I know this place,' he whispered.' Everything about it is familiar. Not in appearance, but . . . '

It came to him then. Memory and understanding.

'There's a man inside who's waiting for us! We help him, and he will be our guide.'

Unstoppable, Jason, Atalanta and Hylas, fired by memories of an earlier quest, stormed across the clearing and entered the stone house. Rubobostes, aware that I hesitated, hesitated too. He followed me when I went to one of the high mounds, stooping to peer into the stone-lined passage that led inwards. The lintel and the uprights were intricately carved; the carvings shifted their shape as I peered at them, forgotten symbols of several ages. These were not simply tombs, they were the entrances and exits to a particular part of the world, one which the Celts knew well.

Lurking, out of sight, huddled in the side passages, were the creatures that were guarding these paths into other worlds.

Jason was calling to me. He called me by the name *Merlin*, something that surprised me. It was an unexpectedly friendly gesture from a man who had once sworn to kill me.

'An old friend is waiting for us,' I reminded Rubobostes, who seemed puzzled by everything that was happening. 'The piper. Do you remember?'

'How can I forget,' the Dacian muttered. He had not been fond of the skirling tones that some people in the world called music.

If I had expected to find the happy-go-lucky, wisecracking man I had once known, however, I was soon disappointed. Grizzled and gaunt, watery-eyed and frightened, the man who huddled on the floor, between the crouching, sympathetic figures of Jason and his argonauts, was a shadow of the robust Hibernian who had guided me from the river watched over by the goddess Daan to the oracle at Arkamon, in Greek Land. Food was piled at one end of the long room—some fresh, mostly decaying, crawling with flies.

The floor was deep in shreds of leather and shards of shattered pipes, both bone and wood.

'What happened? What happened?' I remember muttering as I went to him and took his hands in mine. 'Someone hasn't looked after you. I thought you could sing yourself out of any difficult situation.'

'Merlin,' Elkavar breathed. His grip tightened, a fire came back to his eyes. He searched my face, seeking perhaps to convince himself that this truly *was* the man he'd once aided. 'There are so many tricks and charms in this ocean,' he said, as if reading my concern. 'So many tricks. I fell foul of the trickster god itself!' And again he drew me close, his breath sharp with bile, tears running from the forlorn eyes that had aged even faster than the wretched carcass from which they peered.

'Is it you? Have you found me? Did my song carry? They never, ever let me finish the song! The bastards!' he cried, repeating mournfully, 'Bastards, bastards!'

No one said a word.

'Did my song carry?' he asked again, breaking through his own anguish. He looked furtive then. 'I found a way to get one song out. The pipes at the shore, by the only landing place. They watched me as I built them. From above. They don't go near the sea. If I tried to take proper pipes, they'd stop me; but they didn't stop me carrying wood, great logs, hollowed out. I don't think they understood what I was doing.' He chuckled to himself. 'I set the notes to remind you of that song, remember that song? The one we sang to call Medea back from the underworld? Five notes! And you heard them!'

Good God in Oak! I *had* heard them. That very first day when I'd returned to Taurovinda, to the stronghold's ruins, and found the Three of Awful Boding dangling, bloody, teasing, from the rafters of Urtha's lodge. That tune had been a wisp of sound on the winter's air. I had noticed it and not recognised it: Elkavar's desperate call, from his prison in Ghostland. And on the beach too, though the melody had been too deep, too slow to catch.

'I heard it,' I said to him.

'And I knew you'd come! I knew you wouldn't forget.'

Jason cast me a frosty look. Our presence here had nothing to do with Elkavar. But what was I to do? Lie to the poor wretch whose life was suddenly alive again?

Elkavar struggled to his feet and looked around. 'You I know,' he said to Jason, 'Greetings.'

'Greetings to you. You're a thin man for so much food stacked up so revoltingly. Do you never eat?'

'I never eat,' the Hibernian said, looking at Atalanta and Hylas. 'I don't know who you are, but welcome to my humble home.'

'It could do with a good clean out,' Atalanta said through me. 'With so much food, *why* do you never eat?'

'Well, I eat sometimes,' Elkavar replied. 'They taunt me with food, so much I can't cope with it. I take what I need, but the rest—carcasses, stews, broths, soups, fruits, flagons of wine—they build up, day after day. If I try to throw it away, they bring it back. I am entombed with nourishment, but they deny my music!'

'Entombed with nourishment?' came Rubobostes' voice from the doorway. 'This is my sort of inn. A little rancid, though. Do you have anything fresh?'

'Rubobostes!' Elkavar cried. 'Now I *know* I'm not dreaming. I'm saved: I have charm from Merlin, guile from Jason and strength from you. My friends. My old friends.' He turned in a circle, withered arms trembling, feet doing a small dance. 'Help me stitch the bag for my pipes, help me play, and I'll lead you anywhere you wish to go! It's a certain skill of mine,' he boasted at us enthusiastically, despite our uncertain glances at each other, 'that I can find passages through the Otherworlds. Isn't that so, Merlin?'

'You managed it once, as I remember,' I reminded him. 'Just the once.'

'Well . . . that's true. But it means I can do it again. Doesn't it? But first: eat! Take what you want. There's more food here than could be burned at Beltagne. Danu's kiss! If I stacked the roast pigs on top of each other I could lick the face of the moon. Go on, go on. They'll bring more in a while, more to throw on the pile.'

We decided to wait for a while. At least the meat would be fresh.

And as we waited, we gently drew from Elkavar the story of his presence on this island, in the middle of an ocean, in the middle of Ghostland. Rubobostes was very keen to remind me, in a whisper, that: not everything was as it seemed. He was concerned that this was not Elkavar at all, but some trick, a beguilement designed to confound us.

'To what end?'

'To what end what?'

'Why should we be confounded? Who is doing the confounding?'

'I've heard talk of a Warped Man.'

'So have I.'

'The Warped Man is confounding us.'

'The Warped Man is very likely confounding us. But I'd know this man anywhere. This is Elkavar. Elkavar is as confounded by the Warped Man as are we.'

The Dacian leaned close to me, tugging at the right side of his unkempt moustache. 'I hope you're right.'

Elkavar was very alert. As if blind, he gathered the ripped and ruined fragments of his pipes around him, clawing them in as a mouse claws at its nest.

'There is only one way out of here,' he said. 'And to find the right exit I need to play the right melody. Each time I play it I feel the breeze of freedom, the escape from this desperate place, but those *creatures* swarm on me, bees on honey, and they shred my pipe-bag and break my pipes. I remake them. They shred and shatter them. They try to feed me until my bowels would burst. And they keep me here, trapped. And all because . . .'

He hesitated, frowning.

Jason, remembering a similar encounter with a blind man on his first quest, suggested: 'And all because you challenged a god. The god has punished you. You questioned his judgement! Or was it a *she*-god? That would be worse. But it doesn't matter. I can imagine what happened. You arrogantly assumed that in human terms you were wiser than a god. But so you are! Damn them! Zeus, Athena, Apollo. All gods can be appeased in the right way. I'm weary of these deities. Mightier, all knowing, thunderous, yes! But what *do* they know? Which god did you offend? I remember poor Phineus, the seer, we met him on our way for the fleece. He'd been blinded by Zeus and denied the delicious food that was brought to him every day because of attacks by two *Harpies*, who ate their fill of the feast, then pissed on the rest. And all because he had dared to suggest that he could read the portents of mortal fate more quickly than the god. No lengthy trips to oracles, no cash changing hands, no priests milking the unwary. Poor Phineus. Though it turned out that there *was* a problem with upsetting Zeus. But Zeus is Zeus: indefatigable in his lust for vengeance, almighty, even a god to strangers. He's one of a kind. You don't argue with Zeus. But he's not here now. And your gods are nowhere near as terrible as ours. We can help you.'

Elkavar's face was a picture of puzzlement and desperation. His quick glance at me was a search for reassurance. Jason's enthusiastic declamation waned as fast as a cat's interest in its murdered prey. He was suddenly surly again, all grim and hard-eyed.

Elkavar said (and I swear he sounded nervous at contradicting the older man), 'But I didn't upset a god. Not even a demi-god. I didn't upset anyone. I give you my word on it. A madman has done this to me. A man whose laugh was like a sneer, whose face was pretty in a boyish way until he laughed, and was then warped and twisted, like the image of beauty in a battered silver shield. But that name . . . the name you just used. Phineus. That's what he called me! "You are my Phineus," he said. "Phineus was one of the best parts in the story. So we must make sure you have a fine house and good food; and appropriate little helpers." Yes. That's what he said. You are my Phineus . . . '

CHAPTER TWENTY

—

To Strive, To Seek, To Find

This is what Elkavar told us:

> He sailed into the bay in a very strange ship; there were others
> aboard, but they stayed quite still at the oars. He came ashore and I
> was convinced he had come to rescue me from this island. I hadn't
> dared leave by the route I'd arrived by.
>
> Instead, he disappeared inland, but later came to fetch me. This
> house had suddenly appeared among the tombs. It hadn't been here
> before, I'm certain of it. I came through one of those mounds on to
> the island in the first place! But he persuaded me that I simply hadn't
> seen it, that it was a house that only showed itself at certain times.
>
> We sheltered here and ate exquisite food, brought to us by young
> people from the other side of the island. This went on for several
> days. I told him all about my life and troubles, and Argo and Greek
> Land. He seemed very interested in Greek Land. In that time he
> often went back to the cliffs, above the bay where his ship was
> moored—what did those other men eat or drink, I wonder? They
> never left the vessel as far as I could see. He kept gazing to the east,
> becoming more and more frustrated. He was waiting for something,
> but whatever it was it kept eluding him.

Then he began to taunt me, about my little weakness, my habit of getting lost in the passages under the earth. He started to find something very funny. He had changed. Now he became warped. I was frightened. I thought of a quick escape, back the way I'd come, though that was just as frightening, and he must have detected my fear. He asked me to play the bagpipes. I took my chance and played the melody that would open the 'way down', the gate back into the underworld. I thought I would take a chance on escape. But as I did so, the shutters on the door and windows burst open and creatures from a nightmare flew in and tore the bag to pieces before fleeing. One of them crunched through each of the wooden pipes as if searching for musical marrow.

The mad man laughed loudly and tossed me a joint of meat. As he ran from the house, he shouted, 'At least you won't go hungry. But you must wait for a ship that has taken an Age to get here before you can again find the pathway out of here! My Phineus!'

I followed him frantically to the bay, but he was a fast runner and had already struck away from the island when I reached the beach, nosing the vessel to the setting sun. That was when I saw, in the distance, ahead of him, a vast fleet of ships, dark-sailed and indistinct in the haze of sea and sun, but long vessels, war-galleys, I'm certain of it. Many ships, catching a vigorous wind and slipping steadily out of sight. I have no idea where they were going.

He played me for a fool. It was part of a game, a cruel game.

'What emblem was displayed on his sail?' I asked when it was clear that Elkavar had nothing more to say.

'The sail was cloth-of-black with red-embroidered edges, and the green head of a woman at its centre; her hair was a tangle of serpents; her eyes were hollow.'

'Medusa,' Jason muttered. 'This gets stranger by the moment.'

'But you *are* the ship that has taken an Age to get here,' Elkavar breathed. 'I'd hardly dared think that Argo would be the beginning of my release.'

We all looked to Jason as Elkavar spoke these words. Jason had engineered the release of the blind seer Phineus from the tormenting harpies. But he had had the assistance of argonauts Zetes and Calais, the fleet sons of the Thracian Boreas, who had chased the demons as far as the Sky Floating Isle and cut off their tail feathers, marooning them.

We soon discovered that we could not penetrate more than a shadow's length into the stone-lined passages of these *sidhs*, as Elkavar called them. When we tried to set a net to catch the elementals, after Elkavar had repaired his pipes and begun to play, they were quicker than we could act, doing their damage despite the amazing speed with which Atalanta despatched her arrows at them.

It was Rubobostes who came to our rescue. He had understood the problem, despite his doubts about Elkavar's mortal existence, and with Ruvio had dragged the huge carved pipes from the beach to the hill top and the woodland clearing.

'All we need now is a bag big enough to blow these things, and if instinct serves me right, we'll blast the elementals so far back into those mounds that they'll take a season to return. By that time we can have released the *bagpipe-man* from his curse . . . '

The words were said with the implication that this would be to release a greater curse on to us.

He added, 'There's a legend among my own people that is very similar to this situation, which is why it came to mind. I can't remember the details, though an amount of sorcery was involved. We're a little short on sorcery these days, it seems, so we'll just have to improvise.'

Elkavar had fashioned each new wind-bag from the animal skin pouches in which his food had been brought, using bone needles and twine made from strands of ivy, softened by chewing, for stitching. The meat and skin must have come from somewhere, and Urtha was called up from the ship. He and several marauders from among the old argonauts scoured the far side of the island, eventually returning with a pile of uncured hides stacked on Ruvio's back.

'Odd people,' was how he described the community they had discovered. He was speaking with difficulty, slurring his words. 'They seem dedicated to no other purpose than to supply food and drink for passing ships; there's no harbour over there; they lower packages of supplies down a sheer cliff and haul back up, by exchange, whatever it is that they need for themselves. About forty of them are women, and twenty men; no children. When they're not making food they're making love. They're all very fit and young; it's close to paradise except that none of them speak, only using fingers and gestures. Though they seem to get by very well with just fingers and gestures.'

'Did you see many ships?' I asked.

'Three very large, heading west; and a fourth still receiving supplies.'

Urtha too had received supplies, from the smell on his breath and the odours emanating from the others; they were extremely drunk.

Two days later, as the wind-bag approached completion and the tall pipes were inserted and bound in place, the absurdity of the situation began to infect us. Though Jason went very quiet, Niiv laughed as I had never seen her laugh before, Urtha and Tisaminas sharing the amusement. Rubobostes seemed furious that the mood of hilarity had begun to overwhelm his vision, and when he proposed feeding his majestic and unnatural steed on long grass, to make it pass more wind and thus help to inflate the bag, it was more than most of us could endure.

I wish I could record a more sophisticated resolution to Elkavar's plight, but the fact is, at dusk on the third day of our labours, giant musical pipes, played by squeezing a wind-filled leather bag of huge dimension, flattened by straps under the pull of the Dacian's indefatigable horse, blasted a wailing gale into each of the mounds, a noise so abominable, so raucous, so shattering, that the building in which Elkavar had sheltered developed cracks in the stone, parts of the cliff above the bay fell on to the beach, and a group of adventuring men, two women, and one horse, were blown off their feet by the shock of it; and by the resulting odour.

After that, all was silence.

Though for a while only.

When Elkavar then sounded an appropriate melody on his own set of man-sized pipes, the new goat's-skin wind-bag squeezed between his elbow and his ribs, the sorcery that had trapped him in this place fell away, and though nothing appeared to change, save that the entrances to the mounds closed up, as if Time had healed them, and the stone building collapsed into rubble, the Hibernian was free; free to pass beyond the beach and back to Ocean. The elementals had fled downwards. The game with him was ended.

We took him on board our unexpectedly nervous ship, our

reluctant vessel, an Argo who was suddenly whispering caution. Like any traveller, her experiences with the many worlds she had seen had still not given her full confidence in this new one. Jason and Urtha, heady and half blinded with the strange brew of adventure, took turns to reassure her. She did not punish them for their lies.

Meanwhile, we made sure our sleek-hulled friend was well provisioned from the community that had serviced the glade and its erstwhile captive, then cast off, following the ghostly fleet.

Chasing the Warped Man.

This was a strange ocean. No sooner had we left the Isle of the Wailing Man behind than another island began to loom upon us, its sheer green slopes split by a fall of water that surged into the sea, throwing up a haze of spume and mist. Elkavar urged us to sail south.

'The Warped Man told me of this place. The Island of the Stripped Dogs. Look, there!'

We had come in sight of a strand backed by dunes and low hills, with several paths leading inwards. The creatures that raced along the sand, barking at us, were gruesome, a pack of them, once fine hounds now stripped of their skins.

This was another wailing island, though this time the sound that rose and fell as it shifted with the wind was the sound of a thousand dogs baying and whining. As Argo moved slowly round the coast, we could see the great sail erected on its highest point, a sheet of skins stitched together, the hollow eyes and mouths of the boneless heads opening and closing with the gusts, emitting the most forlorn of cries.

Niiv was entranced. She shimmered in the same way as Munda, when the girl had been possessed by *imbas forasnai*. She was hearing something more than this preternatural howling; I realised she could hear a song within the sound.

'Oh, it's beautiful. It's beautiful!' she cried. 'Merlin, come and listen.'

'What are they singing?'

I suspected that she was not using charm to hear the houndsong. It would have been too great an irony if, as my own powers faded, hers remained. I suspected she was born for such a task.

Indeed, she said, 'I have heard the song of reindeer and snow wolf, I have heard lynx and lark and eagle. But this lament is the most beautiful. Can't you hear it? This is so old. I've only ever heard fragments of it, each time a dog howls at the moon. But this is the whole song.'

'What are they lamenting?'

She took my hand and pressed it. 'These are hounds from the first coming of people. These are the lost; they never knew the leash nor the warmth of fire. These were the old dogs who watched their young cubs taken and tamed. Now they wish they had not nervously hugged the forest edges, but had come close to the fire and shared the warmth and the songs of people. This is their own island. We should land and play with them for a while. They have seen play, but never known it. It would be a kind thing to do.'

Rubobostes' grimace seemed to say it all: play with those skinless, blood-matted creatures, slavering at the edge of the strand? Thank you, but no.

I was more aware of Niiv's deliberate look at me, the pressure of her fingers on my own. *Play for a while. It would be a kind thing to do.*

As if suddenly aware that I had grown cold against her, she loosened her grip, smiled sadly and said, 'There is something else in the song. I can't quite make it out. There's a low moan like a voice intoning a warning, or a direction . . . something about the Father Calling Place. It will rise over our horizon, but it is unsafe for more than one man to land on it.'

Rubobostes had been listening to the exchange without fully understanding Niiv's meaning. When I translated for him, his brow furrowed and his eyes quickened.

'This is another trick,' he said. 'Not the girl, but what the girl has heard. Leashes? We've all been tied around the neck, and someone is gently tugging us along.'

I could not have agreed with him more, of course, and told him so. But I needed to speak to the ship.

Jason, despite Mielikki's hate for him, and Argo's disappointment in his actions, was as proprietary as ever, blocking my way as I tried to approach the birchwood face of the goddess. The ship rocked as the wind tossed us, the sail cracking, whip-like, as it caught and strained below the strengthening breeze.

'What has Mielikki said to you?' I asked him.

'Concerning what?'

'Concerning these islands. This voyage.'

'Nothing. She's silent and angry.'

'I need to know what she knows. At the next island where we make landfall, only one of us can go ashore.'

Jason smiled coldly, scenting the aroma of what he loved: the unknown and danger. His look suggested: what of it? I am the captain; I step ashore.

Urtha, understanding what was being said, murmured, 'If only one of us can go ashore, then Merlin knows more than we do, and he alone should go.'

Urtha, as I would come to discover with increasing frequency and affection, was as pragmatic as he was proud.

But he asked me pointedly, 'Why do you need to talk to the ship?'

'Reassurance.'

'Reassurance? You? Now I *am* worried. Hey, Greeklander! Stand back from that lovely face. Let the man have his reassurance.'

Jason's hostile gaze never left my own, but he was aware that Urtha's words, sounding friendly, were not meant lightly.

If Jason hesitated, it was for a moment only, long enough to notice, too quick to offer insult. He stepped aside.

Mielikki called me down to the Spirit of the Ship, huddled in the stern below her grim visage. At this threshold the breeze was tinged with winter frost. As ever, the Northland Lady was missing her home.

My question to the goddess was simple: Niiv had understood a great deal about the last island, facts that seemed to me to beyond what should have been apparent to her; perhaps the goddess knew more. This ocean had no real business being here, not, at least, in the form in which we were seeing it. If not Mielikki, then perhaps Argo herself was aware of what lay ahead. And why my charm had deserted me.

'There is a smell of Time in the ocean,' Argo told me through her incumbent. 'But new hands have played with the form of the land that floats here. I don't understand why your charm has been taken from you. Your enchantment is designed to work in a charmless world, perhaps. But if Fierce Eyes is here, then charm has deserted her too. You are two of a kind. All she will have is her guile.'

'Are we sailing into a trap?'

'Yes. Of course. Though whose trap—that of Fierce Eyes, or this spectral Warped Man—I cannot tell. I can't get a clear idea. There are too many ghosts, an abundance of ghosts, evident from their memories in the ocean. They follow us like spouting, chattering fish, though they have no form. But you are approaching the Island of the Wicker Men; and beyond that is the Island of the Stone Giants; beyond that, the Island of the Iron Grail. Beyond that, all is warped to the old wood of my eyes.'

'Is someone "warping" you?' I asked anxiously, and certainly naively.

'No,' she replied. 'Nothing like that. Only that I have seen this situation too many times before. My hull has been repaired so many times; I have plunged, under good and courageous captains, into seas every bit as strange as this one. It is familiarity that makes me weary. I am half blinded by the knowledge of just knowing what next to expect.'

I had never known her so forthcoming.

'I tell you this, Merlin, because I know you will come to understand. You are no more than a ship yourself. Wood outlasts men. Age never shows until it shows, and then it comes with harrowing decay. You have lasted for millennia; you will rot in moments, though I hope this doesn't happen yet. When it comes to your rotting, I will carry you in comfort to a place that not even you can imagine. I will be your bier, your pyre and your grave. You will be the last captain of this ship. But not for a long time yet. There is too much to do, as far as you are concerned.

'And since you are the strangest captain I will have known, I can also tell you that for all of you who row at the benches, everything is lost, and everything is to be gained. The Island of the Iron Grail has nothing to plunder. But it will show you everything.'

She went quiet, then, an oracle that had given all it was prepared to give.

'Are you reassured?' Urtha asked me as I left the Spirit of the Ship and returned to my bench, gripping the wet binding of my oar with two blistered hands.

'I don't know what I am,' is all I could think to reply at the time. 'But our ship is in a black mood.'

Islands appeared before us as if Ocean herself was raising them in our path. We rowed hard around bleak crags, caught the breeze where we could and tacked past rough and jagged shores and coasts that were crowded with the strangest of creatures: giant horses that chased each other, as if being raced by men, but bloodily biting any flank that became vulnerable; an island where men and women poured to the shore, laughing and playing the sort of games that appealed hugely to Urtha. It was all we could do to hold him back, but at last he remembered the old story: that any man who beached there would start to laugh and play without mind, without reason.

One island, terraced and green with trees, was home to giant birds whose plumage was rich with reds and greens, usually a sign that they can be eaten. Atalanta had shot down three of them at a great distance before we realised that each was not just large, but almost as large as Argo. We anchored off-shore for a day, cutting up the meat and storing it, while the huntress defended us against the attacks of the angry flocks.

But by then we had become low on meat, and this rich feast was welcome, Elkavar cooking strips of bird flesh in a fire created in an upturned shield. Elkavar was a wonderful cook. He had forgotten to remove the shield's leather grips, and although they were demolished along with the meat, whoever ate them failed to notice.

We came to an island where a long row of crouching wooden statues stared out to sea, warriors behind their shields. Urtha recognised them at once. He went ashore. As he approached each figure, so it rose and greeted him; men of oak and ash and elm, oiled and polished. These were the Coritani who had fallen in battle over the generations. Whenever they went to war they left such effigies behind in their homeland, a fragment of their spirit in each idol, a ritual that had been imposed on them in unhappier times, when their druids had been more powerful. Those who returned burned the effigy in celebration. Those who did not walked and sailed the effigies to this Otherworldly island, where they waited for such moments as this to send messages of greeting and love back to their families.

Urtha told us this as he clambered aboard again. He spent the next little while memorising the words and thoughts of King Vortingoros's dead.

An island loomed into view a day later, a place of gentle hills inland and a warm, wide strand of soft sand gently touched by the surf. Dark-haired and beautiful women lined the water's edge, waving to us, laughing delightfully. Their dress was strange, a figure-hugging robe of gleaming lace, dark grey with speckles of white. This time it was all we could do to stop Rubobostes leaping from Argo and swimming for a short spell of 'rest and recreation', as he termed it, an expression that made us laugh so much that it took all our strength to haul him back to Argo's safety. Niiv and Urtha knew what they were witnessing, and as we rowed Argo hard and fast away from the pleasant-looking island so Rubobostes became aware—as did we all—of the danger that had threatened. The strand faded and the sharp, sea-swept rocks of the true shore became clear; the women slithered on their bellies, fat and glistening, whiskered faces staring after us as they seal-cried their annoyance.

'What in the world of bad dreams were *they*?' the Dacian demanded.

'Selkies,' Urtha explained. 'Seal-like creatures that can warp and develop into the human shape of women.'

Rubobostes stared at him, bemused. 'Why would they do that?'

'To attract their blood-lunch; they need blood to maintain the woman in the seal. The rest of the time they have to feed on fish. Didn't you smell the stench of rotting fish?'

'Yes,' Rubobostes said in a forlorn voice. He returned his gaze to the island.

'Didn't that warn you of danger?' Urtha asked him.

'Danger? In my country, rotting fish is used to make a great delicacy. For a moment I felt at home.'

The big man's disappointment didn't last long.

Argo ploughed her way through a sea that rose against us, a

defiant sea, crashing against our flanks, fighting against the sail. A landfall on which we had set our sights, where a gleam of green and white suggested a palace, seemed to come no closer as time passed. It was blurred, now, in a haze of sea-spray, but it was clear that it remained as far away as ever.

Jason was frustrated, Urtha anxious. Even the argonauts whose lives were still tied to their stolen kolossoi seemed to despair as they crouched gloomily over their raised oars, or heaved at them when the wind shifted to blow against us and the sail was lowered.

It was Urtha's anxiety, however, that proved to be the source of both comfort and warning. Hylas and I translated where necessary. Hylas had a skill with languages.

'This sea is strange, but I've heard of it before. We are not the first ship to sail it. These islands are like the holes in Elkavar's pipes: they can be played differently to make new melodies. The ocean is using us to make the words that go with the tune. Nothing is as it seems, but everything is familiar. In a story my father Ambaros told me, the sea-reiver Maeldun came close to despair, searching these islands for some trace of the life he'd lost. At the end of his voyage, he found home. We are sailing towards home, but don't expect to reach it easily.'

The long-dead Greeklander Tisaminas now stood up, braced against the heaving sea by clutching hard with both hands at Rubobostes' left arm, an arm already under strain as the Dacian used brute strength to hang on to the ropes that held the sail. 'When Odysseus sailed on a similar journey, after the sack of Troy, he too reached home,' he reminded his companions as sea-spray whipped at his beard. 'But his home had to be reclaimed. Twenty years lost! That man had been adrift for twenty years. And in twenty years much changes. Men were looting his land. What he had lost he had to fight to claim back for himself and his family. If we are sailing for home, we must expect a fight.'

Urtha shouted through the gale, 'Home is always a struggle! It's a cauldron whose fire must be constantly watched. But home is the only cauldron that matters. Cauldrons have always been important to us. The Good God, Dagda, knows this, which is why he carries his own! What you put into the cauldron is what you take out of it. In goes flesh, out comes stew. In goes death, out comes life. Everything the same, everything different. Whatever the hardship, whatever the struggle, the important thing is to get there. We can do nothing but brace ourselves against the waves until we get there.'

'Home is where the heart is,' Hylas laughed, quoting from the sheaves of doggerel that Heracles, his one-time master and lover, had written with amazing energy between his adventures.

Home is where the gates are, I thought to myself, as this conversation of encouragement and courage went on. I could remember all too well so many gates closed against me as I'd wandered along the long Path around the world.

Niiv's voice cut through the stormy air like a scolding mother's. 'If I might beg your attention: we're about to run aground!'

An island of spectacular beauty had suddenly loomed before us. Jason's skill and Rubobostes' strength allowed us to miss the rocks and drop our sea anchor in the shallows, close to a cove where an arch of shining, translucent stone spanned the gap between the cliffs.

A boy, dressed in a tunic of white cloth embroidered with the earthy green of tarnished bronze, stood on a narrow ledge, hands on his hips as if impatient; as if he had been waiting. His long, dark hair was tied back and he wore thick-soled sandals. The surging sea blew spray against him, but he stood impassive, smiling; and, catching my eye, he beckoned me to the shore, then turned and jumped from rock to rock, below the arch and out of sight.

Argo whispered through her incumbent: *Follow him.*

Robert Holdstock

ath, out comes life. Everything the same, everything differ

CHAPTER TWENTY-ONE

—

Iron Grail

I swam to the beach, my clothes wrapped in oilskin. Dressed again, and unarmed, I clambered over the rocks that bordered the cove and passed below the strange marble bridge. Almost at once I was hailed.

'Antiokus! Antiokus! Come and see what I've built!'

Kinos waited for me at a distance. Then, just as I slipped and skidded on the wet marble, he turned and ran further through the cove; I followed. His own wet tracks led through the wooded path to a meadow, bright with flowers, heady with the scent of summer. Cloud shadow chased across the field. The boy raised his hands as he faced me, a smile of delight on his face. He was sea-crusted and ragged in his torn, white tunic, I saw now, but the child shone from the guileless eyes. He was only six or seven years old, salty hair tied into a tight top-knot, as had been the fashion in Iolkos seven hundred years ago.

'You are just as I remember you, Antiokus. You've changed nothing but your clothes. Older in the eye. Otherwise the same.'

'And you are just as I remember *you*. Little Dreamer. A little taller perhaps? But then, perhaps not. I'm not sure. Less dreamy in the eye? I'm not sure of that either.'

'I dream! I dream!' the child cried to me excitedly. 'I can make such wonderful things. You must come and see what I've built. My father will come and find me soon. I know he will. I've built a place in which he can sit and feast. Come and see! Come and see!'

He turned again and ran quickly through the summer woods, following a path lined with briar rose and hawthorn, a boy bursting with excitement. When a rock face loomed before us, he laughed out loud, clapping his hands. There was a shallow cave below the overhang, almost buried in thorn. He had painted the gaping mouth with squares and triangles in green and red. Inside, he had laid skins and mats of woven grass to make a warm and comfortable floor. He had built low stools out of shaved and polished wood, and two of them sat on either side of a wide, narrow table carved from olive. In the middle of the table was a pottery bowl, crudely made, intricately detailed. In the bowl he had placed two pieces of fruit.

'They rot quite quickly. I have to keep replacing them. But when he comes, they'll be fresh. One for each of us. My father is sailing. He's away, gathering more golden trophies. The quest is to the north, I expect. Among savages and beasts beyond imagination. He's lost at the moment, but all winds can change. He told me that. Some winds change for the better, some bring storms. My father is wise, though; he knows the sea. He can smell which of Boreas's children is gusting up in anger. I think he must be wounded, though. That's why he is coming home so slowly.'

'Is this the Father Calling Place?'

'It is! It is!'

'You played in a place like this with a boy called Kymon, the son of a king.'

'Yes! I remember him. And his sister. He was a fighter too. He used to tell me what he would do to the enemies of his father when they became his slaves. His world was a muddy fortress, and it meant the world to him.'

'Where is Munda now? Where is his sister?'

Kinos looked edgy, then shrugged. 'Don't know. Look, Antiokus! Everything that is important is here.'

He showed me ten small dolls, each made of wicker and grass, each clothed in strips of black hide or grey pelt that were cut to look like armour. I was immediately intrigued by them. Was it possible that the kolossoi were hidden among them? There were tiny ships, fashioned from wood and clay, and they were arranged as if in a fleet, sailing across the mat and animal-skin floor of this cave. One model stood apart, the symbol of Iolkos, Jason's city, crudely painted on the dried leaf that acted as a sail.

'Everything is here. Everything is here. All my father's stories. Look. This is Phineus. Phineus was the best bit of the story of the golden ram . . .'

He picked up a small, tattered figurine and waved it at me, grinning. His other hand was behind his back. When he brought it out he was holding a dead bat, its wings stretched and held in place by twigs and twine. The creature's belly had erupted with decay. It made swooping motions on to the figure of Phineus. Harpies attacking the blind man, he explained, though I had already made the connection.

'Gnash, gnash, gnash,' he growled as the dead bat savaged the wicker doll.

'Phineus was blind and half mad,' He said suddenly, pausing in the attacking movements. 'But he still knew enough to know what was to come. He guided my father onwards. Sometimes you don't need eyes to see. Sometimes you just need to dream . . .'

His own eyes glowed with excitement. Again he made the bat swoop on the straw figure, then he placed them down, lay down himself beside the ships, and touched each one with a finger, just enough to move it along a fraction.

'Here they go. Here they go. Do you see, Antiokus? Seeking. Seeking. Blow wind blow! Up sail!' he cried as he played. 'Ship oars, and shit over the side. Quickly, quickly, while you have the chance. The gods alone know what might be down there watching. The wind might drop. Catch the breeze. Jason sails the great unknown. My mother waits. My mother waits. Over here, Antiokus, in Hydraland. Do you see?'

A woman's effigy in straw draped in black moleskin stood on a lump of red granite. 'Boiling up her strange brew. Making the smoke that gives you dreams. Ready for rescue from the warped king who keeps her prisoner.'

He sang a little song.

'Mother's charms, and father's arms,
Hold me tight, through each long night.
Charms that sing,
Arms that ring,
Time will tell.
All *must* be well.'

He seemed very happy as he played with his toys. I asked him if he had seen the ship in the bay and he shrugged.

'I see many ships.'

'Didn't you recognise this one?'

'No. Why should I? I recognised you, though.'

Had he seen his father? Would he even have recognised the man? I asked him carefully whether he had noticed anything strange about the rest of the crew, peering over the sides of the vessel.

'Just ghosts,' he said. 'The sea here is full of ghosts.' He sat up suddenly. 'Let's eat the fruit. I have plenty. And I can always get more for my father when he comes. And then I have something else to show you. A wild rose,' he added with a little laugh. 'Here you are . . . ' and he tossed one of the plump plums towards me, stuffing the other into his mouth with a great burst of crimson juice, laughing through the mashing of the pulp.

I was about to pursue the subject of Munda when, unexpectedly, Niiv appeared on the path, calling to me. Kinos was at once annoyed.

'Who's she? I didn't invite her here!'

'She's a friend. She means no harm,' I assured him.

But he rushed to a basket in the corner of the cave, fetched out two ripe plums from his hidden store and flung them at the Pohjolan woman. One struck her on the face and she screeched with shock and anger, but stood her ground. Kinos threw a tantrum. 'I don't know you,' he shouted at Niiv, and then looking at me through tear-filled eyes. 'Why did you bring her? I wanted to show you this place alone. This is my special place. This is the *Father Calling* Place, Antiokus. You told me you had lost your own father when you were young. I thought you were my special friend. It was only for your eyes.'

And with that moment of astonishingly disappointed outrage, he ran from the cave, fleet as a hound, and was lost among the whispering trees.

Niiv wiped the juice from her face, picked up the broken plum and ate it. 'Who was *that* little brat?' she asked. She seemed more interested in her meal than in the question.

'Jason's son. Little Dreamer.'

'What? Not old enough. He'd be a man by now.'

'I know. What are you doing here?'

'He can't have been Jason's son,' she repeated. 'The other son was only slightly older than this one, and when we saw him he was a grown and angry man.'

'I know. We're in a world of phantoms. What are you doing here?'

'I was worried about you.' She was transparently lying. She was intrigued by what I might have been discovering. I let it pass.

On impulse, I went back into the shallow cave and picked up the woven-grass figure of Phineus. I put it back, but gathered up the effigies of the argonauts. I stole them all. They felt like desiccated grass and dried skin, but they might have been hiding the kolossoi of my old friends.

Without my old wits I couldn't tell, so reason suggested that I should leave nothing to chance.

My belt stuffed with crumbling dolls, Niiv and I went back to the cove, where Argo waited. The boy followed us, lurking in the undergrowth, but he neither revealed himself nor railed against the theft.

Later, Mielikki whispered to me: *She says they are not the souls you seek.*

Once aboard, Argo cast off and found deeper water, following the line of the cliffs. I expected Jason to ask me about the boy, but he was implacable and dark. Urtha, looking relaxed at his oar, a king who had cast off his cloak of royalty, whispered, 'Who was he? That lad?'

'The image of Jason's second son.'

'I thought as much. There is a smell of Greek Land in this place. And Jason knows what he saw, he simply doesn't accept it. He referred to the boy as a ghost. He knows he's searching for a man. Was he a ghost?'

'No.'

'But not the son.'

I didn't answer the question. I didn't know how to at that moment. Yes, it was the son. Everything was the son. Everything was Little Dreamer. The crushed dolls in my waistband seemed to pinch at my flesh. Perhaps I had stolen them as much because I didn't want to leave this island as to see if they were my friends' kolossoi. There was more to learn on this intriguing sea-fortress.

I had no doubt that I'd set foot on the Island of the Wicker Men.

The wind gusted and Argo shifted on the swelling sea. The cliffs rode dramatically past, light flashing from polished marble high up among the dense trees that crowded the edges. And after a while, another bay came into sight. A youth, sitting astride a small white horse, waited there. The young man was wearing a green tunic with black edges. He wore a Greeklander helmet tipped back on his head to show his face; the helmet's crest flowed proudly down his back, a wild horse's mane of red. His legs, gripping the animal's flanks, shone where they were encased in silver greaves.

As Argo dropped anchor again this young warrior turned on the beach, marking a pattern in the sand before kicking his way towards the narrow defile leading inland and disappearing from view.

I looked at Jason. He had seen everything I had seen, but he had not responded. His face was a scowl, but as he gripped the rail his hands were white.

'Do you think that might have been your *grail*?' I asked the man, using a word fashionable among warrior-mercenaries.

'My what?'

'Your small copper bowl of hope.'

'The small copper bowl of hope and desire,' he corrected. 'Apollo's *krater*, emptied of wine, filled with dreams. You mean Little Dreamer, of course.'

'Was that your son?'

'No,' was Jason's blunt reply. 'Not him. Not that one. I'll know him when I see him; he'll know me.' He gave me a searching look. 'But I have the feeling that we'll not sail on until you've been ashore. Are you learning something from this place?'

'I am,' I confirmed.

'Then go ashore.'

I waded to the white sand of the cove and had hardly set foot on dry land before Niiv slipped over the side of the ship and followed.

The rider clattered back to the entrance of the defile and grinned at me, helmet now held in his hand. He had long hair and engaging eyes, a young man at ease, delighted with this new company.

'Antiokus, as I live, laugh and cry! It's you. Again. Years have passed, but you don't change! Read what I marked in the sand . . . then come and see what I've built. Come and see what I've built! Who's that?' He craned forward over his steed's nape, face glowing with curiosity as Niiv, naked, stepped on to the sand and dropped her dry robe over her head.

'A friend of mine,' I told the youth.

'Hah!' Niiv exclaimed behind me. Kinos was puzzled for a moment, then laughed.

'You wild rover! She's young. I think I understand. But if I don't, who cares anyway? Come and see what I've built. Both of you.'

Niiv raced past me and held on to the horse's tail as Kinos led us to his new and strange domain. Niiv was fluent in his language, and whispered to him as he rode, but Little Dreamer had ears only for my own progress through a difficult terrain, ensuring my safety; though he had eyes for the woman, eyes that shone.

Only once did our path bring us back in view of the sea and the strand. I glanced down again at the face of Medusa, roughly stamped out by the hooves of the horse. Kinos saw me looking. 'My mother's mark!' he called back. 'I don't understand it; but it comforts me to make it. She liked snakes; and their venom; and strange herbs, potent herbs. My mother protected me at a time of great danger. She protected me often, my brother too. She gave us drinks that took us to the stars, Antiokus! I have journeyed to the stars with my mother's help.'

'Where is your mother now?' I challenged him as we continued along the path.

'Long dead, bless her heart. But she saved my life. My brother's too. A man disguised himself as my father and tried to kill us. This was a long time ago, in the great city of Iolkos, when we were children.' He turned on the thin saddle to look at me, riding in awkward fashion, but with ease. 'Mother hid us carefully. My brother decided to leave this hiding place; I agreed to stay, to wait for Jason. I know he'll come and find me. I've been calling for him. You were my father's friend. Come and see what I've built for him.'

He turned back to a proper riding position, kicked the horse and cantered ahead, Niiv stumbling behind him. As she realised the animal might kick her, she let go of the poor beast. I caught up with her and she clung to me. 'Where are we going?'

I had no words nor time to reassure her. I said only, 'Step by step into a darker place than even the realm where Persephone rules.'

'I don't understand. Who's Persephone?'

'Never mind. Just watch and listen; you may see things that pass me by.'

'What are you two chattering about?' the brash young man called back. It was a question addressed in a mild manner. I replied that we were breathless with the pace. He grinned, slowed to a walk and led us through an olive wood, away from the sea.

After a while he swung down from the horse and tossed his helmet aside, watching us with obvious pleasure. He seemed to notice at once that Niiv's black hair was falsely coloured, but was clearly excited by the pale tint of her eyes.

'We have to be careful here,' he cautioned. 'We're entering a dangerous valley. Keep as quiet as possible. You'll hear the sound of a forge. Ignore it. I should have ignored it, but alas I didn't, and there are some unpleasant creatures hunting the woods and gullies.'

As we walked along the narrow path, we were aware that we were being followed. Our pursuers were furtive. Occasionally, a gleaming gaping metal maw would peer out through the underbrush, some bright, some tarnished a dull green. Though we didn't hear the sound of a forge as we journeyed, I caught the whiff of smelting, the occasional warm draught from a furnace somewhere close. And although the sounds from the crowded woodland were animal and hoarse, Niiv whispered to me: 'Some of them sound as if they're calling his name.'

At the far end of this uncomfortable gorge, Kinos looked back, clearly relieved that we had left the path behind.

'They are quite alone, and some escape to the edge of the world, but they are always drawn back to me.'

'What are they?' I asked him, remembering the snapping jaws, taking a carrion bird, as we had first sailed through Ghostland.

'Wild friends,' he replied. 'I didn't really know what I was doing when I had them made. I needed friends. But *this* I must show you. Look here—'

And he led us a little further, leading the horse by the reins.

We had come out of the wood to face a high, rock wall, stretching away to left and right. The rock was carved in horizontal striations, like the planking of a ship's hull.

With a start of surprise, I realised that that was exactly what it was.

Kinos touched an appreciative hand to Niiv's damp cheek, tugging at a lock of her hair, then turned to me, indicating the high wall. 'Do you see what it is?'

'A ship?'

'My father's ship! Just as I remember it from the harbour; the great ship, the ship of the fleece, the ship of the argonauts! Come inside, Antiokus. Come inside and remember. This is what I have made for my father.'

The structure was enormous. As we approached, it seemed to grow in length and height. Enormous eyes had been carved on the bow; decorated round shields ran along below the rail. The images were vaguely recognisable: Hydra, Cyclops, helmets, riders, lizards, whales . . . all were eerily unreal. Yet recognisable.

Kinos tethered his horse, then led us to the doorway into the stone hull. We entered what, in Argo out at sea, was the Spirit of the Ship, the hidden place where fragments of all the old ships that lay at Argo's heart were fitted into the keel. I don't know if Kinos knew of this ancient connection, but this part of his gigantic model was rich with engraved vessels, a fleet of ships carved as if sailing to battle, fish leaping beside them, seabirds circling above their decks.

Stone men sat at benches. Each was the height of a tree. They were fashioned from white stone. Though they were shown holding the leather grips of their oars, no oars penetrated the hull. It was as if we walked through a temple of great gods as we passed between the two ranks of straining, struggling men, towards the figurehead looming from the stern, and the towering figure of a man at the steering oar, braced against the heave of the tide, stubble-chinned face set grim.

There was no mistaking Jason in those features. Nor, in the narrow, calculating eyes of the beautiful face carved as figurehead, was there any mistaking Medea.

Kinos raised his arms to indicate the argonauts. 'I sculpted them as I remembered them, though many had left before I met them, so I used other men's faces. But look, there is Tisaminas, there Antigos. The one with the harp is Orpheus. That one, with the lion skin, is Heracles. I heard all the stories from my father. I heard all the names. I knew of all the argonauts, even though I didn't meet them all. Do you see that crouching man? That's Phineus. He was the best part of the story. He betrayed the gods. They blinded him and tormented him, but he never gave up hope. He knew he would be rescued. His salvation lay in the hands of men, not gods. Though my father left him behind, in a happier state, I've included him on board. There, then. Do you think he'll be pleased when he sees it?'

'You could find out, if you wish. Your father is in the bay, on his new ship.'

Kinos shook his head, rubbing his hands together. He was suddenly tense and distressed. 'That is not my father. I was warned to be wary of tricks. A shade of my father stalks me, to do me harm. My true father is coming closer. I will recognise him when I see him. As long as that man stays in the bay, I shan't harm him.'

Before I could respond, Niiv whispered to me, 'I can see Atalanta; and Hylas . . . but where are you?'

Her simple observation took my mind off what Kinos—if indeed this young man was the true son of Jason—was saying.

It was true. No towering stone figure of Jason's last recruit—myself—sat on the benches. I walked back between the two rows of figures, staring up at each oarsman's face, feeling a chill as old friends seemed to wink at me, to strain through their megalithic forms to turn and greet me.

There was no Antiokus. No Merlin. No enchanter. But one of the benches was empty.

Kinos was watching me, expectantly and perhaps a little anxious. I called to him, 'You've left a space for me, but not filled it.'

'I did fill it,' he called back. 'I promise you. I made you very carefully. You were the best of the statues; you were the only one looking forward, all the rest look down, if you notice.'

'What happened?'

He came up to me, speaking more softly, looking concerned. 'One day, the statue just got up and walked away. I followed it for a while, but you take long strides, Antiokus. I could see you above the tree tops, but you had walked through the woods before I could catch you. I don't know where you went, but I missed you sitting there. I had meant to make memories only; but I made you as a living thing. I didn't mean to. I think you must be a god in disguise. You work magic. You never grow old.'

But I always walk away.

He slapped me on the shoulder, then, grinning. 'I'll make a new model of you, if it would cheer you up. That's a clouded face if ever I saw one. Save clouds for the sky. I have never seen eyes like yours! So beautiful . . . '

This last was addressed to Niiv, I'm glad to say.

'Like the sea itself,' he added.

Niiv was surprised and upset. As the young man looked at her with interest, she slapped his face. 'You are just a shadow!' she exclaimed, turning to run from the stone ship. 'Just a shadow. Not a man at all.'

Startled, Kinos rubbed his cheek. 'She said such welcome things to me on the path to this monument. What did I say that was wrong?'

'Nothing wrong. I believe she just saw through you. It was something of a shock.'

He was puzzled. 'Then I have something to learn. Am I insubstantial?'

The question, with its two possible meanings, took me by surprise. Was Little Dreamer playing games with me?

'Not insubstantial . . . Kinos. Just too young. She was looking for someone older.'

'I *am* older. But this is when I was happiest,' he said sharply, softening the tone as he added, 'This is the time in my life when everything began to come clear. What had been stories, told by my father and mother, now became real to me. Instead of mere names, his friends became people. Instead of being old men remembered, I could almost speak to them, hear their own stories, feel their pain, their joy. Everything they had been, and everything they had seen, became clear to me. I realised that the best of life is life that has gone before, its memories, its secrets. That *is* the secret of life! I can think of no other life worth living. That's when I *truly* started to build, Antiokus. And I want you to see it. Sail on; sail on with the man who pretends to be my father. All of you, go ashore when you see an island with a palace of green marble rising from the plain beyond its wide beach. Be wary, though. The city is under siege.'

He ran past me and was already mounted up by the time I reached the doorway. He kicked the horse and chased after Niiv, but the girl had fled, frightened by her own glimpse of the true Little Dreamer on this part of the island. I could see her far away below, running to the bay. Kinos, arms folded, stood on a promontory watching her in disappointment, the wind from the sea blowing against him but not moving him, as if he were one of his own childish statues.

Once they were in the deep haven, they furled the sail and stowed it within the sea-crusted ship and lowered the mast by the forestays, bringing it to rest in the crutch. Then with oars they went on and backed her into the shallows, threw the anchor-stone from the bow, tied her up from the stern on the beach, and stepped out themselves on the shore of the sea.

The words of a storyteller I had once met during my travels began to speak to me, images from a lost time, words from a charismatic man. And I was not surprised.

The beach was dense with painted ships, war-galleys all, drawn up by the stern, crowded so closely together it was hard to see a way to pass them. Their eyes watched us as the living eyes of so many sleek-hulled creatures. The plain beyond was alive with tents and fires, and the gleam of weapons and armour, stacked carefully, ready for use.

A citadel of green and shining beauty rose beyond the plain, sprawled across the top of a broad hill, defended by concentric circles of white walls and looming towers. Banners of every colour blew out from the turrets across the dark, rocky slopes with their shimmering tangles of silver-green olive and oak.

I noticed five gates through the walls, the same as at Taurovinda.

As Argo drifted on the swell, running slowly along the line of the beach, we searched for the army that had debouched from these galleys, but there was no sign of human life, either in its living form or its shade.

The small crew at once debated where that army might be hiding.

'In the tents,' was Rubobostes' uncertain suggestion.

'In the ships, below the benches,' Urtha proposed.

'In shallow sand holes,' Hylas offered. 'They're easy to dig.'

'Inside the city already,' Jason grunted. 'Hiding in the shadows. Waiting to strike.'

'Or in a trophy ship,' Tisaminas contributed. 'This reminds me of the siege of Troy. Odysseus and others entered the city concealed inside a trophy ship, hanging by straps inside a double hull.'

'It was a horse,' Elkavar snapped at him. 'A giant wooden horse. I sing songs about it. I should know.'

Everybody laughed, to the man's irritation.

'A story told for children,' I whispered to him. 'The ship was dedicated to Poseidon, sea-thunderer, sea horse, god of the stampeding waves. But it was a cleverly constructed, up-turned ship.'

He laughed dismissively. 'Really? I prefer the horse. Besides, "horse" is easier to rhyme than "trophy ship".'

'On a more practical note,' Atalanta said, 'those ships mean a lot of men. This terrain cannot hide a lot of men. They must be somewhere. Hidden in the ships might well be the answer.'

But the ships were empty, creaking hulks, many of them waterlogged, stinking of brine and pitch, their oars and masts coated with the white shit of seabirds.

While Jason threw down the sea anchor, Rubobostes tethered Argo to the shore, swimming between two galleys, crawling in the narrow space where their hulls scraped together in the shifting sea, knocking in the post with his fist. We all went ashore

then, armed and wary. Those of us without shields took them
from the stacks; I took a spear that was shorter than my height;
Niiv selected one that was twice her height, and though she
struggled with its weight, she clung on to it.

'I like its distance,' she explained when I criticised her
choice. I presume she meant the distance between herself and
the killing end. 'If I have to make it fly, I'll make it fly.'

We moved towards the hill and the palace of green marble.
At one point, when I stood in awe, staring up at the massive
ramparts, Jason caught up with me and stood beside me. If I
was aware of him, it didn't seem to matter. I remember only
that I murmured words from that same old tale-teller, who had
wonderfully described the siege and sacking of Troy, an event
from before Jason's time. The city was known by several
names; Troy was fashionable.

'Now which of the gods, my trickster, has again been plot-
ting with you?'

I had Kinos on my mind; and Medea. But it was Jason who
heard my whisper.

The old warrior's hand clutched my shoulder; ever-youthful
eyes gleamed through the face-guard of his purloined helmet.

'I've been thinking the same thought myself. Though concerning you. But I believe the trickster in you has been left
behind.' He'd realised I'd lost my magic.

'Yes. I'll get it back. For the moment all that matters is what
lies beyond these walls.'

'My son,' he said, staring up the slope of the hill. 'This *must*
be the place.'

Medea, I thought to myself, though without my own 'trickster' I was no longer sure of anything. But I was glad of that
moment of reconciliation in Jason's touch.

All the argonauts but Tisaminas had come ashore. Tisaminas
stayed with the ship at his own suggestion. He had intuited
Argo's impatience to return home and thought that if it least
one of us stayed within her hollow hull she would not slip her
moorings.

My own feeling was that with Niiv ashore, the Northland
Lady would stay true to us. She couldn't leave without the
charmed girl from her own country.

The rest of us now came close to the first of the gates, intending to begin the steady climb to whatever lay above us. At that moment came the sound of baying hounds. We fell back, looking for cover, as a pack of bronze dogs came bounding through the gate, forming a snarling barking line before us. I counted twenty, each as high as a man's waist. When their bodies touched, the metal rang; when they moved, they groaned and creaked like rusting hinges. Behind them, a bronze stallion cantered into view, riderless, reins dangling.

It looked at me and pawed the ground, then turned side on.

I walked towards the horse. When Jason tried to follow, four of the hounds leapt forward and threatened to tear him apart. He backed away hastily. But the dogs allowed me to pass through their rank, and I swung over the cold metal back of this strange beast.

Hanging on to the cold flanks of the neck, I was cantered through each of the gates in the outer walls and into the palace grounds. I had time to glimpse the spiralling towers and rich façades of temples and halls before the mechanical creature stopped so abruptly that I was flung forward, crashing to the ground below its steaming nostrils. It looked down at me with unblinking but sympathetic eyes.

My groin ached and my heels were bruised where I had gripped the steed, trying to slow it down.

'Welcome, Antiokus,' came a familiar voice, speaking slowly and gently. A man's shadow stooped over me and a rough hand hauled me to my feet. Armoured, dark eyes watching from that same Greekland helmet, a thin smile breaking through the dense growth of beard that swathed the face. The grip on my arm could have snapped the bone. I could see battle wounds on the face, streaks of grey in the beard, a cut across the nose; the helmet was dented. The arm that supported me, partly sheathed in leather, had several times been cut through to the bone, the wounds roughly healed and ugly.

'Why did the girl run from me? That time, all those years ago. Why did she run?'

As he asked the question, he removed the helmet, saying, 'I'm glad to see you again. You were a good friend of my father's.'

Time was up to no good, here. In three days I had seen Kinos as young, youth and now warrior. But all of the apparitions had seemed to have lived the intervening years. Looking at Little Dreamer, hardened, scarred, and still so vulnerable, I was unsure whether to believe that this was the true man, or just another shadow.

Was an even older Kinos waiting? Or was another hand at work on these Otherworldly islands, sowing the seeds of confusion, as the poet had put it?

'Why did she run?' Kinos asked again. 'She was so lovely. I suppose I was too bold. When she sneered at you, when you introduced her as a friend of yours, I assumed that she wanted to be anything but. You had plans for her, but she was keeping you at a distance. Perhaps I was wrong . . . '

Oh yes. Very wrong.

What could I say? In a strange world, surrounded by all the trappings of madness, without my wits, uncertain of Medea's location, anxious for my friends on the beach, I fumbled for the right thing to say. I remembered the old maxim that if in doubt, keep it simple. I had sailed too many seas to be afraid of drowning in cliché.

'You were too bold,' I tried to persuade him. 'She was too young.'

'You're a liar,' he said with a grin. 'But then, so am I. So are dreams. Come and see what I've dreamed for my father, when he finally comes to join me on the great adventure!'

He clapped his hands and the metal horse shook its head, turned and cantered across the wide plaza. Two of the hounds came scampering in, wailing, wounded, anxious for affection from their creator, receiving only a harsh command. They whimpered and fled out of sight. They seemed to be bleeding. I imagined the argonauts were fighting hard to get through that bestial barricade of biting bronze.

He led me across the courtyard towards the massive doors of the towering palace. Everything about it echoed Medea's palace in Iolkos, except its scale and its uniformity of colour. The doors were carved with the plants and animals that Medea had found useful for her own particular enchantments.

Inside, the hall was vast and airy, and utterly empty. Our footsteps echoed as we crossed the space. We went down corridors; Kinos showed off the rooms laid out to left and right, just as they had been in his Iolkon home.

'The baths, there.'

There were baths big enough to take a squadron of knights, but no decoration.

'The sleeping chamber. My room; my brother's room. My father's chamber; this is where the musicians entertained us . . .'

All vast, all echoing, all empty of anything except the sound of our passage through them. He seemed so proud of the creation, constantly glancing at me to see if I was impressed. He even said, 'I put my heart into this place. I grew up here. This is where my heart is, Antiokus. I know I was just a child when I lived here, in Iolkos, but I never forgot its beauty.'

I felt very sad for him.

There were two chambers that were full of life and death, however. The first was what he called his 'war room', a dimly illuminated chamber whose walls moved with phosphorescent images of ships and armies.

A helmet-masked statue of Pallas Athena, protector of cities, stood in a niche at the side of the room, cool eyes regarding the wide table on which a model of the island was displayed, the palace central, on its hill, the five wide beaches that surrounded it, in their inlets, covered with model ships and tents, and small wooden figures representing the besieging armies. Only one beach was 'alive' at this moment, the rest were untidy and abandoned. I noticed that a small model of Argo was set out at sea from one of these abandoned shores.

Life-sized, motionless bronze figures in full armour stooped to stare at the map of the city. Proud Kinos, helmet still held below his left arm, walked around the group, introducing them as if they were alive. 'This is Aeneas, a very reckless man, but he is destined for great things. This is Pandarus, and this Polydamus. Here Paris, a wily general, and a good shot with a bow. You'll recognise Hector. When Hector's blood is up, there's no stopping him. Gentlemen: Antiokus, a wanderer, an enchanter, my father's friend, an adventurer and a guest in my house.'

The perfect brazen forms, these echoes of Trojan champions, rippled with the yellow light from the shafting, illusory walls. Their eyes, narrow and thoughtful, remained on the game strategy spread out before them.

Kinos waved a hand towards the goddess. 'Pallas Athena.

She watches over all of this. She protects cities and armies. No matter how I try to make her face, she is always masked! But watch her eyes, Antiokus. She watches and listens. This is my war room. This is where I planned the invasion of a part of Ghostland that had been stolen from us in the past. This is where I united the Dead and the Unborn into an army that could pass across to the living world.'

He was waiting for a word from me, some expression of wonder or approving disbelief. But I had no time for games. 'Why,' I asked him, 'have you, an Achaean, a Greeklander, made effigies of the Trojans as your commanders? These men were your enemies!'

He seemed confused by the question. 'It's how we used to play the siege, my brother and I, as children. You above all should remember! You often took part. I was wild-speared Hector, or watchful Paris—Thesokorus played hot-tempered Achilles, or wily Odysseus. The fourth courtyard of our palace was turned into Troy, and sometimes it fell and sometimes it prevailed. Everything was drawn from my father's wonderful stories. And we played the siege game under my mother's watchful eye. That's how we got our names, Antiokus. My brother was reckless— "always jumping over the bull". I was thoughtful; my dreaming could be my constant companion as I waited for the war to begin.'

And then he had found his own war, a true war: the reclamation of the shadow fortress of Taurovinda, isolated from Ghostland when the winding river had changed its course.

'Yes,' he said when I suggested this to him. 'It was something I discovered that the Dead of this place wanted. They are furious and frustrated at the loss of their land. It had—has—a special significance for them. I don't understand this Otherworld. The Dead wanted their territory back; I had reckoned without the Unborn. To them, Taurovinda is a place of kings in the world of the living. They see it as their inheritance. They soon deserted me. At the siege, if you remember. That ship—Argo, unmistakable! She sang to me, songs of the past. I was shocked and melancholy. I had to leave the battle. And she talked to the leaders of the Unborn. She gave them the resolve to turn against us. And now, they wait for me, down below.'

His moment's melancholy quickly passed. He brightened, pointed to the active beach. 'I'll show you. Come with me. The best room is yet to come,' he added in an alluring tone of voice.

We marched along a passage which reminded me of the approach to Medea's private sanctuary, where she had taken her children and pretended to kill them. It takes a great deal to over-awe me, but the bronze, barred gates he had created, a perfect replica of those which separated the sanctuary from the corridor, were astonishing. They stretched high above us, shining in the sunlight from the openings in the roof. The intricate details of animals and fighting men, ships at sea and chariots charging, flowed as if alive, just as in his 'war room'. The gates opened at his approach and we stepped out over an arching ramp, made of the same highly polished marble, carved with steps to help us keep our grip, and just as well. The space over which this ramp passed was depthless, a great plunging chasm, glinting with light even in unfathomable deep. Booming and moaning sounds rose ponderously from the void. After a moment I realised that it was the distant, rumbling echo of the sea.

Kinos marched over the bridge, helmet tucked under his arm, his backward glances to me full of pride and pleasure at my astonishment and curiosity.

'This was here before I came,' he said as he walked, pointing to the shaft. 'I built the palace around it. Stronger hands than mine brought this bridge and the void into existence. Gods, I expect. This is a work of great power. It helped me build the palace. Below us is a sea, but no sea you can ever imagine. I've seen it once, reflected in a shield in a deep sanctuary. And there are places where it speaks through the earth. The creatures that swim in it are monstrous. Or wonderful?' He glanced back again. 'I suppose it depends on how you look at them.'

The boy who could dream for all of Greek Land.

I remembered Jason's words, angrily spoken when he challenged me in the dark, dank confines of Taurovinda, in Urtha's royal house.

Kinos had certainly been busy with that skill.

And yet he had made nothing.

Ahead of us now rose a second set of gates, not bronze this time, but iron, encrusted with rust. They stood open for us and inside Kinos showed me the shrine and the tomb he had created for his parents.

Two effigies, hand in hand, loomed over us, looking down to where we stood: Jason and Medea, benign of face, dressed for comfort not war, the Colchean enchantress shown without the heavy veils and robes that had usually adorned her, but in a simple dress, draped with herbs and a necklace of the small dishes she used to measure out her powders. Jason was as Kinos would have remembered him from his childhood: still youthful in face and eye, lightly bearded, strong-limbed, a circlet holding back his hair.

They were also made of iron. As with the gates, corrosion was spreading like dried blood across the once bright sheen. I remembered how blood had drenched Medea when she had mimed the slaughter of her sons. There had been such hatred in that act, not for the boys but for the helpless man who had watched, barred by the gates to the sanctuary.

Kinos had given the effigies of his parents the happiness that had been denied them by his father's betrayal. The rust on the figures spoke volumes: the corruption of love; the corrosion of hope.

But Kinos said, 'I like this metal. Iron. I discovered it here. It's stronger than bronze. This tarnishing, the colour change, seems to bring them alive.'

Indeed. He had been right. Perhaps it was how you looked at things. This was his iron grail.

Not three islands, then, but one—wicker, stone and iron. An island of three brothers—Munda's dream—but all the same man. The tangled web of Time was a powerful snare in this Otherworld.

He stood proudly before the statues, staring up at them. 'I miss them so much, Antiokus. You can have no idea. I am happy here; and sad at the same time. Sometimes when I stand here I feel encouraged; sometimes I feel despair. The statues are the two sides of a door, and when they open, and I walk beyond them,' he looked at me warningly, repeating, 'when they open and I walk beyond them, I am a different man. I have to be. Be on your guard, Antiokus. A warped man waits on the wide beach below, where the fighting is furious.'

He reached up to touch the statue of Medea. 'Here at least I can find a little peace. I remember running through the palace with my mother, a game I thought, a game of pursuit, my father chasing us with other men, my first taste of training for the field of battle, for the life of adventure that lay ahead. I had heard my father's stories. I couldn't wait. And suddenly, I woke one morning to find myself a stranger in this strange land. All I had was memory. All I could do was dream those stories. I was sustained by them. I still am. That man, Jason, will find me. There will be reconciliation and renewal. Will my brother be with him? I have no way of telling. My mother? Though it sounds strange, Antiokus, I feel she has been watching over me all these years. Sometimes I wake to find tears on my cheeks, too fresh to be my own.'

He turned back to me, helmet held under his left arm, right hand resting lightly on the hilt of his sword. He hesitated for a moment, then said quietly: 'Yes, I am truly loved and guarded; my fragile life is not discarded; eternity shapes the way we breathe; eternity shapes the way we leave . . . '

Though he spoke the words, watching me with glistening eyes, I recognised the song. Medea's mourning song; I had often heard it, though I had never been privy to the various deaths which were being mourned, inside her walls, inside the private part of the palace she had shared with Jason until his betrayal of her.

But Kinos was not speaking the words as a funeral dirge. To him they were the straw of life and hope to which he clung. His toys were not enough.

I missed Taurovinda very much at that moment, the muddy, bustling, noisy town behind its high walls, where life and pleasure, anger and procreation continued apace, despite the despoliation and desolation that had dealt it such a blow. Here was a citadel of pristine beauty, exquisite stone, shining halls, vast and empty save for toys, toys made from a mind, and for a man, made desolate by solitude.

The stuff of dreams.

How could Medea, the boy's protecting mother, have let her son come to be so mad?

'I have one thing more for you,' Kinos said at last. His spirits had lifted, he held the helmet by its straps, altogether more relaxed. When he smiled, he bore a striking resemblance to his father, though Jason at his age had not had a face so patterned with half-healed wounds.

He led the way to the side of the sanctuary, pushing open a small iron door and inviting me to precede him into the pleasant water garden beyond. The garden was long, lined by olive and pines. A narrow stream of azure blue flowed slowly from a temple at the far end to a shallow fall where we stood; it was tranquil and clean, bright as blue crystal. The water splashed gently.

A model ship, no longer than my sword, was being rowed towards us, following the sluggish flow of the ornamental lake. Kinos led me to a small mooring place on the marble edge of the water and the ship turned to approach us. Six tiny figures fashioned in bronze, heaved on the oars.

The ship was Argo; everything about it told me so, from the look in the bow-eyes to the smiling figurehead of Athena, rising high on its stern.

The metal argonauts shipped oars as the vessel nosed to the intricately modelled quayside, and one of them—a perfect image of Tisaminas—leapt to the 'shore'. He tethered the vessel. The other five figures threw down a ramp and scurried to dry land. I recognised them all. Hylas even waved at me. Atalanta fussed with her minute bow.

Kinos said, 'You'll need to carry them securely. Take out your sword and hide them in the sheath. You'll need to carry the sword anyway, when we go beyond the iron shrine.'

I did as he suggested. I knew what he was giving me. The six bronze kolossoi hauled themselves up the leather stitching and slid down into the oiled and tarnished gloom where the blade had rested.

'The kolossoi are inside them,' Little Dreamer added. 'I made the armour out of bronze because it appealed to me, and because it will help protect them as they find their owners on the beach. If they've survived.'

By 'armour', he meant the figurines themselves.

'Where did you find them? The kolossoi?'

'The girl brought them. The chieftain's daughter. I didn't know what they were, at first. Kolossoi are very strange; each one is different. They had been hidden by Argo, that proud old ship, in the place of the exiles. They told me themselves. I used to play there with the chieftain's children. I could wrestle Kymon into the ground. I was very fond of Munda. But the women who watched over the children chased me away when they saw me. I was a different sort of exile.'

'I saw the Father Calling Place you made with each of them. Little caves with little dreams.'

'The girl went back there when I sent for her. She was only half aware of what was happening to her—a game, she thought. I made her think it was a game. She went back to the place of exiles and found the kolossoi. She picked them up without knowing what they were and brought them here.'

'Where is Munda now?'

His look was hard; his look was disappointed. 'Asleep,' he said, looking down at me. 'I'm sorry.'

I rose to my feet, tilting the scabbard of my sword carefully. 'Asleep?'

'You were close enough to hear her breathing. I remember how you stole the small dolls she'd made, those manikins. Wicker and straw. On the side of this island where you first came ashore alone. I liked to see her make them. I liked to watch her play. That's why I sent for her, to keep me company.'

'And now she sleeps.'

'Until she wakes. Among the briar rose. I was sorry for what I'd done. I had no business stealing the child. But I was lonely. I wanted someone to play with. Don't forget: I was very young, and very lost.'

The way he spoke, stiffly, only occasionally meeting my gaze, suggested this was something he needed to talk about, in search, perhaps, of absolution. 'When two strange men, in the cloaks of wolves, appeared on the island, claiming to know Kymon and Munda, I showed them how to cross the river. I sent them to fetch the girl. I was too young to know better, Antiokus. They said they'd seen my father, but that's not possible.'

'Your father. Jason. He's on the beach at this very moment. You know so much. You surely know that!'

'That is not my father on the beach,' Kinos replied coldly. 'He is not the one. My father would never have played with life and lives like that man on the beach. That man on the beach steals lives. You have six lives in your scabbard. Return them.'

The anger in his voice allowed no argument. He was so quick to deny the possibility of truth. It was as if he couldn't even bear to *think* of his father being close. Perhaps the man on the ship did not fit the memory of the man. Perhaps memory was all that mattered.

I asked quietly, 'And Munda?'

'The girl? As I said, you were close enough to hear her breathing. Close enough to hear her breathing.'

And with that he walked away, back to the iron shrine, his last and most desperate place of calling, waving a hand to me summoning me to follow.

He closed the small door. We again faced the rusting iron statues of his parents. And again he said, 'When we go through go away from me. Please, Antiokus. You were a friend to me when I was a child—I loved to have your company. To lose you in the way I did was also very difficult. It has been wonderful to find you again. Goodbye, Antiokus. Don't judge me only by my dreams.'

The iron figures split apart. Sunlight spilled from a cloudless sky. A chariot thundered up to the exit and Kinos climbed into the car. Below us, on the wide beach, a battle was raging.

The air was full of screaming.

CHAPTER TWENTY-TWO

—

And yet to yield

On the narrow plain below the steep slopes of the citadel, bordering the silver gleam of the ocean, two armies were drawn up facing each other, chariots, horsemen, men on foot, all striking their shields with their swords, all restless below the billowing banners caught in the strong wind from the sea. The horses were nervous, the charioteers struggling to hold position. I could see at once that Kinos drove down among the forces of the Dead. The attacking army—five hundred strong, I estimated—was a legion of the Unborn.

The clamour rose as Kinos was driven along the ranks, his sword held high, his hair streaming from below his gleaming helmet.

He was Hector. This was his Troy. He had created the great siege from the stories his father had told him. He was living a dream in the world of the Dead. He was truly mad.

I had hardly had time to take in the vision below me when the Dead began their attacking run, chariots to the fore, horsemen spreading out to the flanks, squadrons of spearmen marching in columns behind. The Unborn, spread out, remained on their ground, ready to receive the charge. I could see tall men in rich

armour, riding huge horses. I recognised Pendragon as one o
them, but a moment later the flash of gold distracted me.

As the two armies met with the din of metal on metal an
that sustained gull-scream of fury, so a golden-sided charic
was whipped up the winding path to the ramparts, a young ma
bent low over the reins, urging the white horses to take th
slope, his companion, stripped to the waist, hair streaming
holding firmly to the rails, a short spear held defensively. H
was staring up at the ramparts, and when he saw me he grinnec
raising the spear in salute.

The Cymbrii! The sons of the great god Llew, Conan an
Gwyrion. I had thought them long since strangled an
deposited in the cold earth by their angry father. But here the
were, approaching me.

Conan drew on the reins so hard that Gwyrion was throw
from the car, and for a moment he was furious with his brothe
The horses steamed in the bright air, the dust settling aroun
them. This chariot was magnificent, gold leaf on the wicke
sides, and iron rims on the perfect wheels.

'Isn't she beautiful?' Conan exclaimed as he saw my admir
ing glances.

'Your father's?'

The two youths burst out laughing, Gwyrion dabbing at hi
bleeding nose with his finger. 'By the time he notices it's miss
ing, we'll have it back. He sleeps so much these days, he'
hardly aware of the world around him.'

'I thought he was going to punish you!'

'He did,' said Conan. 'But the twenty years is up. When he le
us out, it was as if Time had stood still. Have we aged?'

Twenty years? I had been with them less than two seasons ago

I looked at the two brash sons of the god and only huma
insight pointed out the shadows in their eyes. Fair-haired an
fine-featured, with smiles that dazzled, these two youths ha
been subjected to a torment that no hero could have withstood
They had a sheen about them that was the armour of immortal
ity. They had been hurt, now they could not wait to get on wit
what they did best.

Stealing chariots!

'Get in. We have to get you down to your friends.'

'How did you know I was here?' I shouted as Conan slewed the chariot round and Gwyrion shoved me into the car.

'The mad man who rules here. He sent a messenger to us. He seems to regard you as a friend.'

The wild youths drove me around the battle, towards the line of tents behind the lines. Urtha's pennant fluttered from one of them. Indeed, Urtha sat inside, scowling and sulking, his weapons laid out before him. Niiv stood behind him, arms crossed. Her face brightened when I entered the enclosure.

'That man! That Unborn bastard. How dare he confine me to the tent! But he says it's necessary. Why is it necessary, Merlin? Who in the name of Thunder is he?'

He was talking about Pendragon. As Urtha rose to his feet, strapping on his sword, the resemblance between the two men flashed again, from his eyes, from the set of his mouth, from the iron look.

'I believe he needs you to survive. He'll want to tell tales of you in times to come.'

Urtha nodded sagely, the mood lifting. 'Yes. Merlin, you have a sharp eye, even if your wits have deserted you for the moment. Which son of which of my grandsons will he be, I wonder.'

A future king, I told him; it was all I could tell him. It was too costly to look so far ahead, and I had resisted the temptation whilst in Taurovinda. But I added, 'And a king who will never forget his ancestor, not if I'm around to remind him.'

Urtha looked at me from the corner of his eye. Chariots thundered past outside the tent, axles screeching; the stink of sweat lay heavy on the air. Urtha was deciding whether I was flattering him or appeasing him. He clearly liked the idea of being remembered. It was in the nature of these rough warriors to enjoy the thought of future notoriety.

'Don't tell him *everything* you know about me.'

'Of course not.'

'The shield of Diadara . . . '

'You found it. The quest was well done.'

'As indeed it might yet be. There is still time. But never mind that. What of Munda? Is she a captive of this warped man? Is she alive?'

When I told him that she was the pain in his face blew awa[y] like a breeze. There was a sparkle in his eyes again. 'Is she i[n] the palace?'

I told him what I knew; I used the words that Kinos had use[d.] Urtha stepped outside the tent and stared across the ocean. 'D[o] you know,' he said, 'when you first went ashore, I could hav[e] sworn I heard her calling. I should have gone with you.'

A spear sliced through the air, piercing the canvas of the ten[t] and all three of us flung ourselves to the ground. 'I knew thes[e] were pitched too close,' the chieftain muttered as we stoo[d] again. But a shadow fell over us, the harsh breathing of a tire[d] horse. A broad-shouldered man, protected in leather and iro[n] towered over us, staring down. It was hard to see his face agains[t] the brilliant azure of the sky, but a moment later he smiled. [It] was not the Pendragon, as I'd first suspected.

'Is my brother well?' Gorgodumnos asked. 'I've not see[n] him here, so I imagine he survived the siege. There are other[s] who didn't.'

'Morvodugnos is brash, loud and feeding well,' Urth[a] retorted. 'His is a good sword hand to have in Taurovinda. A[s] was yours. What happened to you?'

'A spear in the back happened to me,' Gorgodumnos replied[.] 'I'm particularly keen to meet up with *that* bastard again. My horse came back without me, I hope. You should have known [I] had not deserted.'

'Yes,' I said to him. 'We knew that you had died. You wer[e] missed very much. Ambaros called you the best of us. So ar[e] you fighting with the Dead?'

He shook his head, adjusting his position on the broad sad-dle. 'No. Too recently dead to have been recruited by the mad-man. There are many of us here who followed the Greeklander[,] but who are not in his control. But we are not Unborn either, s[o] we have no status.'

'Mercenaries?'

'Not even that. Scavengers. Followers. This world is upside[-] down. We follow the smell of the afterlife, even if we don'[t] understand it.'

He turned his mount left side on. 'This is a strange world, my lord Urtha. Delay your crossing for as long as you can.'

'I shall. Be in no doubt of that.'

'And the same message to that younger brother of mine, that great bull, Morvodugnos. When it comes to his time to cross at the Ford of the Last Farewell, I'll be waiting for him. But tell him: not until he has achieved the Feat of the Nine Whirling Women!'

Gorgodumnos laughed, saluted us and cantered heavily towards the sea. He joined a small, sorry band of riders, and they all raised their weapons towards us. They were the fallen of Urtha's Cornovidi and of the Coritani who had come to his assistance during the siege of Taurovinda. Where they rode after that, and for whom they fought, if they fought at all, I couldn't tell.

Kinos's 'Trojans', far outnumbering the ranks of the Unborn, made a sudden push and the forces under the various commanders, Pendragon included, wheeled about and repositioned further down the dunes, towards the sea. Men and horses swarmed through the lines of tents, scattering canvas and stores of spears. Urtha, Niiv and I fled along with the retreat, pausing only in our flight when the clans turned back to the hill and formed a solid line again, using shields and the gut-wrenching spears with five sets of recurved teeth to make a stabbing wall that turned the tide of the battle. As the flow of fighting moved back towards the palace of green marble, the shuddering corpses of both Dead and Unborn were revealed, so many thrashing, bleeding fish after a cruel catch.

I had imagined that Jason and his argonauts were in the thick of the fray, pushing forward to pierce the defensive lines and seek out Kinos. But the man and his war band appeared out of the sun's glare from the direction of the ocean, Tisaminas carrying the flopping body of Atalanta. The broken shaft of a thin dart was stuck in her chest, but her eyes were still aware. Jason, in his dark cloak, looked dreadful, his long hair matted with sweat and blood, his tunic spattered with gore.

'There you are, Antiokus! We need all the help we can get if we're to storm the palace.' He grinned without humour, glancing up at the rising walls. 'A familiar sight, if you remember. And this time, no Medea to bar our entry. Kinos is in there, and I'll fetch him out.'

'Kinos is on the battlefield. He's the only Greeklander you'll see, the argonauts apart.'

'I've seen the *sciamach*,' Jason said with a shake of his head.

'He was also on the plain beyond the Thunder Hill. Medea's trickery, no doubt. A good likeness, but not the man himself.'

I would have laughed had it not been so tragic; twice Jason had been in his living son's presence, and twice he had rejected the young man's identity, preferring to think of him as a shadow warrior, a *sciamath*. Their eyes were blinded to the truth, both father and son.

Yes, that was Medea's doing.

And where *was* Medea?

And then, like Pallas Athena on the plains of Troy, she seemed to whisper to me, as the goddess had whispered to her favoured champions, *You were close enough to hear me breathing*.

'You look alarmed, Antiokus,' Jason said, frowning. The sweat ran from him and his breathing was heavy. 'Gather your wits, and your weapons. The good, golden boys will take us to the gates.'

The Cymbrii were waiting restlessly close by, watching the ebb and flow of the siege war. Their chariot was only sufficient for two of us; the rest, Jason suggested, should follow on foot.

'The palace will be heavily defended,' someone said, and I heard myself say: 'It's empty. There's nothing there but dreams.'

Except in the war room.

'Dreams, and my son,' Jason corrected out of ignorance. 'My son's dreams. I'll know him when I see him. He'll know me as well. Medea did a good job of hiding him, Antiokus. But seven hundred years is collapsing to a few moments only. Come with me, old friend. Come and search the palace with me.'

I held back; Jason watched me, disappointed, perhaps remembering his vow to kill me, a promise made in pain and anger, suddenly forgotten as he strove to clutch the last straw of his life and happiness in Iolkos. Perhaps he sensed in my hesitation a moment's fear and assumed I would keep my distance. He strode past me to the reckless youths, his head lowered, cloak swirling.

'He has no intention of killing you now,' Urtha whispered. 'He has the lust for life again.'

Whatever the High King was implying, I walked swiftly after the old argonaut, wrenching a spear from the ground on my way, and jumped into the crowded car just as Conan turned the

chariot and whipped the horses. Even with the weight of four
men, the beasts seemed to fly across the ground, swinging
round to avoid the edge of the fighting, plunging through thin
woodland and finding the rough path that wound across the side
of the hill to the gates above. Bones jarred and teeth rattled as
we climbed to the palace, Jason and I clinging to the rope loops
on the sides of the car and watching each other impassively.

As we came to the deserted and unguarded open gates from
the iron sanctuary, I saw the flash of light on bronze below. A
chariot detached itself from the fray, working its way back to
the hill, a lone Greeklander bent low as he thrashed with the
reins.

Kinos was withdrawing.

Jason laughed as he jumped to the ground, staring up at the
gleaming façade of the palace, hair blowing in the dry wind that
streamed from within. He recognised this enlarged and elaborate construction, familiar as Medea's palace, the home where
he and the enchantress had lived for a few years, at least, in harmony and happiness. Niiv, Hylas and Tisaminas came panting
up the road. All young, they had run almost as fast as the horses.
The rest of Jason's band had stayed behind. Niiv's eyes sparkled.
She had never experienced anything like this: alive and fighting
in the world of ghosts; discovering what she imagined to be the
secret landscapes of the dead. She clutched my arm as we
entered the iron sanctuary, but she had her mind on the sight and
smell of the place, only the child in her clutching at the familiar
and comforting skin of the man she loved and needed.

Jason turned in a circle where he stood. 'Good gods! I should
know this place, but where's the bull? There should be a bull
where those bloody statues stand.'

Then he saw the faces, noticing the features below the corrosion, the watchful eyes, the youthful smiles, the clean lines of
faces not yet scarred by war or tortured by grief.

'It's me!' he declaimed, and added, laughing, 'High and
mighty.' Then grimly: 'And the woman of my fever dreams . . .'

But he was impressed by what he saw, as if there was welcome and dignity in being represented in this way, even in the
company of a wife he despised. The images were massive; he
felt them to be triumphal. Kinos had called to him, and he had
answered the call.

His son would be waiting for him.

Our footsteps echoed through the empty halls as Jason led us at a steady trot, searching the bright corners for evidence of the boy he was convinced was hiding here. He had hesitated at the bridge, staring down into the booming, chthonic reaches, but had run over the marble arch with confidence. Not so Niiv, who clung to me in horror. I had not realised that she had a terror of falling.

'The place is empty!' Jason cried at last. There was confusion and dismay in his tone of voice. 'It's just a shell!'

He took off towards the main entrance, Hylas in tow. I turned back on my tracks and with Niiv hurrying after me, her spear clutched nervously in both hands, her pale eyes wide with caution, I retraced my earlier steps and found the war room.

'Wait here,' I told Niiv. 'Don't cross the threshold—'

'Why not?'

'And don't ask questions!'

'What is this place?' The moving lights, the images on the walls, were reflected in her eyes. 'Who are those men?' she whispered, her gaze flickering between each of the stooped, hunched, thoughtful bronze warriors grouped around the map table.

'They're only toys,' I reassured her. 'Stay here.'

She sat down against the outside wall of the dark room, peering round the open door every so often, struggling to understand.

I went to the concealed shrine. The brazen statue of Pallas Athena regarded me dully through the eye slits of its face-hugging helmet.

'You played a fine trick on me in the hinterland. But I wonder: has your own enchantment faded, this deep in the Otherworld?'

Cold metal eyes caught the movement of light; but there was no light of their own deeper than the bronze.

'He doesn't even know you're here,' I went on. I was quite determined to have my say, even if the inhabiting spirit of the ikon chose to remain aloof. 'You must have some token charm left in your body to have been able to stay so close to him, and so out of sight. He's felt your kisses and your tears. He's used the power of the earth itself to turn his memories into this monstrous structure. Your son is mad, Medea. You are aware of that, I'm sure. For all your protection, you couldn't stop him losing everything that mortal men call wits. He's just a dog, howling at the moon. He acts by instinct. He's no more alive than the toys he's made in memory of his father's stories.'

Cold metal eyes; no light of their own. Perhaps I was wrong.

'But then, why am I surprised that he's mad?' I taunted. 'His mother was full of confusion. Medea! Priestess of the Ram, yet her sanctuary in Iolkos was built around the figure of a bull. She could have hidden him in any country of her wish, but she flung him into the future, into a land of the dead. He was doomed from that moment on. Doomed to madness as his mother is doomed to fail in her protection. You hide as Athena, Protectress of Cities. You protect nothing but your own need to have the vestige of a son. Your son is dead.'

Cold eyes. Without light.

I rapped my fingers against the tarnished breast, where the heart might lie. 'If the betrayal had been yesterday, or last season, a year ago, I could understand how you could hold such hate in your heart. But you have lived the centuries, waiting. Seven centuries, Medea. It's seven centuries since you sent Kinos to this unfortunate location, to hide him from his father's eyes. You've waited, lived, waited, eaten, drunk, slept, walked, mourned, and waited. Seven centuries! How can hate live so long? I don't understand. How can any living being hate for so long?'

The eyes grew alive!

'Did seven centuries diminish your love for Jason? You fool. We live in twilight. Time slows at twilight.'

The voiced rasped from the metal. The words shocked me as much by their sudden expression as by their content. Medea was right: seven centuries after I had known Jason I had jumped at the chance to raise him from his grave in the Northlands lake. There are some feelings that live as if immortal, despite the thousands of encounters that come and go along the way

My question had been naive. Interestingly, to issue a challenge on the persistence of her hate for her husband had been the charm that enticed the soul out of the statue. She tipped back the helmet, threw off the bronze. She seemed to flow from the hard metal into soft, dark-robed warmth. Here was the old woman again, the beautiful woman, my first lover, faded yet not diminished by the passage of time through her bones and flesh. The shrinking of her body was testimony to the power of enchantment that she had used to make one life among so many lives in her endless existence. As before, I failed to see the age, only breathed the scent of first passion, reaping again the memory of youthful love before we had been set apart along the Path.

I wanted to take her in my arms. We were close enough to kiss. But she kept a distance between us, only a smear of sadness suggesting that she, too, was remembering older days, before Jason, before her truest love, before her fragile life had been shattered by Jason's betrayal of her.

Did she read my mind? I was powerless, beyond intuition. My bones slept; all the carvings there, all the charms that made me so powerful in the outside world, slept comfortably, glad of a rest. Did she read my mind? She could surely have no skill in this land; then again, perhaps, like her son, she was drawing on the echoes of older magic still preserved on this strange island, in the middle of the Realm of the Shadows of Heroes.

'You can have no idea of the horror of my life as Priestess of the Ram in Colchis. Something had taken away my charm. It was a dead place, and I was rotting. That's why I built a sanctuary to a better god—a bull god—in Iolkos! It had all gone wrong in Colchis; Jason did not abduct me, as the silly story goes: he rescued me. There is a saying, somewhere in the world of Ocean, that when a ship founders in a storm, its crew will clutch for life at broken spars. Jason was my broken spar, not perfect, but enough to keep me living. How greedily I clutched at him. He gave me back my life. He was a spar of wood. But he was rotten at the core. When the spar decayed, I sank down into the deep.'

'Taking your two sons with you.'

'I couldn't leave them. Jason was a brutal man. Think what he would have done to them!'

'I know what you've done to them. One wanders the world, selling his skills with weapons, confused and lonely, haunted by the past. The other is a madman, drawing on old forces to re-create a life as a man that is nothing but childishness. You've killed them both, Medea. What solace do you get from being near Little Dreamer? The boy doesn't even know you're here.'

But all the fight had gone from Medea. She might have blazed at me, struck me, found new words in a harsh voice to justify what she had done in Iolkos seven hundred years ago. Only sadness touched the once fair features. And loneliness. 'You don't understand,' she whispered. Then she glanced sharply to the door. 'Who is out there?'

'Only the girl. Niiv.'

'No. Beyond her.'

I could hear the sound of men running. Hylas came skidding into the war room, momentarily astonished by what he saw, breathless, then shouting, 'Antiokus! They're killing each other. Come and stop them!' He could only have been talking about Jason and Kinos.

'They don't recognise each other,' I said to Medea, trying to plead with her to make the fog fall from their eyes.

'I know,' is all she said, closing her arms across her chest, dropping her head slightly, though her gaze remained on mine.

I left her there and followed Hylas. I could hear the ring of metal on metal, the screaming of two men, their words two chants of denial, repeated endlessly. The empty palace was filled beyond echoing with the sounds of fury and despair. As we ran, we became lost. The thunder of rage came at us from every corridor, grim elemental sound that turned us this way and that until we had to stop, exhausted, confused and helpless as the bright world shrank around us.

When I finally found my way to the bridge over the void, the encounter was almost at its end. Kinos, naked save for his helmet, chest-plate and greaves, fighting in the fashion of the Greeklanders of old, took a blow from Jason that knocked him back to the edge of the bridge.

Both men were striped with crimson.

Jason seemed almost startled that his blade had struck so easily. A hank of hair, lank and grey and bloodied, cut from his temple, dangled obscenely from his cloak, fibres caught in the weft. The near side of his face was darkly crusted. The up-draught from the void made his black cloak flow about his shaking figure. He was leaning towards his son, sword held defensively, but his naked hand reaching for the tarnished man.

Kinos looked at me. Through his pain he shouted, 'I'm confused. Antiokus! I'm confused. Help me understand. Is this my father? If he is, why don't I recognise him? Not that it matters any more.'

'Take his hand!' I shouted back. 'Don't fall!'

'Is he the one? Why don't I recognise him?'

'Hold on, Kinos. You built the Father Calling Place. You built so many of them. You forgot only that your father would age. He *is* the one. Take his hand! Don't fall!'

The dying man stared at his father, then pulled off his helmet, let it drop away. 'I waited so long. I began to forget the sound of your laughter. I began to despair. But I see now that you *are* that man, the man I called for. Why do my eyes open just as they are doomed to close?'

'Close them,' Jason said coldly, even though his free hand still reached towards the tottering younger man. 'You are not my son. I would know Kinos, I would know him at any age.'

Kinos laughed and looked at me. He let his sword drop into the void. 'There you have it. Don't you see, Antiokus? I've already fallen. You don't understand. And when all's said and done, all I'm doing is going home . . . '

He blew a sad kiss to his father and tipped himself backwards. He was silent as he descended into the booming depths. The gleam of his breastplate flashed for a long time, but eventually the dark sea below claimed him.

'It's ended,' a voice behind me whispered. I glanced round to see Medea shrinking back, burying herself below the veils of her clothing.

The fight had gone out of Jason, just as it seemed to have deserted Medea. The two of them regarded each other at a distance, but there was no anger, no hate, no hostility in that long gaze; perhaps just weariness and regret.

'Antiokus,' Jason said to me quietly. He pointed his sword into the chasm. 'If the gods are not blinding me for their own purposes, I will say it again: that was not Kinos.'

'Then who was it?'

'I don't know.'

Medea said, 'It was the small part of Kinos that I took to

keep his brother company. A little shadow, that grew like the man. I called him back, but I let him live for a while.'

Jason stepped across the bridge, dark face vile with blood, his eyes wet. 'Then where is Kinos himself?'

Medea didn't move as Jason approached, but she shouted, 'No further!' The man stopped. Niiv clutched my arm nervously, resisting the temptation to chatter at this difficult moment.

'If I take you to him, will you leave this place to its memories? Will you go away peacefully? I am prepared to be kind to you, Jason. But you must go away afterwards; you must leave me alone afterwards.'

'I agree,' the old Greeklander whispered. He sheathed his sword, instructed me to do the same. Only the sound of small voices, urgently warning me from the scabbard, stopped me slaughtering the kolossoi. I slipped my own bronze blade through my belt.

'Then follow me,' Medea said. 'I'll take you to where your dream comes true.'

She ran ahead of us, veils flowing, bone and bronze rattling on the long chains around her waist. She took us into a darker part of the palace, down wide stairs and through labyrinthine passages; there was a feeling of life, here; and death. The walls writhed with animals, painted in luxuriant blues and greens. The scents of incense and burning herbs constantly greeted us. This was the living part of the dead palace: Medea's lair.

At its end was the mortuary room. She stood facing us from its far side, pressed against the black marble wall. Kinos lay on the wooden bier in the centre of the place, his arms by his sides, his armour polished, his hair lovingly braided; flowers were scattered on his breast; his greaves were made of woven grass. The smell of cinnamon was strong, and other oily, musky odours, the stink of preservation.

Jason stepped up to the bier and stared down at the pale, sweet face. There were no scars on this one, though he was a man, much older than the youthful Kinos who had built the stone ship and its monstrous crew.

Medea spoke quietly. 'After he built the palace he went into a war rage. He created siege after siege on the beaches, on the narrow plains around the hill. The Dead of this realm flocked to him; the Unborn were frightened of him. To die before you are born affects the future very much. He played his games with the champions of a thousand ages. I dread to think of the destruction he has caused in future Time.'

'How did he die?' Jason asked. The man was shaking where he stood, his head lowered, his eyes fixed on the waxy skin of the poor boy.

'He died in battle,' Medea answered. 'He created wars for his own amusement. It was always a risk. He was killed in one of the first of the violent encounters.'

'And the other Kinos, the one who has been attacking me ever since I came her . . . ?'

'A small ghost that I made to help his brother, the young Bull Leaper.'

'Thesokorus . . . I found out he hates me too.' There was unexpected defeatism in Jason's voice.

'Thesokorus is still alive,' I whispered to him, intending to imply that there would be another chance for him. Medea heard the whisper and laughed.

'Lost and wandering,' she added. 'I stole his brother from him. I brought back the ghost. This place, this palace, draws on a source of deep enchantment. It was easy to give the small ghost a full life; illusion, but comfortable illusion. But he was always doomed to die at his father's hand.'

Jason bent down to the corpse and lifted it in his arms, embracing memory, hugging the past, but saying goodbye, speaking so softly that I have no words from father to son to record.

Then he let Kinos lie down again and stepped back from the bier.

Did he glance at Medea? Behind her veil her eyes glistened. But at which one of us was she staring? When Jason turned back to me his face was hard. 'The past is gone,' he said. 'There's nowhere to go but forward. I see that now. How do we find Argo?'

'Argo will find us herself.'

'Nowhere else to go,' he added sadly, and with a curious expression on his face.

He left the room. When I looked back at Medea she was slipping into the shadows, to some dark corner of the palace, along another passage, leading away from the echoing tomb that Kinos had built on top of the old hill.

'Goodbye, Fierce Eyes. Goodbye, Medea,' I whispered after her shade.

And I heard a whisper in reply: *I also died when my son died. I waited so long. Don't pity me, Merlin! But understand me. You of all people.*

She and I were not yet finished, I was certain of it. But if she stayed hidden in this *keltoi* Ghostland, finding her again would be hard in the extreme. Able to watch me, despite her weakened state, she would always have the advantage.

Tisaminas found us as we made our way from the palace, retracing my earlier steps towards the beach where the deserted ships from another siege lay rotting. The man was breathless. 'It's all ended. The battle is ended. The two armies are dispersing in ships. None of us can make any sense of it, but the others have gone to the landing place.'

'That's our destination too,' Jason said, slapping the older man on the shoulder. Tisaminas seemed startled by this sudden display of comradeship.

The bronze dogs lay quiet as we passed them; they were at the inner gate, alive, growling deeply, but immobile. On the beach we found the man called Pendragon, and seven others. Their cloaks, in shades of green, red and purple, were tied at the shoulder; their helmets slung from their belts; their battered faces smiling through their beards as we approached.

'You'll need a few more hands to row your strange ship. Here we are!'

'Welcome,' Urtha shouted. 'What's your destination?'

'Back to the river. We feel more comfortable back at the river.'

'We need to make a stop along the way, but you're welcome aboard, all of you.'

Pendragon introduced his burly companion. 'We believe we will all be kings. We have all dreamed our names. Maudraud here thinks he'll be the best of us, but he likes his food too much!'

Maudraud scowled as the others laughed, but he was enjoying the tease. He had slate-grey eyes and a wild smile. I noticed that his hands were shaking, the one on his sword, the other holding a fold of his cloak.

As to this group of men, I will write about them another time, since it was my fortune and qualified pleasure to become involved with them again. They were not all from the same future; some of the men who swam to Argo and found themselves a place at the benches were each other's fathers and grandfathers. In this timeless place, where the map was still unfurled, it didn't matter.

We rowed back to the beach where the child Kinos had shown himself.

I led Urtha and Jason to the low cave where Kinos had drawn the images and made the models that had sustained him in his first years of isolation. Jason stayed there, crouched and hunched, holding the small, straw figure of Phineus. I had lost the other figures during the confusion on the wide beach below the palace.

'She is close enough for us to hear her breathing,' I said to Urtha as we surveyed the tangle of wood and briar around us.

'This is rose briar,' the king said knowingly. 'It's the sort of tangle where we children are sent to sleep for Nemetona, goddess of the groves. We make a drink from the hips, a year later. Blood rose and young dreams to keep the groves vibrant.' He looked at me with a frown. 'There is sleeping and sleeping . . . '

'Yes. I understand. You search that way, I'll enter here.'

We parted company, hacking through the tangled woodland. And after what seemed an age of strangulation in the grasping thorn, grazed and cut and breathless with the humid air, I heard Urtha's delighted cry from somewhere close to me. When we emerged, Jason was waiting for us, his eyes vacant, his mind elsewhere, until he saw us and smiled with genuine pleasure as he beheld the murmuring girl, still in her rough cloak, curled tightly in her father's arms. The half lunula dangled at her neck.

In her right hand she was holding the small elf-shot, the arrowhead that her friend Atanta had given her on crossing the river. As if at peace, now, no longer in need of protection, her fingers unfurled. Urtha took the sharp stone point and tucked it in his belt.

Jason reached out to Munda, stroking her brow and tumble of hair. 'The secret of life,' he said quietly.

'One of the secrets of life,' Urtha replied. 'An important one, but there are others.'

'Yes. I think that's right. Well done. I'm pleased for you.'

Urtha kissed the tip of his daughter's nose, looking at her as if for the first time. 'Thank you. But these next few years will be very interesting.'

We exchanged a glance, he and I. 'Will you be around to see them?' he added.

'I imagine I will. There is so much that I don't yet understand. I seem to belong here; but I feel I've arrived too early.'

'Stop it, Merlin. I'm exhausted enough without your wily thoughts. And I'm hungry. And Jason, you have a decision to make when we get back on board your ship.'

But Jason simply bowed to the king. 'I've already made it. I made it the moment I saw the body of my son. When we cross back over that river, what's it called . . . ?'

'Nantosuelta.'

'Yes. When we cross Nantosuelta I'll be gone from here, and from you. The decision is made; all I need to do is find the kolossoi of my friends . . . those that have survived.'

'They have all survived.'

'Atalanta is close to dying. By the time I find the kolossoi, she will have faded.'

I was able to tell him that the kolossoi were 'home'. It was the first thing I had done on returning to Argo. The small, metal-clad elementals had reunited with their owners. At any moment the argonauts could have faded and gone to their own, ancient homes, leaving one spirit world for another. But they would all row with Argo until the Winding One was crossed, and Jason was finally free of the Warped Man, Dealing Death.

All except Atalanta. She would not survive the next few hours. But as she had lain in the Spirit of the Ship, as Argo's guest, she had confided to me that her daughter was already born. 'She is three years old. She will miss me very much. But perhaps I am alive in Ullanna.'

'Urtha is certainly alive in Ullanna.'

'I'm glad to hear it,' she had said, then gripped me tightly. 'I have a little "light of foresight" of my own, Merlin. Her children by Urtha and Urtha's children by Aylamunda will not be the happiest of families. Only you know this, only you can understand this. There will one day be two Speakers for Kings. Their stories will reflect division and hardship. As my father told me: there will be hardship and a long sigh before the land heals. He was talking about an older time, my time, a long way from here. But his words echo from eternity, Merlin. Stay around the fortress.' She laughed at some hidden thought. 'You are a fine healer, and tolerant of sighing.'

'I wish I could heal you.'

'Well you can't. And that's that, as those *keltoi* kings are fond of saying. But take this, and keep it safe. If it ever seems to be whispering to you, pay attention!'

She had slipped the small bronze casing of her kolossoi into my hand. It was just a toy, a charming thing, a little bit of memory after the body had been reunited with its stolen spirit and been drawn back to the grave. But I was glad to have it.

When she died, we wrapped her in Jason's cloak. We made a brief memorial for her on the far side of Nantosuelta, close to the Ford of the Last Farewell, a low mound over a shallow grave, the body covered with stone. For the first time I noticed how many low mounds were scattered, as if randomly, around this crossing place to the Otherworld.

I was the last to leave the graveside. Unlike the others, I had been aware of the sound of voices singing, the distant wail of trumpets, the beating of drums. Echoes from the past. At this moment, seven hundred years before, Atalanta was being put into her tomb as well. But her daughter, tearful at that moment, no doubt, had a full and wonderful life ahead of her.

The great fortress of Taurovinda, its causewayed heights rising steeply from the Plain of MaegCatha, bloody playground of the Battle Crow, seemed to burn with fires of welcome. Torches in the dusk were waved as signals, and riders came loping across the plain, following the ceremonial way, now marked with new trees and new stones. Manandoun led the party, Ullanna and Kymon close behind, and they spread out through the ever-groves, dismounting and running to the river's edge, where Argo was moored.

We had to jump from the ship and walk ashore.

Kymon ran into the water to greet his sister, and the welcoming tussle sent them both sprawling in the shallows. Urtha waded past them, ignoring them completely, his focus on

Ullanna; the woman's smile became sad as Urtha whispered the news of her ancestor's fate.

It was only as I was squeezing water from my trousers that I realised Jason and Rubobostes had not followed us; nor indeed had the five of grim demeanour. Jason and the big Dacian leaned on the deck rail, watching the activities ashore. Rubobostes waved a hand in salute to me. It was not like the man to ignore the certainty of a good roast and strong drink.

'We're going on!' Jason called. 'I've had enough of this country, though I imply no disrespect for the king and his castle.'

Niiv, standing beside me—she always seemed to be following in my shadow!—whispered, 'Mielikki wants to talk to you.'

I immediately waded back to Argo and climbed the rope ladder to the deck, dropping down to the Spirit of the Ship, Jason following, hunkering down beside me.

Summer air gusted from another place, and the Northland Lady, young and lean, beckoned me to the shade of the pine tree where she sat, her sleepy lynx at her side.

'Argo is leaving,' she said. 'Will you come with her? Or stay here for a while? She can take you back to your path, or to Greek Land, whichever you wish.'

To Greek Land? I'd thought Argo was tired; Mielikki homesick. She should be sailing north. I put this thought to her.

'She is tired, and I am homesick,' the goddess agreed. 'But she has softened her heart to Jason. And there are the other five who must be returned to their own land before they can go back to the tomb. Rubobostes will come with us, and in due course slip away to his own country. Elkavar and Niiv are staying behind. I shall miss her for the while, but I have something to ask you.'

I waited patiently. Mielikki took my hand, her pale eyes filled with concern.

'You seem sad, Merlin.'

'I am. A little. What's the favour?'

'Niiv will age and die. Before she dies, bring her back to the lake. Use a little of that concealed charm to tell when death approaches. You will need a full season to travel the distance, and I do want my handmaiden back before her flesh is cold. Do you promise?'

'Take her now. She frightens me.'

'She wants to stay. She loves you.'

'Must I love her in return?'

'Only you can find out whether that is possible. All I insist ⌐
is that you take care of her. There is one thing more. Concerning Argo, and the premonitions of the three Fates whom yc
first encountered.'

Ah yes; the Three of Awful Boding.

I said, 'Jason was the man who threatened me; Urtha was th
man whose need for me would weaken me. By following hin
into Ghostland I lost access to my skills. I was put at risk. Arg
is the rotting ship. I think I understand that too. She will con
for me when I'm dying, and take me to a place where I can sir
into the water, and be at peace. She will not be my coffin, sh
will be the vessel that takes me to the grave.'

'She will die with you,' Mielikki said. 'When the tin
comes, she will die with you. She has to.'

'Argo is as old as time, and will sail for the rest of time; eac
captain builds on her. That's what she told me.'

'The Argo that you see was built by Jason, and rebuilt b
Jason and the Northlands people. What you see is the she
around many older ships, many older ships around the fir
ship.'

I knew this and reminded Mielikki that I knew it, asking he
why she felt it necessary to raise the subject.

'Argo *will* be your grave when you die. She must die wit
you because it was you who built her. At her heart, in the Spir
of the Ship, is the small boat that you built when you were eig
years old. You called her Little Voyager. A simple boat choppe
out of a length of oak. Less than a finger of that first woo
remains, in her heart. But it is still there. All of the childre
built their little boats, and all those ships still sail. Argo wa
yours. To find you again, when you first sailed with Jason fc
the Golden Fleece, was a time of happiness for her. When sh
took Jason to his watery grave in the Northlands it was in th
certain knowledge that you would come in search of her. That
why she kept Jason alive. She sails on now, with or without yo
but she has found you again, and will come to your call whe
night closes in on you, when the magic has almost gone away.

'I don't expect that to be for many years,' I murmured through my astonishment.

'Nor does Argo,' Mielikki said.

I could hardly take in what the goddess was saying. As before, when I had been with Medea, brilliant flashes of childhood memory opened my inner sight, the sounds and smells and brightness of the long-gone. The boat! Of course I remembered the little boat. It had taken me a season to chop and carve and shape and make riverworthy. It had been no more than a hollow wooden bowl, big enough for a small boy, made buoyant with inflated skins attached to its sides, and with a wide blade of hornbeam as a fixed rudder, my own invention. When I stood in it, legs braced apart, and raised my arms and my sheep's wool cloak to catch the breeze, she had bobbed and scurried with the current, faster than the others, my friend's small coracles, spinning and twirling in the swift water. I had travelled far and in safety, and paddled back against the flow in weary triumph.

When my little voyager had been taken from me, I had cried at the loss. How could I have known that she still sailed the world? That she was designed to find me on occasion? That she was a continuing part of my long walk around the Path?

I slapped her hull, the new, good wood, northern birch around the old oak, her latest cloak. 'Good luck. I'll catch up with you again.'

'Goodbye, Merlin,' she replied. 'Jason is waiting for you.'

All the while I had been in the Spirit of the Ship, Jason had been crouching at my shoulder, but not privy to the scene, to the conversation with the protecting entity of the vessel. As I rose to my feet, he helped me up. Joints stiffen in cold and wet, and to tell the truth, I ached in nearly all of them.

'I caught half the conversation,' he said with a frown. 'Your half. I get the impression that you're staying here, with Urtha, in that muddy place, with his roasts and furious women.'

I told him that that was indeed my intention.

'What about you?' I asked the adventurer; this old king out of Time.

'I go on,' he said. 'Like my second son, I went a little mad. I have come to my senses. I have been chasing dreams and chasing ghosts. But I have a first son still alive, and who knows, Antiokus—'

'Merlin!'

'I don't *like* that name. It sounds artificial. Get another, or stick to the one I know. Anyway, Thesokorus might still recognise me. I shall try again. Kinos is dead, I accept that. I don't believe Medea was playing tricks on us, not this time. The boy died of loneliness and moon fever. I need to be in Greek Land to mourn him, not here, not where the air is so vile and damp and cold.'

'This is a *vibrant* place, Jason. Full of life! It has a full, formidable and challenging future.'

'In which, no doubt, you will play your full, formidable part.'

He brightened up and tugged his beard. His teeth were almost black in his mouth. I hadn't realised how decayed he was. But he was in a forward-looking mood. There had been a sudden, dramatic change in his head and his heart.

'God's luck to you!' he said. 'As for me, I have ten years . . . and I won't waste them. Ten years at least, ten good years to sail this good ship on strange waters and find strange places to . . .' He paused, frowning, trying to find the right word.

'Loot?'

'Yes! Loot. It's what I do best,' he agreed with a sour laugh. 'Ten years. Listen out for my story. I have a feeling you will be the only one writing about me. Now get off my ship, unless you wish to join the adventure.'

'Goodbye, Jason. I hope you find what you're looking for.'

Now his laugh was genuine. 'I'm looking for nothing!' he roared at me, as Rubobostes helped me over the side of the vessel. 'All I hope and pray is that Nothing is looking for me! Though I'll know Nothing when I see it, and I'll keep a piece of it for you.'

'He's mad,' Rubobostes whispered as he let me go. 'This next voyage should be very interesting. Are you sure you won't come? We may have to make him disappear . . .'

'He will never disappear, Rubobostes, old friend. And nor will you. Sail well.'

Argo slipped her mooring and drifted down the river towards the distant sea. I could hear the drone of pipes coming from the high walls of Taurovinda: Elkavar patrolling the boundaries of the fortress with his own particular system of wailing defence. Niiv, as ever, clung to my arm. The black dye was growing out from her hair, bright yellow roots gleaming in the dull sunshine.

'Teach me things,' she urged as we walked through the ever-groves. 'Teach me things, and I promise I'll not look into your future. Not ever. Not ever again.'

' 'You give me moon fever,' I told her. 'You terrify me.'

'I know,' she answered. 'But I love you. And I want you to teach me things. Teach me everything! I will do anything you ask . . . '

There will always be a moment when a man must give up the chase, or give up hope, or give up the ghost. Jason had done all these things. I was equal to Jason when it came to giving up the fight.

I put my arm round Niiv, and gave up resistance to her charms.

Afterword

Hill fortresses such as Taurovinda began to appear in Britain (also known as Alba, Albion, the Isle of Mists, and the Isle of Ghosts) about five centuries BCE, at much the same time as the sprawling and opulent Celtic citadels of Western Europe began to fall to marauding armies from the east, or to uprisings by the discontented lower classes.

Hierarchical, tyrannical and greedy for imported luxuries from Greece, Egypt India, and the Levant, the High Kings and Goddess-Queens were either killed, or fled into exile with their armed retinues and druid-priests. It is more than likely that many found haven across the sea channel, in mysterious Alba, and perhaps further west in Ierna (Ireland.)

Most of what we know of Celtic ritual and belief at that time is anecdotal. But in the Irish epic 'The Cattle (or Bull) Raid on Cuailnge' we have a powerful window back to this period of transition in Celtic society from a wise, if remote and sacrifice-obsessed matriarchy, to a boundary- and symbol-obsessed patriarchy, which brought with it the rise of the champion knight, the prophetic *light of foresight*, and the culture of kingly hospitality.

Many of the new hill-top citadels in Alba were built on the remains of far more ancient sites, whose true function remains intriguing and probably unknowable. Other fragments of the 'Merlin Codex' have more to say on this subject.

Robert Holdstock

London, November 2001

About the Author

Robert Holdstock is the author of such novels as *Mythago Wood*, which won the World Fantasy Award; *Lavondyss; Gate of Ivory, Gate of Horn;* and *Celtika,* the first volume of The Merlin Codex. He lives in London.